ALICE'S ADVENTURES IN

WONDERLAND

ALICE'S ADVENTURES IN WONDERLAND

Lewis Carroll

edited by Richard Kelly

broadview literary texts

Canadian Cataloguing in Publication Data

Carroll, Lewis, 1832-1898
     Alice's adventures in Wonderland

(Broadview literary texts)
Includes bibliographical references.
ISBN 1-55111-223-X

I. Kelly, Richard, 1937-   . II. Title. III. Series.

PR4611. A78 2000   823'.8   C00-931753-8

Broadview Press Ltd., is an independent, international publishing house, incorporated in 1985.

North America:
P.O. Box 1243, Peterborough, Ontario, Canada K9J 7H5
3576 California Road, Orchard Park, NY 14127
TEL: (705) 743-8990; FAX: (705) 743-8353;
E-MAIL: customerservice@broadviewpress.com

United Kingdom:
Turpin Distribution Services Ltd.,
Blackhorse Rd., Letchworth, Hertfordshire SG6 1HN
TEL: (1462) 672555; FAX (1462) 480947; E-MAIL: turpin@rsc.org

Australia:
St. Clair Press, P.O. Box 287, Rozelle, NSW 2039
TEL: (02) 818-1942; FAX: (02) 418-1923

www.broadviewpress.com

Broadview Press gratefully acknowledges the financial support of the Book Publishing Industry Development Program, Ministry of Canadian Heritage, Government of Canada.

Broadview Press is grateful to Professor Eugene Benson for advice on editorial matters for the Broadview Literary Texts series.

Text design and composition by George Kirkpatrick
PRINTED IN CANADA

Contents

Acknowledgments

I am grateful to the University of Tennessee, Knoxville, Exhibit, Performance, and Publication Expense Fund for a grant that assisted in the purchase of photographic materials.

I wish to thank the librarians for Rare Books and Special Collections at Princeton University for their assistance in obtaining Carroll's photographs of the Liddell sisters and for permission to reproduce them. Many other of Carroll's photographs from Princeton's collection may be seen at its Portfolio website: http://libserv3.Princeton.EDU/rbsc2/portfolio/portfolio.html.

I am also grateful to Oxford University Press for permission to reprint extracts from *The Letters of Lewis Carroll*, edited by Morton N. Cohen.

I wish to thank Ms. Barbara Conolly of Broadview Press for her patient and helpful responses to my many questions.

Finally, I am indebted to the many remarkable Carrollians, especially Morton N. Cohen, Martin Gardner, Roger Lancyln Green, and Donald Rackin, whose scholarship and critical insights helped make this volume possible.

Lewis Carroll
(Portrait by O.G. Rejlander)

Introduction

Although Lewis Carroll originally told the story of Alice's adventures in Wonderland explicitly to entertain three young children, the tale evolved into a book that has become a treasure for philosophers, literary critics, biographers, clergymen, psychoanalysts, and linguists, not to mention mathematicians, theologians, and logicians. There appears to be something in *Alice's Adventures in Wonderland* for everyone, and there are almost as many explanations of the work as there are commentators. And, indeed, it is helpful for the curious reader to know something about Carroll's linguistic playfulness, his work in logic and mathematics, his religious opinions, his romantic nostalgia for childhood, his unusual sexuality, and his preoccupation with death. The ideal common reader, however, may be one who can judiciously select and balance the various critical approaches to *Alice* without losing sight of its sparkling wit and hilarious humor.

Derek Hudson reminds us that Carroll was primarily a humorist: "The nearest parallel to the humorous method of Lewis Carroll is probably that of the Marx Brothers, whose dialogue not only has many verbal similarities with his but who also, like him, assert one grand false proposition at the outset and so persuade their audiences to accept anything as possible." Hudson goes on to note that it would be as foolish to look for sustained satire in the one as in the other: "Both have been based largely on a play with words, mixed with judicious slapstick, and set within the framework of an idiosyncratic view of the human situation; their purpose is entertainment."[1] Steadied by an awareness of the enduring comic value of Carroll's works, the best critics nevertheless rightfully insist upon exploring the serious psychological and philosophical subtexts that make his writings profoundly relevant to the modern reader.

---

1   Derek Hudson, *Lewis Carroll, An Illustrated Biography* (New York: New American Library, 1978) 128.

The critics fall into several categories: biographical, psycho-analytical, logical-linguistic, esthetic, Jungian, mythic, existential, sociological, philosophical, theological, and historical. Alexander Taylor's *The White Knight* (1952)[1] attempts to explain *Alice's Adventures in Wonderland* as a commentary upon contemporary ecclesiastical history; William Empson's study, "*Alice in Wonderland*: the Child as Swain" (1960),[2] views Alice as symbolic of the phallus, and her trip as a reversion to her mother's womb; and Donald Rackin's essay, "Alice's Journey to the End of Night"(1966),[3] argues that the story is an existential commentary on meaning in a meaningless world. Given such diverse interpretations of *Alice*, one would do well to be eclectic and to reread the story in the light of the various schools of criticism insofar as they clarify or enrich one's own reading – while recognizing that there is no single correct or hidden meaning to the adventures.

The most important children in Carroll's life were the Liddell sisters: Lorina, Alice, and Edith. Soon after Henry George Liddell became dean of Christ Church in 1855 Carroll befriended his three children. He first met Alice on 25 April 1856, when she was approaching her fourth birthday. He and a friend had gone to the deanery to photograph the cathedral, and his diary for that day reads, "The three girls were in the garden most of the time, and we became excellent friends: we tried to group them in the foreground of the picture, but they were not patient sitters." Apparently Carroll was very impressed with the children, for the entry concludes, "I mark this day with a white stone,"[4] a comment he reserved for extraordinary occasions. The attention he subsequently lavished on the children was soon interpreted by some people as an attempt on his part to win the good graces of their governess, a Miss Prickett, and this rumor led him to write that he would "avoid taking

---

1   Alexander L. Taylor, *The White Knight* (London: Oliver and Boyd, 1952).
2   William Empson, "*Alice in Wonderland*: the Child as Swain," in *Some Versions of Pastoral* (New York: New Directions, 1960) 241-82.
3   Donald Rackin, "Alice's Journey to the End of Night," *PMLA*, 81 (Oct., 1966): 313-26.
4   *The Diaries of Lewis Carroll*, ed. Roger Lancelyn Green, 2 vols. (London: Cassell, 1953) I, 83.

any public notice of the children in future, unless any occasion should arise when such an interpretation is impossible."[1] The gossips clearly misread Carroll's motivations, and his infatuation with Alice continued to blossom both publicly and privately.

Between 1856 and 1862 Carroll continued to visit the Liddell children, amuse them with fanciful stories, play croquet with them, and take them on outings. Alice's presence was a dynamic catalyst that married his own childhood to her's. In what may be described as a surreal blending of the adult into the child, Carroll might have echoed Cathy's exclamation in *Wuthering Heights* – "I am Alice!" That epiphanic moment occurred on 4 July 1862, a day that Carroll records in a remarkable understatement in his diary: "Robinson Duckworth and I made an expedition *up* the river to Godstow with the three Liddells: we had tea on the bank there, and did not reach Christ Church again till quarter past eight, when we took them on to my rooms to see my collection of microphotographs, and restored them to the deanery just before nine." On the opposite page Carroll added in February 1863: "On which occasion I told them the fairy-tale of *Alice's Adventures Under Ground*, which I undertook to write out for Alice, and which is now finished (as to the text) though the pictures are not yet nearly done."[2]

Carroll completed writing *Alice's Adventures Under Ground* before February, 1863, but it took him until the autumn of 1864 before he finished illustrating the manuscript. Besides planning this work as his personal gift for Alice Liddell, Carroll had by this time completed a version that expanded the original from 18,000 to 53,000 words to be illustrated by the famous *Punch* artist, John Tenniel. Carroll finally rejected the title *Alice's Adventures Under Ground* as being "too like a lesson book about mines," and considered *Alice's Golden Hours, Alice Among the Elves, Alice's hour in Elf-land*, and *Alice's doings in Elf-land* before finally settling upon *Alice's Adventures in Wonderland*. When Macmillan, the publishers for Oxford University's Clarendon Press, began to issue the first edition of the work,

1   *Ibid.*, 111.
2   *Ibid.*, 181-82.

Tenniel was dissatisfied with the print quality of his illustrations. Carroll acceded to Tenniel's demand to have the book reprinted, and in August 1865 took the work out of the hands of the Clarendon Press and turned it over to the printer Richard Clay, who reset the type. The unbound sheets of the first edition, however, were disposed of to Appleton Publishers, New York, who published them as the second issue of the first edition in 1866. The actual second edition was published in November, 1865, by Clay.

Sales of *Alice's Adventures in Wonderland* began slowly and then gradually increased, and during Carroll's lifetime over 180,000 copies, in various editions, were sold in Great Britain. Reviewers were both pleased and puzzled with the strange new book. The *Pall Mall Gazette* said that "this delightful little book is a children's feast and a triumph of nonsense." The *Reader* declared it "a glorious artistic treasure." Not all reviews, however, were so complimentary. The *Illustrated Times* thought the story was "too extravagantly absurd,"[1] and the *Athenaeum* was put off with both the tale and its illustrations:

> This is a dream-story; but who can, in cold blood, manufacture a dream, with all its loops and ties, and loose threads, and entanglements, and inconsistencies, and passages which lead to nothing at the end of which Sleep's most diligent pilgrim never arrives? Mr. Carroll has laboured hard to heap together strange adventures, and heterogeneous combinations; and we acknowledge the hard labour. Mr. Tenniel, again, is square and grim, and uncouth in his illustrations, howbeit clever, even sometimes to the verge of grandeur, as is the artist's habit. We fancy that any real child might be more puzzled than enchanted by this still, over-wrought story.[2]

Hard words – but the above review assumed *Alice* was simply a book for children and as such, did not satisfy an adult's expecta-

---

1 These quotations are cited in *The Diaries of Lewis Carroll*, ed. Roger Lancelyn Green, 2 vols. (London: Cassell, 1953) I, 236–37.
2 *Athenaeum*, 16 Dec. 1865, 844.

tions. Nevertheless, as can be seen in the various reviews reprinted in Appendix G, Carroll's tale was warmly greeted by most contemporary critics.

Carroll chose not to follow the established pattern of children's books, which demanded realism and moral didacticism, in favor of characteristics of the fairy tale. The Victorian reader expected a children's book to be realistic, to instruct the child in religion and morals and, consequently, to prepare him for a righteous adulthood. Carroll's book not only lacked a realistic framework but openly poked fun at conventional didacticism. Furthermore, few Victorian authors chose to model their stories upon the fairy tale or to embody elements of the fairy tale in their narratives for children. Hans Christian Anderson's fairy tales were translated into English by 1846, but writers of children's fiction were slow to follow his practice.

Carroll's tentative title, *Alice Among the Elves*, suggests that he was aware of his departure from Victorian tradition. Although there are no elves in the books, there are magical transformations and changes in size, talking animals, and magical potions and foods. By choosing a dream structure for his work, Carroll rejects the approach of earlier writers in their appeal to the reason and moral conventions of their readers.

The character of Alice also departs from the conventional girl heroine. The typical Victorian children's book presented "girl angels fated for an early death," or "impossibly virtuous little ladies," or "naughty girls who eventually reform in response to heavy adult pressure."[1] The unruly child in Julia Ewing's "Amelia and the Dwarfs" (see Appendix I), for example, undergoes a rigorous education that transforms her into a proper young girl. Alice, on the other hand, is neither naughty nor excessively nice, but curious and bewildered. She may grow physically; but her experiences do not apparently teach her anything, alter her behavior, or prepare her for adulthood in a conventional way. Compared to the standard literature for children, *Alice's Adventures in Wonderland* was refreshingly anti-didactic. The Duchess, for example, who finds bizarre

---

1   Elsie Leach, "*Alice in Wonderland* in Perspective," in *Aspects of Alice*, ed. Robert Phillips (New York: Vanguard, 1971) 89–90.

morals to every thing, reduces moralizing to the point of absurdity.

Later critics, however, arrived at a different point of view from that of Carroll's many contemporaries, who read the work as a simple children's story. G. K. Chesterton, for example, declared that "it is not children who ought to read the words of Lewis Carroll, they are far better employed making mud-pies."[1] And Jan B. Gordon argues that the two *Alice* volumes "are decadent adult literature rather than children's literature."[2] Most children today, if they know Alice at all, are familiar with the popular and sentimentalized versions of her presented in films and cartoons. Disney has largely replaced Carroll and Tenniel in shaping the story for young minds. The twentieth-century adult mind, however, is very much at home in the violent, nightmarish dream world of the original *Alice*.

In Wonderland all things are possible. It is called Wonderland because, like Alice, the reader is continually astonished, surprised and puzzled. It is a world made up of contradictions, violence, jokes, anxiety, puns, puzzles, rudeness, arbitrary rules and anarchy shaped by a dream vision. The chaos that rules in Wonderland is not unfamiliar to us. It is evident in the behavior of children who have not yet been restrained by the rules of decorum. At the mad tea party, for example, the Hatter and his associates display the antics of troublesome children in their rude treatment of Alice. But since the Hatter is clearly an adult, his behavior does, indeed, appear quite mad. He and the March Hare, like Oxford debaters, bully Alice with their biting wit and startling logic. In Wonderland everyone is mad, as the Cheshire Cat points out, and yet everyone is comic. Alice is faced with a world of adults who behave like children, despite the variety of intellectual sophistication they exhibit. The words and deeds of these underworld creatures are unanticipated, usually arbitrary, and difficult, if not impossible, to relate

---

1 Quoted in the introduction to *The Annotated Snark*, ed. Martin Gardner (New York: Simon and Schuster, 1962) 11.
2 Jan B. Gordon, "The *Alice* Books and the Metaphors of Victorian Childhood," in *Aspects of Alice*, 94.

to one another. Perhaps in that sense, they represent an intensi-
fied vision of adults from the child's perspective.

Alice's Adventures has the fluid structure of a dream vision, a
conventional literary form that dates back to the middle ages.
Alice's dream, however, differs from the traditional form in that
it is distinctly episodic, is rendered from the third person point
of view, and resists a coherent symbolic or allegorical interpretation. Alice's character does not appear to develop or significantly change throughout the tale. One chapter does not nec-
essarily evolve out of the preceding one. In picaresque fashion
the book sets forth a series of discrete encounters between
Alice and the creatures in Wonderland, and she rarely seems
capable of applying what she learned in a past encounter to a
new one and consequently moves through her dream world in
almost constant amazement. Curiosity above all else impels
Alice on to random new adventures.

The first two paragraphs of the book provide an important
frame for the story in their depiction of Alice falling asleep as
her older sister reads a book. Alice peeps into the book and,
seeing no pictures or conversations in it, wonders what possible
use the book can have. Her remark suggests her rebellion
against the boring and didactic Victorian texts used to educate
children. This setting thus establishes the motivation for Alice's
escape into a dreamworld. Like Alice, Carroll was a mental
traveller, intent on transforming his small plot of Victorian
England into a rigorous and extraordinary adventure, whether
playing railroad as a child at Croft Rectory, working puzzles at
Oxford, or telling fabulous stories to little girls. After three
short paragraphs he whisks Alice off the humdrum surface of
the earth and has her plummet into Wonderland.

Like the great real-life adventurers of her day, Alice is
strongly motivated by curiosity. She resembles a Victorian
anthropologist, an explorer encountering strange cultures that
she chooses not to understand. At times she almost seems to be
a disembodied intellect, so cool is she in the face of danger.
While she is falling down the rabbit-hole, for instance, "she had
plenty of time as she went down to look about her, and to

wonder what was going to happen next." (p. 52) As she continues her fall she rather casually removes from a passing shelf a jar of orange marmalade. To her disappointment it is empty and rather than drop it and risk hitting someone below, she places it in a cupboard as she falls past it. Of course, since she was falling, she could not have dropped the jar even if she chose to.

Her composure is extraordinary (to think of food at a time like that) – and yet she has an intellectual appreciation of her fall, for she says that now "I shall think nothing of tumbling down-stairs!" (p. 52). The naivete of her coolness, however, is quietly undermined by a joke the narrator makes about death: "'Why, I wouldn't say anything about it, even if I fell off the top of the house!' (Which was very likely true)" (p. 52). There is a connection in Carroll's (and the narrator's) mind between the death of childhood and the child's sexual awareness. The poem that introduces *Through the Looking-Glass* ("Come, hearken then, ere voice of dread,/ With bitter summons laden,/ Shall summon to unwelcome bed/ A melancholy maiden") supports the sex-death relationship and elicits a comment by Empson: "After all the marriage-bed was more likely to be the end of the maiden than the grave, and the metaphor firmly implied treats them as identical."[1]

A great deal of the humor found in Alice's encounters with the creatures of Wonderland derives from the solemnity of Alice herself. She is almost totally lacking in a sense of humor; and the reader, along with the narrator, is always a step or two ahead of her. Alice is a kind of "straight man" not only to the inhabitants of Wonderland but to the author as well. More often than not the reader sees things through Alice's eyes, but her vision is limited and flawed by her youthful naivete. Carroll's choice of third-person narrative, therefore, gives one the perspective necessary for adult comedy.

The double perspective of the narrative reflects Carroll's own fundamental duality, a constant tension in his thinking and sensibility between such forces as emotion and reason, illusion and reality, and sentiment and wit. He could move with ease

---

1 Empson, *Some Versions of Pastoral*, 256–57.

from the intellectual rigors of mathematics, logic, and wit to the sentimental expression of his feelings in his serious verse. The dreamy, nostalgic romanticism of the opening poem, for example, stands in marked contrast with the cold and loveless world of verbal assaults of Wonderland itself. The story might be viewed as a battle between the sensibilities of the child and those of an adult. Carroll's dream children – embodiments of his own lost childhood – are filled with hope and wonder. They seek love and understanding, believing that their dreams can be realized. The powerful longings of the child within Carroll, however, are relentlessly undermined, denied, or diffused by his cold reason and wit.

It quickly becomes apparent that Wonderland is not a promised land, a place of sleepy fulfilment. Wonderland stimulates the senses and the mind. It is a *monde fatale*, so to speak, one which seduces Alice (and the reader) to seek new sights, new conversations, new ideas, but it never satisfies her. Conventional meaning, understanding, and the fulfilment that comes with illumination are constantly denied her. That is the secret of Wonderland: its disorienting and compelling attractions make it a Wanderland and Alice an addicted wanderer, free of the intellectual and moral burden of ordering her experiences into some meaningful whole. She is never bored because she is never satisfied.

Significantly, she is presented with a stimulating, alluring vision early on in her adventures. Although all the doors around the hall are locked Alice finds a tiny golden key which opens one that leads into a small passage. She kneels down and looks along the passage into "the loveliest garden you ever saw" (p. 55). Because of her size she is unable to get out of the dark hall to "wander about among those beds of bright flowers and those cool fountains" (p. 55). It is not until Chapter VIII that Alice reaches the garden, only to discover that the roses in the garden are painted and its inhabitants either mad or cruel. One critic believes that "the story revolves about the golden key to the enchanted garden and Alice's endless frustrations and wanderings in bypaths until she enters at last," and that the garden is a "rich symbol if we call it adult life viewed by a child, or vice versa."[1] Another critic conjectures on the perspective of the adult: "As sublibrarian of Christ Church, Carroll used a small room overlooking the deanery garden when the Liddell children played croquet. How often he must have watched them, longing to escape from the dark halls of Oxford into the bright flowers, and cool fountains of childhood's Eden!"[2]

More basic than either of these two readings, however, is the theme of desire created by Alice's vision of the garden. It becomes a dream vision within a dream. Too large to enter the passage to the garden, she can only imagine being among its delights. In mythic terms, Alice's dream garden corresponds to a longing for lost innocence, the Garden of Eden. Her desire invests the place with imagined significance. Later, of course, when she actually enters the garden it loses its romantic aspect. In fact, it turns out to be a parodic Garden of Life, a cruel artifice, for the roses are painted, the people are playing cards, and the death-cry "Off with her head!" echoes throughout the croquet grounds.

Alice's dream garden is an excellent example of Carroll's paradoxical duality. Like Alice, he is possessed by a romantic vision of an Edenic childhood more desirable than his own fallen world, but it is a vision that he knows is inevitably corrupted by adult sin and sexuality. Carroll would later combine the innocence of childhood and the sexuality of adulthood in the character of the Mad Gardener in *Sylvie and Bruno*, a child-man bristling with sexual energy. Here, meanwhile, he allows the romantic dream of the garden to fill Alice with hope and joy for a time but he later tramples that pastoral vision with the hatred and fury of the Queen and the artificiality of the roses and the two-dimensional characters. Carroll's paradoxical attitude here is best summarized by the lines from John Donne's "Twickenham Garden": "that this place may thoroughly be thought / True Paradise, I have the serpent brought."

Alice is constantly at odds with the creatures and situations of Wonderland. It is precisely this tension between her expectations and the actuality of Wonderland that makes the book

---

1   Lennon, *Victoria Through the Looking-Glass*, 123.
2   Gardner, *The Annotated Alice*, (1960) 30.

exciting. Alice is "our" representative, bringing the ideals of reason and morality and a desire for meaning into a world of disorder, contradiction, violence, arbitrariness, cruelty, rudeness, frustration, and amorality. Jan B. Gordon wonders "whether Alice's attempt during her *Adventures* to constitute a social family among the animals is not the burden of the Victorian exile."[1] He sees the character of Alice to be determined by the Victorians' equating the child with the adult, an action which has the unfortunate effect of creating an orphan. Many children do, indeed, develop social and family ties by investing their stuffed animals with human sensibilities. Alice, however, is more than an orphan seeking a surrogate family; she is a victim of a seeming conspiracy of animal, plant, and human characters. These diverse characters comprise a hierarchy of heartless adults who bully and issue orders to Alice. Cruel or indifferent, these creatures exhibit neither compassion nor affection. There can be no families where there are no feelings. Everyone is alone and isolated in Wonderland.

James Kincaid's thesis is that Alice is an invader in Wonderland, that she reenacts the betrayal of innocence: "She carries with her the chief barrier between human beings and comic existence: an implicit belief in a world ruled by death and predation and a relentless insistence upon linear progression and completeness."[2] He contends that Carroll adopts an ironic view that questions the value of human innocence altogether and accepts the sophisticated and melancholy corruption of adults as preferable to the cruel selfishness of children.

This interpretation is a valuable corrective to the sentimental view of Alice held by a few uncritical readers, but it seems to go too far in the other direction. Like patient Griselda in Chaucer's "The Clerk's Tale" and Desdemona in Shakespeare's *Othello*, Alice can be made into an interesting villain because she is so apparently innocent. There is no question that she is an imperfect child – too serious, a bit priggish and prissy, rather conventional, and selfish – and that her innocence is ambigu-

---

1   Gordon, "The *Alice* Books and the Metaphors of Victorian Childhood," in *Aspects of Alice*, 102.
2   James R. Kincaid, "Alice's Invasion of Wonderland," *PMLA*, 88 (Jan. 1973): 96.

ous, but she is hardly a dark Darwinian invader of paradise. Nina Auerbach describes Alice's role more accurately: "The ultimate effect of Alice's adventures implicates her, female child though she is, in the troubled human condition."[1]

The first thing Alice has to learn in this strange world is to adjust to unexpected changes, as in female puberty. By drinking from a mysterious bottle and eating from a small cake she experiences great changes in body size until she becomes unsure of her own identity: "'Who in the world am I?' Ah, *that's* the great puzzle!" (p. 60). Throughout her adventures Alice is confronted with the problem of her shifting identity, a problem aggravated and in large part caused by the inconsistencies of Wonderland. The theme of maturation is also in evidence here: "Children like to think of being so small that they could hide from grown-ups and so big that they could control them, and to do this dramatises the great topic of growing up, which both Alices keep to consistently."[2]

The "nearly universal belief in permanent self-identity is put to the test and eventually demolished in Wonderland."[3] Alice finally overcomes the threat to her selfhood at the conclusion of the story, when, having grown to her full size, she asserts "You're nothing but a pack of cards!" (p. 154). This capability for sudden changes in body size can be seen as an ominous and destructive process that undermines one's sense of natural growth and predictable size. Through the destruction of stability, Wonderland asserts its mad sanity.

Carroll typically grants his heroine incredible powers of distraction, as if to demonstrate that the mind has remarkable defenses against the panic inherent in the human condition. After vainly puzzling over her identity, Alice finds herself swimming in a pool of tears which she wept when she was nine feet tall. Earlier Alice thought about marmalade instead of death during her fall and now she distracts herself from the prospect of drowning by worrying about the proper way to

1   Nina Auerbach, "Alice in Wonderland: A Curious Child," *Victorian Studies*, 17 (Sept. 1973): 46–47.
2   Empson, *Some Versions of Pastoral*, 255.
3   Rackin, "Alice's Journey to the End of Night," 316.

address a mouse she finds swimming in her tears. The image of the tears as a sea supplants in dream-like fashion the actual hall in which Alice stands weeping – for the mouse and Alice, magically joined by birds and other animals, swim "to the shore."

Carroll's need to bring emotion under the reins of reason seems to be the major driving force behind this episode. For centuries poets have seen tears as the essence of human emotion, whether they be tears of sorrow or of joy. John Donne, however, intellectualized this emotional symbol through his metaphysical wit in such poems as "The Canonization" and "A Valediction: of Weeping." Carroll employs a similar wit and comic perspective by threatening to drown his heroine in her own tears. By treating such hyperbole literally (and reinforcing the image through the illustration), Carroll humorously demonstrates the inherent dangers of uncontrolled emotion, of reckless romanticism.

Alice's immersion in her own tears has led some critics to see an underlying image of sexuality. William Empson, for example, reads this scene in Freudian terms: "The symbolic completeness of Alice's experience is I think important. She runs the whole gamut; she is a father in getting down the hole, a foetus at the bottom, and can only be born by becoming a mother and producing her own amniotic fluid."[1] Empson's reading gives a whole new meaning to Wordsworth's line, "The Child is father of the Man" and suggests a genealogy beyond imagining.

Alice's concern for the correct form of address to the mouse is a reminder that nonsense is a game of words, and Chapter III reinforces this aspect of the story. The mouse proposes to dry Alice and the other animals by relating to them a piece of dry history. When the mouse states that "Stigand, the patriotic archbishop of Canterbury, found it advisable" (p. 67), the Duck interrupts to ask what the antecedent of "it" is: "I know what 'it' means well enough, when I find a thing … it's generally a frog, or a worm" (p. 67). Such analysis and questioning is obviously detrimental to communication; but since the mouse's

---

1 Empson, *Some Versions of Pastoral*, 260.

purpose in relating this history is to dry off his fellow creatures, such an attack upon grammatical ambiguity is doubly ridiculous.

The Dodo finally settles upon a Caucus-race to dry everyone off. The Dodo represents Carroll's comic view himself, for when he said his name, his stammer caused it to come out "Do-Do-Dodgson." When Alice asks what kind of a race that is, the Dodo replies that "the best way to explain it is to do it" (p. 68), a remark that suggests the inadequacy of language to explain all things. After the race is run everybody is declared the winner and all are awarded prizes, which seems like a perfectly acceptable democratic arrangement considering that everyone has gotten dry. Like so many anxious children, the animals all crowd around Alice, calling out "Prizes! Prizes!" The Dodo solemnly awards Alice her own thimble, perhaps a fantasy enactment of Carroll's proposal of engagement to Alice.[1] The animals all take this ceremony very seriously and cause Alice to look as solemn as she can. The Caucus-race and the award ceremony seem incomprehensible to Alice because she is an outsider, unfamiliar with the other creatures' games and language system. Similarly, one wonders the extent to which Alice Liddell was aware of the depth of Carroll's feelings towards her.

Carroll may have intended the Caucus-race to satirize the activities of political parties. As one critic suggests, Carroll might have been poking fun at "the fact that committee members generally do a lot of running around in circles, getting nowhere, and with everybody wanting a political plum."[2] The Caucus-race may more significantly be read, however, as a metaphor for the entire story, indeed, for life itself. Many authors, including Saint Paul, have compared life to a race. The

---

1   Morton Cohen's comment on the alleged proposal is relevant here: "He [Carroll] would certainly not have proposed to Alice directly or even asked her parents for her hand then and there.... The most he would have undertaken would have been to suggest that perhaps, in the future, if her affection for him did not diminish, he would be happy to propose an alliance." See *Lewis Carroll* (New York: Knopf, 1995) 100–04.

2   Gardner, *The Annotated Alice*, 31.

circularity and arbitrariness of the Caucus-race, however, undermines the conventional metaphor. By making drying off the motive for the race, Carroll subverts the usual purpose of such a contest, namely, to select the fastest runner. The circle eliminates the finish line and without a goal there can be no losers and no winners. If such is life, then its goals are arbitrary and capricious (though bizarrely practical in the short run). An epistemological equivalent to the Caucus-race occurs in Carroll's satiric poem "The Three Voices," where the sententious old hag observes: "And thus the chain, that sages sought, / Is to a glorious circle wrought, / For Notion hath its source in Thought." Carroll's humor in all of this must not be forgotten, for it provides him with a psychological defense against such a self-reflexive conception of life. His comedy here, as in *The Hunting of the Snark*, diffuses rather than confronts such terribly serious issues as the limits of knowledge and the elusive purpose of life.

The Mouse's tale is still another instance of language as play. "Tale" is confused with "tail," "not" with "knot," and the shape of the verse depicts a tail in Alice's mind. When one thinks back on this chapter he realizes that despite all the dialogue Alice has learned very little from her associates and vice-versa. The strategy of Wonderland is to defeat different systems of logic, to keep details from culminating into some meaningful order. The language, characters, and scenes in Wonderland are all essentially discrete. Attempts to fuse them lead to misunderstanding. Consequently, the reader, not to mention Alice, cannot evaluate past experiences and can only look forward to new and more unusual ones. In the case of the Mouse's tale, however, there is a faint foreshadowing of the trial at the end of the book. Both satirize the legal system by presenting a Kafkaesque vision of justice.

Moving away from the intellectual emphasis upon language, Chapter IV focuses upon Alice's body and her physical space. After drinking from the magical bottle she grows so large that her body fills the entire house. The illustration reveals a powerful sense of claustrophobia, as if a child had somehow gotten into her doll house and cannot get out. Empson finds in this

scene a nightmare theme of the birth-trauma,[1] an idea supported by the fact that in Carroll's drawing of Alice she is much
more in the fetal position than she is in the Tenniel illustration.
This theme is first introduced when Alice, grown large, long-
ingly looks through the small door that leads into the garden.
Alice's response to her entrapment, which would be terrifying
to an ordinary child, is unexpected. Her curiosity and simple
bewilderment are expressed in a remarkably detached tone: "it's
rather curious, you know, this sort of life!" (p. 76). Her reality
becomes a kind of fiction: "When I used to read fairy tales, I
fancied that kind of thing never happened, and now here I am
in the middle of one!" (p. 76). Carroll thus draws a significant
parallel between the strangeness of life and that of fiction. Life
mirrors fiction; both are fabrications that create the illusion of
purpose and meaning. Alice's adventures, however, ultimately
reveal no such purpose and meaning, and her experiences in
Wonderland are fundamentally different from those of children
in fairy tales. She achieves no particular goal in her adventures
nor does she learn a morally uplifting lesson. Indeed, the reader
discovers in her dream the terrifying vision of the void that
underlies the comfortable structures of the rational world.

Carroll's conclusion to this chapter is singularly disappoint-
ing. The difficulties Alice experienced as a giant are now balanced by her encounter with an enormous puppy that threatens her life in its exuberant playfulness. Somehow a puppy
seems out of place in Wonderland. It barks instead of speaks, it
chases a stick, pants, and jumps in the air. It is simply an over-
sized creature from the familiar world above ground and its
presence disfigures the character of Wonderland that has
already been established. There is a little too much of second-
rate *Gulliver's Travels* in this chapter to make it memorable; and
one is happily relieved when Alice finally comes upon the mysterious large blue caterpillar quietly smoking a long hookah,
for here, indeed, is the discomforting dream quality of Wonderland again.

The Caterpillar has a multi-faceted significance in the story.

---

1   Empson, *Some Versions of Pastoral*, 259.

It fuses the themes of sexuality, changing body forms, and the mystery of personal identity. The illustration is replete with phallic images: the Caterpillar himself, the mushroom on which he sits and those beneath him, and Alice's mushroom-shaped dress. As a symbol of sexuality, he represents a threat to Alice's childhood innocence. Enclosed in the chrysalis-like circle of his pipe, he also represents an image of the mysterious transformation of body form. Alice, who literally has to look up to this hooded creature, has come upon her high priest, who presumably will impart his great wisdom and initiate her into the mysteries of life. Of course, he does nothing of the kind, except by indirection.

Like so many of the creatures Alice meets, the Caterpillar treats her rudely, almost contemptuously. What makes this encounter unsettling is that the author provides absolutely no motivation for the Caterpillar's aggressiveness towards Alice. His insults are gratuitous, funny and intimidating. Alice, however, expects to be treated in the polite manner customary above ground. The Caterpillar's first question to her – "Who are *You?*" – is not only contemptuous but especially unnerving considering Alice's previous difficulty in answering that question. It is almost as if the Caterpillar had read her anxieties and set this question to torment her. He does, after all, possess extra-sensory perception. As he gets down from the mushroom he tells her that eating one side will make her grow taller and the other side will make her grow shorter. "'One side of *what*? The other side of *what?*' thought Alice to herself. 'Of the mushroom,' said the Caterpillar, just as if she had asked it aloud" (p. 89).

The issue of Alice's identity is carried into her next encounter. The Pigeon, believing Alice is a serpent, asks, "Well! *What* are you?" and the best that Alice can come up with is "I – I'm a little girl" (p. 90). But Alice's elongated neck suggests convincingly that she looks more serpentine than girlish to the Pigeon – and, furthermore, since girls as well as serpents eat eggs, it really makes no difference to the Pigeon, for then girls are a kind of serpent. Defining an entire creature by a single action has a particular logic from the Pigeon's point of view, and the newness of the idea silences Alice. Wonderland thus reveals again its logical subtext, one that poses a constant challenge to Alice's more conventional reasoning. The Caterpillar's and now the Pigeon's aggressive attack seriously threaten Alice's assumption of a permanent identity. Later, when the White Rabbit orders her about like his servant, Alice imagines that her new identity will surface in the world above when her cat Dinah will command her in the same manner. Empson goes behind the question of identity raised in this section to observe, "Alice knows several reasons why she should object to growing up, and does not at all like being an obvious angel, a head out of contact with its body that has to come down from the sky, and gets mistaken for the Paradisal serpent of the knowledge of good and evil, and by the pigeon of the Annunciation, too."[1]

The peculiar behavior of the creatures in Wonderland, possessed of their unique form of logic and reason, is further developed in Chapter VI. The Frog-Footman sitting on the step of the Duchess' house takes for granted the chaos around him. When a plate flies out of the door and breaks against one of the trees behind him, he continues talking "exactly as if nothing had happened" (p. 94). The surface image of aristocratic order implied by the livery of the Frog-Footman and the Fish-Footman and by the pillared porch of the Duchess' house is subverted by the raucous noise from within and by the Footman's detachment from the interior mayhem.

This is the home of chaos. Once inside, Alice meets the Duchess, one of the most unwholesome characters in the book. She is incredibly ugly, masculine, sadistic, moralistic, and sexually aggressive. The fact that she is first pictured nursing a baby makes her appear even more grotesque, for she is the antithesis of a maternal figure. The Cheshire Cat with its unnerving grin adds still another element of the grotesque to this caricature of domesticity. There is pepper in the air and the cook is throwing everything within her reach at the Duchess and the baby. When Alice attempts to control the situation the Duchess

---

25 *Ibid.*, 258.

quickly puts her in her place: "If everybody minded their own business ... the world would go round a deal faster than it does" (p. 96). And when Alice starts talking about the world spinning on its axis, the Duchess, by way of a pun, escalates the violence: "Talking of axes ... chop off her head!" (p. 96). But her violence is aimless and quickly turns upon the baby: "she began nursing her child again, singing a sort of lullaby to it as she did so, and giving it a violent shake at the end of every line" (p. 96). She then tosses the baby violently up and down "and the poor little thing howled so" (p. 97) that Alice could hardly hear the words of the lullaby. Alice is left to nurse the baby as the Duchess prepares to play croquet with the Queen.

The extended parody of motherhood is finally terminated when the baby turns into a pig. Alice thinks to herself, "If it had grown up ... it would have made a dreadfully ugly child: but it makes rather a handsome pig, I think" (p. 99). Here again is another reminder that in Wonderland the essence of any-thing is unstable. If a baby boy can turn into a pig, then perhaps the Pigeon was correct in seeing Alice as a serpent. There are no familiar rules, conventions, or categories – the comedy of seeming chaos reigns supreme. Without stable points of refer-ence, reason is helpless to defend one against disorder. Alice ultimately comes to realize this at the end of the tale where the culmination of her frustrations leads her to deny the meaning-less world around her. Meanwhile, her conversation with the Cheshire Cat takes her a step further into the confusion.

In a world devoid of structure and permanent landmarks Alice rather naturally asks directions: "Would you tell me, please, which way I ought to go from here?" The Cat replies, "That depends a good deal on where you want to get to." When Alice hesitates with "I don't much care where – " the Cat quickly interrupts, "Then it doesn't matter which way you go." Alice goes on to complete her remark saying " – so long as I get *somewhere*" (p. 100) but one surmises that Wonderland has already spoken in its usual unsettling tone. Alice seemingly cannot escape the madness of chaos that surrounds her. She protests that she does not want to go among mad people, but the Cat knowingly replies, "we're all mad here. I'm mad. You're mad" (p. 100). The term "mad" seems relative to Carroll: the creatures of Wonderland, with their unique rules and logic, seem mad to Alice, and Alice, with her conventional thinking, appears mad to the Cheshire Cat. Alice, in any case, does not believe that her coming to Wonderland proves her mad. She never comprehends the Cat's revelations about its strange world and persists in her subsequent adventures to expect conventional behavior from the inhabitants of Wonderland.

There is no question that the Cheshire Cat registers its momentary hold upon Alice and the reader. Like the grin of a madman it may have no logical significance whatsoever but the sane observer will of necessity try to interpret it even as a reader of nonsense feels compelled to make some sense of it. Unlike the "Mona Lisa" or the Sphinx, the Cat can speak and poses a threat to Alice with its teeth and sharp claws. Its smile, however, is its most unnerving aspect. The Cat's eyes and smile suggest that it knows something that Alice (and the reader) does not. Curiosity may have killed the legendary cat, but here the tables are turned and the Cat makes Alice curious. Alice's curiosity is quickly beaten down by the domineering Duchess, who boldly asserts that all cats can grin. She proceeds to insult Alice, who quickly changes the subject. Like so many previous issues, the question about the Cat's motivation for grinning is forgotten. In a world without meaning, everything is important and everything is trivial. Wonderland forces memory, judgment, and reason into submission.

Carroll enhances the enigmatic nature of the Cheshire Cat by first granting it what appears to be an all-knowing mind and then later undermining its presumed omniscience. After the Cat vanishes it suddenly reappears to ask what became of the baby. Alice replies that it turned into a pig and the Cat remarks, "I thought it would" (p. 101) and vanishes. It is curious that the Cat should be concerned with the fate of the baby; and its lack of surprise that the boy turned into a pig suggests a disquieting omniscience. The Cat vanishes and again reappears to ask if Alice said "pig" or "fig," a question that suggests, in typical Wonderland fashion, that it really does not matter what happened to the baby after all.

In her own detached and amused aspect, Alice is very much like the Cheshire Cat herself. As the Cat gradually vanishes again its grin remains suspended among the branches of its tree, leading Alice to think: "Well! I've often seen a cat without a grin ... but a grin without a cat! It's the most curious thing I ever saw in all my life!" (p. 101). The "seemingly indestructible bond between subject and attribute — has been graphically subverted by the appearance of a cat's grin without a cat."[1] Nevertheless, Alice maintains a remarkable coolness in the face of such a bizarre experience. The word "curious," the most frequent adjective used to describe her behavior, suggests a quiet, detached interest in the occurrences surrounding her, an intellectual rather than an emotional response to fantastic sights. Alice is seldom amazed, excited, or dreadfully afraid.

Despite her equanimity, Alice is no match for the Hatter, who demonstrates that life in Wonderland is like a puzzle in which the pieces refuse to fit together. He challenges her logic with an answerless riddle: "Why is a raven like a writing-desk?" When Alice gives up and asks the Hatter the answer, he replies that he hasn't the slightest idea. In Wonderland it is appropriate that the riddle should have no solution,[2] for it keeps the dream and disorder side of the mind in play. Carroll himself admitted that the riddle, as originally invented, had no answer at all. Like Alice's question to the Duchess as to why her cat grins, this one also has no answer. As questioner, Alice is bullied by the Duchess, and as the one questioned, she is bullied by the Hatter.

Having presented her with an interesting riddle ("'Come, we shall have some fun now!' thought Alice,") the Hatter attacks her use of language and never allows her the opportunity to return to solving the riddle. The March Hare interrupts to tell Alice to say what she means. She replies that "at least I mean what I say — that's the same thing, you know." But the Hatter retaliates with, "Not the same thing a bit!... Why, you might just as well say that 'I see what I eat' is the same thing as 'I eat what I see'!" (p. 104). As Roger W. Holmes points out,

1   Rackin, "Alice's Journey to the End of Night," 320.
2   Elizabeth Sewell, *The Field of Nonsense*, 113.

Carroll the philosopher-logician is at work here: "We know that if all apples are red, it does not follow that red things are apples: the logician's technical description of this is the non-convertability *simpliciter* of universal propositions."[1]

Alice's sense of time as well as her grammar are undermined in the subsequent dialogue, which is full of puns based upon the nonsensical personification of time. Time itself is defined by and is an extension of the incomprehensible manner of the tea party. The scene Alice has come upon has no beginning and apparently no end. The personified time will not obey the Hatter; consequently it is always six o'clock, always tea time. The disordered conversation, like the ceaseless movement around the table, is endless. Life in Wonderland is indeed a Caucus-race.

In the midst of the boisterous tea party is the sleepy dormouse, whose imperturbability appears to anger the March Hare and the Hatter. When the Dormouse drowses off to sleep in the midst of its own story the Hatter pinches it, and as Alice walks away from the interminable confusion she looks back and sees the Hare and the Hatter trying to force the Dormouse into the teapot. There is no explanation offered for any of their actions, and since Wonderland offers no key to understanding its social conventions, this act of gratuitous violence appears as logical as any to conclude the chapter.

Donald Rackin believes that at this point in the narrative "the destruction of the foundations of Alice's old order is practically complete."[2] While it is true that most of the conventions which Alice and the reader subscribe to have been challenged and subverted by the inhabitants of Wonderland, it is not Alice but the reader who discovers this fact. In order to maintain the playful tension between the chaos of Wonderland and the conventional assumptions that Alice brings from her orderly world above ground, Carroll has to take care that Alice's understanding of her dream world does not develop, for that would bring an abrupt end to the nonsense. In this respect the nonsense is a form of irony implicit throughout the entire narrative.

---

1   Roger W. Holmes, "The Philosopher's *Alice in Wonderland*," in *Aspects of Alice*, 161.
2   Rackin, "Alice's Journey to the End of Night," 321.

The rose garden is a parodic garden of life. The only living creatures besides Alice are the flamingo, the hedgehog, and the Cheshire Cat, all animals. The "people" are cards. Furthermore, the flamingo and hedgehogs, which are living, are employed as surrogates for inanimate things, namely a croquet mallet and croquet balls. Life, as such, is inherently detrimental to the game of croquet where consistency and rigidity are required. Such consistency and rigidity, on the other hand, are to be found in the Queen of Hearts, who constantly calls out "Off with her head," and the King of Hearts, whose paper heart has long been trampled flat by his single-minded wife. As Alice says, "you've no idea how confusing it is all the things being alive" (p. 119).

Against the threat of life to the game of croquet is the constant mock-threat of death to Alice, the soldiers, and the Cheshire Cat. The Queen's cry for beheadings finally materializes in the person of the executioner, who has been summoned to cut off the head of the Cat. Wonderland neutralizes its own tension at this point, for the Cheshire Cat's body has vanished, leaving only its grinning head and the metaphysical question, whether one can cut off a head when there is no body from which to cut it off. Although the chapter ends with an academic consideration of execution, the subject of death is turned into an inane intellectual argument, whereby Carroll once again defends himself and the reader against the emotional prospect of mortality.

The Duchess's preoccupation with finding morals in everything parodies the temper of the self-righteous moralists of Victorian England and ironically contrasts with her own sexual aggressiveness. She foolishly applies a moral axiom to everything that Alice says. As Elsie Leach observes, "When Dodgson makes a ridiculous character like the Duchess praise and practice moralizing in this manner, he clearly indicates his attitude toward didacticism directed against children."[1] It is possible that Carroll had in mind the popular children's book by Oliver Goldsmith, *Little Goody Two Shoes*. In that work the wise and

---

1   Leach, "*Alice in Wonderland* Perspective," in *Aspects of Alice*, 91-92.

mature heroine Margery draws morals from every accident, as when the death of a pet dormouse gives her the opportunity of reading to the children a lecture on the uncertainty of life and the necessity of always being prepared for death.[1]

Carroll's depiction of the Duchess, however, goes far beyond parodying Victorian moralists: she represents a terrifying sexual threat to childhood innocence. Alice is made very uneasy by the Duchess's overtures: "Alice did not much like her keeping so close to her: first, because the Duchess was *very* ugly; and secondly, because she was exactly the right height to rest her chin on Alice's shoulder, and it was an uncomfortably sharp chin" (p. 122-23). Walking with her arm tucked "affectionately into Alice's," (p. 122) she shifts the subject to romance: "'Tis so … and the moral of that is – 'Oh, 'tis love, 'tis love, that makes the world go round!'" (p. 123). The Duchess digs her chin further into Alice's shoulder and escalates her sexual overtures: "I dare say you're wondering why I don't put my arm round your waist" (p. 124). Since Alice is still carrying her flamingo, the Duchess remarks, "I'm doubtful about the temper of your flamingo. Shall I try the experiment?" "He might bite" (p. 124), Alice cautiously replies, not at all interested in the offer. The word "experiment" to describe putting her arm around Alice's waist seems to be a sinister euphemism for the act of seduction. William Empson, on the other hand, suggests that the scene depicts Carroll's fear of being seduced by a middle-aged woman.[2] Given the heavy masculine features of the Duchess, the scene rather suggests a seduction by a grotesque man in drag. Her noble stature as duchess, her coy behavior, her elaborate feminine clothes, and her moralizing create a disturbing social, ethical and sexual ambiguity. As she digs her chin further into Alice's shoulder and offers her morals to her as a present, Carroll disrupts this nightmarish sexual encroachment by having the Queen suddenly appear to overpower the Duchess.

At last, it seems, Alice finds someone with whom she can

---

1   *Ibid.*, 92. Carroll was obviously fascinated by *Goody Two Shoes*, for in 1873 and 1877 he attended several theatrical productions in which children acted out the story in pantomime.

2   Empson, *Some Versions of Pastoral*, 263-64.

actually communicate and who will show her compassion. Free from the oppressive Duchess, Alice next meets the Mock Turtle and the Gryphon. Whereas most of the Wonderland creatures are lacking in the emotions of love, compassion, or friendship, here, at last, she seems to have come upon two inhabitants of the mad world who are capable of human feeling and understanding.

In Wonderland, however, it is never safe to judge a creature's mental state based on its behavior; in fact, there may be no mind to judge, no more than can be found in a clever puppet. Carroll describes the Mock Turtle in terms of human emotions: "They [the Gryphon and Alice] had not gone far before they saw the Mock Turtle in the distance, sitting sad and lonely on a little ledge of rock, and, as they came nearer, Alice could hear him sighing as if his heart would break. She pitied him deeply" (p. 127). With one terse remark the Gryphon deconstructs the narrator's emotive description ("sitting sad and lonely") and Alice's deep pity. "It's all his fancy, that: he hasn't got no sorrow, you know," the Gryphon declares. Although the double negative may leave the meaning of this sentence ambiguous, the thrust of the Gryphon's response is a firm reminder that theater should not be mistaken for inner reality.

The recurrent theme of the fear of being eaten dominates this episode. Alice's rendition of "'Tis the voice of the sluggard" concludes with a panther feasting upon an owl. The theme continues in the Mock Turtle's song in which he ironically celebrates the beautiful soup he is destined to become. The idea of death in both cases is distanced by the rhymes and regular meters of the poetry and by Carroll's comic logic that argues that there must be such a creature as a mock turtle to account for the soup made after it.

Many of the creatures who gather at the court for the trial of the Knave of Hearts Alice has met before, suggesting a final assemblage for the approaching conclusion. The time-obsessed White Rabbit appears again, with a trumpet in one hand and a scroll in the other, standing near the King. The conduct of the judge, jurors, and witnesses is, not surprisingly, totally civilized (and far too similar to our own legal system). Form takes precedence over substance, and insignificant details are stressed and important ones overlooked. Justice is as arbitrary as it is whimsical. What is on trial is the law itself.[1] It is another example of a system that asserts its authority within the framework of its arbitrary rules and regulations. It creates order and meaning only within its limited boundaries. From the perspective of an outsider like Alice, however, Wonderland seems indiscriminately to introduce mayhem into everything she observes, from the game of croquet to legal trials. And as in the Queen's croquet grounds, the threat of execution is constantly present in the courtroom.

Shane Leslie's parody of the excesses of Carrollian criticism views the trial as an allegorical satire of the Oxford Movement. He argues as follows: the tarts represent the Thirty-Nine Articles of the Anglican faith; a "knavish Ritualist" (John Henry Newman) is accused of "having removed their natural sense"; and the Hatter (High Church) and the March Hare (Low Church) are called as witnesses against him. Leslie concludes: "it is interesting that the King's words to the Knave were exactly those which had been hurled at Newman and at everybody who had tried to equivocate on the Articles. 'You must have meant some mischief or else you would have signed your name like an honest man.'"[2] It is not impossible, of course, that Carroll quietly alludes to Newman in this section, but the real impact of the trial scene lies in its Kafkaesque absurdity. Following the idea of life as a circular race, the trial of the Knave of Hearts subverts the normal linear progression for one that demands a verdict from the jury before the evidence is heard.

Alice begins to rebel and her increasing size threatens Wonderland with the ultimate disorder – annihilation. She upsets the jury box, spilling the animals onto the floor. The King objects that the trial cannot proceed until all the jurymen are back in their proper places. Such pointless formality in the midst of gross disorder is commonplace at this point. The Queen calls for the Knave of Hearts to be sentenced before the jury submits their verdict. Alice challenges the Queen with

---

1   Rackin, "Alice's Journey to the End of Night," 324.
2   Shane Leslie, "Lewis Carroll and the Oxford Movement," in *Aspects of Alice*, 216.

"Stuff and nonsense!," a statement that dangerously threatens to unravel the substance of Wonderland. When the Queen shouts "Off with her head!" Alice makes her climactic protest: "Who cares for *you*?... You're nothing but a pack of cards!" (p. 154). With this exclamation she annihilates Wonderland as if by word magic, and the suspension of disbelief is at an end. From a child's perspective the rules and regulations of adults may seem as arbitrary and capricious as those enunciated in the trial scene. In Alice's calling the bluff of the Queen there emerges the theme of a child's rebellion: the "rejection of adult authority, a vindication of the rights of the child, even the right of the child to self-assertion."[1]

Alice's dream becomes her nightmare. A novelty at first, Wonderland becomes increasingly oppressive to Alice as she is faced with its fundamental disorder. Everything there, including her own body size, is in a state of flux. She is treated rudely, bullied, asked questions with no answers, and denied answers to asked questions. Her recitation of poems turns them into parodies, a baby turns into a pig, and a cat turns into a grin. The essence of time and space is called into question and her romantic notion of an idyllic garden of life turns out to be a paper wasteland. Whether Alice, as some critics argue, is an alien who invades and contaminates Wonderland or is an innocent contaminated by it, one important fact remains the same: she has a vision that shows the world to be chaotic, meaningless, a terrifying void. In order to escape that oppressive and disorienting vision, she denies it with her outcry, "You're nothing but a pack of cards!," and happily regains the morally intelligible and emotionally comfortable world of her sister.

The systems of the Wonderland creatures may be logical, in the sense of being self consistent, but Carroll's point is that they bear no relation to the underlying meaningless of their world any more than our systems relate to the meaningless of our world. Alice's rejection of Wonderland therefore signals her return to the defenses of Victorian society which, though perhaps no more valid than those of Wonderland, at least afford

---

1   Leach, "*Alice in Wonderland* in Perspective," 92.

her familiar conventions of thought and behavior. As one critic astutely observes, "She becomes for many modern readers what she undoubtedly was for Dodgson: a naive champion of the doomed human quest for ultimate meaning and Edenic order."[1]

Contrasting with the uncertainties and anxieties of Wonderland is Alice's sister's idyllic imagination: "Lastly she pictured to herself how this same little sister of hers would, in the after-time, be herself a grown woman; and how she would keep, through all her riper years, the simple and loving heart of her childhood" (p. 156). The nightmarish tone of the story changes at the conclusion into sentimentality and an idyllic affirmation of innocence. This peaceful, wistful conclusion, with its hope for the preservation of Alice's simple joys and childhood innocence, suppresses the image of Alice's aggressive self. She has met and withstood all the challenges of Wonderland and emerges from the violent dislocation of her dream world totally unaware of the significance of her journey. Equipped with conventional expectations, proper manners, and a moral superiority, Alice possesses powerful defenses against the onslaughts of Wonderland. By denying the nightmare of disorder, by relegating her underground adventures to her subconscious, she is free to enjoy the illusion of order in her waking moments.

Even in the fair gardens of Oxford, however, Alice Liddell would grow up and abandon the pleasant dream of her admirer. Carroll's story is obviously concerned with the anxieties of maturity and the mystery of one's true identity. He poses those anxieties throughout the story, but particularly in the Caterpillar's rough questioning of Alice. Nevertheless, Carroll fails to deal with the subject of sexual maturity in its totality. Once recognizing the pain of growth, he refuses to follow out its implications — for that would be to make Alice's character develop, to replace her innocence with the sexuality of adolescence, and to lose her (as the White Knight does) to other interests. The dream of Alice's sister, then, is the dream of

---

1   Donald Rackin, "Blessed Rage: Lewis Carroll and the Modern Quest for Order," in *Lewis Carroll: A Celebration*, ed. Edward Guiliano (New York: Clarkson N. Potter, 1982) 18.

Carroll himself, who, in his anticipation of Alice Liddell's maturity, may well echo the conclusion of the book, that Alice would "find a pleasure in all their [other children's] simple joys, remembering her own child-life, and the happy summer days" (p. 156).

Through Bergson's Looking-Glass

Scholars, critics, psychoanalysts, and logicians have all scrutinized Carroll's writings; but few of them have offered an explanation of why or how his creations are funny. The problem with any serious discussion of humor, of course, is that the analysis inevitably destroys the fun. How much more satisfying it is to elucidate Hamlet's melancholy than to explain Falstaff's jokes! Nevertheless, humor is at the very heart of Carroll's major works, and no discussion of them could be complete without an examination of some of the principles of that humor, especially as they apply to *Alice's Adventures in Wonderland*.

Henri Bergson's essay on *Laughter*, published in 1900, is a classic statement of the principles of humor. Although his analysis focuses upon the comedy of manners, it is applicable to Carroll's humor as well. Like Carroll, Bergson lived through the technological revolution that made the duality of man and machine a vital concern of philosophers, novelists, poets, and humorists. Bergson believed that life is a vital impulse, not to be understood by reason alone, and sees the comical as something encrusted on the living.

Early in his essay Bergson observes that laughter and emotion are incompatible: "It seems as though the comic could not produce its disturbing effect unless it fell, so to say, on the surface of a soul that is thoroughly calm and unruffled. Indifference is its natural environment, for laughter has no greater foe than emotion."[1] In both his comic poetry and prose Carroll maintains a fairly consistent detachment from his

---

1 Henri Bergson, "Laughter," in *Comedy*, intro. Wylie Sypher (New York: Doubleday, 1956) 63; page numbers for subsequent quotations will be cited in the text.

characters, and his characters likewise usually remain remarkably detached from their environment. The Cheshire Cat best illustrates Bergson's point. The obvious symbol of intellectual detachment, it wears the fixed grin of an amused observer. It can appear as only a head for it is representative of a disembodied intelligence. Alice maintains a similar detachment from her surroundings. She forms no strong or lasting relationships with any of the creatures or persons in Wonderland, not even with the pitiful Mock Turtle, whose excessive weeping is merely all his fancy.

A sentimentalist might have difficulty in appreciating comedy for, as Bergson notes, "to produce the whole of its effect ... the comic demands something like a momentary anesthesia of the heart. Its appeal is to intelligence, pure and simple" (p. 63). Carroll's parodies of the didactic and sentimental verses of Isaac Watts, for example, are funny in so far as the reader is aware of the originals and attentive to the intellectual cleverness involved in reshaping them. The emotions that the moral sentiments originally invoked are repressed by the wit of the parodies.

Bergson refines his observation that laughter appeals to intelligence pure and simple by adding, "this intelligence, however, must always remain in touch with other intelligences." He continues: "The comic will come into being, it appears, whenever a group of men concentrate their attention on one of their number, imposing silence on their emotions and calling into play nothing but their intelligence" (p. 65). Alice provides exactly that focus of concentration for the reader. She is the instrument of humor as Carroll the narrator engages the mind of the reader to share with him the absurdity that arises in her various encounters with the creatures of Wonderland. Carroll invites the reader to conspire with him to laugh at their mutual representative battling with foreign intelligences.

Basic to Bergson's conception of the comic is the tension that exists between rigidity and suppleness: "rigidity is the comic, and laughter is its corrective" (p. 74). He sees a laughable expression of the face as "one that promises nothing more than it gives. It is a unique and permanent grimace. One would say that the person's whole moral life has crystallised into this particular cast of features" (p. 76). He concludes that "automatism, *inelasticity*, habit that has been contracted and maintained are clearly the causes why a face makes us laugh" (p. 76). Tenniel's illustrations are significant in this respect, for they help to fix the expressions of such characters as the Cheshire Cat with its sinister grin and the Queen of Hearts with her perpetual scowl. The Queen's favorite expression, "Off with his head!" or "Off with her head!" likewise is as fixed and predictable as her expression. The sentiment is obviously not funny, but its repetition is.

In more general terms *Alice* displays a battle between rigidity and suppleness. Alice embodies secure conventions and self-assured regulations, and Wonderland is dedicated to undermining those conventions and regulations. Later, in *Through the Looking-Glass* the strict rules of a chess game impose a degree of order upon an unruly set of characters. In this connection another statement by Bergson is revealing: "*The attitudes, gestures and movements of the human body are laughable in exact proportion as that body reminds us of a mere machine*" (p. 79). In *Through the Looking-Glass* Alice and the other characters are treated as chess pieces to be manipulated in a very rational game. In short, they have become things and, as Bergson notes, "*we laugh every time a person gives us the impression of being a thing*" (p. 97). Similarly, the battles between Tweedledee and Tweedledum and between the Lion and the Unicorn are comic because they are repetitive and predictable. Also, Wonderland's Red Queen appears robotic in her repeated, though disregarded, commands for beheadings.

Discussing the humor of disguise, Bergson argues that "any image ... suggestive of the notion of a society disguising itself, or of a social masquerade, so to speak, will be laughable" (p. 89). Both the Caucus-race and the trial of the Knave of Hearts illustrate Bergson's thesis. In the former, all the contestants are awarded prizes, thereby ignoring the substance of the race, namely, finding a winner. In the trial scene, the procedures are of paramount importance, the guilt or innocence of the defendant being of little significance. In both cases a kind of relentless automatism that converts human beings into comic puppets rules supreme.

One final observation by Bergson has relevance to Carroll's humor: "*Any incident is comic that calls our attention to the physical in a person, when it is the moral side that is concerned*" (p. 93). The humor resides in one's perceiving the tension in a "soul tantalised by the needs of the body: on the one hand, the moral personality with its intelligently varied energy, and, on the other, the stupidly monotonous body, perpetually obstructing everything with its machine-like obstinacy" (p. 93). Thus, he argues, we laugh at a public speaker who sneezes just at the most pathetic moment of his speech. Our attention is suddenly recalled from the soul to the body. Alice's frustrations in regulating her body size are cases in point. She longs to enter into "the loveliest garden you ever saw" but "she could not even get her head through the doorway." There are numerous passages in the Alice books, such as Alice's flood of tears and the Duchess' baby's uncontrollable sneezing, in which the human body baffles, betrays and embarrasses the soul.

One of the functions of humor, as Bergson sees it, is to make us human and natural during an age of mechanization. One of Carroll's early poems, "Rules and Regulations," establishes that at the outset of his career he both prized and mocked rigidity. In his fascination with mechanical gadgets he possessed in microcosm a well-ordered, smoothly running universe. In the compulsive tidiness of both his personal life and his writings he achieved an order not inherent in nature. Neither the elusive garden in Wonderland nor the cool geometry of Looking-Glass Land, however, offers more than a temporary oasis in a mutable, biological, and mortal wasteland. Carroll recognized that the machinery of conventions and customs, mathematics and logic, helped to define by contrast and momentarily sustain and comfort the frightened, imperfect, and comic adventurer.

Lewis Carroll: A Brief Chronology

1832   Charles Lutwidge Dodgson born on January 27, at Daresbury, Cheshire; son of Frances Jane Lutwidge and the Reverend Charles Dodgson.

1843   Reverend Dodgson becomes Rector of Croft, Yorkshire, and the family moves there.

1844-45   Attends Richmond Grammar School, Yorkshire.

1845   Produces the family magazine *Useful and Instructive Poetry*.

1846-49   Attends Rugby School.

1850   Studies at home preparing for Oxford; contributes prose, verse, and drawings to *The Rectory Umbrella*; matriculates at Christ Church, Oxford, on 23 May.

1851   Comes into residence as a Commoner at Christ Church on 24 January; mother dies on 26 January.

1852   Student at Christ Church.

1854   Begins to establish himself as a freelance humorist; spends summer with a mathematical reading party at Whitby; contributes poems and stories to the *Oxonian Advertiser* and the *Whitby Gazette*; obtains a First Class in the Final Mathematical School; earns B.A. 18 December.

1855   Becomes Sub-Librarian at Christ Church (holds post until 1857); composes the first stanza of "Jabberwocky," preserved in his scrapbook *Mischmasch*; begins teaching duties at Christ Church as Mathematical Lecturer (until 1881); contributes parodies to the *Comic Times*.

1856   Nom de plume "Lewis Carroll" first appears in *The Train*, a comic paper in which several of his parodies, including "Upon the Lonely Moor," appear; purchases his first camera 18 March; first meets Alice, Edith, and Lorina Liddell on 25 April.

1857   Meets Holman Hunt, John Ruskin, William Makepeace Thackeray, Alfred Tennyson; photographs the Tennyson family; receives his M.A.

1858   *The Fifth Book of Euclid treated Algebraically*, his first published book.

1860   *A Syllabus of Plane Algebraical Geometry* and *Rules for Court Circular*.

1861   Ordained Deacon on 22 December.

1862   On 4 July, makes a boating excursion up the Isis to Godstow in the company of Robinson Duckworth and the three Liddell sisters, to whom he tells the story of Alice; begins writing and revising *Alice's Adventures Under Ground*.

1863   Completes the text of *Alice's Adventures Under Ground* on 10 February; his friend, George Mac-Donald, urges him to publish it.

1864   In April John Tenniel agrees to illustrate, and Macmillan to publish the expanded and renamed (on 10 June) manuscript, *Alice's Adventures in Wonderland*; on 26 November, sends the manuscript of *Alice's Adventures Under Ground* to Alice Liddell.

1865   Sends presentation copy of *Alice's Adventures in Wonderland* to Alice Liddell on 4 July; *Alice's Adventures in Wonderland* first published in July, withdrawn in August and flawed sheets sent to America; the book's true second edition published in England in November by Richard Clay (erroneously dated 1866).

1866   Appleton of New York publishes the second (American) issue of the first edition of *Alice's Adventures in Wonderland*.

1867   Writes "Bruno's Revenge" for *Aunt Judy's Magazine*; tours the Continent and visits Russia with Dr. H. P. Liddon.

1868   Father dies on 21 June; moves his family to Guildford in September; in October moves into rooms in Tom Quad, Oxford, where he resides for the rest of his life.

1869   *Phantasmagoria and Other Poems* published in January.

1871   Completes *Through the Looking-Glass and What Alice Found There*, illustrated by John Tenniel, in January; the volume published in December (though dated 1872).

1875   "Some Popular Fallacies about Vivisection" published in the *Fortnightly Review*.

1876   *The Hunting of the Snark* (March), illustrated by Henry Holiday.

1879   *Euclid and his Modern Rivals.*

1881   Resigns Mathematical Lectureship (but retains his Studentship) to devote more time to writing.

1882   Elected Curator of the Senior Common Room (holds post until 1892).

1883   *Rhyme? and Reason?*, a collection of his verse.

1885   *A Tangled Tale*, a series of mathematical problems in the form of short stories originally printed in the *Monthly Packet*.

1886   Facsimile edition of his original illustrated manuscript of *Alice's Adventures Under Ground*; Theatrical production by Savile Clarke of *Alice in Wonderland* on 23 December.

1887   *The Game of Logic*; "Alice on the Stage," in *The Theatre*.

1888   *Curiosa Mathematica, Part 1*, a highly technical analysis of Euclid's 12th Axiom.

1889   *Sylvie and Bruno.*

1890   *The Nursery Alice.*

1893   *Sylvie and Bruno Concluded*, and *Curiosa Mathematica, Part 2.*

1896   *Symbolic Logic, Part 1*, the last book by Carroll to appear in his lifetime.

1898   Dies on 14 January at his sisters' home at Guildford and is buried there; *Three Sunsets and Other Poems* published posthumously.

A Note on the Text

The text of *Alice's Adventures in Wonderland* is based upon the ninth edition, published by Macmillan in 1897, which represents Carroll's final revised edition of the book.

ALICE'S ADVENTURES

IN WONDERLAND

CONTENTS

All in the golden afternoon[1]
    Full leisurely we glide;
For both our oars, with little skill,
    By little arms are plied,
While little hands make vain pretence
    Our wanderings to guide.

Ah, cruel Three![2] In such an hour,
    Beneath such dreamy weather,
To beg a tale of breath too weak
    To stir the tiniest feather!
Yet what can one poor voice avail
    Against three tongues together?

Imperious Prima flashes forth
    Her edict "to begin it":
In gentler tones Secunda hopes
    "There will be nonsense in it!"
While Tertia interrupts the tale
    Not more than once a minute.

Anon, to sudden silence won,
    In fancy they pursue
The dream-child moving through a land
    Of wonders wild and new,
In friendly chat with bird or beast —
    And half believe it true.

And ever, as the story drained
    The wells of fancy dry,
And faintly strove that weary one
    To put the subject by,
"The rest next time — " "It is next time!"
    The happy voices cry.

---

1   This was the afternoon of July 4, 1862 when Carroll, accompanied by Robinson
    Duckworth and the three Liddell sisters, first told the story of Alice's adventures.
2   The three Liddell sisters. Lorina Charlotte is Prima, the eldest; Alice Pleasance is
    Secunda, the second oldest; and Edith Mary is Tertia, the youngest.

Thus grew the tale of Wonderland:
  Thus slowly, one by one,
Its quaint events were hammered out –
  And now the tale is done,
And home we steer, a merry crew,
  Beneath the setting sun.

Alice! A childish story take,
  And, with a gentle hand,
Lay it where Childhood's dreams are twined
  In Memory's mystic band,
Like pilgrim's wither'd wreath of flowers[1]
  Pluck'd in a far-off land.

---

1 Pilgrims to sacred shrines were known to wear garlands of flowers on their heads.

CHAPTER I.

DOWN THE RABBIT-HOLE.

ALICE was beginning to get very tired of sitting by her sister on the bank, and of having nothing to do: once or twice she had peeped into the book her sister was reading, but it had no pictures or conversations in it, "and what is the use of a book," thought Alice, "without pictures or conversations?"

So she was considering, in her own mind (as well as she could, for the hot day made her feel very sleepy and stupid), whether the pleasure of making a daisy-chain would be worth the trouble of getting up and picking the daisies, when suddenly a White Rabbit with pink eyes ran close by her.

There was nothing so *very* remarkable in that; nor did Alice think it so *very* much out of the way to hear the Rabbit say to itself "Oh dear! Oh dear! I shall be too late!" (when she thought it over afterwards, it occurred to her that she ought to have wondered at this, but at the time it all seemed quite natural); but, when the Rabbit actually *took a watch out of its waistcoat-pocket*, and looked at it, and then hurried on, Alice started to her feet, for it flashed across her mind that she had never before seen a rabbit with either a waistcoat-pocket, or a watch to take out of it, and, burning with curiosity, she ran across the field after it, and was just in time to see it pop down a large rabbit-hole under the hedge.

In another moment down went Alice after it, never once considering how in the world she was to get out again.

The rabbit-hole went straight on like a tunnel for some way, and then dipped suddenly down, so suddenly that Alice had not a moment to think about stopping herself before she found herself falling down what seemed to be a very deep well.

Either the well was very deep, or she fell very slowly, for she had plenty of time as she went down to look about her, and to wonder what was going to happen next. First, she tried to look down and make out what she was coming to, but it was too dark to see anything: then she looked at the sides of the well, and noticed that they were filled with cupboards and book-shelves: here and there she saw maps and pictures hung upon pegs. She took down a jar from one of the shelves as she passed: it was labeled "ORANGE MARMALADE," but to her great disappointment it was empty: she did not like to drop the jar, for fear of killing somebody underneath, so managed to put it into one of the cupboards as she fell past it.[1]

"Well!" thought Alice to herself. "After such a fall as this, I shall think nothing of tumbling down-stairs! How brave they'll all think me at home! Why, I wouldn't say anything about it, even if I fell off the top of the house!" (Which was very likely true.)[2]

Down, down, down. Would the fall *never* come to an end? "I wonder how many miles I've fallen by this time?" she said

---

1 Since Alice is falling at the same rate as the jar of marmalade, she could not drop it if she wanted to, a detail the mathematician author well knew.

2 Carroll's parenthetical dark humor is here directed at Alice's naivete. Later in the story, however, he allows her to ponder her personal annihilation in terms of an extinguished candle flame.

aloud. "I must be getting somewhere near the centre of the earth. Let me see: that would be four thousand miles down, I think —" (for, you see, Alice had learnt several things of this sort in her lessons in the school-room, and though this was not a *very* good opportunity for showing off her knowledge, as there was no one to listen to her, still it was good practice to say it over) " — yes, that's about the right distance — but then I wonder what Latitude or Longitude I've got to?" (Alice had not the slightest idea what Latitude was, or Longitude either, but she thought they were nice grand words to say.)

Presently she began again. "I wonder if I shall fall right *through* the earth! How funny it'll seem to come out among the people that walk with their heads downwards! The antipathies, I think — " (she was rather glad there *was* no one listening, this time, as it didn't sound at all the right word) " — but I shall have to ask them what the name of the country is, you know. Please, Ma'am, is this New Zealand? Or Australia?" (and she tried to curtsey as she spoke — fancy, *curtseying* as you're falling through the air! Do you think you could manage it?) "And what an ignorant little girl she'll think me for asking! No, it'll never do to ask: perhaps I shall see it written up somewhere."

Down, down, down. There was nothing else to do, so Alice soon began talking again. "Dinah'll miss me very much to-night, I should think!" (Dinah[1] was the cat.) "I hope they'll remember her saucer of milk at tea-time. Dinah, my dear! I wish you were down here with me! There are no mice in the air, I'm afraid, but you might catch a bat, and that's very like a mouse, you know. But do cats eat bats, I wonder?" And here Alice began to get rather sleepy, and went on saying to herself, in a dreamy sort of way, "Do cats eat bats? Do cats eat bats?" and sometimes "Do bats eat cats?", for, you see, as she couldn't answer either question, it didn't much matter which way she put it. She felt that she was dozing off, and had just begun to dream that she was walking hand in hand with Dinah, and was saying to her, very earnestly, "Now, Dinah, tell me the truth: did you ever eat a bat?", when suddenly, thump! thump!

---

1   Dinah was the name of the Liddells' tabby cat, Alice's favorite pet.

down she came upon a heap of sticks and dry leaves, and the fall was over.

Alice was not a bit hurt, and she jumped up on to her feet in a moment: she looked up, but it was all dark overhead: before her was another long passage, and the White Rabbit was still in sight, hurrying down it. There was not a moment to be lost: away went Alice like the wind, and was just in time to hear it say, as it turned a corner, "Oh my ears and whiskers, how late it's getting!" She was close behind it when she turned the corner, but the Rabbit was no longer to be seen: she found herself in a long, low hall, which was lit up by a row of lamps hanging from the roof.

There were doors all round the hall, but they were all locked; and when Alice had been all the way down one side and up the other, trying every door, she walked sadly down the middle, wondering how she was ever to get out again.

Suddenly she came upon a little three-legged table, all made of solid glass: there was nothing on it but a tiny golden key, and Alice's first idea was that this might belong to one of the doors of the hall; but, alas! either the locks were too large, or the key was too small, but at any rate it would not open any of them. However, on the second time round, she came upon a low curtain she had not noticed before, and behind it was a little door about fifteen inches high: she tried the little golden key in the lock, and to her great delight it fitted!

Alice opened the door and found that it led into a small passage, not much larger than a rat-hole: she knelt down and looked along the passage into the loveliest garden you ever saw. How she longed to get out of that dark hall, and wander about among those beds of bright flowers and those cool fountains, but she could not even get her head through the doorway; "and even if my head *would* go through," thought poor Alice, "it would be of very little use without my shoulders. Oh, how I wish I could shut up like a telescope! I think I could, if I only knew how to begin." For, you see, so many out-of-the-way things had happened lately, that Alice had begun to think that very few things indeed were really impossible.

There seemed to be no use in waiting by the little door, so she went back to the table, half hoping she might find another key on it, or at any rate a book of rules for shutting people up like telescopes: this time she found a little bottle on it ("which certainly was not here before," said Alice),[1] and tied round the neck of the bottle was a paper label, with the words "DRINK ME" beautifully printed on it in large letters.

It was all very well to say "Drink me," but the wise little Alice was not going to do *that* in a hurry. "No, I'll look first,"

---

1 Assuming Alice is correct in observing that the bottle was not on the table when she first took the key, one suspects an eerie authorial presence that manipulates the scene.

she said, "and see whether it's marked '*poison*' or not"; for she had read several nice little stories[1] about children who had got burnt, and eaten up by wild beasts, and other unpleasant things, all because they *would* not remember the simple rules their friends had taught them: such as, that a red-hot poker will burn you if you hold it too long; and that, if you cut your finger *very* deeply with a knife, it usually bleeds; and she had never forgotten that, if you drink much from a bottle marked "poison," it is almost certain to disagree with you, sooner or later.

However, this bottle was *not* marked "poison," so Alice ventured to taste it, and, finding it very nice (it had, in fact, a sort of mixed flavour of cherry-tart, custard, pine-apple, roast turkey, toffy, and hot buttered toast), she very soon finished it off.[2]

★　★　★　★

★　★　★　★

"What a curious feeling!" said Alice. "I must be shutting up like telescope!"

And so it was indeed: she was now only ten inches high, and her face brightened up at the thought that she was now the right size for going through the little door into that lovely garden. First, however, she waited for a few minutes to see if she was going to shrink any further: she felt a little nervous about this; "for it might end, you know," said Alice herself, "in my going out altogether, like a candle.[3] I wonder what I should be like then?" And she tried to fancy what the flame of a candle looks like after the candle is blown out, for she could not remember ever having seen such a thing.

After a while, finding that nothing more happened, she decided going into the garden at once; but, alas for poor Alice!

1　Didactic and moralistic stories aimed at creating obedient and dutiful children were popular during the nineteenth century. See "Amelia and the Dwarfs" in Appendix I for an example of such tales.

2　Carroll's insertion of asterisks appear after Alice drinks or eats, indicating that she will undergo a sudden change in size.

3　This grim thought is echoed later in *Through the Looking-Glass* when the Tweedle brothers assault Alice with the idea that she is merely a sort of thing in the Red King's dream, and that were the King to wake, she would "go out – bang! – just like a candle!"

when she got the door, she found she had forgotten the little golden key, and when she went back to the table for it, she found she could not possibly reach it: she could see it quite plainly through the glass, and she tried her best to climb up one of the legs of the table, but it was too slippery; and when she had tired herself out with trying, the poor little thing sat down and cried.

"Come, there's no use in crying like that!" said Alice to herself rather sharply, "I advise you to leave off this minute!" She generally gave herself very good advice (though she very seldom followed it), and sometimes she scolded herself so severely as to bring tears into her eyes; and once she remembered trying to box her own ears for having cheated herself in a game of croquet she was playing against herself, for this curious child was very fond of pretending to be two people. "But it's no use now," thought poor Alice, "to pretend to be two people! Why, there's hardly enough of me left to make *one* respectable person!"

Soon her eye fell on a little glass box that was lying under the table: she opened it, and found in it a very small cake, on which the words "EAT ME" were beautifully marked in currants. "Well, I'll eat it," said Alice, "and if it makes me grow larger, I can reach the key; and if it makes me grow smaller, I can creep under the door: so either way I'll get into the garden, and I don't care which happens!"

She ate a little bit, and said anxiously to herself "Which way? Which way?", holding her hand on the top of her head to feel which way it was growing; and she was quite surprised to find that she remained the same size. To be sure, this is what generally happens when one eats cake; but Alice had got so much into the way of expecting nothing but out-of-the-way things to happen, that it seemed quite dull and stupid for life to go on in the common way.

So she set to work, and very soon finished off the cake.

★   ★   ★   ★

★   ★   ★   ★

CHAPTER II.

THE POOL OF TEARS.

"CURIOUSER and curiouser!" cried Alice (she was so much surprised, that for the moment she quite forgot how to speak good English). "Now I'm opening out like the largest telescope that ever was! Good-bye, feet!" (for when she looked down at her feet, they seemed to be almost out of sight, they were getting so far off). "Oh, my poor little feet, I wonder who will put on your shoes and stockings for you now, dears? I'm sure *I* sha'n't be able! I shall be a great deal too far off to trouble myself about you: you must manage the best way you can – but I must be kind to them," thought Alice, "or perhaps they wo'n't walk the way I want to go! Let me see. I'll give them a new pair of boots every Christmas."

And she went on planning to herself how she would manage it. "They must go by the carrier," she thought; "and how funny it'll seem, sending presents to one's own feet! And how odd the directions will look!

> Alice's Right Foot, Esq.
> Hearthrug,
> near the Fender,[1]
> (with Alice's love).

Oh dear, what nonsense I'm talking!"

Just at this moment her head struck against the roof of the hall: in fact she was now rather more than nine feet high, and she at once took up the little golden key and hurried off to the garden door.

Poor Alice! It was as much as she could do, lying down on one side, to look through into the garden with one eye; but to get through was more hopeless than ever: she sat down and began to cry again.

"You ought to be ashamed of yourself," said Alice, "a great girl like you," (she might well say this), "to go on crying in this way! Stop this moment, I tell you!" But she went on all the same, shedding gallons of tears, until there was a large pool around her, about four inches deep, and reaching half down the hall.

After a time she heard a little pattering of feet in the distance, and she hastily dried her eyes to see what was coming. It was the White Rabbit returning, splendidly dressed, with a pair of white kid-gloves in one hand and a large fan in the other: he came trotting along in a great hurry, muttering to himself, as he

---

1   A fender is a screen between the hearthrug and an open fireplace.

came, "Oh! The Duchess, the Duchess! Oh! *Wo'n't* she be savage if I've kept her waiting!" Alice felt so desperate that she was ready to ask help of any one: so, when the Rabbit came near her, she began, in a low, timid voice, "If you please. Sir –" The Rabbit started violently, dropped the white kid-gloves and the fan, and skurried away into the darkness as hard as he could go.

Alice took up the fan and gloves, and, as the hall was very hot, she kept fanning herself all the time she went on talking. "Dear, dear! How queer everything is to-day! And yesterday things went on just as usual. I wonder if I've been changed in the night? Let me think: was I the same when I got up this morning? I almost think I can remember feeling a little different. But if I'm not the same, the next question is 'Who in the world am I?' Ah, *that's* the great puzzle!" And she began thinking over all the children she knew that were of the same age as herself, to see if she could have been changed for any of them.

"I'm sure I'm not Ada," she said, "for her hair goes in such long ringlets, and mine doesn't go in ringlets at all; and I'm sure I ca'n't be Mabel, for I know all sorts of things, and she, oh, she knows such a very little! Besides, *she's* she, and I'm *I*, and – oh dear, how puzzling it all is! I'll try if I know all the things I used to know. Let me see: four times five is twelve, and four times six is thirteen, and four times seven is – oh dear! I shall never get to twenty at that rate![1] However, the Multiplication-Table doesn't signify: let's try Geography. London is the capital of Paris, and Paris is the capital of Rome, and Rome – no, *that's* all wrong. I'm certain! I must have been changed for Mabel! I'll try and say '*How doth the little* – ',", and she crossed her hands on her lap, as if she were saying lessons, and began to repeat it, but her voice sounded hoarse and strange, and the words did not come the same as they used to do: –

> *"How doth the little crocodile*
> *Improve his shining tail,*
> *And pour the waters of the Nile*
> *On every golden scale!*
>
> *"How cheerfully he seems to grin,*
> *How neatly spreads his claws,*
> *And welcomes little fishes in,*
> *With gently smiling jaws!"*[2]

"I'm sure those are not the right words," said poor Alice, and her eyes filled with tears again as she went on, "I must be Mabel after all, and I shall have to go and live in that poky little house, and have next to no toys to play with, and oh, ever so many lessons to learn! No, I've made up my mind about it: if

---

1 Martin Gardner, in his *Annotated Alice*, explains that since the traditional multiplication table ends with the 12's, if you continue the nonsense progression you end with 4 times 12 (the highest she can go) is 19, one short of twenty.
2 A parody of "Against Idleness and Mischief" by Isaac Watts (1674-1748), reprinted in Appendix H.

I'm Mabel, I'll stay down here! It'll be no use their putting their heads down and saying 'Come up again, dear!' I shall only look up and say 'Who am I, then? Tell me that first, and then, if I like being that person, I'll come up: if not, I'll stay down here till I'm somebody else' – but, oh dear!" cried Alice, with a sudden burst of tears, "I do wish they *would* put their heads down! I am so *very* tired of being all alone here!"

As she said this she looked down at her hands, and was surprised to see that she had put on one of the Rabbit's little white kid-gloves while she was talking. "How *can* I have done that?" she thought. "I must be growing small again." She got up and went to the table to measure herself by it, and found that, as nearly as she could guess, she was now about two feet high, and was going on shrinking rapidly: she soon found out that the cause of this was the fan she was holding, and she dropped it hastily, just in time to save herself from shrinking away altogether.

"That *was* a narrow escape!" said Alice, a good deal frightened at the sudden change, but very glad to find herself still in existence. "And now for the garden!" And she ran with all speed back to the little door; but, alas! the little door was shut again, and the little golden key was lying on the glass table as before, "and things are worse than ever," thought the poor child, "for I never was so small as this before, never! And I declare it's too bad, that it is!"

As she said these words her foot slipped, and in another moment, splash! she was up to her chin in salt-water. Her first idea was that she had somehow fallen into the sea, "and in that case I can go back by railway," she said to herself. (Alice had been to the seaside once in her life, and had come to the general conclusion that, wherever you go to on the English coast, you find a number of bathing-machines[1] in the sea, some children digging in the sand with wooden spades, then a row of lodging-houses, and behind them a railway station.) However,

---

[1] Bathing machines are horse-drawn caravans in which bathers would change into their swimming clothes. The horses would back the caravans into the water so that the bathers could exit down the steps directly into the sea.

she soon made out that she was in the pool of tears which she had wept when she was nine feet high.

"I wish I hadn't cried so much!" said Alice, as she swam about, trying to find her way out. "I shall be punished for it now, I suppose, by being drowned in my own tears![1] That *will* be a queer thing, to be sure! However, everything is queer to-day."

Just then she heard something splashing about in the pool a little way off, and she swam nearer to make out what it was: at first she thought it must be a walrus or hippopotamus, but then she remembered how small she was now, and she soon made out that it was only a mouse, that had slipped in like herself.

"Would it be of any use, now," thought Alice, "to speak to this mouse? Everything is so out-of-the-way down here, that I should think very likely it can talk: at any rate, there's no harm in trying." So she began: "O Mouse, do you know the way out of this pool? I am very tired of swimming about here, O Mouse!" (Alice thought this must be the right way of speaking to a mouse: she had never done such a thing before, but she remembered having seen, in her brother's Latin Grammar, "A mouse – of a mouse – to a mouse – a mouse – O mouse!")[2] The mouse looked at her rather inquisitively, and seemed to her to wink with one of its little eyes, but it said nothing.

---

1 One of the recurrent themes in Carroll's writings is the fear of disorder and emotional excess, a fear kept in check through humor and wit.
2 The Latin cases for nouns: nominative, genitive, dative, accusative, and vocative.

"Perhaps it doesn't understand English," thought Alice. "I daresay it's a French mouse, come over with William the Conqueror." (For, with all her knowledge of history, Alice had no very clear notion how long ago anything had happened.) So she began again: "Où est ma chatte?", which was the first sentence in her French lesson-book. The Mouse gave a sudden leap out of the water, and seemed to quiver all over with fright. "Oh, I beg your pardon!" cried Alice hastily, afraid that she had hurt the poor animal's feelings. "I quite forgot you didn't like cats."

"Not like cats!" cried the Mouse in a shrill, passionate voice. "Would *you* like cats, if you were me?"

"Well, perhaps not," said Alice in a soothing tone: "don't be angry about it. And yet I wish I could show you our cat Dinah. I think you'd take a fancy to cats, if you could only see her. She is such a dear quiet thing," Alice went on, half to herself, as she swam lazily about in the pool, "and she sits purring so nicely by the fire, licking her paws and washing her face – and she is such a nice soft thing to nurse – and she's such a capital one for catching mice – oh, I beg your pardon!" cried Alice again, for this time the Mouse was bristling all over, and she felt certain it must be really offended. "We wo'n't talk about her any more, if you'd rather not."

"We, indeed!" cried the Mouse, who was trembling down to the end of its tail. "As if I would talk on such a subject! Our family always *hated* cats: nasty, low, vulgar things! Don't let me hear the name again!"

"I wo'n't indeed!" said Alice, in a great hurry to change the subject of conversation. "Are you – are you fond – of – of dogs?" The Mouse did not answer, so Alice went on eagerly: "There is such a nice little dog, near our house, I should like to show you! A little bright-eyed terrier, you know, with oh, such long curly brown hair! And it'll fetch things when you throw them, and it'll sit up and beg for its dinner, and all sorts of things – I ca'n't remember half of them – and it belongs to a farmer, you know, and he says it's so useful, it's worth a hundred pounds! He says it kills all the rats and – oh dear!" cried Alice in a sorrowful tone. "I'm afraid I've offended it again!" For the Mouse was swimming away from her as hard as it could go, and making quite a commotion in the pool as it went.

So she called softly after it, "Mouse dear! Do come back again, and we wo'n't talk about cats, or dogs either, if you don't like them!" When the Mouse heard this, it turned round and swam slowly back to her: its face was quite pale (with passion, Alice thought), and it said, in a low trembling voice, "Let us get to the shore, and then I'll tell you my history, and you'll understand why it is I hate cats and dogs."

It was high time to go, for the pool was getting quite crowded with the birds and animals that had fallen into it: there was a Duck and a Dodo, a Lory and an Eaglet, and several other curious creatures.[1] Alice led the way, and the whole party swam to the shore.

---

1   The Duck is Reverend Robinson Duckworth, Fellow of Trinity College, Oxford, and later Chaplain to the Queen and Canon of Westminster. He was present on the rowing party on July 4, 1862, when Carroll first told the Liddell sisters the story of Alice. The Dodo (a large, awkward, flightless bird that once lived on the island of Mauritius but which has been extinct since the seventeenth century) is Carroll, himself. When he stammered Carroll's name would come out as "Do-Do-Dodgson." The Lory (a brightly colored Australasian parrot) represents Lorina Liddell. The Eaglet is Edith Liddell. The "other curious creatures" may refer to Carroll's sisters, Frances and Elizabeth, and his Aunt Lucy Lutwidge, all of whom went with Carroll and the three Liddell sisters on a rowing party to Nuneham on June 17, 1862. A heavy downpour of rain caused them to leave their boat and walk three miles through the storm. This drenching may have been the inspiration for Alice's pool of tears.

CHAPTER III.

A CAUCUS-RACE AND A LONG TALE.

THEY were indeed a queer-looking party that assembled on the bank-the birds with draggled feathers, the animals with their fur clinging close to them, and all dripping wet, cross, and uncomfortable.

The first question of course was, how to get dry again: they had a consultation about this, and after a few minutes it seemed quite natural to Alice to find herself talking familiarly with them, as if she had known them all her life. Indeed, she had quite a long argument with the Lory, who at last turned sulky, and would only say, "I'm older than you, and must know better." And this Alice would not allow, without knowing how old it was, and, as the Lory positively refused to tell its age, there was no more to be said.

At last the Mouse, who seemed to be a person of some authority among them, called out "Sit down, all of you, and listen to me! *I'll* soon make you dry enough!" They all sat down at once, in a large ring, with the Mouse in the middle. Alice kept her eyes anxiously fixed on it, for she felt sure she would catch a bad cold if she did not get dry very soon.

"Ahem!" said the Mouse with an important air. "Are you all ready? This is the driest thing I know. Silence all round, if you please! 'William the Conqueror, whose cause was favoured by the pope, was soon submitted to by the English, who wanted leaders, and had been of late much accustomed to usurpation and conquest. Edwin and Morcar, the earls of Mercia and Northumbria —'"[1]

"Ugh!" said the Lory, with a shiver.

"I beg your pardon!" said the Mouse, frowning, but very politely. "Did you speak?"

"Not I!" said the Lory, hastily.

"I thought you did," said the Mouse. "I proceed. 'Edwin and Morcar, the earls of Mercia and Northumbria, declared for him; and even Stigand, the patriotic archbishop of Canterbury, found it advisable – '"

"Found *what*?" said the Duck.

"Found *it*," the Mouse replied rather crossly: "of course you know what 'it' means."[2]

"I know what 'it' means well enough, when *I* find a thing," said the Duck: "it's generally a frog, or a worm. The question is, what did the archbishop find?"

The Mouse did not notice this question, but hurriedly went on, "' – found it advisable to go with Edgar Atheling to meet William and offer him the crown. William's conduct at first was moderate. But the insolence of his Normans –' How are you getting on now, my dear?" it continued, turning to Alice as it spoke.

---

1 In his edition of the Alice books, Roger Lancelyn Green identifies this rather pompous and dry quotation as coming from Havilland Chepmell's *A Short Course of History* (1862), a book used by the Liddell sisters' governess to instruct them.

2 This is one of many examples in the story of the deconstruction of ordinary discourse. Rather than getting on with the business of communication, some of the creatures in Wonderland prefer to play with issues of grammar, linguistics, and logic.

"As wet as ever," said Alice in a melancholy tone: "it doesn't seem to dry me at all."

"In that case," said the Dodo solemnly, rising to its feet, "I move that the meeting adjourn, for the immediate adoption of more energetic remedies – "

"Speak English!" said the Eaglet. "I don't know the meaning of half those long words, and, what's more, I don't believe you do either!" And the Eaglet bent down its head to hide a smile: some of the other birds tittered audibly.

"What I was going to say," said the Dodo in an offended tone, "was, that the best thing to get us dry would be a Caucus-race."[1]

"What *is* a Caucus-race?" said Alice; not that she much wanted to know, but the Dodo had paused as if it thought that *somebody* ought to speak, and no one else seemed inclined to say anything.

"Why," said the Dodo, "the best way to explain it is to do it." (And, as you might like to try the thing yourself, some winter-day, I will tell you how the Dodo managed it.)

First it marked out a race-course, in a sort of circle, ("the exact shape doesn't matter," it said,) and then all the party were placed along the course, here and there. There was no "One, two, three, and away!", but they began running when they liked, and left off when they liked, so that it was not easy to know when the race was over. However, when they had been running half an hour or so, and were quite dry again, the Dodo suddenly called out "The race is over!", and they all crowded round it, panting, and asking "But who has won?"

This question the Dodo could not answer without a great deal of thought, and it stood for a long time with one finger pressed upon its forehead (the position in which you usually

---

1   *Caucus* is an American term for a meeting of local members of a political party especially to select delegates to a convention or register preferences for candidates running for office. In the 1760's there was a Caucus Club of Boston, its name possibly derived from the Medieval Latin term for a drinking vessel, *caucus*. In his *Annotated Alice* Martin Gardner suggests that Carroll might have intended his Caucus-race to represent the fact that committee members frequently run around in circles, getting nowhere, and with everyone wanting a political plum. More simply, perhaps, he chose the name because it was both mysterious and alliterative.

see Shakespeare, in the pictures of him), while the rest waited in silence. At last the Dodo said "*Everybody* has won, and *all* must have prizes."

"But who is to give the prizes?" quite a chorus of voices asked.

"Why, *she*, of course," said the Dodo, pointing to Alice with one finger; and the whole party at once crowded round her, calling out, in a confused way, "Prizes! Prizes!"

Alice had no idea what to do, and in despair she put her hand in her pocket, and pulled out a box of comfits[1] (luckily the salt water had not got into it), and handed them round as prizes. There was exactly one a-piece, all round.

"But she must have a prize herself, you know," said the Mouse.

"Of course," the Dodo replied very gravely. "What else have you got in your pocket?" it went on, turning to Alice.

"Only a thimble,"[2] said Alice sadly.

---

1   A comfit is a confection of sugar-covered fruit, seed, or nut.
2   Thimbles appear to hold a special significance to Carroll. In his book *Lewis Carroll* Derek Hudson notes (p. 44) that when a loose floor board in the nursery floor at Croft Rectory (where the Dodgsons moved in 1843 when Carroll was eleven years

"Hand it over here," said the Dodo.

Then they all crowded round her once more, while the Dodo solemnly presented the thimble, saying "We beg your acceptance of this elegant thimble"; and, when it had finished this short speech, they all cheered

Alice thought the whole thing very absurd, but they all looked so grave that she did not dare to laugh; and, as she could not think of anything to say, she simply bowed, and took the thimble, looking as solemn as she could.

The next thing was to eat the comfits: this caused some noise and confusion, as the large birds complained that they could not taste theirs, and the small ones choked and had to be patted on the back. However, it was over at last, and they sat down again in a ring, and begged the Mouse to tell them something more.

"You promised to tell me your history, you know," said Alice, "and why it is you hate — C and D," she added in a whisper, half afraid that it would be offended again.

"Mine is a long and a sad tale! "said the Mouse, turning to Alice, and sighing.

"It is a long tail, certainly," said Alice, looking down with wonder at the Mouse's tail; "but why do you call it sad?" And she kept on puzzling about it while the Mouse was speaking, so that her idea of the tale was something like this:[1]

---

old) was taken up during renovation in 1950 the workmen discovered several items hidden away, including a child's white glove, a child's left-hand shoe, and a thimble. Later, in Carroll's long poem *The Hunting of the Snark*, a zany crew with unusual instruments go in search of a Snark: "They sought it with thimbles, they sought it with care;/ They pursued it with forks and hope." It has been suggested that Alice's reception of the thimble as her prize looks towards her future domesticity. Might one not see, however, in the Dodo's serious presentation of the "elegant thimble" to Alice a tantalizing subtext: Carroll's proposal of marriage to Alice Liddell? (See Morton Cohen's *Lewis Carroll*, pp. 101-04, for a discussion of the issue of a marriage proposal).

1   The mouse's tale is a recasting of the poem in *Alice's Adventures Under Ground* reprinted in the Appendix. Shaped verse has a long tradition that includes such writers as George Herbert and Robert Herrick. Carroll's revision of his original poem introduces a satire on the law, thus anticipating the bizarre trial of the Knave of Hearts.

"Fury said to
a mouse, That
he met in the
house, 'Let
us both go
to law: I
will prose-
cute *you*. —
Come, I'll
take no de-
nial: We
must have
the trial;
For really
this morn-
ing I've
nothing
to do.'
Said the
mouse to
the cur,
'Such a
trial, dear
sir, With
no jury
or judge,
would
be wast-
ing our
breath.'
'I'll be
judge,
I'll be
jury,'
said
cun-
ning
old
Fury:
'I'll
try
the
whole
cause,
and
con-
demn
you to
death'."

"You are not attending!" said the Mouse to Alice, severely. "What are you thinking of?"

"I beg your pardon," said Alice very humbly: "you had got to the fifth bend, I think?"

"I had *not*!" cried the Mouse, sharply and very angrily.

"A knot!" said Alice, always ready to make herself useful, and looking anxiously about her "Oh, do let me help to undo it!"

"I shall do nothing of the sort," said the Mouse, getting up and walking away. "You insult me by talking such nonsense!"

"I didn't mean it!" pleaded poor Alice. "But you're so easily offended, you know!"

The Mouse only growled in reply.

"Please come back, and finish your story!" Alice called after it. And the others all joined in chorus "Yes, please do!" But the Mouse only shook its head impatiently, and walked a little quicker.

"What a pity it wouldn't stay!" sighed the Lory, as soon as it was quite out of sight. And an old Crab took the opportunity of saying to her daughter "Ah, my dear! Let this be a lesson to you never to lose *your* temper!" "Hold your tongue, Ma!" said the young Crab, a little snappishly. "You're enough to try the patience of an oyster!"

"I wish I had our Dinah here, I know I do!" said Alice aloud, addressing nobody in particular. "She'd soon fetch it back!"

"And who is Dinah, if I might venture to ask the question?" said the Lory.

Alice replied eagerly, for she was always ready to talk about her pet: "Dinah's our cat. And she's such a capital one for catching mice, you ca'n't think! And oh, I wish you could see her after the birds! Why, she'll eat a little bird as soon as look at it!"

This speech caused a remarkable sensation among the party. Some of the birds hurried off at once: one old Magpie began wrapping itself up very carefully, remarking "I really must be getting home: the night-air doesn't suit my throat!" And a Canary called out in a trembling voice, to its children, "Come away, my dears! It's high time you were all in bed!" On various pretexts they all moved off, and Alice was soon left alone.

"I wish I hadn't mentioned Dinah!" she said to herself in a melancholy tone. "Nobody seems to like her, down here, and I'm sure she's the best cat in the world! Oh, my dear Dinah! I wonder if I shall ever see you any more!" And here poor Alice began to cry again, for she felt very lonely and low-spirited. In a little while, however, she again heard a little pattering of footsteps in the distance, and she looked up eagerly, half hoping that the Mouse had changed his mind, and was coming back to finish his story.

CHAPTER IV.

THE RABBIT SENDS IN A LITTLE BILL.

It was the White Rabbit, trotting slowly back again, and looking anxiously about as it went, as if it had lost something; and
she heard it muttering to itself, "The Duchess! The Duchess!
Oh my dear paws! Oh my fur and whiskers! She'll get me executed, as sure as ferrets are ferrets! Where *can* I have dropped
them, I wonder?" Alice guessed in a moment that it was looking for the fan and the pair of white kid-gloves, and she very
good-naturedly began hunting about for them, but they were
nowhere to be seen – everything seemed to have changed since
her swim in the pool; and the great hall, with the glass table and
the little door, had vanished completely.

Very soon the Rabbit noticed Alice, as she went hunting
about, and called out to her, in an angry tone, "Why, Mary
Ann,[1] what *are* you doing out here? Run home this moment,
and fetch me a pair of gloves[2] and a fan! Quick, now!" And
Alice was so much frightened that she ran off at once in the
direction it pointed to, without trying to explain the mistake
that it had made.

"He took me for his housemaid," she said to herself as she
ran. "How surprised he'll be when he finds out who I am! But
I'd better take him his fan and gloves – that is, if I can find
them." As she said this, she came upon a neat little house,
on the door of which was a bright brass plate with the name
"W. RABBIT" engraved upon it. She went in without

---

1   According to Roger Lancyln Green the name "Mary Ann" was a common equiva-
    lent for "servant girl" in the nineteenth century.
2   Like thimbles, gloves held a special meaning to Carroll. As a child he appears to
    have hidden a white glove beneath the floor board of his room at Croft Rectory.
    Isa Bowman, the child actress who became one of Carroll's closest child friends late
    in his life, recalls: "he had a curious habit of always wearing, in all seasons of the
    year, a pair of grey cotton gloves" (*Lewis Carroll As I Knew Him*, p. 9). Certainly the
    Liddell children would recognize the parallels between people they knew and the
    creatures in the story.

knocking, and hurried upstairs, in great fear lest she should meet the real Mary Ann, and be turned out of the house before she had found the fan and gloves.

"How queer it seems," Alice said to herself, "to be going messages for a rabbit! I suppose Dinah'll be sending me on messages next!" And she began fancying the sort of thing that would happen: "'Miss Alice! Come here directly, and get ready for your walk!' 'Coming in a minute, nurse! But I've got to watch this mouse-hole till Dinah comes back, and see that the mouse doesn't get out.' Only I don't think," Alice went on, "that they'd let Dinah stop in the house if it began ordering people about like that!"

By this time she had found her way into a tidy little room with a table in the window, and on it (as she had hoped) a fan and two or three pairs of tiny white kid-gloves: she took up the fan and a pair of the gloves, and was just going to leave the room, when her eye fell upon a little bottle that stood near the looking-glass. There was no label this time with the words "DRINK ME," but nevertheless she uncorked it and put it to her lips. "I know *something* interesting is sure to happen," she said to herself, "whenever I eat or drink anything: so I'll just see what this bottle does. I do hope it'll make me grow large again, for really I'm quite tired of being such a tiny little thing!"

It did so indeed, and much sooner than she had expected: before she had drunk half the bottle, she found her head pressing against the ceiling, and had to stoop to save her neck from being broken. She hastily put down the bottle, saying to herself "That's quite enough – I hope I sha'n't grow any more – As it is, I ca'n't get out at the door – I do wish I hadn't drunk quite so much!"

Alas! It was too late to wish that! She went on growing, and growing, and very soon had to kneel down on the floor: in another minute there was not even room for this, and she tried the effect of lying down with one elbow against the door, and the other arm curled round her head. Still she went on grow-ing, and, as a last resource, she put one arm out of the window, and one foot up the chimney, and said to herself "Now I can do no more, whatever happens. What *will* become of me?"

Luckily for Alice, the little magic bottle had now had its full effect, and she grew no larger: still it was very uncomfortable, and, as there seemed to be no sort of chance of her ever getting out of the room again, no wonder she felt unhappy.

"It was much pleasanter at home," thought poor Alice, "when one wasn't always growing larger and smaller, and being ordered about by mice and rabbits. I almost wish I hadn't gone down that rabbit-hole – and yet – and yet – it's rather curious, you know, this sort of life! I do wonder what *can* have happened to me! When I used to read fairy tales, I fancied that kind of thing never happened, and now here I am in the middle of one![1] There ought to be a book written about me, that there ought! And when I grow up, I'll write one – but I'm grown up now," she added in a sorrowful tone: "at least there's no room to grow up any more *here*."

---

1   Despite the fact that Alice's experiences are cast in the form of a dream, she always carries a "passport" home. In this instance she reveals that she is conscious that she is in a dream world, and throughout her travels in Wonderland she constantly alludes to the comfortable and understandable Victorian world from which she came, a safe harbor of sanity in what appears a mad world. Her self-consciousness finally gives her control over her dream and allows her to emerge from it when she shouts out in the courtroom "You're nothing but a pack of cards!"

"But then," thought Alice, "shall I *never* get any older than I am now? That'll be a comfort, one way – never to be an old woman – but then – always to have lessons to learn! Oh, I shouldn't like *that*!"

"Oh, you foolish Alice!" she answered herself. "How can you learn lessons in here? Why, there's hardly room for *you*, and no room at all for any lesson-books!"

And so she went on, taking first one side and then the other, and making quite a conversation of it altogether; but after a few minutes she heard a voice outside, and stopped to listen.

"Mary Ann! Mary Ann!" said the voice. "Fetch me my gloves this moment!" Then came a little pattering of feet on the stairs. Alice knew it was the Rabbit coming to look for her, and she trembled till she shook the house, quite forgetting that she was now about a thousand times as large as the Rabbit, and had no reason to be afraid of it.

Presently the Rabbit came up to the door, and tried to open it; but, as the door opened inwards, and Alice's elbow was pressed hard against it, that attempt proved a failure. Alice heard it say to itself "Then I'll go round and get in at the window."

"*That* you wo'n't!" thought Alice, and, after waiting till she fancied she heard the Rabbit just under the window, she suddenly spread out her hand, and made a snatch in the air. She did not get hold of anything, but she heard a little shriek and a fall, and a crash of broken glass, from which she concluded that it was just possible it had fallen into a cucumber-frame, or something of the sort.

Next came an angry voice – the Rabbit's – "Pat! Pat! Where are you?" And then a voice she had never heard before, "Sure then I'm here! Digging for apples, yer honour!"[1]

"Digging for apples, indeed!" said the Rabbit angrily. "Here! Come help me out of *this*!" (Sounds of more broken glass.)

"Now tell me, Pat, what's that in the window?"

"Sure, it's an arm, yer honour!" (He pronounced it "arrum.")

---

[1] The uneducated speech of Pat, an Irishman, conveys a humorous stereotype of the lower class. The sensitivity of the British ear to class differences makes for easy fun, as does the reversal of roles between the White Rabbit and Alice (aka "Mary Ann").

"An arm, you goose! Who ever saw one that size? Why, it fills the whole window!"

"Sure, it does, yer honour: but it's an arm for all that."

"Well, it's got no business there, at any rate: go and take it away!"

There was a long silence after this, and Alice could only hear whispers now and then; such as "Sure, I don't like it, yer honour, at all, at all!" "Do as I tell you, you coward!", and at last she spread out her hand again, and made another snatch in the air. This time there were *two* little shrieks, and more sounds of broken glass. "What a number of cucumber-frames there must be!" thought Alice. "I wonder what they'll do next! As for pulling me out of the window, I only wish they *could*! I'm sure *I* don't want to stay in here any longer!"

She waited for some time without hearing anything more: at last came a rumbling of little cart-wheels, and the sound of a good many voices all talking together: she made out the words: "Where's the other ladder? – Why, I hadn't to bring but one. Bill's got the other – Bill! Fetch it here, lad! – Here, put 'em up at this corner – No, tie 'em together first – they don't reach half high enough yet – Oh, they'll do well enough. Don't be particular – Here, Bill! Catch hold of this rope – Will the roof bear? – Mind that loose slate – Oh, it's coming down! Heads below!" (a loud crash) – "Now, who did that? – It was Bill, I fancy – Who's to go down the chimney? – Nay, I sha'n't! *You* do it! – That I wo'n't, then! – Bill's got to go down – Here, Bill! The master says you've got to go down the chimney!"[1]

"Oh! So Bill's got to come down the chimney, has he?" said Alice to herself. "Why, they seem to put everything upon Bill! I wouldn't be in Bill's place for a good deal: this fireplace is narrow, to be sure; but I *think* I can kick a little!"

She drew her foot as far down the chimney as she could, and waited till she heard a little animal (she couldn't guess of what sort it was) scratching and scrambling about in the chimney close above her: then, saying to herself "This is Bill", she gave one sharp kick, and waited to see what would happen next.

The first thing she heard was a general chorus of "There goes Bill!" then the Rabbit's voice alone – "Catch him, you by the hedge!" then silence, and then another confusion of voices – "Hold up his head – Brandy now – Don't choke him – How was it, old fellow? What happened to you? Tell us all about it!"

Last came a little feeble, squeaking voice ("That's Bill," thought Alice), "Well, I hardly know – No more, thank ye; I'm better now – but I'm a deal too flustered to tell you – all I know is, something comes at me like a Jack-in-the-box, and up I goes like a sky-rocket!"

"So you did, old fellow!" said the others.

---

1 It is interesting to note that during this scene Carroll presents the madcap proceedings from Alice's limited perspective. She has to unscramble the excited talk and odd noises in order to figure out what is going on outside the house.

"We must burn the house down!" said the Rabbit's voice. And Alice called out, as loud as she could, "If you do, I'll set Dinah at you!"

There was a dead silence instantly, and Alice thought to herself "I wonder what they *will* do next! If they had any sense, they'd take the roof off." After a minute or two, they began moving about again, and Alice heard the Rabbit say "A barrowful will do, to begin with."

"A barrowful of *what*?" thought Alice. But she had not long to doubt, for the next moment a shower of little pebbles came rattling in at the window, and some of them hit her in the face. "I'll put a stop to this," she said to herself, and shouted out "You'd better not do that again!", which produced another dead silence.

Alice noticed, with some surprise, that the pebbles were all turning into little cakes as they lay on the floor, and a bright idea came into her head. "If I eat one of these cakes," she thought, "it's sure to make *some* change in my size; and, as it ca'n't possibly make me larger, it must make me smaller, I suppose."

So she swallowed one of the cakes, and was delighted to find that she began shrinking directly. As soon as she was small enough to get through the door, she ran out of the house, and found quite a crowd of little animals and birds waiting outside. The poor little Lizard, Bill, was in the middle, being held up by two guinea-pigs, who were giving it something out of a bottle. They all made a rush at Alice the moment she appeared; but she ran off as hard as she could, and soon found herself safe in a thick wood.

"The first thing I've got to do," said Alice to herself, as she wandered about in the wood, "is to grow to my right size again; and the second thing is to find my way into that lovely garden. I think that will be the best plan."

It sounded an excellent plan, no doubt, and very neatly and simply arranged: the only difficulty was, that she had not the smallest idea how to set about it; and, while she was peering about anxiously among the trees, a little sharp bark just over her head made her look up in a great hurry.

An enormous puppy was looking down at her with large round eyes, and feebly stretching out one paw, trying to touch her. "Poor little thing!" said Alice, in a coaxing tone, and she tried hard to whistle to it; but she was terribly frightened all the time at the thought that it might be hungry, in which case it would be very likely to eat her up in spite of all her coaxing.

Hardly knowing what she did, she picked up a little bit of stick, and held it out to the puppy: whereupon the puppy jumped into the air off all its feet at once, with a yelp of delight, and rushed at the stick, and made believe to worry it: then Alice dodged behind a great thistle, to keep herself from being run over; and, the moment she appeared on the other side, the puppy made another rush at the stick, and tumbled head over heels in its hurry to get hold of it: then Alice, think-ing it was very like having a game of play with a cart-horse, and

expecting every moment to be trampled under its feet, ran round the thistle again: then the puppy began a series of short charges at the stick, running a very little way forwards each time and a long way back, and barking hoarsely all the while, till at last it sat down a good way off, panting, with its tongue hanging out of its mouth, and its great eyes half shut.

This seemed to Alice a good opportunity for making her escape: so she set off at once, and ran till she was quite tired and out of breath, and till the puppy's bark sounded quite faint in the distance.

"And yet what a dear little puppy it was!" said Alice, as she leant against a buttercup to rest herself, and fanned herself with one of the leaves. "I should have liked teaching it tricks very much, if – if I'd only been the right size to do it! Oh dear! I'd nearly forgotten that I've got to grow up again! Let me see – how *is* it to be managed? I suppose I ought to eat or drink something or other; but the great question is 'What?'"

The great question certainly was "What?". Alice looked all round her at the flowers and the blades of grass, but she could not see anything that looked like the right thing to eat or drink under the circumstances. There was a large mushroom growing near her, about the same height as herself; and, when she had looked under it, and on both sides of it, and behind it, it occurred to her that she might as well look and see what was on top of it.

She stretched herself up on tiptoe, and peeped over the edge of the mushroom, and her eyes immediately met those of a large blue caterpillar,[1] that was sitting on the top, with its arms folded, quietly smoking a long hookah, and taking not the smallest notice of her or of anything else.

---

1 Like Tenniel's illustrations, Wonderland is a rather colorless place. The White Rabbit and his white kid gloves, of course, can be depicted in Tenniel's black-and-white drawings. The color red appears in the name of the Red Queen and King, and the gardeners busily paint the white roses red (black in the illustration). The color blue, however, stands out in this stark landscape and gives a mysterious character to the Caterpillar. Unlike the red associated with the raging Queen, the cool color of blue suggests a dreary, laconic, contemplative mood. In the *Nursery Alice* Tenniel colored his illustrations (only twenty of the forty two original drawings are included), creating a warmer and more genial world for very young children.

CHAPTER V.

ADVICE FROM A CATERPILLAR.

THE caterpillar and Alice looked at each other for some time in silence: at last the Caterpillar took the hookah out of its mouth, and addressed her in a languid, sleepy voice.

"Who are *you*?"[1] said the Caterpillar.

This was not an encouraging opening for a conversation. Alice replied, rather shyly, "I – I hardly know, Sir, just at present

---

1   This is one of many challenges to Alice's sense of her identity. In Chapter 2, after experiencing dramatic changes in her body size, Alice puts the fundamental question: "Who in the world am I? Ah, *that's* the great puzzle!" Later in Chapter 5, the Pigeon accuses her of being a serpent, and the best defense of her selfhood Alice can come up with is the dubious assertion: "I'm a little girl."

– at least I know who I *was* when I got up this morning, but I think I must have been changed several times since then."

"What do you mean by that?" said the Caterpillar, sternly. "Explain yourself!"

"I ca'n't explain *myself*, I'm afraid, Sir," said Alice, "because I'm not myself, you see."

"I don't see," said the Caterpillar.

"I'm afraid I ca'n't put it more clearly," Alice replied, very politely, "for I ca'n't understand it myself, to begin with; and being so many different sizes in a day is very confusing."

"It isn't," said the Caterpillar.

"Well, perhaps you haven't found it so yet," said Alice; "but when you have to turn into a chrysalis[1] – you will some day, you know – and then after that into a butterfly, I should think you'll feel it a little queer, wo'n't you?"

"Not a bit," said the Caterpillar.

"Well, perhaps *your* feelings may be different," said Alice: "all I know is, it would feel very queer to *me*."

"You!" said the Caterpillar contemptuously. "Who are *you*?"

"Which brought them back again to the beginning of the conversation. Alice felt a little irritated at the Caterpillar's making such *very* short remarks, and she drew herself up and said, very gravely, "I think you ought to tell me who *you* are, first."

"Why?" said the Caterpillar.

Here was another puzzling question; and, as Alice could not think of any good reason, and the Caterpillar seemed to be in a *very* unpleasant state of mind, she turned away.

"Come back!" the Caterpillar called after her. "I've something important to say!"

This sounded promising, certainly. Alice turned and came back again.

"Keep your temper," said the Caterpillar.

"Is that all?" said Alice, swallowing down her anger as well as she could.

"No," said the Caterpillar.

---

1   In the illustration of this scene Tenniel has drawn the tube of the hookah so as to encase the Caterpillar, thereby suggesting the chrysalis mentioned by Alice.

Alice thought she might as well wait, as she had nothing else to do, and perhaps after all it might tell her something worth hearing. For some minutes it puffed away without speaking; but at last it unfolded its arms, took the hookah out of its mouth again, and said "So you think you're changed, do you?"

"I'm afraid I am, Sir," said Alice. "I ca'n't remember things as I used – and I don't keep the same size for ten minutes together!"

"Ca'n't remember *what* things?" said the Caterpillar.

"Well, I've tried to say '*How doth the little busy bee*,' but it all came different!" Alice replied in a very melancholy voice.

"Repeat '*You are old, Father William*,'"[1] said the Caterpillar.

Alice folded her hands, and began: –

"*You are old, Father William*," *the young man said,*
   "*And your hair has become very white;*
And yet you incessantly stand on your head –
   Do you think, at your age, it is right?"

---

1   "You Are Old, Father William" is a parody of Robert Southey's pious and didactic poem, "The Old Man's Comforts, and How He Gained Them" (1799), reprinted in Appendix H.

"In my youth," Father William replied to his son,
 "I feared it might injure the brain;
But, now that I'm perfectly sure I have none,
 Why, I do it again and again."

"You are old," said the youth, "as I mentioned before,
 And have grown most uncommonly fat;
Yet you turned a back-somersault in at the door —
 Pray, what is the reason of that?"

"In my youth," said the sage, as he shook his grey locks,
 "I kept all my limbs very supple
By the use of this ointment — one shilling the box —
 Allow me to sell you a couple?"

"You are old," said the youth, "and your jaws are too weak
 For anything tougher than suet;
Yet you finished the goose, with the bones and the beak —
 Pray, how did you manage to do it?"

"In my youth," said his father, "I took to the law,
And argued each case with my wife;
And the muscular strength, which it gave to my jaw
Has lasted the rest of my life."

"You are old, "said the youth, "one would hardly suppose
That your eye was as steady as ever;
Yet you balanced an eel on the end of your nose –
What made you so awfully clever?"

"I have answered three questions, and that is enough,"
Said his father, "Don't give yourself airs!
Do you think I can listen all day to such stuff?
Be off, or I'll kick you down-stairs!"

"That is not said right," said the Caterpillar.

"Not *quite* right, I'm afraid," said Alice, timidly: "some of the words have got altered."

"It is wrong from beginning to end," said the Caterpillar, decidedly; and there was silence for some minutes.

The Caterpillar was the first to speak. "What size do you want to be?" it asked.

"Oh, I'm not particular as to size," Alice hastily replied; "only one doesn't like changing so often, you know."

"I *don't* know," said the Caterpillar.

Alice said nothing: she had never been so much contradicted in all her life before, and she felt that she was losing her temper.

"Are you content now?" said the Caterpillar.

"Well, I should like to be a *little* larger, Sir, if you wouldn't mind," said Alice: "three inches is such a wretched height to be."

"It is a very good height indeed!" said the Caterpillar angrily, rearing itself upright as it spoke (it was exactly three inches high).

"But I'm not used to it!" pleaded poor Alice in a piteous tone. And she thought to herself "I wish the creatures wouldn't be so easily offended!"

"You'll get used to it in time," said the Caterpillar; and it put the hookah into its mouth, and began smoking again.

This time Alice waited patiently until it chose to speak again. In a minute or two the Caterpillar took the hookah out of its mouth, and yawned once or twice, and shook itself. Then it got down off the mushroom, and crawled away into the grass, merely remarking, as it went, "One side will make you grow taller, and the other side will make you grow shorter."

"One side of *what*? The other side of *what*?" thought Alice to herself.

"Of the mushroom," said the Caterpillar, just as if she had asked it aloud; and in another moment it was out of sight.[1]

Alice remained looking thoughtfully at the mushroom for a minute, trying to make out which were the two sides of it; and, as it was perfectly round, she found this a very difficult question. However, at last she stretched her arms round it as far as they would go, and broke off a bit of the edge with each hand.

"And now which is which?" she said to herself, and nibbled a little of the right-hand bit to try the effect. The next moment she felt a violent blow underneath her chin: it had struck her foot!

She was a good deal frightened by this very sudden change, but she felt that there was no time to be lost, as she was shrinking rapidly: so she set to work at once to eat some of the other bit. Her chin was pressed so closely against her foot, that there was hardly room to open her mouth; but she did it at last, and managed to swallow a morsel of the left-hand bit.

★   ★   ★   ★

★   ★   ★   ★

"Come, my head's free at last!" said Alice in a tone of delight, which changed into alarm in another moment, when she found that her shoulders were nowhere to be found: all she could see, when she looked down, was an immense length of neck, which seemed to rise like a stalk out of a sea of green leaves that lay far below her.

"What *can* all that green stuff be?" said Alice. "And where *have* my shoulders got to? And oh, my poor hands, how is it I ca'n't see you?" She was moving them about, as she spoke, but no result seemed to follow, except a little shaking among the distant green leaves.

---

1   Apparently the Caterpillar is capable of reading Alice's thoughts, the ultimate invasion of her privacy.

As there seemed to be no chance of getting her hands up to her head, she tried to get her head down to *them*, and was delighted to find that her neck would bend about easily in any direction, like a serpent. She had just succeeded in curving it down into a graceful zigzag, and was going to dive in among the leaves, which she found to be nothing but the tops of the trees under which she had been wandering, when a sharp hiss made her draw back in a hurry: a large pigeon had flown into her face, and was beating her violently with its wings.

"Serpent!" screamed the Pigeon.

"I'm *not* a serpent!" said Alice indignantly. "Let me alone!"

"Serpent, I say again!" repeated the Pigeon, but in a more sub-dued tone, and added, with a kind of sob, "I've tried every way, but nothing seems to suit them!"

"I haven't the least idea what you're talking about," said Alice.

"I've tried the roots of trees, and I've tried banks, and I've tried hedges," the Pigeon went on, without attending to her; "but those serpents! "There's no pleasing them!"

Alice was more and more puzzled, but she thought there was no use in saying anything more till the Pigeon had finished.

"As if it wasn't trouble enough hatching the eggs," said the Pigeon; "but I must be on the look-out for serpents, night and day! Why, I haven't had a wink of sleep these three weeks!"

"I'm very sorry you've been annoyed," said Alice, who was beginning to see its meaning.

"And just as I'd taken the highest tree in the wood," contin-ued the Pigeon, raising its voice to a shriek, "and just as I was thinking I should be free of them at last, they must needs come wriggling down from the sky! Ugh, Serpent!"

"But I'm *not* a serpent, I tell you!" said Alice. "I'm a – I'm a – "

"Well! *What* are you?" said the Pigeon. "I can see you're try-ing to invent something!"

"I – I'm a little girl," said Alice, rather doubtfully, as she remembered the number of changes she had gone through, that day.

"A likely story indeed!" said the Pigeon, in a tone of the deepest contempt. "I've seen a good many little girls in my time, but never *one* with such a neck as that! No, no! You're a serpent; and there's no use denying it. I suppose you'll be telling me next that you never tasted an egg!"

"I *have* tasted eggs, certainly," said Alice, who was a very truthful child; "but little girls eat eggs quite as much as serpents do, you know."

"I don't believe it," said the Pigeon; "but if they do, why, then they're a kind of serpent: that's all I can say."

This was such a new idea to Alice, that she was quite silent for a minute or two, which gave the Pigeon the opportunity of adding "You're looking for eggs, I know *that* well enough; and what does it matter to me whether you're a little girl or a serpent?"

"It matters a good deal to *me*," said Alice hastily; "but I'm not looking for eggs, as it happens; and, if I was, I shouldn't want *yours*: I don't like them raw."

"Well, be off, then!" said the Pigeon in a sulky tone, as it settled down again into its nest. Alice crouched down among the trees as well as she could, for her neck kept getting entangled among the branches, and every now and then she had to stop and untwist it. After a while she remembered that she still held the pieces of mushroom in her hands, and she set to work very carefully, nibbling first at one and then at the other, and growing sometimes taller, and sometimes shorter, until she had succeeded in bringing herself down to her usual height.

It was so long since she had been anything near the right size, that it felt quite strange at first; but she got used to it in a few minutes, and began talking to herself, as usual, "Come, there's half my plan done now! How puzzling all these changes are! I'm never sure what I'm going to be, from one minute to another! However, I've got back to my right size: the next thing is, to get into that beautiful garden – how is that to be done, I wonder?" As she said this, she came suddenly upon an open place, with a little house in it about four feet high. "Whoever lives there," thought Alice, "it'll never do to come upon them *this* size: why, I should frighten them out of their wits!" So she began nibbling at the right-hand bit again, and did not venture to go near the house till she had brought herself down to nine inches high.

CHAPTER VI.

PIG AND PEPPER.

FOR a minute or two she stood looking at the house, and wondering what to do next, when suddenly a footman in livery came running out of the wood – (she considered him to be a footman because he was in livery: otherwise, judging by his face only, she would have called him a fish) – and rapped loudly at the door with his knuckles. It was opened by another footman in livery, with a round face, and large eyes like a frog; and both footmen, Alice noticed, had powdered hair that curled all over their heads. She felt very curious to know what it was all about, and crept a little way out of the wood to listen.

The Fish-Footman began by producing from under his arm a great letter, nearly as large as himself, and this he handed over to the other, saying, in a solemn tone, "For the Duchess. An invitation from the Queen to play croquet." The Frog-Footman repeated, in the same solemn tone, only changing the order of the words a little, "From the Queen. An invitation for the Duchess to play croquet."

Then they both bowed low, and their curls got entangled together.

Alice laughed so much at this, that she had to run back into the wood for fear of their hearing her; and, when she next peeped out, the Fish-Footman was gone, and the other was sitting on the ground near the door, staring stupidly up into the sky.

Alice went timidly up to the door, and knocked.

"There's no sort of use in knocking," said the Footman, "and that for two reasons. First, because I'm on the same side of the door as you are: secondly, because they're making such a noise inside, no one could possibly hear you." And certainly there *was* a most extraordinary noise going on within – a constant howling and sneezing, and every now and then a great crash, as if a dish or kettle had been broken to pieces.

"Please, then," said Alice, "how am I to get in?"

"There might be some sense in your knocking," the Footman went on, without attending to her, "if we had the door between us. For instance, if you were *inside*, you might knock, and I could let you out, you know." He was looking up into the sky all the time he was speaking, and this Alice thought decidedly uncivil. "But perhaps he ca'n't help it," she said to herself; "his eyes are so *very* nearly at the top of his head. But at any rate he might answer questions. – How am I to get in?" she repeated, aloud.

"I shall sit here," the Footman remarked, "till to-morrow – "

At this moment the door of the house opened, and a large plate came skimming out, straight at the Footman's head: it just grazed his nose, and broke to pieces against one of the trees behind him.

"— or next day, maybe," the Footman continued in the same tone, exactly as if nothing had happened.

"How am I to get in?" asked Alice again, in a louder tone.

"*Are* you to get in at all?" said the Footman. "That's the first question, you know."

It was, no doubt: only Alice did not like to be told so. "It's really dreadful," she muttered to herself, "the way all the creatures argue. It's enough to drive one crazy!"

The Footman seemed to think this a good opportunity for repeating his remark, with variations. "I shall sit here," he said, "on and off, for days and days."

"But what am *I* to do?" said Alice.

"Anything you like," said the Footman, and began whistling.

"Oh, there's no use in talking to him," said Alice desperately: "he's perfectly idiotic!" And she opened the door and went in.

The door led right into a large kitchen, which was full of smoke from one end to the other: the Duchess[1] was sitting on a

---

[1] Tenniel's depiction of the Duchess may be based upon a painting by Quinten Massys, a Flemish painter of the Renaissance. The clothing, especially the head-dress, bears a remarkable similarity to Tenniel's depiction. The face of Massys' woman, however, is much more grotesque than that of Tenniel's duchess, and

three-legged stool in the middle, nursing a baby: the cook was leaning over the fire, stirring a large cauldron which seemed to be full of soup.

"There's certainly too much pepper in that soup!" Alice said to herself, as well as she could for sneezing.

There was certainly too much of it in the *air*. Even the Duchess sneezed occasionally; and as for the baby, it was sneezing and howling alternately without a moment's pause. The only two creatures in the kitchen, that did *not* sneeze, were the cook, and a large cat, which was lying on the hearth and grinning from ear to ear.

"Please would you tell me," said Alice, a little timidly, for she was not quite sure whether it was good manners for her to speak first, "why your cat grins like that?"

"It's a Cheshire-Cat,"[1] said the Duchess, "and that's why. Pig!"

She said the last word with such sudden violence that Alice quite jumped; but she saw in another moment that it was addressed to the baby, and not to her, so she took courage, and went on again: —

"I didn't know that Cheshire-Cats always grinned; in fact, I didn't know that cats *could* grin."

"They all can," said the Duchess; "and most of 'em do."

"I don't know of any that do," Alice said very politely, feeling quite pleased to have got into a conversation.

"You don't know much," said the Duchess; "and that's a fact."

Alice did not at all like the tone of this remark, and thought it would be as well to introduce some other subject of conversation. While she was trying to fix on one, the cook took the

---

resembles a horrific animal gargoyle. Tenniel gives his duchess a striking masculine face with a head totally out of proportion to her body.

1 "Grin like a Cheshire cat" was a common saying in Carroll's day. The origin of the phrase is unknown but it has been speculated that it derives from the painted grinning lions that appeared on signboards of pubs in the county of Cheshire (where Carroll was born). Also, Cheshire cheeses were once made in the form of cats. This speculation appeared in *Notes and Queries* between 1850 and 1852, and as Roger Lancyln Green points out in his edition of *Wonderland*, Carroll subscribed to this journal from its inception until his death.

cauldron of soup off the fire, and at once set to work throwing everything within her reach at the Duchess and the baby – the fire-irons came first; then followed a shower of saucepans, plates, and dishes. The Duchess took no notice of them even when they hit her; and the baby was howling so much already, that it was quite impossible to say whether the blows hurt it or not.

"Oh, *please* mind what you're doing!" cried Alice, jumping up and down in an agony of terror. "Oh, there goes his *precious* nose!", as an unusually large saucepan flew close by it, and very nearly carried it off.

"If everybody minded their own business," the Duchess said, in a hoarse growl, "the world would go round a deal faster than it does."

"Which would *not* be an advantage," said Alice, who felt very glad to get an opportunity of showing off a little of her knowledge. "Just think what work it would make with the day and night! You see the earth takes twenty-four hours to turn round on its axis – "

"Talking of axes," said the Duchess, "chop off her head!"

Alice glanced rather anxiously at the cook, to see if she meant to take the hint; but the cook was busily stirring the soup, and seemed not to be listening, so she went on again: "Twenty-four hours, I *think*; or is it twelve? I – "

"Oh, don't bother *me*!" said the Duchess. "I never could abide figures!" And with that she began nursing her child again, singing a sort of lullaby to it as she did so, and giving it a violent shake at the end of every line: –

> "*Speak roughly to your little boy,*
> *And beat him when he sneezes:*
> *He only does it to annoy,*
> *Because he knows it teases.*"

CHORUS

(in which the cook and the baby joined): –

"Wow! Wow! Wow!"

While the Duchess sang the second verse of the song, she kept tossing the baby violently up and down, and the poor little thing howled so, that Alice could hardly hear the words: –

> *"I speak severely to my boy,*
> *I beat him when he sneezes;*
> *For he can thoroughly enjoy*
> *The pepper when he pleases!"*

CHORUS

"Wow! wow! wow!"[1]

"Here! You may nurse it a bit, if you like!" the Duchess said to Alice, flinging the baby at her as she spoke. "I must go and get ready to play croquet with the Queen," and she hurried out of the room. The cook threw a frying-pan after her as she went, but it just missed her.

Alice caught the baby with some difficulty, as it was a queer-shaped little creature, and held out its arms and legs in all directions, "just like a star-fish," thought Alice. The poor little thing was snorting like a steam-engine when she caught it, and kept doubling itself up and straightening itself out again, so that altogether, for the first minute or two, it was as much as she could do to hold it.

As soon as she had made out the proper way of nursing it (which was to twist it up into a sort of knot, and then keep tight hold of its right ear and left foot, so as to prevent its undoing itself), she carried it out into the open air. "If I don't take this child away with me," thought Alice, "they're sure to kill it in a day or two. Wouldn't it be murder to leave it behind?" She said the last words out loud, and the little thing grunted in reply (it had left off sneezing by this time). "Don't grunt," said Alice; "that's not at all a proper way of expressing yourself."

The baby grunted again, and Alice looked very anxiously

---

1   "Speak Roughly" is a parody of "Speak Gently," by David Bates (published in 1848), reprinted in Appendix H.

into its face to see what was the matter with it. There could be no doubt that it had a *very* turn-up nose, much more like a snout than a real nose: also its eyes were getting extremely small for a baby: altogether Alice did not like the look of the thing at all. "But perhaps it was only sobbing," she thought, and looked into its eyes again, to see if there were any tears.

No, there were no tears. "If you're going to turn into a pig,[1] my dear," said Alice, seriously, "I'll have nothing more to do with you. Mind now!" The poor little thing sobbed again (or grunted, it was impossible to say which), and they went on for some while in silence.

Alice was just beginning to think to herself, "Now, what am I to do with this creature, when I get it home?" when it grunted again, so violently, that she looked down into its face in some alarm. This time there could be *no* mistake about it: it was neither more nor less than a pig, and she felt that it would be quite absurd for her to carry it any further.

---

1 In his *Annotated Alice* Martin Gardner suggests that this transformation reflects Carroll's distaste for little boys. In his novel, *Sylvie and Bruno*, Carroll depicts a horrid little boy named Uggug as having "the expression of a prize-pig." At the end of the story Uggug (his name speaks for itself) turns into a porcupine. Note that in Tenniel's illustrations neither the Duchess nor Alice look at their infant, but rather stare out at the reader.

So she set the little creature down, and felt quite relieved to see it trot away quietly into the wood. "If it had grown up," she said to herself, "it would have made a dreadfully ugly child: but it makes rather a handsome pig, I think." And she began thinking over other children she knew, who might do very well as pigs, and was just saying to herself "if one only knew the right way to change them – "[1] when she was a little startled by seeing the Cheshire-Cat sitting on a bough of a tree a few yards off.

The Cat only grinned when it saw Alice. It looked good-natured, she thought: still it had *very* long claws and a great many teeth, so she felt that it ought to be treated with respect.

"Cheshire-Puss," she began, rather timidly, as she did not at all know whether it would like the name: however, it only grinned a little wider. "Come, it's pleased so far," thought Alice,

---

[1] Alice's fleeting fantasy of power perhaps suggests Circe, who turned Odysseus's men into swine.

and she went on. "Would you tell me, please, which way I ought to go from here?"

"That depends a good deal on where you want to get to," said the Cat.

"I don't much care where – " said Alice.

"Then it doesn't matter which way you go," said the Cat.

"– so long as I get *somewhere*," Alice added as an explanation.

"Oh, you're sure to do that," said the Cat, "if you only walk long enough."

Alice felt that this could not be denied, so she tried another question. "What sort of people live about here?"

"In *that* direction," the Cat said, waving its right paw round, "lives a Hatter: and in *that* direction," waving the other paw, "lives a March Hare. Visit either you like: they're both mad."[1]

"But I don't want to go among mad people," Alice remarked.

"Oh, you ca'n't help that," said the Cat: "we're all mad here. I'm mad. You're mad."

"How do you know I'm mad?" said Alice.

"You must be," said the Cat, "or you wouldn't have come here."

Alice didn't think that proved it at all: however, she went on: "And how do you know that you're mad?"

"To begin with," said the Cat, "a dog's not mad. You grant that?"

"I suppose so," said Alice.

"Well, then," the Cat went on, "you see a dog growls when it's angry, and wags its tail when it's pleased. Now *I* growl when I'm pleased, and wag my tail when I'm angry. Therefore I'm mad."

---

1   The phrases "as mad as a Hatter" and "as mad as a March hare" were both well-known sayings in Carroll's day. Hares typically mate in March and, according to folk belief, exhibit frenzied behavior during this period. The madness of hatters may due to their use of mercury in preparing the felt for making hats. Mercury poisoning can produce symptoms of mental disorder. Carroll's Hatter may have been suggested by Theophilus Carter, a furniture dealer in Oxford. According to Green (*Lewis Carroll*, p. 258), Carter was known in Oxford as the Mad Hatter. He dressed like Prime Minister Gladstone and stood at the door of his shop, wearing a top hat. Tenniel is said to have come to Oxford to sketch him for the book.

"*I* call it purring, not growling," said Alice.

"Call it what you like," said the Cat. "Do you play croquet with the Queen to-day?"

"I should like it very much," said Alice, " but I haven't been invited yet."

"You'll see me there," said the Cat, and vanished.

Alice was not much surprised at this, she was getting so well used to queer things happening. While she was still looking at the place where it had been, it suddenly appeared again.

"By-the-bye, what became of the baby?" said the Cat. "I'd nearly forgotten to ask."

"It turned into a pig," Alice answered very quietly, just as if the Cat had come back in a natural way.

"I thought it would," said the Cat, and vanished again.

Alice waited a little, half expecting to see it again, but it did not appear, and after a minute or two she walked on in the direction in which the March Hare was said to live. "I've seen hatters before," she said to herself: "the March Hare will be much the most interesting, and perhaps, as this is May, it wo'n't be raving mad – at least not so mad as it was in March." As she said this, she looked up, and there was the Cat again, sitting on a branch of a tree.

"Did you say 'pig,' or 'fig'?"[1] said the Cat.

"I said 'pig,'" replied Alice; "and I wish you wouldn't keep appearing and vanishing so suddenly: you make one quite giddy!"

"All right," said the Cat; and this time it vanished quite slowly, beginning with the end of the tail, and ending with the grin, which remained some time after the rest of it had gone.

"Well! I've often seen a cat without a grin," thought Alice; "but a grin without a cat! It's the most curious thing I ever saw in all my life!"

She had not gone much farther before she came in sight of the house of the March Hare: she thought it must be the right house, because the chimneys were shaped like ears and the roof

1   The Cat's reappearance to ask this question comically undercuts his seeming omni-science. Just moments earlier he said that he thought the baby would turn into a pig.

was thatched with fur. It was so large a house, that she did not like to go nearer till she had nibbled some more of the left-hand bit of mushroom, and raised herself to about two feet high: even then she walked up towards it rather timidly, saying to herself "Suppose it should be raving mad after all! I almost wish I'd gone to see the Hatter instead!"

CHAPTER VII.

A MAD TEA-PARTY.

THERE was a table set out under a tree in front of the house, and the March Hare and the Hatter were having tea at it: a Dormouse[1] was sitting between them, fast asleep, and the other two were using it as a cushion, resting their elbows on it, and talking over its head. "Very uncomfortable for the Dormouse," thought Alice; "only as it's asleep, I suppose it doesn't mind."

The table was a large one, but the three were all crowded together at one corner of it. "No room! No room!" they cried out when they saw Alice coming. "There's *plenty* of room!" said Alice indignantly, and she sat down in a large arm-chair at one end of the table.

"Have some wine," the March Hare said in an encouraging tone.

---

1   A dormouse is a nocturnal rodent that lives in trees and hibernates during the winter. Its name derives from the Latin *dormire*, to sleep.

Alice looked all round the table, but there was nothing on it but tea. "I don't see any wine," she remarked.

"There isn't any," said the March Hare.

"Then it wasn't very civil of you to offer it," said Alice angrily.

"It wasn't very civil of you to sit down without being invited," said the March Hare.

"I didn't know it was *your* table," said Alice: "it's laid for a great many more than three."

"Your hair wants cutting," said the Hatter. He had been looking at Alice for some time with great curiosity, and this was his first speech.

"You should learn not to make personal remarks," Alice said with some severity: "it's very rude."

The Hatter opened his eyes very wide on hearing this; but all he *said* was "Why is a raven like a writing-desk?"[1]

"Come, we shall have some fun now!" thought Alice. "I'm glad they've begun asking riddles – I believe I can guess that," she added aloud.

"Do you mean that you think you can find out the answer to it?" said the March Hare.

"Exactly so," said Alice.

"Then you should say what you mean," the March Hare went on. "I do," Alice hastily replied; "at least – at least I mean what I say – that's the same thing, you know."

"Not the same thing a bit!" said the Hatter. "Why, you might just as well say that 'I see what I eat' is the same thing as 'I eat what I see'!"

---

1   From Carroll's day to the present many people have speculated about the answer to this famous riddle. Carroll, himself, weighed in on the fun by supplying an answer in the preface to the 1896 edition of the story: "Because it can produce a few notes, tho they are *very* flat; and it is nevar [*sic, raven* spelled backwards] put with the wrong end in front." See Denis Crutch, *Jabberwocky* (Winter, 1976). When Alice asks the riddling Hatter for the answer, his response that he hasn't the slightest idea appears well suited to his madcap world. Wonderland is a place of words, fragments, and questions that resist the mind's relentless attempt to discover order and meaning. Martin Gardner, in his *More Annotated Alice*, provides Aldous Huxley's fascinating answers to the riddle: because there's a *b* in *both* and because there's an *n* in *neither*. Like the big questions in life (Is there a God? Is there free will?), the riddle is about words, not reality.

"You might just as well say," added the March Hare, "that 'I like what I get' is the same thing as 'I get what I like'!"

"You might just as well say," added the Dormouse, which seemed to be talking in its sleep, "that 'I breathe when I sleep' is the same thing as 'I sleep when I breathe'!"

"It *is* the same thing with you," said the Hatter, and here the conversation dropped, and the party sat silent for a minute, while Alice thought over all she could remember about ravens and writing-desks, which wasn't much.

The Hatter was the first to break the silence. "What day of the month is it?" he said, turning to Alice: he had taken his watch out of his pocket, and was looking at it uneasily, shaking it every now and then, and holding it to his ear.

Alice considered a little, and then said "The fourth."[1]

"Two days wrong!" sighed the Hatter. "I told you butter wouldn't suit the works!" he added, looking angrily at the March Hare.

"It was the *best* butter," the March Hare meekly replied.

"Yes, but some crumbs must have got in as well," the Hatter grumbled: "you shouldn't have put it in with the bread-knife."

The March Hare took the watch and looked at it gloomily: then he dipped it into his cup of tea, and looked at it again: but he could think of nothing better to say than his first remark, "It was the *best* butter, you know."

Alice had been looking over his shoulder with some curiosity. "What a funny watch!" she remarked. "It tells the day of the month, and doesn't tell what o'clock it is!"

"Why should it?" muttered the Hatter. "Does *your* watch tell you what year it is?"

"Of course not," Alice replied very readily: "but that's because it stays the same year for such a long time together."

"Which is just the case with *mine*," said the Hatter.

Alice felt dreadfully puzzled. The Hatter's remark seemed to her to have no sort of meaning in it, and yet it was certainly English. "I don't quite understand you," she said, as politely as she could.

---

1   May 4, 1852 was the date of Alice Liddell's birth. At the end of the previous chapter Alice remarks that the month is May.

"The Dormouse is asleep again," said the Hatter, and he poured a little hot tea upon its nose.

The Dormouse shook its head impatiently, and said, without opening its eyes, "Of course, of course: just what I was going to remark myself."

"Have you guessed the riddle yet?" the Hatter said, turning to Alice again.

"No, I give it up," Alice replied. "What's the answer?"

"I haven't the slightest idea," said the Hatter.

"Nor I," said the March Hare.

Alice sighed wearily. "I think you might do something better with the time," she said, "than wasting it in asking riddles that have no answers."

"If you knew Time as well as I do," said the Hatter, "you wouldn't talk about wasting *it*. It's *him*."

"I don't know what you mean," said Alice.

"Of course you don't!" the Hatter said, tossing his head contemptuously. "I dare say you never even spoke to Time!"

"Perhaps not," Alice cautiously replied; "but I know I have to beat time when I learn music."

"Ah! That accounts for it," said the Hatter. "He wo'n't stand beating. Now, if you only kept on good terms with him, he'd do almost anything you liked with the clock. For instance, suppose it were nine o'clock in the morning, just time to begin lessons: you'd only have to whisper a hint to Time, and round goes the clock in a twinkling! Half-past one, time for dinner!"

("I only wish it was," the March Hare said to itself in a whisper.)

"That would be grand, certainly," said Alice thoughtfully; "but then – I shouldn't be hungry for it, you know."

"Not at first, perhaps," said the Hatter: "but you could keep it to half-past one as, long as you liked."

"Is that the way *you* manage?" Alice asked.

The Hatter shook his head mournfully. "Not I!" he replied. "We quarreled last March – just before *he* went mad, you know –" (pointing with his teaspoon at the March Hare,) "– it was at the great concert given by the Queen of Hearts, and I had to sing

'Twinkle, twinkle, little bat!
How I wonder what you're at!'

You know the song, perhaps?"

"I've heard something like it," said Alice.

"It goes on, you know," the Hatter continued, "in this way: –

'Up above the world you fly,
Like a tea-tray in the sky.
Twinkle, twinkle – '"[1]

Here the Dormouse shook itself, and began singing in its sleep "*Twinkle, twinkle, twinkle, twinkle –* " and went on so long that they had to pinch it to make it stop.

"Well, I'd hardly finished the first verse," said the Hatter, "when the Queen bawled out 'He's murdering the time! Off with his head!'"

"How dreadfully savage!" exclaimed Alice.

"And ever since that," the Hatter went on in a mournful tone, "he wo'n't do a thing I ask! It's always six o'clock now."

---

1   "Twinkle, twinkle little bat" is a parody of Jane Taylor's poem "The Star" (in *Rhymes for the Nursery*, 1806), reprinted in Appendix H. Professor Bartholomew Price, a friend and tutor of Carroll, was nicknamed the "Bat."

A bright idea came into Alice's head. "Is that the reason so many tea-things are put out here?" she asked.

"Yes, that's it," said the Hatter with a sigh: "it's always tea-time, and we've no time to wash the things between whiles."

"Then you keep moving round, I suppose?" said Alice.

"Exactly so," said the Hatter: "as the things get used up."

"But what happens when you come to the beginning again?"[1] Alice ventured to ask.

"Suppose we change the subject," the March Hare interrupted, yawning. "I'm getting tired of this. I vote the young lady tells us a story."

"I'm afraid I don't know one," said Alice, rather alarmed at the proposal.

"Then the Dormouse shall!" they both cried. "Wake up, Dormouse!" And they pinched it on both sides at once.

The Dormouse slowly opened its eyes. "I wasn't asleep," it said in a hoarse, feeble voice, "I heard every word you fellows were saying."

"Tell us a story!" said the March Hare.

"Yes, please do!" pleaded Alice.

"And be quick about it," added the Hatter, "or you'll be asleep again before it's done."

"Once upon a time there were three little sisters," the Dormouse began in a great hurry; "and their names were Elsie, Lacie, and Tillie;[2] and they lived at the bottom of a well – "

"What did they live on?" said Alice, who always took a great interest in questions of eating and drinking.

"They lived on treacle,"[3] said the Dormouse, after thinking a minute or two.

"They couldn't have done that, you know," Alice gently remarked. "They'd have been ill."

---

1   The image of circularity here, as in the Caucus-race, suggests that in Wonderland, frozen in time at six o'clock, it is difficult to get anywhere.

2   The three Liddell sisters: Elsie is Lorina Charlotte (L.C., pronounced "Elsie"); Lacie is an anagram of Alice; and Tillie was short for Matilda, the family's nickname for Edith.

3   According to Martin Gardner (*More Annotated Alice*), before "treacle" became a common term for molasses, it referred to medicinal compounds. Wells that contained healing waters were called treacle wells.

"So they were," said the Dormouse; "*very* ill."

Alice tried a little to fancy to herself what such an extraordinary way of living would be like, but it puzzled her too much: so she went on: "But why did they live at the bottom of a well?"

"Take some more tea," the March Hare said to Alice, very earnestly.

"I've had nothing yet," Alice replied in an offended tone: "so I ca'n't take more."

"You mean you ca'n't take *less*," said the Hatter: "it's very easy to take *more* than nothing."

"Nobody asked *your* opinion," said Alice.

"Who's making personal remarks now?" the Hatter asked triumphantly.

Alice did not quite know what to say to this: so she helped herself to some tea and bread-and-butter, and then turned to the Dormouse, and repeated her question. "Why did they live at the bottom of a well?"

The Dormouse again took a minute or two to think about it, and then said "It was a treacle-well."

"There's no such thing!" Alice was beginning very angrily, but the Hatter and the March Hare went "Sh! Sh!" and the Dormouse sulkily remarked "If you ca'n't be civil, you'd better finish the story for yourself."

"No, please go on!" Alice said very humbly. "I wo'n't interrupt you again. I dare say there may be *one*."

"One, indeed!" said the Dormouse indignantly. However, he consented to go on. "And so these three little sisters – they were learning to draw, you know – "

"What did they draw?" said Alice, quite forgetting her promise.

"Treacle," said the Dormouse, without considering at all, this time.

"I want a clean cup," interrupted the Hatter: "let's all move one place on."

He moved on as he spoke, and the Dormouse followed him: the March Hare moved into the Dormouse's place, and Alice rather unwillingly took the place of the March Hare. The Hatter was the only one who got any advantage from the change; and Alice was a good deal worse off than before, as the March Hare had just upset the milk-jug into his plate.

Alice did not wish to offend the Dormouse again, so she began very cautiously: "But I don't understand. Where did they draw the treacle from?"

"You can draw water out of a water-well," said the Hatter; "so I should think you could draw treacle out of a treacle-well – eh, stupid?"

"But they were *in* the well," Alice said to the Dormouse, not choosing to notice this last remark.

"Of course they were," said the Dormouse: "well in."

This answer so confused poor Alice, that she let the Dormouse go on for some time without interrupting it.

"They were learning to draw," the Dormouse went on, yawning and rubbing its eyes, for it was getting very sleepy; "and they drew all manner of things – everything that begins with an M –"

"Why with an M?" said Alice.

"Why not?" said the March Hare.

Alice was silent.

The Dormouse had closed its eyes by this time, and was going off into a doze; but, on being pinched by the Hatter, it woke up again with a little shriek, and went on: "– that begins with an M, such as mouse-traps, and the moon, and memory, and muchness – you know you say things are 'much of a muchness'[1] – did you ever see such a thing as a drawing of a muchness!"

"Really, now you ask me," said Alice, very much confused, "I don't think – "

"Then you shouldn't talk," said the Hatter.

This piece of rudeness was more than Alice could bear: she got up in great disgust, and walked off: the Dormouse fell asleep instantly, and neither of the others took the least notice of her going, though she looked back once or twice, half

---

1 "Much of a muchness" is a British phrase that means two things are essentially the same.

hoping that they would call after her: the last time she saw them, they were trying to put the Dormouse into the teapot.[1]

"At any rate I'll never go *there* again!" said Alice, as she picked her way through the wood. "It's the stupidest tea-party I ever was at in all my life!"

Just as she said this, she noticed that one of the trees had a door leading right into it. "That's very curious!" she thought. "But everything's curious to-day. I think I may as well go in at once." And in she went.

Once more she found herself in the long hall, and close to the little glass table. "Now, I'll manage better this time," she said to herself, and began by taking the little golden key, and unlocking the door that led into the garden. Then she set to work nibbling at the mushroom (she had kept a piece of it in her pocket) till she was about a foot high: then she walked down the little passage: and *then* – she found herself at last in the beautiful garden, among the bright flower-beds and the cool fountains.

1 According to Roger Lancelyn Green in his edition of the Alice books, Victorian children often kept dormice as pets, and a favorite nest was a teapot filled with grass and moss.

CHAPTER VIII.

THE QUEEN'S CROQUET-GROUND.

A LARGE rose-tree stood near the entrance of the garden: the roses growing on it were white, but there were three gardeners at it, busily painting them red. Alice thought this a very curious thing, and she went nearer to watch them, and, just as she came up to them, she heard one of them say "Look out now, Five! Don't go splashing paint over me like that!"

"I couldn't help it," said Five, in a sulky tone. "Seven jogged my elbow."

On which Seven looked up and said "That's right, Five! Always lay the blame on others!"

"You'd better not talk!" said Five. "I heard the Queen say only yesterday you deserved to be beheaded."

"What for?" said the one who had spoken first.

"That's none of *your* business, Two!" said Seven.

"Yes, it *is* his business!" said Five. "And I'll tell him – it was for bringing the cook tulip-roots instead of onions."

Seven flung down his brush, and had just begun "Well, of all the unjust things – " when his eye chanced to fall upon Alice, as she stood watching them, and he checked himself suddenly: the others looked round also, and all of them bowed low.

"Would you tell me, please," said Alice, a little timidly, "why you are painting those roses?"

Five and Seven said nothing, but looked at Two. Two began, in a low voice, "Why, the fact is, you see, Miss, this here ought to have been a *red* rose-tree, and we put a white one in by mistake; and, if the Queen was to find it out, we should all have our heads cut off, you know. So you see, Miss, we're doing our best, afore she comes, to – " At this moment, Five, who had been anxiously looking across the garden, called out "The Queen! The Queen!", and the three gardeners instantly threw themselves flat upon their faces. There was a sound of many footsteps, and Alice looked round, eager to see the Queen.

First came ten soldiers carrying clubs: these were all shaped like the three gardeners, oblong and flat, with their hands and feet at the corners: next the ten courtiers: these were ornamented all over with diamonds, and walked two and two, as the soldiers did. After these came the royal children: there were ten of them, and the little dears came jumping merrily along, hand in hand, in couples: they were all ornamented with hearts. Next came the guests, mostly Kings and Queens, and among them Alice recognised the White Rabbit: it was talking in a hurried nervous manner, smiling at everything that was said, and went by without noticing her. Then followed the Knave of Hearts,[1] carrying the King's crown on a crimson

---

1 Note Tenniel's illustration of this scene. Michael Hancher (in *The Tenniel Illustrations*) has done some interesting detective work in observing a link between the Knave's red nose (indicated by Tenniel's cross hatching in this illustration and in the next-to-last illustration in Chapter 12) and the stolen tarts. Although Carroll makes no mention of the Knave's nose, Tenniel's illustrations suggest that the peppery tarts are the source of the Knave's irritated nose – his guilt being clear as the nose on his face.

velvet cushion; and, last of all this grand procession, came THE KING AND THE QUEEN OF HEARTS.

Alice was rather doubtful whether she ought not to lie down on her face like the three gardeners, but she could not remember ever having heard of such a rule at processions; "and besides, what would be the use of a procession," thought she, "if people had all to lie down on their faces, so that they couldn't see it?" So she stood where she was, and waited.

When the procession came opposite to Alice, they all stopped and looked at her, and the Queen said, severely, "Who is this?" She said it to the Knave of Hearts, who only bowed and smiled in reply.

"Idiot!" said the Queen, tossing her head impatiently; and, turning to Alice, she went on: "What's your name, child?"

"My name is Alice, so please your Majesty," said Alice very politely; but she added, to herself, "Why, they're only a pack of cards, after all. I needn't be afraid of them!"[1]

"And who are *these*?" said the Queen, pointing to the three gardeners who were lying round the rose-tree; for, you see, as they were lying on their faces, and the pattern on their backs was the same as the rest of the pack, she could not tell whether they were gardeners, or soldiers, or courtiers, or three of her own children.

"How should *I* know?" said Alice, surprised at her own courage. "It's no business of *mine*."

The Queen turned crimson with fury, and, after glaring at her for a moment like a wild beast, began screaming "Off with her head! Off with — "[2]

"Nonsense!" said Alice, very loudly and decidedly, and the Queen was silent.

---

1   In reassuring herself of her safety by noting that the people around her are merely cards, Alice once again appears to recognize that she is in a dreamworld, one which she can ultimately dissolve, as evidenced in the final chapter where her proclamation, "You're nothing but a pack of cards!" ends the dream and returns her to reality.

2   "Off with her head" echoes the line from *Richard III*, "Off with his head! So much for Buckingham!" This line appears in Colley Cibber's version of Shakespeare's play. This eighteenth-century adaptation of the play remained popular in Carroll's day.

The King laid his hand upon her arm, and timidly said "Consider, my dear: she is only a child!"

The Queen turned angrily away from him, and said to the Knave "Turn them over!"

The Knave did so, very carefully, with one foot.

"Get up!" said the Queen in a shrill, loud voice, and the three gardeners instantly jumped up, and began bowing to the King, the Queen, the royal children, and everybody else.

"Leave off that!" screamed the Queen. "You make me giddy." And then, turning to the rose-tree, she went on "What *have* you been doing here?"

"May it please your Majesty," said Two, in a very humble tone, going down on one knee as he spoke, "we were trying – "

"*I* see!" said the Queen, who had meanwhile been examining the roses. "Off with their heads!" and the procession moved on, three of the soldiers remaining behind to execute the unfortunate gardeners, who ran to Alice for protection.

"You sha'n't be beheaded!" said Alice, and she put them into a large flower-pot that stood near. The three soldiers wandered about for a minute or two, looking for them, and then quietly marched off after the others.

"Are their heads off?" shouted the Queen.

"Their heads are gone, if it please your Majesty!" the soldiers shouted in reply.

"That's right!" shouted the Queen. "Can you play croquet?"

The soldiers were silent, and looked at Alice, as the question was evidently meant for her. "Yes!" shouted Alice.

"Come on, then!" roared the Queen, and Alice joined the procession, wondering very much what would happen next.

"It's — it's a very fine day!" said a timid voice at her side. She was walking by the White Rabbit, who was peeping anxiously into her face.

"Very," said Alice. "Where's the Duchess?"

"Hush! Hush!" said the Rabbit in a low hurried tone. He looked anxiously over his shoulder as he spoke, and then raised himself upon tiptoe, put his mouth close to her ear, and whispered "She's under sentence of execution."

"What for?" said Alice.

"Did you say 'What a pity!'?" the Rabbit asked.

"No, I didn't," said Alice. "I don't think it's at all a pity. I said 'What for?'"

"She boxed the Queen's ears – " the Rabbit began. Alice gave a little scream of laughter. "Oh, hush!" the Rabbit whispered in a frightened tone. "The Queen will hear you! You see she came rather late, and the Queen said – "

"Get to your places!" shouted the Queen in a voice of thunder, and people began running about in all directions, tumbling up against each other: however, they got settled down in a minute or two, and the game began.

Alice thought she had never seen such a curious croquet-ground[1] in her life: it was all ridges and furrows: the croquet balls were live hedgehogs, and the mallets live flamingoes, and the soldiers had to double themselves up and stand on their hands and feet, to make the arches.

The chief difficulty Alice found at first was in managing her flamingo: she succeeded in getting its body tucked away, comfortably enough, under her arm, with its legs hanging down, but generally, just as she had got its neck nicely straightened out, and was going to give the hedgehog a blow with its head, it *would* twist itself round and look up in her face, with such a puzzled expression that she could not help bursting out laughing; and, when she had got its head down, and was going to begin again, it was very provoking to find that the hedgehog had unrolled itself, and was in the act of crawling away: besides all this, there was generally a ridge or a furrow in the way wherever she wanted to send the hedgehog to, and, as the

---

1   Carroll often played croquet with the Liddell children in the deanery garden. In 1863 he published *Croquet Castles*, a complicated version of ordinary croquet, to enhance their mutual enjoyment of the game.

doubled-up soldiers were always getting up and walking off to other parts of the ground, Alice soon came to the conclusion that it was a very difficult game indeed.[1]

The players all played at once, without waiting for turns, quarreling all the while, and fighting for the hedgehogs; and in a very short time the Queen was in a furious passion, and went stamping about, and shouting "Off with his head!" or "Off with her head!" about once in a minute.

Alice began to feel very uneasy: to be sure, she had not as yet had any dispute with the Queen, but she knew that it might happen any minute, "and then," thought she, "what would become of me? They're dreadfully fond of beheading people here: the great wonder is, that there's any one left alive!"

She was looking about for some way of escape, and wondering whether she could get away without being seen, when she noticed a curious appearance in the air: it puzzled her very much at first, but after watching it a minute or two she made it out to be a grin, and she said to herself "It's the Cheshire-Cat: now I shall have somebody to talk to."

"How are you getting on?" said the Cat, as soon as there was mouth enough for it to speak with.

Alice waited till the eyes appeared, and then nodded. "It's no use speaking to it," she thought, "till its ears have come, or at least one of them." In another minute the whole head appeared, and then Alice put down her flamingo, and began an account of the game, feeling very glad she had some one to listen to her. The Cat seemed to think that there was enough of it now in sight, and no more of it appeared.

"I don't think they play at all fairly," Alice began, in rather a complaining tone, "and they all quarrel so dreadfully one ca'n't hear oneself speak – and they don't seem to have any rules in

---

1   Ever since he was a child, Carroll was fascinated by rules and regulations, the essential architecture of order. Games, of course, are shaped and controlled by rules. In croquet, the rigidity and stability of mallets, balls, and hoops are assumed before the rules can go into effect. The suppleness and instability in the Wonderland version of croquet, however, dissolve the game into anarchy. Like the Caucus-race, it is impossible to go forward in this anti-game.

particular: at least, if there are, nobody attends to them – and you've no idea how confusing it is all the things being alive: for instance, there's the arch I've got to go through next walking about at the other end of the ground – and I should have croqueted the Queen's hedgehog just now, only it ran away when it saw mine coming!"

"How do you like the Queen?" said the Cat in a low voice.

"Not at all," said Alice: "she's so extremely – " Just then she noticed that the Queen was close behind her, listening: so she went on " – likely to win, that it's hardly worth while finishing the game."

The Queen smiled and passed on.

"Who *are* you talking to?" said the King, coming up to Alice, and looking at the Cat's head with great curiosity.

"It's a friend of mine – a Cheshire-Cat," said Alice: "allow me to introduce it."

"I don't like the look of it at all," said the King: "however, it may kiss my hand, if it likes." "I'd rather not," the Cat remarked.

"Don't be impertinent," said the King, "and don't look at me like that!" He got behind Alice as he spoke.

"A cat may look at a king,"[1] said Alice. "I've read that in some book, but I don't remember where."

"Well, it must be removed," said the King very decidedly; and he called to the Queen, who was passing at the moment, "My dear! I wish you would have this cat removed!"

The Queen had only one way of settling all difficulties, great or small. "Off with his head!" she said without even looking round.

"I'll fetch the executioner myself," said the King eagerly, and he hurried off.

Alice thought she might as well go back and see how the game was going on, as she heard the Queen's voice in the distance, screaming with passion. She had already heard her sentence three of the players to be executed for having missed their turns, and she did not like the look of things at all, as the

---

1   "A cat may look at a king" is a proverbial expression.

game was in such confusion that she never knew whether it was her turn or not. So she went off in search of her hedgehog.

The hedgehog was engaged in a fight with another hedgehog, which seemed to Alice an excellent opportunity for croqueting one of them with the other: the only difficulty was that her flamingo was gone across the other side of the garden, where Alice could see it trying in a helpless sort of way to fly up into a tree.

By the time she had caught the flamingo and brought it back, the fight was over, and both the hedgehogs were out of sight: "but it doesn't matter much," thought Alice, "as all the arches are gone from this side of the ground." So she tucked it away under her arm, that it might not escape again, and went back to have a little more conversation with her friend.

When she got back to the Cheshire-Cat, she was surprised to find quite a large crowd collected round it: there was a dispute going on between the executioner, the King, and the Queen, who were all talking at once, while all the rest were quite silent, and looked very uncomfortable.

The moment Alice appeared, she was appealed to by all three to settle the question, and they repeated their arguments to her, though, as they all spoke at once, she found it very hard to make out exactly what they said.

The executioner's argument was, that you couldn't cut off a head unless there was a body to cut it off from: that he had never had to do such a thing before, and he wasn't going to begin at *his* time of life.

The King's argument was that anything that had a head could be beheaded, and that you weren't to talk nonsense.

The Queen's argument was that, if something wasn't done about it in less than no time, she'd have everybody executed, all round. (It was this last remark that had made the whole party look so grave and anxious.) Alice could think of nothing else to say but "It belongs to the Duchess: you'd better ask *her* about it."

"She's in prison," the Queen said to the executioner: "fetch her here." And the executioner went off like an arrow.

The Cat's head began fading away the moment he was gone, and, by the time he had come back with the Duchess, it had entirely disappeared: so the King and the executioner ran wildly up and down, looking for it, while the rest of the party went back to the game.

CHAPTER IX.

THE MOCK TURTLE'S STORY.

"You ca'n't think how glad I am to see you again, you dear old thing!" said the Duchess, as she tucked her arm affectionately into Alice's, and they walked off together.

Alice was very glad to find her in such a pleasant temper, and thought to herself that perhaps it was only the pepper that had made her so savage when they met in the kitchen.

"When *I'm* a Duchess," she said to herself (not in a very hopeful tone, though), "I wo'n't have any pepper in my kitchen *at all*. Soup does very well without – Maybe it's always pepper that makes people hot-tempered," she went on, very much pleased at having found out a new kind of rule, "and vinegar that makes them sour – and camomile[1] that makes them bitter – and – and barley-sugar[2] and such things that make children sweet-tempered. I only wish people knew *that*: then they wouldn't be so stingy about it, you know – "

She had quite forgotten the Duchess by this time, and was a little startled when she heard her voice close to her ear. "You're thinking about something, my dear, and that makes you forget to talk. I ca'n't tell you just now what the moral of that is, but I shall remember it in a bit."

"Perhaps it hasn't one," Alice ventured to remark.

"Tut, tut, child!" said the Duchess. "Everything's got a moral, if only you can find it."[3] And she squeezed herself up closer to Alice's side as she spoke.

Alice did not much like her keeping so close to her: first, because the Duchess was *very* ugly; and secondly, because she was exactly the right height to rest her chin on Alice's shoulder,

---

1   Camomile was a bitter medicine, made from the herb of the same name, used as a tonic and as a cure for bile attacks.
2   Barley-sugar is a hard candy made by boiling cane sugar with a barley mixture.
3   The Duchess's compulsive moralizing is a *reductio ad absurdum* of the conventional moralizing found in the popular children's books in the nineteenth century.

and it was an uncomfortably sharp chin. However, she did not like to be rude: so she bore it as well as she could.

"The game's going on rather better now," she said, by way of keeping up the conversation a little.

"'Tis so," said the Duchess: "and the moral of that is – 'Oh, 'tis love, 'tis love, that makes the world go round!'"[1]

"Somebody said," Alice whispered, "that it's done by everybody minding their own business!"

"Ah well! It means much the same thing," said the Duchess, digging her sharp little chin into Alice's shoulder as she added "and the moral of *that* is – 'Take care of the sense, and the sounds will take care of themselves.'"[2]

"How fond she is of finding morals in things!" Alice thought to herself.

---

1 According to Roger Lancyln Green, this line comes from a popular song called "The Dawn of Love."
2 A play on the proverb, "Take care of the pence and the pounds will take care of themselves."

"I dare say you're wondering why I don't put my arm round your waist," the Duchess said, after a pause: "the reason is, that I'm doubtful about the temper of your flamingo. Shall I try the experiment?"[1]

"He might bite," Alice cautiously replied, not feeling at all anxious to have the experiment tried.

"Very true," said the Duchess: "flamingoes and mustard both bite. And the moral of that is – 'Birds of a feather flock together.'"

"Only mustard isn't a bird," Alice remarked.

"Right, as usual," said the Duchess: "what a clear way you have of putting things!"

"It's a mineral, I *think*," said Alice.

"Of course it is," said the Duchess, who seemed ready to agree to everything that Alice said: "there's a large mustard-mine near here. And the moral of that is – 'The more there is of mine, the less there is of yours.'"

"Oh, I know!" exclaimed Alice, who had not attended to this last remark. "It's a vegetable. It doesn't look like one, but it is."

"I quite agree with you," said the Duchess; "and the moral of that is – 'Be what you would seem to be' – or, if you'd like it put more simply – 'Never imagine yourself not to be otherwise than what it might appear to others that what you were or might have been was not otherwise than what you had been would have appeared to them to be otherwise.'"

"I think I should understand that better," Alice said very politely, "if I had it written down: but I ca'n't quite follow it as you say it."

"That's nothing to what I could say if I chose," the Duchess replied, in a pleased tone.

"Pray don't trouble yourself to say it any longer than that," said Alice.

---

1   There is something chilling about this scene. The Duchess, a grotesque female with the face of a man, relentlessly invades Alice's space. Her use of the word "experiment" and her concern for the temper of Alice's flamingo seem to veil a sexual innuendo.

"Oh, don't talk about trouble!" said the Duchess. "I make you a present of everything I've said as yet."

"A cheap sort of present!" thought Alice. "I'm glad people don't give birthday-presents like that!" But she did not venture to say it out loud.

"Thinking again?" the Duchess asked, with another dig of her sharp little chin.

"I've a right to think," said Alice sharply, for she was beginning to feel a little worried.

"Just about as much right," said the Duchess, "as pigs have to fly; and the m – "

But here, to Alice's great surprise, the Duchess's voice died away, even in the middle of her favourite word 'moral,' and the arm that was linked into hers began to tremble. Alice looked up, and there stood the Queen in front of them, with her arms folded, frowning like a thunderstorm.

"A fine day, your Majesty!" the Duchess began in a low, weak voice.

"Now, I give you fair warning," shouted the Queen, stamping on the ground as she spoke; "either you or your head must be off, and that in about half no time! Take your choice!"

The Duchess took her choice, and was gone in a moment.

"Let's go on with the game," the Queen said to Alice; and Alice was too much frightened to say a word, but slowly followed her back to the croquet-ground.

The other guests had taken advantage of the Queen's absence, and were resting in the shade: however, the moment they saw her, they hurried back to the game, the Queen merely remarking that a moment's delay would cost them their lives.

All the time they were playing the Queen never left off quarreling with the other players, and shouting "Off with his head!" or "Off with her head!" Those whom she sentenced were taken into custody by the soldiers, who of course had to leave off being arches to do this, so that, by the end of half an hour or so, there were no arches left, and all the players, except the King, the Queen, and Alice, were in custody and under sentence of execution.

Then the Queen left off, quite out of breath, and said to Alice, "Have you seen the Mock Turtle yet?"

"No," said Alice. "I don't even know what a Mock Turtle is." "It's the thing Mock Turtle Soup[1] is made from," said the Queen.

"I never saw one, or heard of one," said Alice.

"Come on, then," said the Queen, "and he shall tell you his history."

As they walked off together, Alice heard the King say in a low voice, to the company generally, "You are all pardoned." "Come, *that's* a good thing!" she said to herself, for she had felt quite unhappy at the number of executions the Queen had ordered.

They very soon came upon a Gryphon,[2] lying fast asleep in the sun. (If you don't know what a Gryphon is, look at the picture.) "Up, lazy thing!" said the Queen, "and take this young lady to see the Mock Turtle, and to hear his history. I must go back and see after some executions I have ordered"; and she walked off, leaving Alice alone with the Gryphon. Alice did

---

1 Mock turtle soup is usually made of veal, and thus Tenniel draws the creature as a composite of a calf and a turtle.

2 A gryphon is a mythical monster with the head and wings of an eagle and the lower torso of a lion. It often appeared on medieval heraldry. The Liddell children collected heraldic crests for which Carroll provided names.

not quite like the look of the creature, but on the whole she thought it would be quite as safe to stay with it as to go after that savage Queen: so she waited.

The Gryphon sat up and rubbed its eyes: then it watched the Queen till she was out of sight: then it chuckled. "What fun!" said the Gryphon, half to itself, half to Alice.

"What *is* the fun?" said Alice.

"Why, *she*," said the Gryphon. "It's all her fancy, that: they never executes nobody, you know. Come on!"

"Everybody says 'come on!' here," thought Alice, as she went slowly after it: "I never was so ordered about before, in all my life, never!"[1]

They had not gone far before they saw the Mock Turtle in the distance, sitting sad and lonely on a little ledge of rock, and, as they came nearer, Alice could hear him sighing as if his heart would break. She pitied him deeply. "What is his sorrow?" she asked the Gryphon. And the Gryphon answered, very nearly in the same words as before, "It's all his fancy, that: he hasn't got no sorrow, you know. Come on!"[2]

So they went up to the Mock Turtle, who looked at them with large eyes full of tears, but said nothing.

"This here young lady," said the Gryphon, "she wants for to know your history, she do."

"I'll tell it her," said the Mock Turtle in a deep, hollow tone. "Sit down, both of you, and don't speak a word till I've finished."

So they sat down, and nobody spoke for some minutes. Alice thought to herself "I don't see how he can *ever* finish, if he doesn't begin." But she waited patiently.

---

1   What may make her being ordered about even more exasperating is that the Gryphon is of the lower class, as revealed by his speech.

2   The Gryphon's remark is a telling one. In Wonderland, it is not possible for Alice to make meaningful assumptions about the creatures' motives, feelings, or thoughts based upon external observations. There may, in fact, be no inner emotional core to these creatures and any attempt to interpret their inner life by judging their behavior leads to erroneous conclusions. In *Through the Looking-Glass* Alice finds herself misreading the tears of the Walrus as sorrow for eating the baby oysters. To Alice's dismay, Tweedledee points out that the Walrus ate more oysters than the Carpenter.

"Once," said the Mock Turtle at last, with a deep sigh, "I was a real Turtle."

These words were followed by a very long silence, broken only by an occasional exclamation of "Hjckrrh!" from the Gryphon, and the constant heavy sobbing of the Mock Turtle. Alice was very nearly getting up and saying, "Thank you, Sir, for your interesting story," but she could not help thinking there *must* be more to come, so she sat still and said nothing.

"When we were little," the Mock Turtle went on at last, more calmly, though still sobbing a little now and then, "we went to school in the sea. The master was an old Turtle – we used to call him Tortoise – "

"Why did you call him Tortoise, if he wasn't one?" Alice asked.

"We called him Tortoise because he taught us," said the Mock Turtle angrily. "Really you are very dull!"

"You ought to be ashamed of yourself for asking such a simple question," added the Gryphon; and then they both sat silent and looked at poor Alice, who felt ready to sink into the earth. At last the Gryphon said to the Mock Turtle "Drive on, old fellow! Don't be all day about it!", and he went on in these words: —

"Yes, we went to school in the sea, though you mayn't believe it — "

"I never said I didn't!" interrupted Alice.

"You did," said the Mock Turtle.

"Hold your tongue!" added the Gryphon, before Alice could speak again. The Mock Turtle went on.

"We had the best of educations — in fact, we went to school every day — "

"*I've* been to a day-school, too," said Alice. "You needn't be so proud as all that."

"With extras?" asked the Mock Turtle, a little anxiously.

"Yes," said Alice: "we learned French and music."

"And washing?"[1] said the Mock Turtle. "Certainly not!" said Alice indignantly.

"Ah! Then yours wasn't a really good school," said the Mock Turtle in a tone of great relief. "Now, at *ours*, they had, at the end of the bill, 'French, music, *and washing* — extra.'"

"You couldn't have wanted it much," said Alice; "living at the bottom of the sea."

"I couldn't afford to learn it," said the Mock Turtle with a sigh. "I only took the regular course."

"What was that?" inquired Alice.

---

1 According to Martin Gardner (*Annotated Alice*), the phrase "French, music, and washing — extra" often appeared on boarding school bills. The meaning is simply that there was an extra charge to teach French and music, and to have one's clothes washed by the school. The Mock Turtle, however, asks Alice if washing was one of the subjects taught at her school, an idea obviously repugnant to a middle-class assumptions.

"Reeling and Writhing,[1] of course, to begin with," the Mock Turtle replied; "and then the different branches of Arithmetic – Ambition, Distraction, Uglification, and Derision."

"I never heard of 'Uglification,'" Alice ventured to say. "What is it?"

The Gryphon lifted up both its paws in surprise. "Never heard of uglifying!" it exclaimed. "You know what to beautify is, I suppose?"

"Yes," said Alice doubtfully: "it means – to – make – anything – prettier."

"Well, then," the Gryphon went on, "if you don't know what to uglify is, you *are* a simpleton."

Alice did not feel encouraged to ask anymore questions about it: so she turned to the Mock Turtle, and said "What else had you to learn?"

"Well, there was Mystery," the Mock Turtle replied, counting off the subjects on his flappers, – "Mystery, ancient and modern, with Seaography: then Drawling – the Drawling-master[2] was an old conger-eel, that used to come once a week: he taught us Drawling, Stretching, and Fainting in Coils."

"What was *that* like?" said Alice.

"Well, I ca'n't show it you, myself," the Mock Turtle said: "I'm too stiff. And the Gryphon never learnt it."

"Hadn't time," said the Gryphon: "I went to the Classical master, though. He was an old crab, *he* was."

"I never went to him," the Mock Turtle said with a sigh. "He taught Laughing and Grief, they used to say."

"So he did, so he did," said the Gryphon, sighing in his turn; and both creatures hid their faces in their paws.

"And how many hours a day did you do lessons?" said Alice, in a hurry to change the subject.

"Ten hours the first day," said the Mock Turtle: "nine the next, and so on."

---

1 All of the Mock Turtle's subjects are puns on traditional courses of study: reading, writing, addition, subtraction, multiplication, division, history, geography, drawing, sketching, painting in oils, Latin, and Greek.

2 The "Drawling-master" may be based upon the famous art critic, John Ruskin, who visited the Liddell children weekly to teach them drawing.

"What a curious plan!" exclaimed Alice.

"That's the reason they're called lessons," the Gryphon remarked: "because they lessen from day to day."

This was quite a new idea to Alice, and she thought it over a little before she made her next remark. "Then the eleventh day must have been a holiday?"

"Of course it was," said the Mock Turtle.

"And how did you manage on the twelfth?"[1] Alice went on eagerly.

"That's enough about lessons," the Gryphon interrupted in a very decided tone. "Tell her something about the games now."

---

1   The eleventh day was a holiday because the hours have been reduced to zero. The Gryphon ends the discussion when Alice asks about the twelfth day because, as Martin Gardner points out (*More Annotated Alice*), she introduces the possibility of mysterious negative numbers, something of a mind boggler in the context of diminishing lessons.

CHAPTER X.

THE LOBSTER-QUADRILLE.

THE Mock Turtle sighed deeply, and drew the back of one flapper across his eyes. He looked at Alice and tried to speak, but, for a minute or two, sobs choked his voice. "Same as if he had a bone in his throat," said the Gryphon; and it set to work shaking him and punching him in the back. At last the Mock Turtle recovered his voice, and, with tears running down his cheeks, he went on again: –

"You may not have lived much under the sea – " ("I haven't," said Alice) – "and perhaps you were never even introduced to a lobster – "(Alice began to say "I once tasted –" but checked herself hastily, and said "No, never") " – so you can have no idea what a delightful thing a Lobster-Quadrille is!"[1]

"No, indeed," said Alice. "What sort of a dance is it?"

"Why," said the Gryphon, "you first form into a line along the seashore – "

"Two lines!" cried the Mock Turtle. "Seals, turtles, salmon, and so on: then, when you've cleared all the jelly-fish out of the way – "

"*That* generally takes some time," interrupted the Gryphon.

" – you advance twice – "

"Each with a lobster as a partner!" cried the Gryphon.

"Of course," the Mock Turtle said: "advance twice, set to partners – "

" – change lobsters, and retire in same order," continued the Gryphon.

"Then, you know," the Mock Turtle went on, "you throw the – "

"The lobsters!" shouted the Gryphon, with a bound into the air.

---

1   A quadrille is a square dance of French origin composed of five figures and per-
    formed by four couples. This dance, which was fashionable during Carroll's day,
    was taught to the Liddell children by a private tutor.

" – as far out to sea as you can – "

"Swim after them!" screamed the Gryphon.

"Turn a somersault in the sea!" cried the Mock Turtle, capering wildly about.

"Change lobsters again!" yelled the Gryphon at the top of its voice.

"Back to land again, and – that's all the first figure," said the Mock Turtle, suddenly dropping his voice; and the two creatures, who had been jumping about like mad things all this time, sat down again very sadly and quietly, and looked at Alice. "It must be a very pretty dance," said Alice timidly.

"Would you like to see a little of it?" said the Mock Turtle.

"Very much indeed," said Alice.

"Come, let's try the first figure!" said the Mock Turtle to the Gryphon. "We can do it without lobsters, you know. Which shall sing?"

"Oh, *you* sing," said the Gryphon. "I've forgotten the words."

So they began solemnly dancing round and round Alice, every now and then treading on her toes when they passed too close, and waving their fore-paws to mark the time, while the Mock Turtle sang this, very slowly and sadly: –

"Will you walk a little faster?" said a whiting to a snail,
"There's a porpoise close behind us, and he's treading on my tail.
See how eagerly the lobsters and the turtles all advance!
They are waiting on the shingle – will you come and join the dance?
  Will you, wo'n't you, will you, wo'n't you, will you join the dance?
  Will you, wo'n't you, will you, wo'n't you, wo'n't you
                                          join the dance?

"You can really have no notion how delightful it will be
When they take us up and throw us, with the lobsters, out to sea!"
But the snail replied "Too far, too far!", and gave a look askance –
Said he thanked the whiting kindly, but he would not join the dance.
  Would not, could not, would not, could not, would not
                                          join the dance.
  Would not, could not, would not, could not, could not
                                          join the dance.

"What matters it how far we go?" his scaly friend replied.
"There is another shore, you know, upon the other side.
The further off from England the nearer is to France –
Then turn not pale, beloved snail, but come and join the dance.
    Will you, wo'n't you, will you, wo'n't you, will you join the dance?
    Will you, wo'n't you, will you, wo'n't you, wo'n't you
                                                    join the dance?"[1]

"Thank you, it's a very interesting dance to watch," said Alice, feeling very glad that it was over at last: "and I do so like that curious song about the whiting!"

"Oh, as to the whiting," said the Mock Turtle, "they – you've seen them, of course?"

---

1   The Mock Turtle's song is a loose parody of Mary Howitt's nursery poem, "The Spider and the Fly," first published in 1834 and reprinted in Appendix H.

"Yes," said Alice, "I've often seen them at dinn – " she checked herself hastily.

"I don't know where Dinn may be," said the Mock Turtle; "but, if you've seen them so often, of course you know what they're like?"

"I believe so," Alice replied thoughtfully. "They have their tails in their mouths – and they're all over crumbs."[1]

"You're wrong about the crumbs," said the Mock Turtle: "crumbs would all wash off in the sea. But they *have* their tails in their mouths; and the reason is – " here the Mock Turtle yawned and shut his eyes. "Tell her about the reason and all that," he said to the Gryphon.

"The reason is," said the Gryphon, "that they *would* go with the lobsters to the dance. So they got thrown out to sea. So they had to fall a long way. So they got their tails fast in their mouths. So they couldn't get them out again. That's all."

"Thank you," said Alice, "it's very interesting. I never knew so much about a whiting before."

"I can tell you more than that, if you like," said the Gryphon. "Do you know why it's called a whiting?"

"I never thought about it," said Alice. "Why?"

"*It does the boots and shoes*," the Gryphon replied very solemnly.

Alice was thoroughly puzzled. "Does the boots and shoes!" she repeated in a wondering tone.

"Why, what are *your* shoes done with?" said the Gryphon. "I mean, what makes them so shiny?"

Alice looked down at them, and considered a little before she gave her answer. "They're done with blacking, I believe."

"Boots and shoes under the sea," the Gryphon went on in a deep voice, "are done with whiting. Now you know."

"And what are they made of?" Alice asked in a tone of great curiosity.

"Soles and eels, of course," the Gryphon replied, rather impatiently: "any shrimp could have told you that."

---

1 Years later, Carroll was told that fishmongers sold whitings with their tails tucked into their eyes, not their mouths. The fish would be fried covered with breadcrumbs.

"If I'd been the whiting," said Alice, whose thoughts were still running on the song, "I'd have said to the porpoise 'Keep back, please! We don't want *you* with us!'"

"They were obliged to have him with them," the Mock Turtle said. "No wise fish would go anywhere without a porpoise."

"Wouldn't it, really?" said Alice, in a tone of great surprise.

"Of course not," said the Mock Turtle. "Why, if a fish came to me, and told me he was going a journey, I should say 'With what porpoise?'"

"Don't you mean 'purpose'?" said Alice.

"I mean what I say," the Mock Turtle replied, in an offended tone. And the Gryphon added "Come, let's hear some of *your* adventures."

"I could tell you my adventures – beginning from this morning," said Alice a little timidly; "but it's no use going back to yesterday, because I was a different person then."

"Explain all that," said the Mock Turtle.

"No, no! The adventures first," said the Gryphon in an impatient tone: "explanations take such a dreadful time."

So Alice began telling them her adventures from the time when she first saw the White Rabbit. She was a little nervous about it, just at first, the two creatures got so close to her, one on each side, and opened their eyes and mouths so *very* wide; but she gained courage as she went on. Her listeners were perfectly quiet till she got to the part about her repeating "*You are old, Father William*," to the Caterpillar, and the words all coming different, and then the Mock Turtle drew a long breath, and said "That's very curious!"

"It's all about as curious as it can be," said the Gryphon.

"It all came different!" the Mock Turtle repeated thoughtfully. "I should like to hear her try and repeat something now. Tell her to begin." He looked at the Gryphon as if he thought it had some kind of authority over Alice.

"Stand up and repeat '*Tis the voice of the sluggard*,'" said the Gryphon. "How the creatures order one about, and make one repeat lessons!" thought Alice. "I might just as well be at school at once." However, she got up, and began to repeat it, but her head was so full of the Lobster-Quadrille, that she hardly knew what she was saying; and the words came very queer indeed: –

> "'Tis the voice of the Lobster: I heard him declare
> 'You have baked me too brown, I must sugar my hair.'
> As a duck with its eyelids, so he with his nose
> Trims his belt and his buttons, and turns out his toes.
> When the sands are all dry, he is gay as a lark,
> And will talk in contemptuous tones of the Shark:
> But, when the tide rises and sharks are around,
> His voice has a timid and tremulous sound."[1]

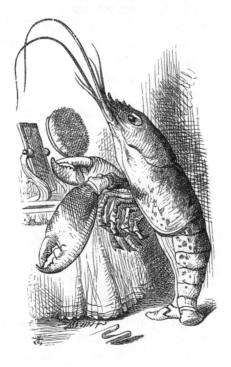

---

1   A parody of Isaac Watt's didactic poem "The Sluggard" (1715), reprinted in Appendix H. Only the first four lines of the parody appeared until the 1886 edition of *Alice*. The next four lines of this stanza and the last six lines of the second stanza were added for Savile Clarke's operetta in 1886 and later added to the edition of *Alice* that same year.

"That's different from what I used to say when I was a child," said the Gryphon.

"Well, *I* never heard it before," said the Mock Turtle; "but it sounds uncommon nonsense."

Alice said nothing: she had sat down with her face in her hands, wondering if anything would *ever* happen in a natural way again.

"I should like to have it explained," said the Mock Turtle.

"She ca'n't explain it," said the Gryphon hastily. "Go on with the next verse."

"But about his toes?" the Mock Turtle persisted. "How *could* he turn them out with his nose, you know?"

"It's the first position in dancing," Alice said; but she was dreadfully puzzled by the whole thing, and longed to change the subject.

"Go on with the next verse," the Gryphon repeated: "it begins '*I passed by his garden.*'"

Alice did not dare to disobey, though she felt sure it would all come wrong, and she went on in a trembling voice: –

> "*I passed by his garden, and marked, with one eye,*
> *How the Owl and the Panther were sharing a pie:*
> *The Panther took pie-crust, and gravy, and meat,*
> *While the Owl had the dish as its share of the treat.*
> *When the pie was all finished, the Owl, as a boon,*
> *Was kindly permitted to pocket the spoon:*
> *While the Panther received knife and fork with a growl,*
> *And concluded the banquet by –* "[1]

"What *is* the use of repeating all that stuff?" the Mock Turtle

---

1   In editions prior to 1886 this verse ended abruptly after the second line and read as follows: "I passed by his garden, and marked, with one eye,/ How the owl and the oyster were sharing a pie." In 1886 Carroll modified and added to the song for Savile Clarke's theatrical version of the Alice books. He changed the oyster to a panther and added the last six lines of the poem. Also of interest is the stanza as it appeared in William Boyd's *Songs from Alice in Wonderland* (1870). Here Carroll added two lines following the one in which the owl and oyster share a pie: "While the Duck and the Dodo, the lizard and cat,/ Were swimming in milk round the brim of a hat."

interrupted, "if you don't explain it as you go on? It's by far the most confusing thing *I* ever heard!"

"Yes, I think you'd better leave off," said the Gryphon, and Alice was only too glad to do so.

"Shall we try another figure of the Lobster-Quadrille?" the Gryphon went on. "Or would you like the Mock Turtle to sing you another song?"

"Oh, a song, please, if the Mock Turtle would be so kind," Alice replied, so eagerly that the Gryphon said, in a rather offended tone, "Hm! No accounting for tastes! Sing her '*Turtle Soup*,' will you, old fellow?"

The Mock Turtle sighed deeply, and began, in a voice choked with sobs, to sing this: –

> "*Beautiful Soup, so rich and green,*
> *Waiting in a hot tureen!*
> *Who for such dainties would not stoop?*
> *Soup of the evening, beautiful Soup!*
> *Soup of the evening, beautiful Soup!*
> *Beau – ootiful Soo – oop!*
> *Beau – ootiful Soo – oop!*
> *Soo – oop of the e – e – evening,*
> *Beautiful, beautiful Soup!*

> *Beautiful Soup! Who cares for fish,*
> *Game, or any other dish?*
> *Who would not give all else for two p*
> *ennyworth only of beautiful Soup?*
> *Pennyworth only of beautiful soup?*
> *Beau – ootiful Soo – oop!*
> *Beau – ootiful Soo – oop!*
> *Soo – oop of the e – e – evening,*
> *Beautiful, beauti – FUL SOUP!*"[1]

---

1   "Turtle Soup" is a parody of "Beautiful Star," a popular song by J.M. Sayles, reprinted in Appendix H. Carroll notes in his diary that he heard Alice and Edith sing "Beautiful Star" in August of 1862.

"Chorus again!" cried the Gryphon, and the Mock Turtle had just begun to repeat it, when a cry of "The trial's beginning!" was heard in the distance.

"Come on!" cried the Gryphon, and, taking Alice by the hand, it hurried off, without waiting for the end of the song.

"What trial is it?" Alice panted as she ran; but the Gryphon only answered "Come on!" and ran the faster, while more and more faintly came, carried on the breeze that followed them, the melancholy words: —

> *"Soo — oop of the e — e — evening,*
> *Beautiful, beautiful Soup!"*

CHAPTER XI.

WHO STOLE THE TARTS?

THE King and Queen of Hearts were seated on their throne when they arrived, with a great crowd assembled about them – all sorts of little birds and beasts, as well as the whole pack of cards: the Knave was standing before them, in chains, with a soldier on each side to guard him; and near the King was the White Rabbit, with a trumpet in one hand, and a scroll of parchment in the other. In the very middle of the court was a table, with a large dish of tarts upon it: they looked so good, that it made Alice quite hungry to look at them – "I wish they'd get the trial done," she thought, "and hand round the refreshments!" But there seemed to be no chance of this; so she began looking at everything about her to pass away the time.

Alice had never been in a court of justice before, but she had read about them in books, and she was quite pleased to find that she knew the name of nearly everything there. "That's the judge," she said to herself, "because of his great wig."

The judge, by the way, was the King; and, as he wore his crown over the wig (look at the frontispiece if you want to see how he did it), he did not look at all comfortable, and it was certainly not becoming.

"And that's the jury-box," thought Alice; "and those twelve creatures," (she was obliged to say "creatures," you see, because some of them were animals, and some were birds,) "I suppose they are the jurors." She said this last word two or three times over to herself, being rather proud of it: for she thought, and rightly too, that very few little girls of her age knew the meaning of it at all. However, "jurymen" would have done just as well.

The twelve jurors were all writing very busily on slates. "What are they doing?" Alice whispered to the Gryphon. "They ca'n't have anything to put down yet, before the trial's begun."

"They're putting down their names," the Gryphon whispered in reply, "for fear they should forget them before the end of the trial."

"Stupid things!" Alice began in a loud indignant voice; but she stopped herself hastily, for the White Rabbit cried out "Silence in the court!", and the King put on his spectacles and looked anxiously round, to make out who was talking.

Alice could see, as well as if she were looking over their shoulders, that all the jurors were writing down "Stupid things!" on their slates, and she could even make out that one of them didn't know how to spell "stupid," and that he had to ask his neighbour to tell him. "A nice muddle their slates'll be in, before the trial's over!" thought Alice.

One of the jurors had a pencil that squeaked. This, of course, Alice could not stand, and she went round the court and got behind him, and very soon found an opportunity of taking it away. She did it so quickly that the poor little juror (it was Bill, the Lizard) could not make out at all what had become of it; so, after hunting all about for it, he was obliged to write with one finger for the rest of the day; and this was of very little use, as it left no mark on the slate."

"Herald, read the accusation!" said the King.

On this the White Rabbit blew three blasts on the trumpet, and then unrolled the parchment-scroll, and read as follows: –

> "*The Queen of Hearts, she made some tarts,*
> *All on a summer day:*
> *The Knave of Hearts, he stole those tarts*
> *And took them quite away!*"[1]

"Consider your verdict," the King said to the jury.

"Not yet, not yet!" the Rabbit hastily interrupted. "There's a great deal to come before that!"

"Call the first witness," said the King; and the White Rabbit blew three blasts on the trumpet, and called out "First witness!"

The first witness was the Hatter. He came in with a teacup

---

1   These lines are taken unchanged from a traditional nursery rhyme.

in one hand and a piece of bread-and-butter in the other. "I beg pardon, your Majesty," he began, "for bringing these in; but I hadn't quite finished my tea when I was sent for."

"You ought to have finished," said the King. "When did you begin?"

The Hatter looked at the March Hare, who had followed him into the court, arm-in-arm with the Dormouse. "Fourteenth of March, I think it was," he said.

"Fifteenth," said the March Hare.

"Sixteenth," said the Dormouse.

"Write that down," the King said to the jury; and the jury eagerly wrote down all three dates on their slates, and then added them up, and reduced the answer to shillings and pence.

"Take off your hat," the King said to the Hatter.

"It isn't mine," said the Hatter.

"*Stolen!*" the King exclaimed, turning to the jury, who instantly made a memorandum of the fact.

"I keep them to sell," the Hatter added as an explanation. "I've none of my own. I'm a hatter."

Here the Queen put on her spectacles, and began staring hard at the Hatter, who turned pale and fidgeted.

"Give your evidence," said the King; "and don't be nervous, or I'll have you executed on the spot."

This did not seem to encourage the witness at all: he kept shifting from one foot to the other, looking uneasily at the Queen, and in his confusion he bit a large piece out of his teacup instead of the bread-and-butter.

Just at this moment Alice felt a very curious sensation, which puzzled her a good deal until she made out what it was: she was beginning to grow larger again, and she thought at first she would get up and leave the court; but on second thoughts she decided to remain where she was as long as there was room for her.

"I wish you wouldn't squeeze so," said the Dormouse, who was sitting next to her. "I can hardly breathe."

"I ca'n't help it," said Alice very meekly: "I'm growing."

"You've no right to grow *here*," said the Dormouse.

"Don't talk nonsense," said Alice more boldly: "you know you're growing too."

"Yes, but *I* grow at a reasonable pace," said the Dormouse: "not in that ridiculous fashion." And he got up very sulkily and crossed over to the other side of the court.

All this time the Queen had never left off staring at the Hatter, and, just as the Dormouse crossed the court, she said, to one of the officers of the court, "Bring me the list of the singers in the last concert!" on which the wretched Hatter trembled so, that he shook off both his shoes.[1]

"Give your evidence," the King repeated angrily, "or I'll have you executed, whether you are nervous or not."

"I'm a poor man, your Majesty," the Hatter began, in a trembling voice, "and I hadn't begun my tea – not above a week or so – and what with the bread-and-butter getting so thin – and the twinkling of the tea – "

"The twinkling of *what*?" said the King.

"It *began* with the tea," the Hatter replied.

"Of course twinkling *begins* with a T!" said the King sharply. "Do you take me for a dunce? Go on!"

"I'm a poor man," the Hatter went on, "and most things twinkled after that – only the March Hare said – "

---

1   The last concert, to which the Queen refers, is mentioned in Chapter 7. The Hatter explains to Alice: " – it was at the great concert given by the Queen of Hearts and I had to sing ['Twinkle, twinkle, little bat!']."

"I didn't!" the March Hare interrupted in a great hurry.

"You did!" said the Hatter.

"I deny it!" said the March Hare.

"He denies it," said the King: "leave out that part."

"Well, at any rate, the Dormouse said – " the Hatter went on, looking anxiously round to see if he would deny it too; but the Dormouse denied nothing, being fast asleep.

"After that," continued the Hatter, "I cut some more bread-and-butter – "

"But what did the Dormouse say?" one of the jury asked.

"That I ca'n't remember," said the Hatter.

"You *must* remember," remarked the King, "or I'll have you executed."

The miserable Hatter dropped his teacup and bread-and-butter, and went down on one knee. "I'm a poor man, your Majesty," he began.

"You're a *very* poor *speaker*," said the King.

Here one of the guinea-pigs cheered, and was immediately suppressed by the officers of the court. (As that is rather a hard word, I will just explain to you how it was done. They had a large canvas bag, which tied up at the mouth with strings: into this they slipped the guinea-pig, head first, and then sat upon it.)

"I'm glad I've seen that done," thought Alice. "I've so often read in the newspapers, at the end of trials, 'There was some attempt at applause, which was immediately suppressed by the officers of the court,' and I never understood what it meant till now."

"If that's all you know about it, you may stand down," continued the King.

"I ca'n't go no lower," said the Hatter: "I'm on the floor, as it is."

"Then you may *sit* down," the King replied.

Here the other guinea-pig cheered, and was suppressed.

"Come, that finishes the guinea-pigs!" thought Alice. "Now we shall get on better."

"I'd rather finish my tea," said the Hatter, with an anxious look at the Queen, who was reading the list of singers.

"You may go," said the King, and the Hatter hurriedly left the court, without even waiting to put his shoes on.

" – and just take his head off outside," the Queen added to one of the officers; but the Hatter was out of sight before the officer could get to the door.

"Call the next witness!" said the King.

The next witness was the Duchess's cook. She carried the pepper-box in her hand, and Alice guessed who it was, even before she got into the court, by the way the people near the door began sneezing all at once.

"Give your evidence," said the King.

"Sha'n't," said the cook.

The King looked anxiously at the White Rabbit, who said, in a low voice, "Your Majesty must cross-examine *this* witness."

"Well, if I must, I must," the King said with a melancholy air, and, after folding his arms and frowning at the cook till his eyes were nearly out of sight, he said, in a deep voice, "What are tarts made of?"

"Pepper, mostly," said the cook.

"Treacle," said a sleepy voice behind her.

"Collar that Dormouse!" the Queen shrieked out. "Behead that Dormouse! Turn that Dormouse out of court! Suppress him! Pinch him! Off with his whiskers!"

For some minutes the whole court was in confusion, getting the Dormouse turned out, and, by the time they had settled down again, the cook had disappeared.

"Never mind!" said the King, with an air of great relief. "Call the next witness." And, he added, in an under-tone to the Queen, "Really, my dear, *you* must cross-examine the next witness. It quite makes my forehead ache!"

Alice watched the White Rabbit as he fumbled over the list, feeling very curious to see what the next witness would be like, "– for they haven't got much evidence yet," she said to herself. Imagine her surprise, when the White Rabbit read out, at the top of his shrill little voice, the name "Alice!"

CHAPTER XII.

ALICE'S EVIDENCE.

"Here!" cried Alice, quite forgetting in the flurry of the moment how large she had grown in the last few minutes, and she jumped up in such a hurry that she tipped over the jury-box with the edge of her skirt, upsetting all the jurymen on to the heads of the crowd below, and there they lay sprawling about, reminding her very much of a globe of goldfish she had accidentally upset the week before.[1]

"Oh, I *beg* your pardon!" she exclaimed in a tone of great dismay, and began picking them up again as quickly as she could, for the accident of the gold-fish kept running in her head, and she had a vague sort of idea that they must be collected at once and put back into the jury-box, or they would die.

"The trial cannot proceed," said the King, in a very grave voice, "until all the jurymen are back in their proper places — *all*," he repeated with great emphasis, looking hard at Alice as he said so.

Alice looked at the jury-box, and saw that, in her haste, she had put the Lizard in head downwards, and the poor little thing was waving its tail about in a melancholy way, being quite unable to move. She soon got it out again, and put it right; "not that it signifies much," she said to herself; "I should think it

---

1 The comparison of the jurors spilled out of the jury box to goldfish spilled out of their tank of water has a lethal implication. The disorder brought about by Alice's sudden growth suggests her power over the scene — and eventually over her dream when, some moments later, she declares, "You're nothing but a pack of cards!" She collects the jurors (as she did the goldfish) to keep them alive for the moment, but with her final declaration she annihilates them along with the pack of cards. In Tenniel's illustration of this scene and in his last illustration in which the cards fly up in the air, he depicts the animals out of dress. The White Rabbit, for example, is no longer wearing his fine clothing but appears as a frightened bunny standing behind Alice. As she violently ends the dream, the humanized creatures lose their characters and become biological animals running for their lives.

would be quite as much use in the trial one way up as the other."

As soon as the jury had a little recovered from the shock of being upset, and their slates and pencils had been found and handed back to them, they set to work very diligently to write out a history of the accident, all except the Lizard, who seemed too much overcome to do anything but sit with its mouth open, gazing up into the roof of the court.

"What do you know about this business?" the King said to Alice.

"Nothing," said Alice.

"Nothing *whatever*?" persisted the King.

"Nothing whatever," said Alice.

"That's very important," the King said, turning to the jury. They were just beginning to write this down on their slates, when the White Rabbit interrupted: "*Un*important, your Majesty means, of course," he said, in a very respectful tone, but frowning and making faces at him as he spoke.

"*Un*important, of course, I meant," the King hastily said, and went on to himself in an under-tone, "important – unimportant – unimportant – important – " as if he were trying which word sounded best.

Some of the jury wrote it down "important," and some "unimportant." Alice could see this, as she was near enough to look over their slates; "but it doesn't matter a bit," she thought to herself.

At this moment the King, who had been for some time busily writing in his note-book, called out "Silence!", and read out from his book, "Rule Forty-two. *All persons more than a mile high to leave the court.*"[1]

Everybody looked at Alice.

"*I'm* not a mile high," said Alice.

"You are," said the King.

"Nearly two miles high," added the Queen.

"Well, I sha'n't go, at any rate," said Alice: "besides, that's not a regular rule: you invented it just now."

"It's the oldest rule in the book," said the King.

"Then it ought to be Number One," said Alice.

The King turned pale, and shut his note-book hastily. "Consider your verdict," he said to the jury, in a low trembling voice.

"There's more evidence to come yet, please your Majesty," said the White Rabbit, jumping up in a great hurry: "this paper has just been picked up."

"What's in it?" said the Queen.

---

1   The number forty-two held a private significance to Carroll. In the Preface to *The Hunting of the Snark* Carroll mentions Rule 42 in a nautical context: "*No one shall speak to the Man at the Helm.*" The forgetful Baker, in the same poem, carefully packed forty-two boxes of his goods, his name painted on each, but neglects having them brought aboard ship. Also, there are forty-two illustrations in *Alice's Adventures in Wonderland*.

"I haven't opened it yet," said the White Rabbit; "but it seems to be a letter, written by the prisoner to – to somebody."

"It must have been that," said the King, "unless it was written to nobody, which isn't usual, you know."

"Who is it directed to?" said one of the jurymen.

"It isn't directed at all," said the White Rabbit: "in fact, there's nothing written on the *outside*." He unfolded the paper as he spoke, and added "It isn't a letter, after all: it's a set of verses."

"Are they in the prisoner's handwriting?" asked another of the jurymen.

"No, they're not," said the White Rabbit, "and that's the queerest thing about it." (The jury all looked puzzled.)

"He must have imitated somebody else's hand," said the King. (The jury all brightened up again.)

"Please your Majesty," said the Knave, "I didn't write it, and they ca'n't prove that I did: there's no name signed at the end."[1]

---

1   Although the King has his own Wonderland logic that allows him to interpret the actions and words of the Knave, simple logic would require the Knave to explain how he knew the letter was not signed if he did not write it.

"If you didn't sign it," said the King, "that only makes the matter worse. You *must* have meant some mischief, or else you'd have signed your name like an honest man."

There was a general clapping of hands at this: it was the first really clever thing the King had said that day.

"That *proves* his guilt, of course," said the Queen: "so, off with – "

"It doesn't prove anything of the sort!" said Alice. "Why, you don't even know what they're about!"

"Read them," said the King.

The White Rabbit put on his spectacles. "Where shall I begin, please your Majesty?" he asked.

"Begin at the beginning," the King said, very gravely, "and go on till you come to the end: then stop."

There was dead silence in the court, whilst the White Rabbit read out these verses: –

> "*They told me you had been to her,*
> *And mentioned me to him:*
> *She gave me a good character,*
> *But said I could not swim.*
>
> *He sent them word I had not gone*
> *(We know it to be true):*
> *If she should push the matter on,*
> *What would become of you?*
>
> *I gave her one, they gave him two,*
> *You gave us three or more;*
> *They all returned from him to you,*
> *Though they were mine before.*
>
> *If I or she should chance to be*
> *Involved in this affair,*
> *He trusts to you to set them free,*
> *Exactly as they were.*

My notion was that you had been
(Before she had this fit)
An obstacle that came between
Him, and ourselves, and it.

Don't let him know she liked them best,
For this must ever be
A secret, kept from all the rest,
Between yourself and me."[1]

"That's the most important piece of evidence we've heard yet," said the King, rubbing his hands; "so now let the jury – "

"If any one of them can explain it," said Alice, (she had grown so large in the last few minutes that she wasn't a bit afraid of interrupting him,) "I'll give him sixpence. *I* don't believe there's an atom of meaning in it."

The jury all wrote down, on their slates, "*She* doesn't believe there's an atom of meaning in it," but none of them attempted to explain the paper.

"If there's no meaning in it," said the King, "that saves a world of trouble, you know, as we needn't try to find any. And yet I don't know," he went on, spreading out the verses on his knee, and looking at them with one eye; "I seem to see some meaning in them, after all. ' – said I *could not swim* – ' you ca'n't swim, can you?" he added, turning to the Knave.

The Knave shook his head sadly. "Do I look like it?" he said. (Which he certainly did *not*, being made entirely of cardboard.)

"All right, so far," said the King; and he went on muttering over the verses to himself: "'*We know it to be true*' – that's the jury, of course – 'If she should push the matter on' – that must be the Queen – '*What would become of you?*' – What, indeed! – '*I*

---

1   The White Rabbit's "evidence" is, of course, a piece of nonsense verse that baffles the mind with its array of confusing pronouns. The verse is a revision of a poem Carroll had written earlier entitled "She's All My Fancy Painted Him," which appeared in the *Comic Times* in 1855 and is reprinted in Appendix H. The first line of the original poem parodies William Mee's sentimental ballad "Alice Gray" (*c.* 1815), also reprinted in Appendix H.

gave her one, they gave him two' – why, that must be what he did with the tarts, you know – "

"But it goes on '*they all returned from him to you,*'" said Alice.

"Why, there they are!" said the King triumphantly, pointing to the tarts on the table. "Nothing can be clearer than *that*. Then again – '*before she had this fit*' – you never had *fits*, my dear, I think?" he said to the Queen.

"Never!" said the Queen, furiously, throwing an inkstand at the Lizard as she spoke. (The unfortunate little Bill had left off writing on his slate with one finger, as he found it made no mark; but he now hastily began again, using the ink, that was trickling down his face, as long as it lasted.)

"Then the words don't *fit* you," said the King, looking round the court with a smile. There was a dead silence.

"It's a pun!" the King added in an angry tone, and everybody laughed. "Let the jury consider their verdict," the King said, for about the twentieth time that day.

"No, no!" said the Queen. "Sentence first – verdict afterwards."

"Stuff and nonsense!" said Alice loudly. "The idea of having the sentence first!"

"Hold your tongue!" said the Queen, turning purple.

"I wo'n't!" said Alice.

"Off with her head!" the Queen shouted at the top of her voice. Nobody moved.

"Who cares for *you*?" said Alice (she had grown to her full size by this time). "You're nothing but a pack of cards!"

At this the whole pack rose up into the air, and came flying down upon her; she gave a little scream, half of fright and half of anger, and tried to beat them off, and found herself lying on the bank, with her head in the lap of her sister, who was gently brushing away some dead leaves that had fluttered down from the trees upon her face.

"Wake up, Alice dear!" said her sister. "Why, what a long sleep you've had!"

"Oh, I've had such a curious dream!" said Alice. And she told her sister, as well as she could remember them, all these strange Adventures of hers that you have just been reading about; and, when she had finished, her sister kissed her, and said "It was a curious dream, dear, certainly; but now run in to your tea: it's getting late." So Alice got up and ran off, thinking while she ran, as well she might, what a wonderful dream it had been.

But her sister sat still just as she left her, leaning her head on her hand, watching the setting sun, and thinking of little Alice and all her wonderful Adventures, till she too began dreaming after a fashion, and this was her dream: –

First, she dreamed about little Alice herself: once again the tiny hands were clasped upon her knee, and the bright eager eyes were looking up into hers – she could hear the very tones of her voice, and see that queer little toss of her head to keep back the wandering hair that *would* always get into her eyes – and still as she listened, or seemed to listen, the whole place around her became alive with the strange creatures of her little sister's dream.

The long grass rustled at her feet as the White Rabbit hurried by – the frightened Mouse splashed his way through the neighbouring pool – she could hear the rattle of the teacups as the March Hare and his friends shared their never-ending meal, and the shrill voice of the Queen ordering off her unfortunate guests to execution – once more the pig-baby was sneezing on the Duchess's knee, while plates and dishes crashed around it – once more the shriek of the Gryphon, the squeaking of the Lizard's slate-pencil, and the choking of the suppressed guinea-pigs, filled the air, mixed up with the distant sob of the miserable Mock Turtle.

So she sat on, with closed eyes, and half believed herself in Wonderland, though she knew she had but to open them again, and all would change to dull reality – the grass would be only rustling in the wind, and the pool rippling to the waving of the reeds – the rattling teacups would change to tinkling sheep-bells, and the Queen's shrill cries to the voice of the shepherd-boy – and the sneeze of the baby, the shriek of the Gryphon, and all the other queer noises, would change (she knew) to the confused clamour of the busy farm-yard – while the lowing of the cattle in the distance would take the place of the Mock Turtle's heavy sobs.

Lastly, she pictured to herself how this same little sister of hers would, in the after-time, be herself a grown woman; and how she would keep, through all her riper years, the simple and loving heart of her childhood; and how she would gather about her other little children, and make *their* eyes bright and eager with many a strange tale, perhaps even with the dream of Wonderland of long ago; and how she would feel with all their simple sorrows, and find a pleasure in all their simple joys, remembering her own child-life, and the happy summer days.

THE END.

Appendix A: *Lewis Carroll*, Alice's Adventures Under Ground

[*Alice's Adventures Under Ground* represents the first version of *Alice's Adventures in Wonderland*. After telling the story of Alice to the Liddell sisters during their boat trip in 1862, Carroll assured Alice that he would write it down for her. On November 26, 1864, he presented to Alice as a Christmas gift the hand-printed volume containing thirty seven of his own drawings. In revising this version for publication by Macmillan, Carroll nearly doubled its size and made numerous changes, adding new characters, episodes, and verse. He added the chapters on the Mad Tea Party and Pig and Pepper, lengthened the trial of the Knave of Hearts to two chapters, added the characters of the Cheshire Cat and the Duchess, and made many other revisions to create a more sophisticated and complex story.

For the sake of clarity, the text that follows is set in typescript rather than in Carroll's script and contains all of the thirty seven drawings. The original manuscript now resides in the British Museum.]

A Christmas Gift to a Dear Child in Memory of a Summer Day.

Chapter I

Alice was beginning to get very tired of sitting by her sister on the bank, and of having nothing to do: once or twice she had peeped into the book her sister was reading, but it had no pictures or conversations in it, and where is the use of a book, thought Alice, without pictures or conversations? So she was considering in her own mind, (as well as she could, for the hot day made her feel very sleepy and stupid,) whether the pleasure of making a daisy-chain was worth the trouble of getting up and picking the daisies, when a white rabbit with pink eyes ran close by her.

There was nothing very remarkable in that, nor did Alice think it so *very* much out of the way to hear the rabbit say to itself "dear, dear! I shall be too late!" (when she thought it over afterwards, it occurred to her that she ought to have wondered at this, but at the time it all seemed quite natural); but when the rabbit actually *took a watch out of its waistcoat-pocket*, looked at it, and then hurried on, Alice started to her feet, for it flashed across her mind that she had never before seen a rabbit with either a waistcoat-pocket or a watch to take out of it, and, full of curiosity, she hurried across the field after it, and was just in time to see it pop down a large rabbit-hole under the hedge. In a moment down went Alice after it, never once considering how in the world she was to get out again.

The rabbit-hole went straight on like a tunnel for some way, and then dipped suddenly down, so suddenly, that Alice had not a moment to think about stopping herself, before she found herself falling down what seemed a deep well. Either the well was very deep, or she fell very slowly, for she had plenty of time as she went down to look about her, and to wonder what would happen next. First, she tried to look down and make out what she was coming to, but it was too dark to see anything: then, she looked at the sides of the well, and noticed that they were filled with cupboards and book-shelves: here and there were maps and pictures hung on pegs. She took a jar down off one of the shelves as she passed: it was labelled "Orange Marmalade," but to her great disappointment it was empty: she did not like to drop the jar, for fear of killing somebody underneath, so managed to put it into one of the cupboards as she fell past it.

"Well!" thought Alice to herself, "after such a fall as this, I shall think nothing of tumbling down stairs! How brave they'll all think me at home! Why, I wouldn't say anything about it, even if I fell off the top of the house!" (which was most likely true.)

Down, down, down. Would the fall *never* come to an end? "I wonder how many miles I've fallen by this time?" said she aloud, "I must be getting somewhere near the centre of the earth. Let me see: that would be four thousand miles down, I think—" (for you see Alice had learnt several things of this sort in her lessons in the schoolroom, and though this was not a *very* good opportunity of showing off her knowledge, as there was no one to hear her, still it was good practice to say it over,) "yes, that's the right distance, but then what Longitude or Latitude-line shall I be in?" (Alice had no idea what Longitude was, or Latitude either, but she thought they were nice grand words to say.)

Presently she began again: "I wonder if I shall fall right *through* the earth! How funny it'll be to come out among the people that walk with their heads downwards! But I shall have to ask them what the name of the country is, you know. Please,

Ma'am, is this New Zealand or Australia?"—and she tried to curtsey as she spoke, (fancy *curtseying* as you're falling through the air! do you think you could manage it?) "and what an ignorant little girl she'll think me for asking! No, it'll never do to ask: perhaps I shall see it written up somewhere."

Down, down, down: there was nothing else to do, so Alice soon began talking again. "Dinah will miss me very much tonight, I should think!" (Dinah was the cat.) "I hope they'll remember her saucer of milk at tea-time! Oh, dear Dinah, I wish I had you here! There are no mice in the air, I'm afraid, but you might catch a bat, and that's very like a mouse, you know, my dear. But do cats eat bats, I wonder?" And here Alice began to get rather sleepy, and kept on saying to herself, in a dreamy sort of way "do cats eat bats? do cats eat bats?" and sometimes, "do bats eat cats?" for, as she couldn't answer either question, it didn't much matter which way she put it. She felt that she was dozing off, and had just begun to dream that she was walking hand in hand with Dinah, and was saying to her very earnestly, "Now, Dinah, my dear, tell me the truth. Did you ever eat a bat?" when suddenly, bump! bump! down she came upon a heap of sticks and shavings, and the fall was over.

Alice was not a bit hurt, and jumped on to her feet directly: she looked up, but it was all dark overhead; before her was another long passage, and the white rabbit was still in sight, hurrying down it. There was not a moment to be lost: away went Alice like the wind, and just heard it say, as it turned a corner, "my ears and whiskers, how late it's getting!" She turned the corner after it, and instantly found herself in a long, low hall, lit up by a row of lamps which hung from the roof.

There were doors all round the hall, but they were all locked, and when Alice had been all round it, and tried them all, she walked sadly down the middle, wondering how she was ever to get out again: suddenly she came upon a little three-legged table, all made of solid glass; there was nothing lying upon it, but a tiny golden key, and Alice's first idea was that it might belong to one of the doors of the hall, but alas! either the locks were too large, or the key too small, but at any rate it would open none of them. However, on the second time round, she came to a low curtain, behind which was a door about eighteen inches high: she tried the little key in the key-hole, and it fitted! Alice opened the door, and looked down a small passage, not larger than a rat-hole, into the loveliest garden you ever saw. How she longed to get out of that dark hall, and wander about among those beds of bright flowers and those cool fountains, but she could not even get her head through the doorway, "and even if my head would go through" thought poor Alice, "it would be very little use without my shoulders. Oh, how I wish I could shut up like a telescope! I think I could, if I only knew how to begin." For, you see, so many out-of-the-way things had happened lately, that Alice began to think very few things indeed were really impossible.

There was nothing else to do, so she went back to the table, half hoping she might find another key on it, or at any rate a book of rules for shutting up people like telescopes: this time there was a little bottle on it—"which certainly was not there before" said Alice—and tied round the neck of the bottle was a paper label with the words DRINK ME beautifully printed on it in large letters.

It was all very well to say "drink me," "but I'll look first," said the wise little Alice, "and see whether the bottle's marked 'poison' or not," for Alice had read several nice little stories about children that got burnt, and eaten up by wild beasts, and other unpleasant things, because they *would* not remember the simple rules their friends had given them, such as, that, if you get into the fire, it will burn you, and that, if you cut your finger very deeply with a knife, it generally bleeds, and she had never forgotten that, if you drink a bottle marked "poison," it is almost certain to disagree with you, sooner or later.

However, this bottle was *not* marked poison, so Alice tasted it, and finding it very nice, (it had, in fact, a sort of mixed flavour of cherry-tart, custard, pine-apple, roast turkey, toffy, and hot buttered toast,) she very soon finished it off.

★   ★   ★   ★   ★

"What a curious feeling!" said Alice, "I must be shutting up like a telescope!"

It was so indeed: she was now only ten inches high, and her face brightened up as it occurred to her that she was now the right size for going through the little door into that lovely garden. First, however, she waited for a few minutes to see whether she was going to shrink any further: she felt a little nervous about this, "for it might end, you know," said Alice to herself, "in my going out altogether, like a candle, and what should I be like then, I wonder?" and she tried to fancy what the flame of a candle is like after the candle is blown out, for she could not remember having ever seen one. However, nothing more happened, so she decided on going into the garden at once, but, alas for poor Alice! when she got to the door, she found she had forgotten the little golden key, and when she went back to the table for the key, she found she could not possibly reach it: she could see it plainly enough through the glass, and she tried her best to climb up one of the legs of the table, but it was too slippery, and when she had tired herself out with trying, the poor little thing sat down and cried.

"Come! there's no use in crying!" said Alice to herself rather sharply, "I advise you to leave off this minute!" (she generally gave herself very good advice, and sometimes scolded herself so severely as to bring tears into her eyes, and once she remembered boxing her own ears for having been unkind to herself in a game of croquet she was playing with herself, for this curious child was very fond of pretending to be two people,) "but it's no use now," thought poor Alice, "to pretend to be two people! Why, there's hardly enough of me left to make one respectable person!"

Soon her eyes fell on a little ebony box lying under the table: she opened it, and found in it a very small cake, on which was lying a card with the words EAT ME beautifully printed on it in large letters. "I'll eat," said Alice, "and if it makes me larger, I can reach the key, and if it makes me smaller, I can creep under the door, so either way I'll get into the garden, and I don't care which happens!"

She ate a little bit, and said anxiously to herself, "which way? which way?" and laid her hand on the top of her head to feel which way it was growing, and was quite surprised to find that she remained the same size: to be sure this is what generally happens when one eats cake, but Alice had got into the way of expecting nothing but out-of-the way things to happen, and it seemed quite dull and stupid for things to go on in the common way.

So she set to work, and very soon finished off the cake.

★　　★　　★　　★　　★

"Curiouser and curiouser!" cried Alice, (she was so surprised that she quite forgot how to speak good English,) "now I'm opening out like the largest telescope that ever was! Goodbye, feet!" (for when she looked down at her feet, they seemed almost out of sight, they were getting so far off,) "oh, my poor little feet, I wonder who will put on your shoes and stockings for you now, dears? I'm sure *I* ca'n't! I shall be a great deal too far off to bother myself about you: you must manage the best way you can—but I must be kind to them," thought Alice, "or perhaps they won't walk the way I want to go! Let me see: I'll give them a new pair of boots every Christmas."

And she went on planning to herself how she would manage it: "they must go by the carrier," she thought, "and how funny it'll seem, sending presents to one's own feet! And how odd the directions will look! **ALICE'S RIGHT FOOT, ESQ.**
THE CARPET,
with ALICE'S LOVE.
oh dear! what nonsense I am talking!"

Just at this moment, her head struck against the roof of the hall: in fact, she was now rather more than nine feet high, and she at once took up the little golden key, and hurried off to the garden door.

Poor Alice! it was as much as she could do, lying down on one side, to look through into the garden with one eye, but to get through was more hopeless than ever: she sat down and cried again.

"You ought to be ashamed of yourself," said Alice, "a great girl like you," (she might well say this,) "to cry in this way! Stop this instant, I tell you!" But she cried on all the same, shedding gallons of tears, until there was a large pool, about four inches deep, all round her, and reaching half way across the hall. After a time, she heard a little pattering of feet in the distance, and dried her eyes to see what was coming.

It was the white rabbit coming back again, splendidly dressed, with a pair of white kid gloves in one hand, and a nosegay in the other. Alice was ready to ask help of any one, she felt so desperate, and as the rabbit passed her, she said, in a low, timid voice, "If you please, Sir—" the rabbit started violently, looked up once into the roof of the hall, from which the voice seemed to come, and then dropped the nosegay and the

white kid gloves, and skurried away into the darkness as hard as it could go.

Alice took up the nosegay and gloves, and found the nosegay so delicious that she kept smelling at it all the time she went on talking to herself—"dear, dear! how queer everything is today! and yesterday everything happened just as usual: I wonder if I was changed in the night? Let me think: was I the same when I got up this morning? I think I remember feeling rather different. But if I'm not the same, who in the world am I? Ah, that's the great puzzle!" And she began thinking over all the children she knew of the same age as herself, to see if she could have been changed for any of them.

"I'm sure I'm not Gertrude," she said, "for her hair goes in such long ringlets, and mine doesn't go in ringlets at all—and I'm sure I ca'n't be Florence, for I know all sorts of things, and she, oh! she knows such a very little! Besides, *she's* she, and *I'm* I, and—oh dear! how puzzling it all is! I'll try if I know all the things I used to know. Let me see: four times five is twelve, and four times six is thirteen, and four times seven is fourteen—oh dear! I shall never get to twenty at this rate! But the Multiplication Table don't signify—let's try Geography. London is the capital of France, and Rome is the capital of Yorkshire, and Paris—oh dear! dear! *that's* all wrong, I'm certain! I must have been changed for Florence! I'll try and say 'How doth the little,'" and she crossed her hands on her lap, and began, but her voice sounded hoarse and strange, and the words did not sound the same as they used to do:

> "How doth the little crocodile
>   Improve its shining tail,
> And pour the waters of the Nile
>   On every golden scale!
>
> How cheerfully it seems to grin!
>   How neatly spreads its claws!
> And welcomes little fishes in
>   With gently-smiling jaws!"

"I'm sure those are not the right words," said poor Alice, and her eyes filled with tears as she thought "I must be Florence after all, and I shall have to go and live in that poky little house, and have next to no toys to play with, and oh! ever so many lessons to learn! No! I've made up my mind about it: if I'm Florence, I'll stay down here! It'll be no use their putting their heads down and saying 'come up, dear!' I shall only look up and say who am I, then? answer me that first, and then, if I like being that person, I'll come up: if not, I'll stay down here till I'm somebody else—but, oh dear!" cried Alice with a sudden burst of tears, "I do wish they *would* put their heads down! I am so tired of being all alone here!"

As she said this, she looked down at her hands, and was surprised to find she had put on one of the rabbit's little gloves while she was talking. "How *can* I have done that?" thought she, "I must be growing small again." She got up and went to the table to measure herself by it, and found that, as nearly as she could guess, she was now about two feet high, and was going on shrinking rapidly: soon she found out that the reason of it was the nosegay she held in her hand: she dropped it hastily, just in time to save herself from shrinking away altogether, and found that she was now only three inches high.

"Now for the garden!" cried Alice, as she hurried back to the little door, but the little door was locked again, and the little gold key was lying on the glass table as before, and "things are worse than ever!" thought the poor little girl, "for I never was as small as this before, never! And I declare it's too bad, it is!"

At this moment her foot slipped, and splash! she was up to her chin in salt water. Her first idea was that she had fallen into the sea: then she remembered that she was under ground, and she soon made out that it was the pool of tears she had wept when she was nine feet high. "I wish I hadn't cried so much!" said Alice, as she swam about, trying to find her way out, "I shall be punished for it now, I suppose, by being drowned in my own tears! Well! that'll be a queer thing, to be sure! However, every thing is queer today." Very soon she saw something splashing about in the pool near her: at first she thought it must be a walrus or a hippopotamus, but then she remembered how small she was herself, and soon made out that it was only a mouse, that had slipped in like herself.

"Would it be any use, now," thought Alice, "to speak to this mouse? The rabbit is something quite out-of-the-way, no

doubt, and so have I been, ever since I came down here, but that is no reason why the mouse should not be able to talk. I think I may as well try."

So she began: "oh Mouse, do you know how to get out of this pool? I am very tired of swimming about here, oh Mouse!" The mouse looked at her rather inquisitively, and seemed to her to wink with one of its little eyes, but it said nothing.

"Perhaps it doesn't understand English," thought Alice; "I daresay it's a French mouse, come over with William the Conqueror!" (for, with all her knowledge of history, Alice had no very clear notion how long ago anything had happened,) so she began again: "où est ma chatte?" which was the first sentence out of her French lesson-book. The mouse gave a sudden jump in the pool, and seemed to quiver with fright: "oh, I beg your pardon!" cried Alice hastily, afraid that she had hurt the poor animal's feelings, "I quite forgot you didn't like cats!"

"Not like cats!" cried the mouse, in a shrill, passionate voice, "would *you* like cats if you were me?"

"Well, perhaps not," said Alice in a soothing tone, "don't be angry about it. And yet I wish I could show you our cat Dinah: I think you'd take a fancy to cats if you could only see her. She is such a dear quiet thing," said Alice, half to herself as she swam

lazily about in the pool, "she sits purring so nicely by the fire, licking her paws and washing her face: and she is such a nice soft thing to nurse, and she's such a capital one for catching mice—oh! I beg your pardon!" cried poor Alice again, for this time the mouse was bristling all over, and she felt certain that it was really offended, "have I offended you?"

"Offended indeed!" cried the mouse, who seemed to be positively trembling with rage, "our family always *hated* cats! Nasty, low, vulgar things! Don't talk to me about them any more!"

"I won't indeed!" said Alice, in a great hurry to change the conversation, "are you—are you—fond of—dogs?" The mouse did not answer, so Alice went on eagerly: "there is such a nice little dog near our house I should like to show you! A little bright-eyed terrier, you know, with oh! such long curly brown hair! And it'll fetch things when you throw them, and it'll sit up and beg for its dinner, and all sorts of things—I ca'n't remember half of them—and it belongs to a farmer, and he says it kills all the rats and—oh dear!" said Alice sadly, "I'm afraid I've offended it again!" for the mouse was swimming away from her as hard as it could go, and making quite a commotion in the pool as it went.

So she called softly after it: "mouse dear! Do come back again, and we won't talk about cats and dogs any more, if you don't like them!" When the mouse heard this, it turned and swam slowly back to her: its face was quite pale, (with passion, Alice thought,) and it said in a trembling low voice "let's get to the shore, and then I'll tell you my history, and you'll understand why it is I hate cats and dogs."

It was high time to go, for the pool was getting quite full of birds and animals that had fallen into it. There was a Duck and a Dodo, a Lory and an Eaglet, and several other curious creatures. Alice led the way, and the whole party swam to the shore.[1]

---

1 See the first entry in Appendix E for a description of the event that may have prompted this watery episode.

They were indeed a curious looking party that assembled on the bank—the birds with draggled feathers, the animals with their fur clinging close to them—all dripping wet, cross, and uncomfortable. The first question of course was, how to get dry: they had a consultation about this, and Alice hardly felt at all surprised at finding herself talking familiarly with the birds, as if she had known them all her life. Indeed, she had quite a long argument with the Lory, who at last turned sulky, and would only say "I am older than you, and must know best," and this Alice would not admit without knowing how old the Lory was, and as the Lory positively refused to tell its age, there was nothing more to be said.

At last the mouse, who seemed to have some authority among them, called out "sit down, all of you, and attend to me! I'll soon make you dry enough!" They all sat down at once, shivering, in a large ring, Alice in the middle, with her eyes anxiously fixed on the mouse, for she felt sure she would catch a bad cold if she did not get dry soon.

"Ahem!" said the mouse, with a self-important air, "are you all ready? This is the driest thing I know. Silence all round, if you please!

"William the Conqueror, whose cause was favoured by the pope, was soon submitted to by the English, who wanted leaders, and had been of late much accustomed to usurpation and conquest. Edwin and Morcar, the earls of Mercia and Northumbria—"

"Ugh!" said the Lory with a shiver.

"I beg your pardon?" said the mouse, frowning, but very politely, "did you speak?"

"Not I!" said the Lory hastily.

"I thought you did," said the mouse, "I proceed. Edwin and Morcar, the earls of Mercia and Northumbria, declared for him and even Stigand, the patriotic archbishop of Canterbury, found it advisable to go with Edgar Atheling to meet William and offer him the crown. William's conduct was at first moderate—how are you getting on now, dear?" said the mouse, turning to Alice as it spoke.

"As wet as ever," said poor Alice, "it doesn't seem to dry me at all."

"In that case," said the Dodo solemnly, rising to his feet, "I move that the meeting adjourn, for the immediate adoption of more energetic remedies—"

"Speak English!" said the Duck, "I don't know the meaning of half of those long words, and what's more, I don't believe you do either!" And the Duck quacked a comfortable laugh to itself. Some of the other birds tittered audibly.

"I only meant to say," said the Dodo in a rather offended tone, "that I know of a house near here, where we could get the young Lady and the rest of the party dried, and then we could listen comfortably to the story which I think you were good enough to promise to tell us," bowing gravely to the mouse.

The mouse made no objection to this, and the whole party moved along the river bank, (for the pool had by this time begun to flow out of the hall, and the edge of it was fringed with rushes and forget-me-nots,) in a slow procession, the Dodo leading the way. After a time the Dodo became impatient, and, leaving the Duck to bring up the rest of the party, moved on at a quicker pace with Alice, the Lory, and the Eaglet, and soon brought them to a little cottage, and there they sat snugly by the fire, wrapped up in blankets, until the rest of the party had arrived, and they were all dry again.

Then they all sat down again in a large ring on the bank, and begged the mouse to begin his story.

"Mine is a long and a sad tale!" said the mouse, turning to Alice, and sighing.

"It *is* a long tail, certainly," said Alice, looking down with wonder at the mouse's tail, which was coiled nearly all round the party, "but why do you call it sad?" and she went on puzzling about this as the mouse went on speaking, so that her idea of the tale was something like this:

We lived beneath the mat
    Warm and snug and fat
        But one woe, & that
           Was the *cat*
             To our joys
               a clog, In
               our eyes a
            fog, On our
          hearts a log
        Was the dog!
      When the
    cat's away,
   Then
  the mice
  will
  play,
    But, alas!
     one day, (*So* they say)
       Came the dog and
            cat, Hunting
              for a
              rat,
             Crushed
            the mice
          all flat;
        Each
      one
      as
     he
      sat
      Underneath
        the mat,
       Warm,
      & snug,
     & fat—
   Think of that!

"You are not attending!" said the mouse to Alice severely, "what are you thinking of?"

"I beg your pardon," said Alice very humbly, "you had got to the fifth bend, I think?"

"I had *not!*" cried the mouse, sharply and very angrily.

"A knot!" said Alice, always ready to make herself useful, and looking anxiously about her, "oh, do let me help to undo it!"

"I shall do nothing of the sort!" said the mouse, getting up and walking away from the party, "you insult me by talking such nonsense!"

"I didn't mean it!" pleaded poor Alice, "but you're so easily offended, you know."

The mouse only growled in reply.

"Please come back and finish your story!" Alice called after it, and the others all joined in chorus "yes, please do!" but the mouse only shook its ears, and walked quickly away, and was soon out of sight.

"What a pity it wouldn't stay!" sighed the Lory, and an old Crab took the opportunity of saying to its daughter "Ah, my dear! let this be a lesson to you never to lose *your* temper!" "Hold your tongue, Ma!" said the young Crab, a little snappishly, you're enough to try the patience of an oyster!"

"I wish I had our Dinah here, I know I do!" said Alice aloud, addressing no one in particular, "*she'd* soon fetch it back!"

"And who is Dinah, if I might venture to ask the question?" said the Lory.

Alice replied eagerly, for she was always ready to talk about her pet, "Dinah's our cat. And she's such a capital one for catching mice, you ca'n't think! And oh! I wish you could see her after the birds! Why, she'll eat a little bird as soon as look at it!"

This answer caused a remarkable sensation among the party: some of the birds hurried off at once; one old magpie began wrapping itself up very carefully, remarking "I really must be getting home: the night air does not suit my throat," and a canary called out in a trembling voice to its children "come away from her, my dears, she's no fit company for you!" On various pretexts, they all moved off, and Alice was soon left alone.

She sat for some while sorrowful and silent, but she was not long before she recovered her spirits, and began talking to herself again as usual: "I do wish some of them had stayed a little longer! and I was getting to be such friends with them—really the Lory and I were almost like sisters! and so was that dear little Eaglet! And then the Duck and the Dodo! How nicely the Duck sang to us as we came along through the water: and if the Dodo hadn't known the way to that nice little cottage, I don't know when we should have got dry again—" and there is no knowing how long she might have prattled on in this way, if she had not suddenly caught the sound of pattering feet.

It was the white rabbit, trotting slowly back again, and looking anxiously about it as it went, as if it had lost something, and she heard it muttering to itself "the Marchioness! the Marchioness! oh my dear paws! oh my fur and whiskers! She'll have me executed, as sure as ferrets are ferrets! Where *can* I have dropped them, I wonder?" Alice guessed in a moment that it was looking for the nosegay and the pair of white kid gloves, and she began hunting for them, but they were now nowhere to be seen—everything seemed to have changed since her swim in the pool, and her walk along the river-bank with its fringe of rushes and forget-me-nots, and the glass table and the little door had vanished.

Soon the rabbit noticed Alice, as she stood looking curiously about her; and at once said in a quick angry tone, "why, Mary Ann! what *are* you doing out here? Go home this moment, and look on my dressing-table for my gloves and nosegay, and fetch them here, as quick as you can run, do you hear?" and Alice was so much frightened that she ran off at once, without saying a word, in the direction which the rabbit had pointed out.

She soon found herself in front of a neat little house, on the door of which was a bright brass plate with the name W. RABBIT, ESQ. She went in, and hurried upstairs, for fear she should meet the real Mary Ann and be turned out of the house before she had found the gloves: she knew that one pair had been lost in the hall, "but of course," thought Alice, "it has plenty more of them in its house. How queer it seems to be going messages for a rabbit! I suppose Dinah'll be sending me messages next!" And she began fancying the sort of things that would happen: "Miss Alice! come here directly and get ready for your walk!" "Coming in a minute, nurse! but I've got to watch this mousehole till Dinah comes back, and see that the mouse doesn't get out—" "only I don't think," Alice went on, "that they'd let Dinah stop in the house, if it began ordering people about like that!"

By this time she had found her way into a tidy little room, with a table in the window on which was a looking-glass and,

(as Alice had hoped,) two or three pairs of tiny white kid gloves: she took up a pair of gloves, and was just going to leave the room, when her eye fell upon a little bottle that stood near the looking-glass: there was no label on it this time with the words "drink me," but nevertheless she uncorked it and put it to her lips: "I know something interesting is sure to happen," she said to herself, "whenever I eat or drink anything, so I'll see what this bottle does. I do hope it'll make me grow larger, for I'm quite tired of being such a tiny little thing!"

It did so indeed, and much sooner than she expected: before she had drunk half the bottle, she found her head pressing against the ceiling, and she stooped to save her neck from being broken, and hastily put down the bottle, saying to herself "that's quite enough—I hope I sha'n't grow any more—I wish I hadn't drunk so much!"

Alas! it was too late: she went on growing and growing, and very soon had to kneel down: in another minute there was not room even for this, and she tried the effect of lying down, with one elbow against the door, and the other arm curled round her head. Still she went on grow-ing, and as a last resource she put one arm out of the window, and one foot up the chimney, and said to herself "now I can do no more—what *will* become of me?"

Luckily for Alice, the little magic bottle had now had its full effect, and she grew no larger: still it was very uncomfortable, and as there seemed to be no sort of chance of ever getting out of the room again, no wonder she felt unhappy. "It was much pleasanter at home," thought poor Alice, "when one wasn't always growing larger and smaller, and being ordered about by mice and rabbits—I almost wish I hadn't gone down that rabbit-hole, and yet, and yet—it's rather curious, you know, this sort of life. I do wonder what *can* have happened to me! When I used to read fairy-tales, I fancied that sort of thing never happened, and now here I am in the middle of one! There ought to be a book written about me, that there ought! and when I grow up I'll write one—but I'm grown up now" said she in a sorrowful tone, "at least there's no room to grow up any more *here*."

"But then," thought Alice, "shall I *never* get any older than I am now? That'll be a comfort, one way—never to be an old woman—but then—always to have lessons to learn! Oh, I shouldn't like *that*!"

"Oh, you foolish Alice!" she said again, "how can you learn lessons in here? Why, there's hardly room for you, and no room at all for any lesson-books!"

And so she went on, taking first one side, and then the other, and making quite a conversation of it altogether, but after a few minutes she heard a voice outside, which made her stop to listen.

"Mary Ann! Mary Ann!" said the voice, "fetch me my gloves this moment!" Then came a little pattering of feet on the stairs: Alice knew it was the rabbit coming to look for her, and she trembled till she shook the house, quite forgetting that she was now about a thousand times as large as the rabbit, and had no reason to be afraid of it. Presently the rabbit came to the door, and tried to open it, but as it opened inwards, and Alice's elbow was against it, the attempt proved a failure. Alice heard it say to itself "then I'll go round and get in at the window."

"That you won't!" thought Alice, and, after waiting till she fancied she heard the rabbit just under the window, she suddenly spread out her hand, and made a snatch in the air. She did not get hold of anything, but she heard a little shriek and a fall and a crash of breaking glass, from which she concluded that it was just possible it had fallen into a cucumber-frame, or something of the sort.

Next came an angry voice—the rabbit's—"Pat, Pat! where are you?" And then a voice she had never heard before, "shure then I'm here! digging for apples, anyway, yer honour!"

"Digging for apples indeed!" said the rabbit angrily, "here, come and help me out of *this*!"—Sound of more breaking glass.

"Now, tell me, Pat, what is that coming out of the window?"

"Shure it's an arm, yer honour!" (He pronounced it "arrum.")

"An arm, you goose! Who ever saw an arm that size? Why, it fills the whole window, don't you see?"

"Shure, it does, yer honour, but it's an arm for all that."

"Well, it's no business there: go and take it away!"

There was a long silence after this, and Alice could only hear whispers now and then, such as "shure I don't like it, yer honour, at all at all!" "do as I tell you, you coward!" and at last she spread out her hand again and made another snatch in the air. This time there were *two* little shrieks, and more breaking glass— "what a number of cucumber-frames there must be!" thought Alice, "I wonder what they'll do next! As for pulling me out of the window, I only wish they *could*! I'm sure *I* don't want to stop in here any longer!"

She waited for some time without hearing anything more: at last came a rumbling of little cart-wheels, and the sound of a good many voices all talking together: she made out the words "where's the other ladder?—why, I hadn't to bring but one; Bill's got the other—here, put 'em up at this corner—no, tie 'em together first—they don't reach high enough yet—oh, they'll do well enough, don't be particular—here, Bill! catch hold of this rope—will the roof bear?—mind that loose slate— oh, it's coming down! heads below!—" (a loud crash) "now, who did that?—it was Bill, I fancy—who's to go down the chimney?—nay, *I* sha'n't! *you* do it!—*that* I won't then—Bill's got to go down—here, Bill! the master says you've to go down the chimney!"

"Oh, so Bill's got to come down the chimney, has he?" said Alice to herself, "why, they seem to put everything upon Bill! I wouldn't be in Bill's place for a good deal: the fireplace is a pretty tight one, but I *think* I can kick a little!"

She drew her foot as far down the chimney as she could, and waited till she heard a little animal (she couldn't guess what sort it was) scratching and scrambling in the chimney close above her: then, saying to herself "this is Bill," she gave one sharp kick, and waited again to see what would happen next.

The first thing was a general chorus of "there goes Bill!" then the rabbit's voice alone "catch him, you by the hedge!" then silence, and then another confusion of voices, "how was it, old fellow? what happened to you? tell us all about it."

Last came a little feeble squeaking voice, ("that's Bill" thought Alice,) which said "well, I hardly know—I'm all of a fluster myself—something comes at me like a Jack-in-the-box,

and the next minute up I goes like a rocket!" "And so you did, old fellow!" said the other voices.

"We must burn the house down!" said the voice of the rabbit, and Alice called out as loud as she could "if you do, I'll set Dinah at you!" This caused silence again, and while Alice was thinking "but how can I get Dinah here?" she found to her great delight that she was getting smaller: very soon she was able to get up out of the uncomfortable position in which she had been lying, and in two or three minutes more she was once more three inches high.

She ran out of the house as quick as she could, and found quite a crowd of little animals waiting outside—guinea-pigs, white mice, squirrels, and "Bill" a little green lizard, that was being supported in the arms of one of the guinea-pigs, while another was giving it something out of a bottle. They all made a rush at her the moment she appeared, but Alice ran her hardest, and soon found herself in a thick wood.

Chapter III

"The first thing I've got to do," said Alice to herself, as she wandered about in the wood, "is to grow to my right size, and the second thing is to find my way into that lovely garden. I think that will be the best plan."

It sounded an excellent plan, no doubt, and very neatly and simply arranged: the only difficulty was, that she had not the smallest idea how to set about it, and while she was peering anxiously among the trees round her, a little sharp bark just over her head made her look up in a great hurry.

An enormous puppy was looking down at her with large round eyes, and feebly stretching out one paw, trying to reach her: "poor thing!" said Alice in a coaxing tone, and she tried hard to whistle to it, but she was terribly alarmed all the while at the thought that it might be hungry, in which case it would probably devour her in spite of all her coaxing. Hardly knowing what she did, she picked up a little bit of stick, and held it out to the puppy: whereupon the puppy jumped into the air off all its feet at once, and with a yelp of delight rushed at the stick, and made believe to worry it: then Alice dodged behind a great thistle to keep herself from being run over, and, the moment she appeared at the other side, the puppy made another dart at the stick, and tumbled head over heels in its hurry to get hold: then Alice, thinking it was very like having a game of play with a cart-horse, and expecting every moment to be trampled under its feet, ran round the thistle again: then the puppy began a series of short charges at the stick, running a very little way forwards each time and a long way back, and barking hoarsely all the while, till at last it sat down a good way off, panting, with its tongue hanging out of its mouth, and its great eyes half shut.

This seemed to Alice a good opportunity for making her escape: she set off at once, and ran till the puppy's bark sounded quite faint in the distance, and till she was quite tired and out of breath.

"And yet what a dear little puppy it was!" said Alice, as she leant against a buttercup to rest herself, and fanned herself with her hat, "I should have liked teaching it tricks, if—if I'd only been the right size to do it! Oh! I'd nearly forgotten that I've got to grow up again! Let me see: how *is* it to be managed? I suppose I ought to eat or drink something or other, but the great question is, what?"

The great question certainly was, what? Alice looked all round her at the flowers and the blades of grass, but could not see anything that looked like the right thing to eat under the circumstances. There was a large mushroom near her, about the same height as herself, and when she had looked under it, and on both sides of it, and behind it, it occurred to her to look and see what was on the top of it.

She stretched herself up on tiptoe, and peeped over the edge of the mushroom, and her eyes immediately met those of a large blue caterpillar, which was sitting with its arms folded, quietly smoking a long hookah, and taking not the least notice of her or of anything else.

For some time they looked at each other in silence: at last the caterpillar took the hookah out of its mouth, and languidly addressed her.

"Who are you?" said the caterpillar.

This was not an encouraging opening for a conversation: Alice replied rather shyly, "I—I hardly know, sir, just at present—at least I know who I *was* when I got up this morning, but I think I must have been changed several times since that."

"What do you mean by that?" said the caterpillar, "explain yourself!"

"I ca'n't explain *myself*, I'm afraid, sir," said Alice, "because I'm not myself, you see."

"I don't see," said the caterpillar.

"I'm afraid I ca'n't put it more clearly," Alice replied very politely, "for I ca'n't understand it myself, and really to be so many different sizes in one day is very confusing."

"It isn't," said the caterpillar.

"Well, perhaps you haven't found it so yet," said Alice, "but when you have to turn into a chrysalis, you know, and then after that into a butterfly, I should think it'll feel a little queer, don't you think so?"

"Not a bit," said the caterpillar.

"All I know is," said Alice, "it would feel queer to *me*—"

"*You!*" said the caterpillar contemptuously, "who are you?"

Which brought them back again to the beginning of the conversation: Alice felt a little irritated at the caterpillar making such *very* short remarks, and she drew herself up and said very gravely "I think you ought to tell me who *you* are, first."

"Why?" said the caterpillar.

Here was another puzzling question: and as Alice had no reason ready, and the caterpillar seemed to be in a *very* bad temper, she turned round and walked away.

"Come back!" the caterpillar called after her, "I've something important to say!"

This sounded promising: Alice turned and came back again.

"Keep your temper," said the caterpillar.

"Is that all?" said Alice, swallowing down her anger as well as she could.

"No," said the caterpillar.

Alice thought she might as well wait, as she had nothing else to do, and perhaps after all the caterpillar might tell her something worth hearing. For some minutes it puffed away at its hookah without speaking, but at last it unfolded its arms, took the hookah out of its mouth again, and said "so you think you're changed, do you?"

"Yes, sir," said Alice, "I ca'n't remember the things I used to know—I've tried to say 'How doth the little busy bee' and it came all different!"

"Try and repeat 'You are old, father William,'" said the caterpillar.

Alice folded her hands, and began:

1.

"You are old, father William," the young man said,
    "And your hair is exceedingly white:
And yet you incessantly stand on your head—
    Do you think, at your age, it is right?"

2.

"In my youth," father William replied to his son,
    "I feared it *might* injure the brain:
But now that I'm perfectly sure I have none,
    Why, I do it again and again."

3.

"You are old," said the youth, "as I mentioned before,
    "And have grown most uncommonly fat:
Yet you turned a back-somersault in at the door—
    Pray what is the reason of that?"

4.

"In my youth," said the sage, as he shook his gray locks,
    "I kept all my limbs very supple.
By the use of this ointment, five shillings the box—
    Allow me to sell you a couple."

5.

"You are old," said the youth, "and your jaws are too weak
    "For anything tougher than suet:
Yet you eat all the goose, with the bones and the beak—
    Pray, how did you manage to do it?"

6.

"In my youth," said the old man, "I took to the law,
    And argued each case with my wife,
And *the muscular strength, which it gave to my jaw,*
    Has lasted the rest of my life."

7.

"You are old," said the youth, "one would hardly suppose
    "That your eye was as steady as ever:
Yet you balanced an eel on the end of your nose—
    What made you so *awfully* clever?"

"I have answered three questions, and that is enough,"
  Said his father, "don't give yourself airs!
"Do you think I can listen all day to such stuff?
  Be off, or I'll kick you down stairs!"

"That is not said right," said the caterpillar.

"Not *quite* right, I'm afraid," said Alice timidly, "some of the words have got altered."

"It is wrong from beginning to end," said the caterpillar decidedly, and there was silence for some minutes: the caterpillar was the first to speak.

"What size do you want to be?" it asked.

"Oh, I'm not particular as to size," Alice hastily replied, "only one doesn't like changing so often, you know."

"Are you content now?" said the caterpillar.

"Well, I should like to be a *little* larger, sir, if you wouldn't mind," said Alice, "three inches is such a wretched height to be."

"It is a very good height indeed!" said the caterpillar loudly and angrily, rearing itself straight up as it spoke (it was exactly three inches high).

"But I'm not used to it!" pleaded poor Alice in a piteous tone, and she thought to herself "I wish the creatures wouldn't be so easily offended!"

"You'll get used to it in time," said the caterpillar, and it put the hookah into its mouth, and began smoking again.

This time Alice waited quietly until it chose to speak again: in a few minutes the caterpillar took the hookah out of its mouth, and got down off the mushroom, and crawled away into the grass, merely remarking as it went: "the top will make you grow taller, and the stalk will make you grow shorter."

"The top of *what*? the stalk of *what*?" thought Alice.

"Of the mushroom," said the caterpillar, just as if she had asked it aloud, and in another moment it was out of sight.

Alice remained looking thoughtfully at the mushroom for a minute, and then picked it and carefully broke it in two, taking the stalk in one hand and the top in the other. "*Which* does the stalk do?" she said, and nibbled a little bit of it to try: the next moment she felt a violent blow on her chin: it had struck her foot!

She was a good deal frightened by this very sudden change, but as she did not shrink any further, and had not dropped the top of the mushroom, she did not give up hope yet. There was hardly room to open her mouth, with her chin pressing against her foot, but she did it at last, and managed to bite off a little bit of the top of the mushroom.

* * * * *

"Come! my head's free at last!" said Alice in a tone of delight, which changed into alarm in another moment, when she found that her shoulders were nowhere to be seen: she looked down upon an immense length of neck, which seemed to rise like a stalk out of a sea of green leaves that lay far below her.

"What *can* all that green stuff be?" said Alice, "and where *have* my shoulders got to? And oh! my poor hands! how is it I ca'n't see you?" She was moving them about as she spoke, but no result seemed to follow, except a little rustling among the leaves. Then she tried to bring her head down to her hands, and was delighted to find that her neck would bend about easily in every direction, like a serpent. She had just suc-ceeded in bending it down in a beautiful zig-zag, and was going to dive in among

the leaves, which she found to be the tops of the trees of the wood she had been wandering in, when a sharp hiss made her draw back: a large pigeon had flown into her face, and was violently beating her with its wings.

"Serpent!" screamed the pigeon.

"I'm *not* a serpent!" said Alice indignantly, "let me alone!"

"I've tried every way!" the pigeon said desperately, with a kind of sob: "nothing seems to suit 'em!"

"I haven't the least idea what you mean," said Alice.

"I've tried the roots of trees, and I've tried banks, and I've tried hedges," the pigeon went on without attending to her, "but them serpents! There's no pleasing 'em!"

Alice was more and more puzzled, but she thought there was no use in saying anything till the pigeon had finished.

"As if it wasn't trouble enough hatching the eggs!" said the pigeon, "without being on the look out for serpents, day and night! Why, I haven't had a wink of sleep these three weeks!"

"I'm very sorry you've been annoyed," said Alice, beginning to see its meaning.

"And just as I'd taken the highest tree in the wood," said the pigeon raising its voice to a shriek, "and was just thinking I was free of 'em at last, they must needs come down from the sky! Ugh! Serpent!"

"But I'm *not* a serpent," said Alice, "I'm a— I'm a—"

"Well! *What* are you?" said the pigeon, "I see you're trying to invent something."

"I— I'm a little girl," said Alice, rather doubtfully, as she remembered the number of changes she had gone through.

"A likely story indeed!" said the pigeon, "I've seen a good many of them in my time, but never *one* with such a neck as yours! No, you're a serpent, I know *that* well enough! I suppose you'll tell me next that you never tasted an egg!"

"I *have* tasted eggs, certainly," said Alice, who was a very truthful child, "but indeed I don't want any of yours. I don't like them raw."

"Well, be off, then!" said the pigeon, and settled down into its nest again. Alice crouched down among the trees, as well as she could, as her neck kept getting entangled among the branches, and several times she had to stop and untwist it. Soon she remembered the pieces of mushroom which she still held in her hands, and set to work very carefully, nibbling first at one and then at the other, and growing sometimes taller and sometimes shorter, until she had succeeded in bringing herself down to her usual size.

It was so long since she had been of the right size that it felt quite strange at first, but she got quite used to it in a minute or two, and began talking to herself as usual: "well! there's half my plan done now! How puzzling all these changes are! I'm never sure what I'm going to be, from one minute to another! However, I've got to my right size again: the next thing is, to get into that beautiful garden—how *is* that to be done, I wonder?"

Just as she said this, she noticed that one of the trees had a doorway leading right into it. "That's very curious!" she thought, "but everything's curious today: I may as well go in." And in she went.

Once more she found herself in the long hall, and close to the little glass table: "now, I'll manage better this time" she said to herself, and began by taking the little golden key, and unlocking the door that led into the garden. Then she set to work eating the pieces of mushroom till she was about fifteen inches high: then she walked down the little passage: and *then*— she found herself at last in the beautiful garden, among the bright flowerbeds and the cool fountains.

A large rose tree stood near the entrance of the garden: the roses on it were white, but there were three gardeners at it, busily painting them red. This Alice thought a very curious thing, and she went near to watch them, and just as she came up she heard one of them say "look out, Five! Don't go splashing paint over me like that!"

"I couldn't help it," said Five in a sulky tone, "Seven jogged my elbow."

On which Seven lifted up his head and said "that's right, Five! Always lay the blame on others!"

"*You'd* better not talk!" said Five, "I heard the Queen say only yesterday she thought of having you beheaded!"

"What for?" said the one who had spoken first.

"That's not your business, Two!" said Seven.

"Yes, it *is* his business!" said Five, "and I'll tell him: it was for bringing tulip-roots to the cook instead of potatoes."

Seven flung down his brush, and had just begun "well! Of all the unjust things—"when his eye fell upon Alice, and he stopped suddenly: the others looked round, and all of them took off their hats and bowed low.

"Would you tell me, please," said Alice timidly, "why you are painting those roses?"

Five and Seven looked at Two, but said nothing: Two began,

in a low voice, "why, Miss, the fact is, this ought to have been a red rose tree, and we put a white one in by mistake, and if the Queen was to find it out, we should all have our heads cut off. So, you see, we're doing our best, before she comes, to—" At this moment Five, who had been looking anxiously across the garden called out "the Queen! the Queen!" and the three gardeners instantly threw themselves flat upon their faces. There was a sound of many footsteps, and Alice looked round, eager to see the Queen.

First came ten soldiers carrying clubs: these were all shaped like the three gardeners, flat and oblong, with their hands and feet at the corners: next the ten courtiers; these were all ornamented with diamonds, and walked two and two, as the soldiers did. After these came the Royal children: there were ten of them, and the little dears came jumping merrily along, hand in hand, in couples: they were all ornamented with hearts. Next came the guests, mostly kings and queens, among whom Alice recognised the white rabbit: it was talking in a hurried nervous manner, smiling at everything that was said, and went by without noticing her. Then followed the Knave of Hearts, carrying the King's crown on a cushion, and, last of all this grand procession, came THE KING AND QUEEN OF HEARTS.

When the procession came opposite to Alice, they all stopped and looked at her, and the Queen said severely "who is

this?" She said it to the Knave of Hearts, who only bowed and smiled in reply.

"Idiot!" said the Queen, turning up her nose, and asked Alice "what's your name?"

"My name is Alice, so please your Majesty," said Alice boldly, for she thought to herself, "why, they're only a pack of cards! I needn't be afraid of them!"

"Who are these?" said the Queen, pointing to the three gardeners lying round the rose tree, for, as they were lying on their faces, and the pattern on their backs was the same as the rest of the pack, she could not tell whether they were gardeners, or soldiers, or courtiers, or three of her own children.

"How should *I* know?" said Alice, surprised at her own courage, "it's no business of *mine*."

The Queen turned crimson with fury, and, after glaring at her for a minute, began in a voice of thunder, "off with her—"

"Nonsense!" said Alice, very loudly and decidedly, and the Queen was silent.

The King laid his hand upon her arm, and said timidly "remember my dear! She is only a child!"

The Queen turned angrily away from him, and said to the Knave "turn them over!"

The Knave did so, very carefully, with one foot.

"Get up!" said the Queen, in a shrill loud voice, and the three gardeners instantly jumped up, and began bowing to the King, the Queen, the Royal children, and everybody else.

"Leave off that!" screamed the Queen, "you make me giddy." And then, turning to the rose tree, she went on "what *have* you been doing here?"

"May it please your Majesty," said Two very humbly, going down on one knee as he spoke, "we were trying—"

"*I* see!" said the Queen, who had been examining the roses, "off with their heads!" and the procession moved on, three of the soldiers remaining behind to execute the three unfortunate gardeners, who ran to Alice for protection.

"You sha'n't be beheaded!" said Alice, and she put them into her pocket: the three soldiers marched once round her, looking for them, and then quietly marched off after the others.

"Are their heads off?" shouted the Queen.

"Their heads are gone," the soldiers shouted in reply, "if it please your Majesty!"

"That's right!" shouted the Queen, "can you play croquet?"

The soldiers were silent, and looked at Alice, as the question was evidently meant for her.

"Yes!" shouted Alice at the top of her voice.

"Come on then!" roared the Queen, and Alice joined the procession, wondering very much what would happen next.

"It's—it's a very fine day!" said a timid little voice: she was walking by the white rabbit, who was peeping anxiously into her face.

"Very," said Alice, "where's the Marchioness?"

"Hush, hush!" said the rabbit in a low voice, "she'll hear you. The Queen's the Marchioness: didn't you know that?"

"No, I didn't," said Alice, "what of?"

"Queen of Hearts," said the rabbit in a whisper, putting its mouth close to her ear, "and Marchioness of Mock Turtles."

"What are *they*?" said Alice, but there was no time for the answer, for they had reached the croquet-ground, and the game began instantly.

Alice thought she had never seen such a curious croquet-ground in all her life: it was all in ridges and furrows: the croquet-balls were live hedgehogs, the mallets live ostriches, and

the soldiers had to double themselves up, and stand on their feet and hands, to make the arches.

The chief difficulty which Alice found at first was to manage her ostrich: she got its body tucked away, comfortably enough, under her arm, with its legs hanging down, but generally, just as she had got its neck straightened out nicely, and was going to give a blow with its head, it *would* twist itself round, and look up into her face, with such a puzzled expression that she could not help bursting out laughing: and when she had got its head down, and was going to begin again, it was very confusing to find that the hedgehog had unrolled itself, and was in the act of crawling away: besides all this, there was generally a ridge or a furrow in her way, wherever she wanted to send the hedgehog to, and as the doubled-up soldiers were always getting up and walking off to other parts of the ground, Alice soon came to the conclusion that it was a very difficult game indeed.

The players all played at once without waiting for turns, and quarrelled all the while at the tops of their voices, and in a very few minutes the Queen was in a furious passion, and went stamping about and shouting "off with his head!" or "off with her head!" about once in a minute. All those whom she sentenced were taken into custody by the soldiers, who of course had to leave off being arches to do this, so that, by the end of half an hour or so, there were no arches left, and all the players, except the King, the Queen, and Alice, were in custody, and under sentence of execution.

Then the Queen left off, quite out of breath, and said to Alice "have you seen the Mock Turtle?"

"No," said Alice, "I don't even know what a Mock Turtle is."

"Come on then," said the Queen, "and it shall tell you its history."

As they walked off together, Alice heard the King say in a low voice, to the company generally, "you are all pardoned."

"Come, that's a good thing!" thought Alice, who had felt quite grieved at the number of executions which the Queen had ordered.

They very soon came upon a Gryphon, which lay fast asleep in the sun: (if you don't know what a Gryphon is, look at the picture): "up, lazy thing!" said the Queen, "and take this young lady to see the Mock Turtle, and to hear its history. I must go back and see after some executions I ordered," and she walked off, leaving Alice with the Gryphon. Alice did not quite like the look of the creature, but on the whole she thought it quite as safe to stay as to go after that savage Queen: so she waited.

The Gryphon sat up and rubbed its eyes: then it watched the Queen till she was out of sight: then it chuckled. "What fun!" said the Gryphon, half to itself, half to Alice.

"What *is* the fun?" said Alice.

"Why, *she*," said the Gryphon; "it's all her fancy, that: they never executes nobody, you know: come on!"

"Everybody says 'come on!' here," thought Alice, as she walked slowly after the Gryphon; "I never was ordered about so before in all my life—never!"

They had not gone far before they saw the Mock Turtle in the distance, sitting sad and lonely on a little ledge of rock, and, as they came nearer, Alice could hear it sighing as if its heart would break. She pitied it deeply: "what is its sorrow?" she asked the Gryphon, and the Gryphon answered, very nearly in the same words as before, "it's all its fancy, that: it hasn't got no sorrow, you know: come on!"

So they went up to the Mock Turtle, who looked at them with large eyes full of tears, but said nothing.

"This here young lady" said the Gryphon, "wants for to know your history, she do."

"I'll tell it," said the Mock Turtle, in a deep, hollow tone, "sit down, and don't speak till I've finished."

So they sat down, and no one spoke for some minutes: Alice thought to herself "I don't see how it can *ever* finish, if it doesn't begin," but she waited patiently.

"Once," said the Mock Turtle at last, with a deep sigh, "I was a real Turtle."

These words were followed by a very long silence, broken only by an occasional exclamation of "hjckrrh!" from the Gryphon, and the constant heavy sobbing of the Mock Turtle. Alice was very nearly getting up and saying, "thank you, sir, for your interesting story," but she could not help thinking there *must* be more to come, so she sat still and said nothing.

"When we were little," the Mock Turtle went on, more calmly, though still sobbing a little now and then, "we went to school in the sea. The master was an old Turtle—we used to call him Tortoise—"

"Why did you call him Tortoise, if he wasn't one?" asked Alice.

"We called him Tortoise because he taught us," said the Mock Turtle angrily, "really you are very dull!"

"You ought to be ashamed of yourself for asking such a simple question," added the Gryphon, and then they both sat silent and looked at poor Alice, who felt ready to sink into the earth: at last the Gryphon said to the Mock Turtle, "get on, old fellow! Don't be all day!" and the Mock Turtle went on in these words:

"You may not have lived much under the sea—" ("I haven't," said Alice,) "and perhaps you were never even introduced to a lobster—" (Alice began to say "I once tasted—" but hastily checked herself, and said "no, never," instead,) "so you

can have no idea what a delightful thing a Lobster Quadrille is!"

"No, indeed, said Alice, "what sort of a thing is it?"

"Why," said the Gryphon, "you form into a line along the sea shore—"

"Two lines!" cried the Mock Turtle, "seals, turtles, salmon, and so on—advance twice:—"

"Each with a lobster as partner!" cried the Gryphon.

"Of course," the Mock Turtle said, "advance twice, set to partners—"

"Change lobsters, and retire in same order—"interrupted the Gryphon.

"Then, you know," continued the Mock Turtle, "you throw the—"

"The lobsters!" shouted the Gryphon, with a bound into the air.

"As far out to sea as you can—"

"Swim after them!" screamed the Gryphon.

"Turn a somersault in the sea!" cried the Mock Turtle, capering wildly about.

"Change lobsters again!" yelled the Gryphon at the top of its voice, "and then—"

"That's all," said the Mock Turtle, suddenly dropping its voice, and the two creatures, who had been jumping about like mad things all this time, sat down again very sadly and quietly, and looked at Alice.

"It must be a very pretty dance," said Alice timidly.

"Would you like to see a little of it?" said the Mock Turtle.

"Very much indeed," said Alice.

"Come, let's try the first figure!" said the Mock Turtle to the Gryphon, "we can do it without lobsters, you know. Which shall sing?"

"Oh! *you* sing!" said the Gryphon, "I've forgotten the words."

So they began solemnly dancing round and round Alice, every now and then treading on her toes when they came too close, and waving their fore-paws to mark the time, while the Mock Turtle sang, slowly and sadly, these words:

"Beneath the waters *of* the sea
Are lobsters thick as thick can be—
They love to dance with you and me,
   My own, my gentle Salmon!"

The Gryphon joined in singing the chorus, which was:

"Salmon come up! Salmon go down!
Salmon come twist your tail around!
Of all the fishes *of* the sea
   There's none so good as Salmon!"

"Thank you," said Alice, feeling very glad that the figure was over.

"Shall we try the second figure?" said the Gryphon, or would you prefer a song?"

"Oh, a song, please!" Alice replied, so eagerly, that the Gryphon said, in a rather offended tone, "hm! no accounting for tastes! Sing her 'Mock Turtle Soup,' will you, old fellow!"

The Mock Turtle sighed deeply, and began, in a voice sometimes choked with sobs, to sing this:

"Beautiful Soup, so rich and green,
Waiting in a hot tureen!
Who for such dainties would not stoop?

Soup of the evening, beautiful Soup!
Soup of the evening, beautiful Soup!
    Beau—ootiful Soo—oop!
    Beau—ootiful Soo—oop!
  Soo—oop of the e—e—evening,
    Beautiful beautiful Soup!"

"Chorus again!" cried the Gryphon, and the Mock Turtle had just begun to repeat it, when a cry of "the trial's beginning!" was heard in the distance.

"Come on!" cried the Gryphon, and, taking Alice by the hand, he hurried off, without waiting for the end of the song.

"What trial is it?" panted Alice as she ran, but the Gryphon only answered "come on!" and ran the faster, and more and more faintly came, borne on the breeze that followed them, the melancholy words:

> "Soo—oop of the e—e—evening,
>   Beautiful beautiful Soup!"

The King and Queen were seated on their throne when they arrived, with a great crowd assembled around them: the Knave was in custody: and before the King stood the white rabbit, with a trumpet in one hand, and a scroll of parchment in the other.

"Herald! read the accusation!" said the King.

On this the white rabbit blew three blasts on the trumpet, and then unrolled the parchment scroll, and read as follows:

> "The Queen of Hearts she made some tarts
>   All on a summer day:
> The Knave of Hearts he stole those tarts,
>   And took them quite away!"

"Now for the evidence," said the King, "and then the sentence."

"No!" said the Queen, "first the sentence, and then the evidence!"

"Nonsense!" cried Alice, so loudly that everybody jumped, "the idea of having the sentence first!"

"Hold your tongue!" said the Queen.

"I won't!" said Alice, "you're nothing but a pack of cards! Who cares for you?"

At this the whole pack rose up into the air, and came flying down upon her: she gave a little scream of fright, and tried to beat them off, and found herself lying on the bank, with her head in the lap of her sister, who was gently brushing away some leaves that had fluttered down from the trees on to her face.

"Wake up! Alice dear!" said her sister, "what a nice long sleep you've had!"

"Oh, I've had such a curious dream!" said Alice, and she told her sister all her Adventures Under Ground, as you have read them, and when she had finished, her sister kissed her and said "it *was* a curious dream, dear, certainly! But now run in to your tea: it's getting late."

So Alice ran off, thinking while she ran (as well she might) what a wonderful dream it had been.

But her sister sat there some while longer, watching the setting sun, and thinking of little Alice and her Adventures, till she too began dreaming after a fashion, and this was her dream:

She saw an ancient city, and a quiet river winding near it along the plain, and up the stream went slowly gliding a boat with a merry party of children on board—she could hear their voices and laughter like music over the water—and among them was another little Alice, who sat listening with bright eager eyes to a tale that was being told, and she listened for the words of the tale, and lo! it was the dream of her own little sister. So the boat wound slowly along, beneath the bright summer-day, with its merry crew and its music of voices and laughter, till it passed round one of the many turnings of the stream, and she saw it no more.

Then she thought, (in a dream within the dream, as it were,) how this same little Alice would, in the after-time, be herself a grown woman: and how she would keep, through her riper years, the simple and loving heart of her childhood: and how she would gather around her other little children, and make *their* eyes bright and eager with many a wonderful tale, perhaps even with these very adventures of the little Alice of long-ago: and how she would feel with all their simple sorrows, and find a pleasure in all their simple joys, remembering her own child-life, and the happy summer days.

THE END

Appendix B: *Lewis Carroll,* The Nursery Alice

[Carroll began writing the text of *The Nursery Alice* in December of 1888. Tenniel agreed to color twenty of the pictures he drew for *Alice's Adventures in Wonderland* to include in this children's edition. Finding the printed pictures too bright and gaudy, Carroll cancelled Macmillan's entire edition of ten thousand copies and had another ten thousand printed. The book finally appeared for Easter of 1890. The volume was about one quarter of the original *Alice,* with the twenty colored illustrations by Tenniel. Morton Cohen (in *Lewis Carroll, a Biography*) observes that Carroll "did more than merely condense the story; he tried to explain the story and teach the child about the characters. The text is really addressed to the mothers acting as (Carroll's) surrogates in bringing the book, the text, and the pictures to the child's awareness."]

PREFACE

(ADDRESSED TO ANY MOTHER.)

I HAVE reason to believe that "Alice's Adventures in Wonderland" has been read by some hundreds of English Children, aged from Five to Fifteen: also by Children, aged from Fifteen to Twenty-five: yet again by Children, aged from Twenty-five to Thirty-five: and even by Children – for there *are* such – Children in whom no waning of health and strength, no weariness of the solemn mockery, and the gaudy glitter, and the hopeless misery, of Life has availed to parch the pure fountain of joy that wells up in all child-like hearts – Children of a "certain" age, whose tale of years must be left untold, and buried in respectful silence.

And my ambition *now* is (is it a vain one?) to be read by Children aged from Nought to Five. To be read? Nay, not so! Say rather to be thumbed, to be cooed over, to be dogs'-eared, to be rumpled, to be kissed, by the illiterate, ungrammatical, dimpled Darlings, that fill your Nursery with merry uproar, and your inmost heart of hearts with a restful gladness!

Such, for instance, as a child I once knew, who – having been carefully instructed that *one* of any earthly thing was enough for any little girl and that to ask for *two* buns, *two* oranges, *two* of anything, would certainly bring upon her the awful charge of being "greedy" – was found one morning sitting up in bed, solemnly regarding her *two* little naked feet, and murmuring to herself, softly and penitently, "deedy!"

Easter-tide, 1890

I.

THE WHITE RABBIT.

ONCE upon a time, there was a little girl called Alice; and she had a very curious dream.

Would you like to hear what it was that she dreamed about?

Well, this was the *first* thing that happened. A White Rabbit came running by, in a great hurry; and, just as it passed Alice, it stopped, and took its watch out of its pocket.

Wasn't *that* a funny thing? Did *you* ever see a Rabbit that had a watch, and a pocket to put it in? Of course, when a Rabbit has a watch, it *must* have a pocket to put it in; it would never do to carry it about in its mouth – and it wants its hands sometimes, to run about with.

Hasn't it got pretty pink eyes (I think *all* White Rabbits have pink eyes); and pink ears; and a nice brown coat; and you can just see its red pocket-handkerchief peeping out of its coat-pocket: and, what with its blue neck-tie and its yellow waistcoat, it really is *very* nicely dressed.

"Oh dear, oh dear!" said the Rabbit. "I shall be too late!" *What* would it be too late *for*, I wonder? Well, you see, it had to go and visit the Duchess (you'll see a picture of the Duchess, soon, sitting in her kitchen): and the Duchess was a very cross old lady; and the Rabbit *knew* she'd be very angry indeed if he kept her waiting. So the poor thing was as frightened as frightened could be (Don't you see how he's trembling? Just shake the book a little, from side to side, and you'll soon see him tremble), because he thought the Duchess would have his head cut off for a punishment. That was what the Queen of Hearts used to do, when *she* was angry with people (you'll see a picture of *her*, soon): at least she used to *order* their heads to be cut off, and she always *thought* it was done, though they never *really* did it.

And so, when the White Rabbit ran away, Alice wanted to see what would happen to it: so she ran after it: and she ran, and she ran, till she tumbled right down the rabbit-hole.

And then she had a very long fall indeed. Down, and down, and down, till she began to wonder if she was going right *through* the world, so as to come out on the other side!

It was just like a very deep well: only there was no water in it. If anybody *really* had such a fall as that, it would kill them, most likely: but you know it doesn't hurt a bit to fall in a *dream*, because, all the time you *think* you're falling, you really *are* lying somewhere, safe and sound, and fast asleep!

However, this terrible fall came to an end at last, and down came Alice on a heap of sticks and dry leaves. But she wasn't a bit hurt, and up she jumped, and ran after the Rabbit again.

And so that was the beginning of Alice's curious dream. And, next time you see a White Rabbit, try and fancy *you're* going to have a curious dream, just like dear little Alice.

II.

HOW ALICE GREW TALL.

AND so, after Alice had tumbled down the rabbit-hole, and had run a long long way underground, all of a sudden she found herself in a great hall, with doors all around it.

But all the doors were locked: so, you see, poor Alice couldn't get out of the hall: and that made her very sad.

However, after a little while, she came to a little table, all made of glass, with three legs (There are *two* of the legs in the picture, and just the *beginning* of the other leg, do you see?), and on the table was a little key: and she went round the hall, and tried if she could unlock any of the doors with it.

Poor Alice! The key wouldn't unlock *any* of the doors. But at last she came upon a tiny little door: and oh, how glad she was, when she found the key would fit it!

So she unlocked the tiny little door, and she stooped down and looked through it, and what do you think she saw? Oh, such a beautiful garden! And she did so *long* to go into it! But the door was *far* too small. She couldn't squeeze herself through, any more than *you* could squeeze yourself into a mouse-hole!

So poor little Alice locked up the door, and took the key back to the table again: and *this* time she found quite a new thing on it (now look at the picture again), and what do you think it was? It was a little bottle, with a label tied to it, with the words "DRINK ME" on the label.

So she tasted it and it was *very* nice so she set to work, and drank it up. And then *such* a curious thing happened to her! you'll never guess what it was: so I shall have to tell you. She got smaller, and smaller, till at last she was just the size of a little doll!

Then she said to herself "*Now* I'm the right size to get through the little door! "And away she ran. But, when she got there, the door was locked, and the key was on the top of the table, and she couldn't reach it! *Wasn't* it a pity she had locked up the door again?

Well, the next thing she found was a little cake: and it had the words "EAT ME" marked on it. So of course she set to work and ate it up. And *then* what do you think happened to her? No, you'll never guess! I shall have to tell you again.

She grew, and she grew, and she grew. Taller than she was before! Taller than *any* child! Taller than any grown-up person! Taller, and taller, and taller! Just look at the picture, and you'll *see* how tall she got!

Which would *you* have liked the best, do you think, to be a little tiny Alice, no larger than a kitten, or a great tall Alice, with your head always knocking against the ceiling?

III.

THE POOL OF TEARS.

PERHAPS you think Alice must have been very much pleased, when she had eaten the little cake, to find herself growing so tremendously tall? Because of course it would be easy enough, *now*, to reach the little key off the glass table, and to open the little tiny door.

Well of course she could do *that*: but what good was it to get the door open, when she couldn't get *through*? She was worse off than ever, poor thing! She could just manage, by putting her head down, close to the ground, to *look* through with one eye! But that was *all* she could do. No wonder the poor tall child sat down and cried as if her heart would break.

So she cried, and she cried. And her tears ran down the middle of the hall, like a deep river. And very soon there was quite a large Pool of Tears, reaching half-way down the hall.

And there she might have staid, till this very day, if the White Rabbit hadn't happened to come through the hall, on his way to visit the Duchess. He was dressed up as grand as grand could be, and he had a pair of white kid gloves in one hand, and a little fan in the other hand and he kept on muttering to himself "Oh, the Duchess, the Duchess! Oh, *won't* she be savage if I've kept her waiting!"

But he didn't see Alice, you know. So, when she began to say "If you please, Sir – " her voice seemed to come from the top of the hall, because her head was so high up. And the Rabbit was dreadfully frightened: and he dropped the gloves and the fan, and ran away as hard as he could go.

Then a *very* curious thing indeed happened. Alice took up the fan, and began to fan herself with it: and, lo and behold, she got quite small again, and, all in a minute, she was just about the size of a mouse!

Now look at the picture, and you'll soon guess what happened next. It looks just like the sea, doesn't it? But it *really* is the Pool of Tears – all made of *Alice's* tears, you know!

And Alice has tumbled into the Pool: and the Mouse has tumbled in: and there they are, swimming about together.

Doesn't Alice look pretty, as she swims across the picture? You can just see her blue stockings, far away under the water.

But why is the Mouse swimming away from Alice in such a hurry? Well, the reason is, that Alice began talking about cats and dogs: and a Mouse always *hates* talking about cats and dogs! Suppose *you* were swimming about, in a Pool of your own Tears: and suppose somebody began talking to *you* about lesson-books and bottles of medicine, wouldn't *you* swim away as hard as you could go?

IV.

THE CAUCUS-RACE.

WHEN Alice and the Mouse had got out of the Pool of Tears, of course they were very wet: and so were a lot of other curious creatures, that had tumbled in as well. There was a Dodo (that's the great bird, in front, leaning on a walking-stick); and a Duck; and a Lory (that's just behind the Duck, looking over its head); and an Eaglet (that's on the left-hand side of the Lory); and several others.

Well, and so they didn't know how in the world they were to get dry again. But the Dodo – who was a very wise bird – told them the right way was to have a Caucus-Race. And what do you think *that* was?

You *don't know?* Well, you *are* an ignorant child! Now, be very attentive, and I'll soon cure you of your ignorance!

First, you must have a *racecourse*. It ought to be a *sort* of circle, but it doesn't much matter *what* shape it is, so long as it goes a good way round, and joins on to itself again.

Then, you must put all the *racers* on the course, here and there: it doesn't matter *where*, so long as you don't crowd them too much together.

Then, you needn't say "One, two, three, and away" but let them all set off running just when they like, and leave off just when they like.

So all these creatures, Alice and all, went on running round and round, till they were all quite dry again. And then the Dodo said *everybody* had won, and *everybody* must have prizes!

Of course *Alice* had to give them their prizes. And she had nothing to give them but a few comfits she happened to have in her pocket. And there was just one a-piece, all round. And there was no prize for Alice!

So what do you think they did? Alice had nothing left but her thimble. Now look at the picture, and you'll see what happened.

"Hand it over here!" said the Dodo.

Then the Dodo took the thimble and handed it back to Alice, and said "We beg your acceptance of this elegant thimble!" And then all the other creatures cheered.

Wasn't *that* a curious sort of present to give her? Suppose they wanted to give *you* a birthday-present, would you rather they should go to your toy-cupboard, and pick out your nicest doll, and say "Here, my love, here's a lovely birthday-present for you!" or would you like them to give you something *new*, something that *didn't* belong to you before?

V.

BILL, THE LIZARD.

Now I'm going to tell you about Alice's Adventures in the White Rabbit's house.

Do you remember how the Rabbit dropped his gloves and his fan, when he was so frightened at hearing Alice's voice, that seemed to come down from the sky? Well, of course he couldn't go to visit the Duchess *without* his gloves and his fan: so, after a bit, he came back again to look for them.

By this time the Dodo and all the other curious creatures had gone away, and Alice was wandering about all alone.

So what do you think he did? Actually he thought she was his housemaid, and began ordering her about! "Mary Ann!" he said. "Go home this very minute, and fetch me a pair of gloves and a fan! Quick, now!"

Perhaps he couldn't see very clearly with his pink eyes for I'm sure Alice doesn't look very *like* a housemaid, *does* she? However she was a very good natured little girl: so she wasn't a bit offended, but ran off to the Rabbit's house as quick as she could.

It was lucky she found the door open: for, if she had had to ring, I suppose the *real* Mary Ann would have come to open the door: and she would *never* have let Alice come in. And I'm sure it was *very* lucky she didn't meet the real Mary Ann, as she trotted upstairs: for I'm afraid she would have taken Alice for a robber!

So at last she found her way into the Rabbit's room and there was a pair of gloves lying on the table, and she was just going to take them up and go away, when she happened to see a little bottle on the table. And of course it had the words "DRINK ME!" on the label. And of course Alice drank some!

Well, I think that was *rather* lucky, too: don't *you*? For, if she *hadn't* drunk any, all this wonderful adventure, that I'm going to tell you about, wouldn't have happened at all. And wouldn't *that* have been a pity?

You're getting so used to Alice's Adventures, that I daresay you can guess what happened next? If you can't, I'll tell you.

She grew, and she grew, and she grew. And in a very short time the room was full of *Alice*: just in the same way as a jar is full of jam! There was *Alice* all the way up to the ceiling: and *Alice* in every corner of the room!

The door opened inwards: so of course there wasn't any room to open it: so when the Rabbit got tired of waiting, and came to fetch his gloves for himself, of course he couldn't get in.

So what do you think he did? (Now we come to the picture). He sent Bill, the Lizard, up to the roof of the house, and told him to get down the chimney. But Alice happened to have one of her feet in the fire-place: so, when she heard Bill coming down the chimney, she just gave a little tiny kick, and away went Bill, flying up into the sky!

Poor little Bill! Don't you pity him very much? How frightened he must have been!

VI.

THE DEAR LITTLE PUPPY.

WELL, it doesn't look such a very *little* Puppy, does it? But then, you see, Alice had grown very small indeed: and *that's* what makes the Puppy look so large. When Alice had eaten one of those little magic cakes, that she found in the White Rabbit's house, it made her get quite small, directly, so that she could get through the door: or else she could *never* have got out of the house again. Wouldn't *that* have been a pity? Because then she wouldn't have dreamed all the other curious things that we're going to read about.

So it really *was* a *little* Puppy, you see. And isn't it a little *pet*? And look at the way it's barking at the little stick that Alice is holding out for it! You can see she was a *little* afraid of it, all the time, because she's got behind that great thistle, for fear it should run over her. That would have been just about as bad, for *her*, as it would be for *you* to be run over by a waggon and four horses!

Have you got a little pet puppy at *your* home? If you have, I hope you're always kind to it, and give it nice things to eat.

Once upon a time, I knew some little children, about as big as you; and they had a little pet dog of their own; and it was called *Dash*. And this is what they told me about its birthday-treat.

"Do you know, one day we remembered it was Dash's birthday that day. So we said 'Let's give Dash a nice birthday-treat, like what we have on *our* birthdays!' So we thought and we thought 'Now, what is it *we* like best of all, on our birthdays?' And we thought and we thought. And at last we all called out together 'Why, its *oatmeal-porridge*, of course!' So of course we thought Dash would be *quite* sure to like it very much, too.

"So we went to the cook, and we got her to make a saucerful of nice oatmeal-porridge. And then we called Dash into the house, and we said 'Now, Dash, you're going to have your birthday-treat!' We expected Dash would jump for joy: but it didn't, one bit!

"So we put the saucer down before it, and we said 'Now, Dash, don't be greedy! Eat it nicely, like a good dog!'

"So Dash just tasted it with the tip of its tongue: and then it made, oh, such a horrid face! And then, do you know, it did *hate* it so, it wouldn't eat a bit more of it! So we had to put it all down its throat with a spoon!"

I wonder if Alice will give *this* little Puppy some porridge? I don't think she *can*, because she hasn't got any with her. I can't see any saucer in the picture.

VII.

THE BLUE CATERPILLAR.

WOULD you like to know what happened to Alice, after she had got away from the Puppy? It was far too large an animal, you know, for *her* to play with. (I don't suppose *you* would much enjoy playing with a young Hippopotamus, would you? You would always be expecting to be crushed as flat as a pancake under its great heavy feet!) So Alice was very glad to run away, while it wasn't looking.

Well, she wandered up and down, and didn't know what in the world to do, to make herself grow up to her right size again. Of course she knew that she had to eat or drink *something*: that was the regular rule, you know: but she couldn't guess *what* thing.

However, she soon came to a great mushroom, that was so tall that she couldn't see over the top of it without standing on tip-toe. And what do you think she saw? Something that I'm sure *you* never talked to, in all your life!

It was a large Blue Caterpillar.

I'll tell you, soon, what Alice and the Caterpillar talked about but first let us have a good look at the picture.

That curious thing, standing in front of the Caterpillar, is called a "hookah": and it's used for smoking. The smoke comes through that long tube, that winds round and round like a serpent.

And do you see its long nose and chin? At least, they *look* exactly like a nose and chin, don't they? But they really *are* two of its legs. You know a Caterpillar has got *quantities* of legs: you can see some more of them, further down.

What a bother it must be to a Caterpillar, counting over such a lot of legs, every night, to make sure it hasn't lost any of them!

And *another* great bother must be, having to settle which leg it had better move first. I think, if *you* had forty or fifty legs, and if you wanted to go a walk, you'd be such a time in settling which leg to begin with, that you'd never go a walk at all!

And what did Alice and the Caterpillar *talk* about, I wonder?

Well, Alice told it how *very* confusing it was, being first one size and then another.

And the Caterpillar asked her if she liked the size she was, just then.

And Alice said she would like to be just a *little* bit larger – three inches was such a *wretched* height to be! (Just mark off three inches on the wall, about the length of your middle finger, and you'll see what size she was.)

And the Caterpillar told her one side of the mushroom would make her grow *taller*, and the other side would make her grow *shorter*.

So Alice took two little bits of it with her to nibble, and managed to make herself quite a nice comfortable height, before she went on to visit the Duchess.

VIII.

THE PIG-BABY.

WOULD you like to hear about Alice's visit to the Duchess? It was a very interesting visit indeed, I can assure you.

Of course she knocked at the door to begin with: but nobody came: so she had to open it for herself.

Now, if you look at the picture, you'll see exactly what Alice saw when she got inside.

The door led right into the kitchen, you see. The Duchess sat in the middle of the room, nursing the Baby. The Baby was howling. The soup was boiling. The Cook was stirring the Soup. The Cat – it was a *Cheshire* Cat – was grinning, as Cheshire Cats always do. All these things were happening just as Alice went in.

The Duchess has a beautiful cap and gown, hasn't she? But I'm afraid she *hasn't* got a very beautiful *face*.

The Baby – well, I daresay you've seen *several* nicer babies than *that*: and more good-tempered ones, too. However, take a good look at it, and we'll see if you know it again, next time you meet it!

The Cook – well, you *may* have seen nicer cooks, once or twice.

But I'm nearly sure you've *never* seen a nicer *Cat*! Now *have* you? And *wouldn't* you like to have a Cat of your own, just like that one, with lovely green eyes, and smiling so sweetly?

The Duchess was very rude to Alice. And no wonder. Why, she even called her own *Baby* "Pig!" And it *wasn't* a Pig, *was* it? And she ordered the Cook to chop off Alice's head; though of course the Cook didn't do it: and at last she threw the Baby at her! So Alice caught the Baby, and took it away with her: and I think that was about the best thing she could do.

So, she wandered away, through the wood, carrying the ugly little thing with her. And a great job it was to keep hold of it, it wriggled about so. But at last she found out that the *proper* way was, to keep tight hold of its left foot and its right ear.

But don't *you* try to hold on to a Baby like that, my Child! There are not many babies that *like* being nursed in *that* way!

Well, and so the Baby kept grunting, and grunting, so that Alice had to say to it, quite seriously, "If you're going to turn into a *Pig*, my dear, I'll have nothing more to do with you. Mind now!"

And at last she looked down into its face, and what *do* you think had happened to it? Look at the picture, and see if you can guess. Why, *that's* not the Baby that Alice was nursing, is it?

Ah, I *knew* you wouldn't know it again, though I told you to take a good look at it! Yes, it *is* the Baby. And it's turned into a little *Pig*!

So Alice put it down, and let it trot away into the wood. And she said to herself "It was a *very* ugly *Baby* but it makes rather a handsome *Pig*, I think."

Don't you think she was right?

IX.

THE CHESHIRE-CAT.

ALL alone, all alone! Poor Alice! No Baby, not even a *Pig* to keep her company!

So you may be sure she was very glad indeed, when she saw the Cheshire-Cat, perched up in a tree, over her head.

The Cat has a very nice smile, no doubt: but just look what a lot of teeth it's got! Isn't Alice just a *little* shy of it?

Well, yes, a *little*. But then, it couldn't help having teeth, you know: and it *could* have helped smiling, supposing it had been cross, so, on the whole, she was *glad*.

Doesn't Alice look very prim, holding her head so straight up, and with her hands behind her, just as if she were going to say her lessons to the Cat!

And that reminds me. There's a little lesson I want to teach *you*, while we're looking at this picture of Alice and the Cat. Now don't be in a bad temper about it, my dear Child! It's a very *little* lesson indeed!

Do you see that Fox-Glove growing close to the tree? And do you know why it's called a *Fox*-Glove? Perhaps you think its got something to do with a Fox? No indeed! *Foxes* never wear Gloves!

The right word is "*Folk's*-Gloves." Did you ever hear that Fairies used to be called "the good *Folk*"?

Now we've finished the lesson, and we'll wait a minute, till you've got your temper again.

Well? Do you feel quite good natured again? No temper-ache? No crossness about the corners of the mouth? Then we'll go on.

"Cheshire Puss!" said Alice. (*Wasn't* that a pretty name for a Cat?) "Would you tell me which way I ought to go from here?"

And so the Cheshire-Cat told her which way she ought to go, if she wanted to visit the Hatter, and which way to go, to visit the March Hare. "They're both mad!" said the Cat.

And then the Cat vanished away, just like the flame of a candle when it goes out!

So Alice set off, to visit the March Hare. And as she went along, there was the Cat again! And she told it she didn't *like* it coming and going so quickly.

So this time the Cat vanished quite slowly, beginning with the tail, and ending with the grin. Wasn't *that* a curious thing, a Grin without any Cat? Would you like to see one?

If you turn up the corner of this leaf, you'll have Alice looking at the Grin and she doesn't look a bit more frightened than when she was looking at the Cat, *does* she?

X.

THE MAD TEA-PARTY.

THIS is the Mad Tea-Party. You see Alice had left the Cheshire-Cat, and had gone off to see the March Hare and the Hatter, as the Cheshire-Cat had advised her: and she found them having tea under a great tree, with a Dormouse sitting between them.

There were only those three at table, but there were quantities of tea-cups set all along it. You can't see all the table, you know, and even in the bit you *can* see there are nine cups, counting the one the March Hare has got in his hand.

That's the March Hare, with the long ears, and straws mixed up with his hair. The straws showed he was mad – I don't know why. Never twist up straws among *your* hair, for fear people should think you're mad!

There was a nice green arm-chair at the end of the table, that looked as if it was just meant for Alice: so she went and sat down in it.

Then she had quite a long talk with the March Hare and the Hatter. The Dormouse didn't say much. You see it was fast asleep generally, and it only just woke up for a moment, now and then.

As long as it was asleep, it was very useful to the March Hare and the Hatter, because it had a nice round soft head, just like a pillow: so they could put their elbows on it, and lean across it, and talk to each other quite comfortably. You wouldn't like people to use *your* head for a pillow, *would* you? But if you were fast asleep, like the Dormouse, you wouldn't feel it: so I suppose you wouldn't care about it.

I'm afraid they gave Alice *very* little to eat and drink. However, after a bit, she helped herself to some tea and bread-and-butter: only I don't quite see where she *got* the bread-and-butter: and she had no plate for it. Nobody seems to have a plate except the Hatter. I believe the March Hare must have had one as well: because, when they all moved one place on (that was the rule at this curious tea-party), and Alice had to go into the place of the March Hare, she found he had just upset the milk-jug into his plate. So I suppose his plate and the milk-jug are hidden behind that large tea-pot.

The Hatter used to carry about hats to sell: and even the one that he's got on his head is meant to be sold. You see it's got its price marked on it – a "10" and a "6" – that means "ten shillings and sixpence." Wasn't that a funny way of selling hats? And hasn't he got a beautiful neck-tie on? Such a lovely yellow tie, with large red spots.

He has just got up to say to Alice "Your hair wants cutting!" That was a rude thing to say, *wasn't* it? And do you think her hair *does* want cutting? *I* think it's a very pretty length – just the right length.

XI.

THE QUEEN'S GARDEN.

THIS is a little bit of the beautiful garden I told you about. You see Alice had managed at last to get quite small, so that she could go through the little door. I suppose she was about as tall as a mouse, if it stood on its hind-legs: so of course this was a *very* tiny rose-tree: and these are *very* tiny gardeners.

What funny little men they are! But *are* they men, do you think? I think they must be live cards, with just a head, and arms, and legs, so as to *look* like little men. And what are they doing with that red paint, I wonder? Well, you see, this is what they told Alice. The Queen of Hearts wanted to have a red rose-tree just in that corner: and these poor little gardeners had made a great mistake, and had put in a white one instead: and they were so frightened about it, because the Queen was *sure* to be angry, and then she would order all their heads to be cut off!

She was a dreadfully savage Queen, and that was the way she always did, when she was angry with people. "Off with their heads!" They didn't *really* cut their heads off, you know: because nobody ever obeyed her: but that was what she always *said*.

Now can't you guess what the poor little gardeners are trying to do? They're trying to paint the roses *red*, and they're in a great hurry to get it done before the Queen comes. And then *perhaps* the Queen won't find out it was a white rose-tree to begin with: and then *perhaps* the little men won't get their heads cut off!

You see there were *five* large white roses on the tree – such a job to get them all painted red! But they've got three and a half done, now, and if only they wouldn't stop to talk – work away, little men, *do* work away! Or the Queen will he coming before it's done! And if she finds any *white* roses on the tree, do you know what will happen? It will be "Off with their heads!" Oh, work away, my little men! Hurry, hurry!

The Queen has come! And *isn't* she angry? Oh, my poor little Alice!

XII.

THE LOBSTER-QUADRILLE.

DID you ever play at Croquet? There are large wooden balls, painted with different colours, that you have to roll about; and arches of wire, that you have to send them through; and great wooden mallets, with long handles, to knock the balls about with.

Now look at the picture, and you'll see that *Alice* has just been playing a Game of Croquet.

"But she *couldn't* play, with that great red what's–its–name in her arms! Why, how could she hold the mallet?"

Why, my dear Child, that great red what's–its–name (its *real* name is "*a Flamingo*") *is* the mallet. In this Croquet-Game, the balls were live *Hedge-hogs* – you know a hedge-hog can roll itself up into a ball? – and the mallets were live *Flamingos*!

So Alice is just resting from the Game, for a minute, to have a chat with that dear old thing, the Duchess: and of course she keeps her mallet under her arm, so as not to lose it.

But I don't think she *was* a dear old thing, one bit! To call her Baby a *Pig*, and to want to chop off Alice's head!

Oh, that was only a joke, about chopping off Alice's head: and as to the Baby – why, it *was* a Pig, you know! And just look at her *smile*! Why, it's wider than all Alice's head: and yet you can only see half of it!

Well, they'd only had a *very* little chat, when the Queen came and took Alice away, to see the Gryphon and the Mock Turtle. *You don't know what a Gryphon is?* Well! Do you know *anything*? That's the question. However, look at tile picture. That creature with a red head, and red claws, and green scales, is the *Gryphon*. Now you know.

And the other's the *Mock Turtle*. It's got a calf's-head, because calf's-head is used to make *Mock Turtle Soup*. Now you know.

"But what are they *doing*, going round and round Alice like that?"

Why, I thought of *course* you'd know *that*! They're dancing *a Lobster-Quadrille*.

And next time *you* meet a Gryphon and a Mock Turtle, I daresay they'll dance it for *you*, if you ask them prettily. Only don't let them come *quite* close, or they'll be treading on your toes, as they did on poor Alice's.

XIII.

WHO STOLE THE TARTS?

DID you ever hear how the Queen of Hearts made some tarts? And can you tell me what became of them?

"Why, of course I can! Doesn't the song tell all about it?

> *The Queen of Hearts, she made some tarts:*
> *All on a summer day:*
> *The Knave of Hearts, he stole those tarts,*
> *And took them quite away!*"

Well, yes, the *Song* says so. But it would never do to punish the poor Knave, just because there was a Song about him. They had to take him prisoner, and put chains on his wrists, and bring him before the King of Hearts, so that there might be a regular trial.

Now, if you look at the big picture, at the beginning of this book, you'll see what a grand thing a trial is, when the Judge is a King!

The King is very grand, *isn't* he? But he doesn't look very *happy*. I think that big crown, on the top of his wig, must be very heavy and uncomfortable. But he had to wear them *both*, you see, so that people might know he was a Judge *and* a King.

And *doesn't* the Queen look cross? She can see the dish of tarts on the table, that she had taken such trouble to make. And she can see the bad Knave (do you see the chains hanging from his wrists?) that stole them away from her: so I don't think it's any wonder if she *does* feel a *little* cross.

The White Rabbit is standing near the King, reading out the Song, to tell everybody what a bad Knave he is: and the Jury (you can just see two of them, up in the Jury-box, the Frog and the Duck) have to settle whether he's "guilty" or "not guilty."

Now I'll tell you about the accident that happened to Alice.

You see, she was sitting close by the Jury-box and she was called as a witness. You know what a "witness" is? A "witness" is a person who has seen the prisoner do whatever he's accused of; or at any rate knows *something* that's important in the trial.

But *Alice* hadn't seen the Queen *make* the tarts: and she hadn't seen the Knave *take* the tarts: and, in fact, she didn't know anything about it: so why in the world they wanted *her* to be a witness, I'm sure I can't tell you!

Anyhow, they *did* want her. And the White Rabbit blew his big trumpet, and shouted out "Alice!" And so Alice jumped up in a great hurry. And then –

And then what *do* you think happened? Why, her skirt caught against the Jury-box, and tipped it over, and all the poor little Jurors came tumbling out of it!

Let's try if we can make out all the twelve. You know there ought to be twelve to make up a Jury. I see the Frog, and the Dormouse, and the Rat and the Ferret, and the Hedgehog, and the Lizard, and the Bantam-Cock, and the Mole, and the Duck, and the Squirrel, and a screaming bird, with a long beak, just behind the Mole.

But that only makes eleven: we must find one more creature.

Oh, do you see a little white head, coming out behind the Mole, and just under the Duck's beak? That makes up the twelve.

Mr. Tenniel says the screaming bird is a *Storkling* (of course you know what *that* is?) and the little white head is a *Mouseling*. Isn't it a little *darling*?

Alice picked them all up again, very carefully, and I hope they weren't *much* hurt!

XIV.

THE SHOWER OF CARDS.

OH dear, oh dear! What *is* it all about? And what's happening to Alice?

Well, I'll tell you all about it, as well I can. The way the trial ended was this. The King wanted the Jury to settle whether the Knave of Hearts was *guilty* or *not guilty* – that means that they were to settle whether *he* had stolen the Tarts, or if somebody else had taken them. But the wicked *Queen* wanted to have his *punishment* settled, first of all. That wasn't at all fair, *was* it? Because, you know, supposing he never *took* the Tarts, then of course he oughtn't to be punished. Would *you* like to be punished for something you hadn't done?

So Alice said "Stuff and nonsense!"

So the Queen said "Off with her head!" (Just what she always said, when she was angry.)

So Alice said "Who cares for *you*? You're nothing but a pack of cards!"

So they were *all* very angry, and flew up into the air, and came tumbling down again, all over Alice, just like a shower of rain.

And I think you'll *never* guess what happened next. The next thing was, Alice woke up out of her curious dream. And she found that the cards were only some leaves off the tree, that the wind had blown down upon her face.

Wouldn't it be a nice thing to have a curious dream, just like Alice?

The best plan is this. First lie down under a tree, and wait till a White Rabbit runs by, with a watch in his hand: then shut your eyes, and pretend to be dear little Alice.

Good-bye, Alice dear, good-bye !

THE END.

AN EASTER GREETING

TO

EVERY CHILD WHO LOVES "ALICE."

My dear child,

Please to fancy, if you can, that you are reading a real letter, from a real friend whom you have seen, and whose voice you can seem to yourself to hear, wishing you, as I do now with all my heart, a happy Easter.

Do you know that delicious dreamy feeling, when one first wakes on a summer morning, with the twitter of birds in the air, and the fresh breeze coming in at the open window when, lying lazily with eyes half shut, one sees as in a dream green boughs waving, or waters rippling in a golden light? It is a pleasure very near to sadness, bringing tears to one's eyes like a beautiful picture or poem. And is not that a Mother's gentle hand that undraws your curtains, and a Mother's sweet voice that summons you to rise? To rise and forget, in the bright sunlight, the ugly dreams that frightened you so when all was dark – to rise and enjoy another happy day, first kneeling to thank that unseen Friend who sends you the beautiful sun?

Are these strange words from a writer of such tales as "Alice"? And is this a strange letter to find in a book of nonsense? It may be so. Some perhaps may blame me for thus mixing together things grave and gay; others may smile and think it odd that any one should speak of solemn things at all, except in Church and on a Sunday: but I think – nay, I am sure – that some children will read this gently and lovingly, and in the spirit in which I have written it.

For I do not believe God means us thus to divide life into two halves – to wear a grave face on Sunday, and to think it out-of-place to even so much as mention Him on a week-day. Do you think He cares to see only kneeling figures and to hear only tones of prayer – and that He does not also love to see the lambs leaping in the sunlight, and to hear the merry voices of the children, as they roll among the hay? Surely their innocent laughter is as sweet in His ears as the grandest anthem that ever rolled up from the "dim religious light" of some solemn cathedral?

And if I have written anything to add to those stores of innocent and healthy amusement that are laid up in books for the children I love so well, it is surely something I may hope to look back upon without shame and sorrow (as how much of life must then be recalled!) when my turn comes to walk through the valley of shadows.

This Easter sun will rise on you, dear child, "feeling your life in every limb," and eager to rush out into the fresh morning air – and many an Easter-day will come and go, before it finds you feeble and grey-headed, creeping wearily out to bask once more in the sunlight – but it is good, even now, to think sometimes of that great morning when "the Sun of righteousness" shall "arise with healing in his wings."

Surely your gladness need not be the less for the thought that you will one day see a brighter dawn than this – when lovelier sights will meet your eyes than any waving trees or rippling waters – when angel-hands shall undraw your curtains, and sweeter tones than ever loving Mother breathed shall wake you to a new and glorious day – and when all the sadness, and the sin, that darkened life on this little earth, shall be forgotten like the dreams of a night that is past!

Your affectionate Friend,
LEWIS CARROLL.

Appendix C: Lewis Carroll, "Alice on the Stage"

[Henry Savile Clarke's *Alice in Wonderland*, "A Musical Dream Play, in Two Acts, for Children and Others," opened on December 23, 1886, at the Prince of Wales Theatre, London. A very popular production, the play ran for fifty performances, closing on February 26, 1887. The editor of the *Theatre* at that time was looking for essays about the stage and Carroll sent him "*Alice* on the Stage," which led off the series in that publication in April 1887. Carroll hoped that by publishing this essay he could explain what he hoped to achieve in his two Alice books.]

"Look here: here's all this Judy's clothes falling to pieces again." Such were the pensive words of Mr. Thomas Codlin; and they may fitly serve as a motto for a writer who has set himself the unusual task of passing in review a set of puppets that are virtually his own – the stage embodiments of his own dream-children.

Not that the play itself is in any sense mine. The arrangements, in dramatic form, of a story written without the slightest idea that it would be so adapted, was a task that demanded powers denied to me, but possessed in an eminent degree, so far as I can judge, by Mr. Savile Clarke. I do not feel myself qualified to criticise his play, as a play; nor shall I venture on any criticism of the players as players.

What is it, then, I have set myself to do ? And what possible claim have I to be heard? My answer must be that, as the writer of the two stories thus adapted, and the originator (as I believe, for at least I have not *consciously* borrowed them) of the "airy nothings" for which Mr. Saville Clarke has so skilfully provided, if not a name, at least, a "local habitation," I may without boastfulness claim to have a special knowledge of what it was I meant them to be, and so a special understanding of how far that intention has been realised. And I fancied there might be some readers of *The Theatre* who would be interested in sharing that knowledge and that understanding.

Many a day had we rowed together on that quiet stream – the three little maidens and I – and many a fairy tale had been extemporised for their benefit – whether it were at times when the narrator was "i' the vein," and fancies unsought came crowding thick upon him, or at times when the jaded Muse was goaded into action, and plodded meekly on, more because she had to say something than that she had something to say – yet none of these many tales got written down: they lived and died, like summer midges, each in its own golden afternoon until there came a day when, as it chanced, one of my little listeners petitioned that the tale might be written out for her. That was many a year ago, but I distinctly remember, now as I write, how, in a desperate attempt to strike out some new line of fairy-lore, I had sent my heroine straight down a rabbit-hole, to begin with, without the least idea what was to happen afterwards. And so, to please a child I loved (I don't remember any other motive), I printed in manuscript, and illustrated with my own crude designs – designs that rebelled against every law of Anatomy or Art (for I had never had a lesson in drawing) – the book which I have just had published in facsimile. In writing it out, I added many fresh ideas, which seemed to grow of themselves upon the original stock; and many more added themselves when, years afterwards, I wrote it all over again for publication: but (this may interest some readers of "Alice" to know) every such idea and nearly every word of the dialogue, *came of itself*. Sometimes an idea comes at night, when I have had to get up and strike a light to note it down – sometimes when out on a lonely winter walk, when I have had to stop, and with half frozen fingers jot down a few words which should keep the new-born idea from perishing – but whenever or however it comes, *it comes of itself*. I cannot set invention going like a clock, by any voluntary winding up: nor do I believe that any *original* writing (and what other writing is worth preserving?) was ever so produced. If you sit down, unimpassioned and uninspired, and *tell* yourself to write for so many hours, you will merely produce (at least I am sure *I* should merely produce) some of that article which fills, so far as I can judge, two-thirds of most magazines – most easy to write most weary to read – men call it "padding," and it is to my mind one of the most detestable things in modern literature. "Alice" and the "Looking-Glass" are made up almost wholly of bits and scraps, single ideas which came of themselves. Poor they may have been; but at least they were the best I had to offer: and I can desire no higher praise to be written of me than the words of a Poet [Alfred, Lord Tennyson], written of a Poet,

> "He gave the people of his best:
> The worst he kept, the best he gave."

I have wandered from my subject, I know: yet grant me another minute to relate a little incident of my own experience. I was walking on a hillside, alone, one bright summer day, when suddenly there came into my head one line of verse – one solitary line – "For the Snark *was* Boojum, you see." I knew not what it meant, then: I know not what it means, now; but I wrote it down: and, some time afterwards, the rest of the stanza occurred to me, that being its last line: and so by degrees, at odd moments during the next year or two, the rest of the poem pieced itself together, that being its last stanza. And since then, periodically I have received courteous letters from strangers, begging to know whether "The Hunting of the Snark" is an allegory, or contains some hidden moral, or is a political satire: and for all such questions I have but one answer, "*I don't know!*" And now I return to my text, and will wander no more.

Stand forth, then, from the shadowy past, "Alice," the child of my dreams. Full many a year has slipped away, since that "golden afternoon" that gave thee birth, but I can call it up almost as clearly as if it were yesterday – the cloudless blue above, the watery mirror below, the boat drifting idly on its way, the tinkle of the drops that fell from the oars, as they waved so sleepily to and fro, and (the one bright gleam of life in all the slumberous scene) the three eager faces, hungry for news of fairy-land, and who would not be said "nay" to: from whose lips "Tell us a story, please," had all the stern immutability of Fate!

What wert thou, dream-Alice, in thy foster-father's eyes? How shall he picture thee? Loving, first, loving and gentle: loving as a dog (forgive the prosaic simile, but I know no earthly love so pure and perfect), and gentle as a fawn: then courteous – courteous to *all*, high or low, grand or grotesque, King or Caterpillar, even as though she were herself a King's daughter, and her clothing of wrought gold: then trustful, ready to accept the wildest impossibilities with all that utter trust that only dreamers know; and lastly, curious – wildly curious, and with the eager enjoyment of Life that comes only in the happy hours of childhood, when all is new and fair, and when Sin and Sorrow are but names – empty words signifying nothing!

And the White Rabbit, what of *him*? Was *he* framed on the "Alice" lines, or meant as a contrast? As a contrast, distinctly. For *her* "youth," "audacity," "vigour," and "swift directness of purpose," read "elderly," "timid," "feeble," and "nervously shilly-shallying," and you will get *something* of what I meant him to be. I *think* the White Rabbit should wear spectacles. I am sure his voice should quaver, and his knees quiver, and his whole air suggests a total inability to say "Bo" to a goose!

But I cannot hope to be allowed, even by the courteous Editor of *The Theatre*, half the space I should need (even if my *reader's* patience would hold out) to discuss each of my puppets one by one. Let me cull from the two books a Royal Trio – the Queen of Hearts, the Red Queen, and the White Queen. It was certainly hard on my Muse, to expect her to sing of *three* Queens, within such brief compass, and yet to give to each her own individuality. Each, of course, had to preserve, through all her eccentricities, a certain queenly *dignity*. *That* was essential. And for distinguishing traits, I pictured to myself the Queen of Hearts as a sort of embodiment of ungovernable passion – a blind and aimless Fury. The Red Queen I pictured as a Fury, but of another type; *her* passion must be cold and calm; she must be formal and strict, yet not unkindly; pedantic to the tenth degree, the concentrated essence of all governesses! Lastly, the White Queen seemed, to my dreaming fancy, gentle, stupid, fat and pale; helpless as an infant; and with a slow, maundering, bewildered air about her just *suggesting* imbecility, but never quite passing into it; that would be, I think, fatal to any comic effect she might otherwise produce. There is a character strangely like her in Wilkie Collins' novel "No Name": by two different converging paths we have somehow reached the same ideal, and Mrs. Wragg and the White Queen might have been twin-sisters.

As it is no part of my present purpose to find fault with any of those who have striven so zealously to make this "dream-play" a waking success, I shall but name two or three who seemed to me specially successful in realising the characters of the story.

None, I think was better realised than the two undertaken by Mr. Sydney Harcourt, "the Hatter" and "Tweedledum." To see him enact the Hatter was a weird and uncanny thing, as though some grotesque monster, seen last night in a dream, should walk into the room in broad daylight, and quickly say "Good morning!" I need not try to describe what I meant the Hatter to be, since, so far as I can now remember, it was exactly what Mr. Harcourt has made him: and I may say nearly the same of Tweedledum: but the Hatter surprised me most – perhaps only because it came first in the play.

There were others who realised my ideas nearly as well; but I am not attempting a complete review: I will conclude with a few words about the two children who played "Alice" and "the Dormouse."

Of Miss Phoebe Carlo's performance it would be difficult to speak too highly. As a mere effort of memory, it was surely a marvellous feat for so young a child, to learn no less than two hundred and fifteen speeches – nearly three times as many as Beatrice in "Much Ado About Nothing." But what I admired most, as realising most nearly my ideal heroine, was her perfect assumption of the high spirits, and readiness to enjoy *everything*, of a child out for a holiday. I doubt if any grown actress, however experienced, could have worn this air so perfectly; *we* look before and after, and sigh for what is not; a child never does *this*: and it is only a child that can utter from her heart the words poor Margaret Fuller Ossoli [American author and feminist, 1810-1850] so longed to make her own, "I am all happy *now!*"

And last (I may for once omit the time-honoured addition "not least," for surely no tinier maiden ever yet achieved so genuine a theatrical success?) comes our dainty Dormouse. "Dainty" is the only epithet that seems to me exactly to suit her: with her beaming baby-face, the delicious crispness of her speech, and the perfect realism with which she makes herself the embodied essence of Sleep, she is surely the daintiest Dormouse that ever yet told us "I sleep when I breathe!" With the first words of that her opening speech, a sudden silence falls upon the house (at least it has been so every time *I* have been there), and the baby tones sound strangely clear in the stillness. And yet I doubt if the charm is due only to the incisive clearness of her articulation; to me there was an even greater charm in the utter self-abandonment and conscientious *thoroughness* of her acting. If Dorothy ever adopts a motto, it ought to be "thorough." I hope the time may soon come when she will have a better part than "Dormouse" to play – when some enterprising manager will revive the "Midsummer Night's Dream" and do his obvious duty to the public by securing Miss Dorothy d'Alcourt as "Puck"!

It would be well indeed for our churches if some of the clergy could take a lesson in enunciation from this little child; and better still, for "our noble selves," if *we* would lay to heart some things that she could teach us, and would learn by her example to realise, rather more than we do, the spirit of a maxim I once came across in an old book, "Whatsoever thy hand findeth to do, *do it with thy might.*"

[Source: "*Alice* on the Stage," reprinted in *The Unknown Lewis Carroll*, ed. Stuart Dodgson Collingwood (New York: Dover, 1961) 163-74.]

Appendix D: From Lewis Carroll, Symbolic Logic

[In *Symbolic Logic, Part I*, published in 1896, Carroll hoped to educate young people to think logically by popularizing the rigorous subject of logic. He presents the logical problems to be solved in whimsical terms that are reminiscent of the humor in *Alice's Adventures*.]

... Mental recreation is a thing that we all of us need for our mental health; and you may get much healthy enjoyment, no doubt, from Games, such as Backgammon, Chess, and the new Game "Halma." But, after all, when you have made yourself a first-rate player at any one of these Games, you have nothing real to *show* for it, as a *result*! You enjoyed the Game, and the victory, no doubt, *at the time*: but you have no *result* that you can treasure up and get real *good* out of. And, all the while, you have been leaving unexplored a perfect *mine* of wealth. Once master the machinery of Symbolic Logic, and you have a mental occupation always at hand, of absorbing interest, and one that will be of real *use* to you in *any* subject you may take up. It will give you clearness of thought – the ability to *see your way* through a puzzle – the habit of arranging your ideas in an orderly and get-at-able form – and, more valuable than all, the power to detect *fallacies*, and to tear to pieces the flimsy illogical arguments, which you will so continually encounter in books, in newspapers, in speeches, and even in sermons, and which so easily delude those who have never taken the trouble to master this fascinating Art. *Try it.* That is all I ask of you!

February 21, 1896.

Sets of Concrete Propositions, proposed as Premisses for Sorites. *
Conclusions to be found.

I

(1)   Babies are illogical;
(2)   Nobody is despised who can manage a crocodile;
(3)   Illogical persons are despised.

Univ. "persons"; a = able to manage a crocodile; b = babies;
c = despised; d = logical.

2

(1)   My saucepans are the only things I have that are made of
      tin;
(2)   I find all *your* presents very useful;
(3)   None of my saucepans are of the slightest use.

Univ. "things of mine"; a = made of tin; b = my saucepans;
c = useful; d = your presents.

3

(1)   No potatoes of mine, that are new, have been boiled;
(2)   All my potatoes in this dish are fit to eat;
(3)   No unboiled potatoes of mine are fit to eat.

Univ. "my potatoes"; a = boiled; b = eatable; c = in this dish;
d = new.

---

*   Sorites is a form of argument in which a series of incomplete syllogisms is so
    arranged that the predicate of each premise forms the subject of the next until the
    subject of the first is joined with the predicate of the last in the conclusion.

4

(1)   There are no Jews in the kitchen;
(2)   No Gentiles say "shpoonj";
(3)   My servants are all in the kitchen.

Univ. "persons"; a = in the kitchen; b = Jews; c = my servants;
d = saying "shpoonj."

5

(1)   No ducks waltz;
(2)   No officers ever decline to waltz;
(3)   All my poultry are ducks.

Univ. "creatures"; a = ducks; b = my poultry; c = officers;
d = willing to waltz.

6

(1)   Every one who is sane can do Logic;
(2)   No lunatics are fit to serve on a jury;
(3)   None of *your* sons can do Logic.

Univ. "persons"; a = able to do Logic; b = fit to serve on a
jury; c = sane; d = your sons.

7

(1)   There are no pencils of mine in this box;
(2)   No sugar-plums of mine are cigars;
(3)   The whole of my property, that is not in this box, consists
      of cigars.

Univ. "things of mine"; a = cigars; b = in this box; c = pencils;
d = sugar-plums.

(1) No kitten, that loves fish, is unteachable;
(2) No kitten without a tail will play with a gorilla;
(3) Kittens with whiskers always love fish;
(4) No teachable kitten has green eyes;
(5) No kittens have tails unless they have whiskers.

Univ. "kittens"; a = green–eyed; b = loving fish; c = tailed; d = teachable; e = whiskered; h = willing to play with a gorilla.

Answers

1.   Babies cannot manage crocodiles.
2.   *Your* presents to me are not made of tin.
3.   All my potatoes in this dish are old ones.
4.   My servants never say "shpoonj."
5.   My poultry are not officers.
6.   None of *your* sons are fit to serve on a jury.
7.   No pencils of mine are sugar-plums.
40. No kitten with green eyes will play with a gorilla.

[Source: *The Complete Works of Lewis Carroll* (New York, Vintage, 1976) 1241-42, 1253.]

Appendix E: From Lewis Carroll's Diaries and Letters

1. Diaries

June 17. (Tu). [1862]
Expedition to Nuneham. Duckworth (of Trinity) and Ina, Alice and Edith came with us. We set out about 12.30 and got to Nuneham about 2: dined there, then walked in the park and set off for home about 4:30. About a mile above Nuneham heavy rain came on, and after bearing it a short time I settled that we had better leave the boat and walk: three miles of this drenched us all pretty well. I went on first with the children, as they could walk much faster than Elizabeth [Carroll's sister], and took them to the only house I knew in Sandford, Mrs. Broughton's, where Ranken lodges. I left them with her to get their clothes dried, and went off to find a vehicle, but none was to be had there, so on the others arriving, Duckworth and I walked on to Iffley, whence we sent them a fly. We all had tea in my rooms about 8:30, after which I took the children home, and we adjourned to Bayne's rooms for music and singing.

July 3. (Th). [1862]
… Atkinson [Rev. Francis Home Atkinson, a clergyman on vacation at Oxford] and I went to lunch at the Deanery, after which we were to have gone down the river with the children, but as it rained, we remained to hear some music and singing instead – the three sang "Sally come up" [an American minstrel song by T. Ramsey and E.W. Mackney] with great spirit. Then croquet, at which Duckworth joined us, and he and Atkinson afterwards dined with me. I mark this day with a white stone.

July 4. (F). [1862]
Atkinson brought over to my rooms some friends of his, a Mrs. and Miss Peters, of whom I took photographs, and who afterwards looked over my album and staid [sic] to lunch. They

then went off to the Museum, and Duckworth and I made an expedition *up* the river to Godstow with the three Liddells: we had tea on the bank there, and did not reach Ch. Ch. [Christ Church] again till quarter past eight, when we took them on to my rooms to see my collection of micro-photographs, and restored them to the Deanery just before nine.

[Carroll appended to this entry the following comment and notes:]

On which occasion I told them the fairy-tale of "Alice's Adventures Under Ground," which I undertook to write out for Alice, and which is now finished (as to the text) though the pictures are not yet nearly done. February 10, 1863

nor yet. March 12, 1864

"Alice's Hour in Elfland"? June 9, 1864

"Alice's Adventures in Wonderland"? June 28.

July 5. (Sat). [1862]
Left, with Atkinson, for London at 9.02, meeting at the station the Liddells, who went up by the same train. [On Sept. 13, 1864 (the day on which he finished the pictures), Carroll commented that the headings for *Alice's Adventures Under Ground* "were written out (on my way to London) July 5, 1862." The text was not finished until November 13, 1862.]

Aug: 1. (F). [1862]
As the Dean's children are still here, Harcourt [Augustus Harcourt, an Oxford tutor in chemistry] and I went over to see if they could come on the river today or tomorrow, and remained a short time, for me to write the names in the books for crests etc. which I have given to Alice and Edith, and to hear them play their trio and sing "Beautiful Star."

Aug: 6. (W). [1862]

In the afternoon Harcourt and I took the three Liddells up to Godstow, where we had tea: we tried the game of "the Ural Mountains" on the way, but it did not prove very successful, and I had to go on with my interminable fairy-tale of "Alice's Adventures." We got back soon after 8, and had supper in my rooms, the children coming over for a short while. A very enjoyable expedition, the last, I should think, to which Ina is likely to be allowed to come. [Carroll adds in brackets: "her fourteenth time."]

Nov: 13. (Th). [1862]

On returning to Ch. Ch. [Christ Church] I found Ina, Alice and Edith in the quadrangle, and had a little talk with them – a rare event of late. [Carroll adds in brackets: "Began writing the fairy-tale for Alice, which I told them July 4, going to Godstow – I hope to finish it by Xmas."]

May 9. (Sat.) [1863]

Heard from Mrs. MacDonald about "Alice's Adventures Under Ground," which I had lent them to read, and which they wish me to publish. [Louisa MacDonald, wife of George MacDonald, novelist and poet, and author of *The Light Princess* and other stories for children.]

Dec: 19. (Sat). [1863]

At 5 went over to the Deanery, where I staid [sic] till 8, making a sort of dinner at their tea. The nominal object of my going was to play croquet, but it never came to that, music, talk, etc. occupying the whole of a *very* pleasant evening. The Dean was away: Mrs. Liddell was with us part of the time. It is nearly six months (June 25th) since I have seen anything of them, to speak of. I mark this day with a white stone.

[Source: *Lewis Carroll's Diaries: the Private Journals of Charles Lutwidge Dodgson*, ed. Edward Wakeling. 4 vols (The Lewis Carroll Society: Luton, Beds, 1997): v.4, 81-82, 92-96, 110, 115, 141, 197, 266, 271-72, 284, 297, 298, 311, 347.]

Jan: 25. (M). [1864]

Called at the "Board of Health" and saw Mr. Tom Taylor [popular playwright and staff officer at *Punch* at this time]. He gave me a note of introduction to Mr. Tenniel (to whom he had before applied, for me, about pictures for *Alice's Adventures*). Then I called ... at Mr. Tenniel's, whom I found at home: he was very friendly, and seemed to think favourably of undertaking the pictures, but must see the book before deciding.

April 5. (Tu). [1864]

Heard from Tenniell [*sic*] that he consents to draw the pictures for "Alice's Adventures Under Ground."

May 2. (M). [1864]

Sent Tenniell [*sic*] the first piece of slip set up for *Alice's Adventures*, from the beginning of Chap. III.

May 6. (F). [1864]

Sent to the Press [Oxford University Press] a batch of MS. from the first chapter of *Alice's Adventures*.

June 21. (Tu). [1864]

Called on Macmillan [Alexander Macmillan, Carroll's publisher], who strongly advised my altering the size of the page of my book, and adopting that of *The Water Babies* [a fairy tale by Charles Kingsley, published in 1863].... Then called on Tenniell [*sic*], who agreed to the change of page.

Aug: 2. (Tu). [1864]

Sent off to Mr. Combe [an employee of Clarendon Press] Chapter III of *Alice's Adventures*.

Sept. 13. (Tu). [1864]

At Croft. Finished drawing the pictures in the MS. copy of *Alice's Adventures*. [Carroll later added to this entry: "MS. finally sent to Alice, Nov: 26, (Sat.) 1864."]

Oct: 12. (W). [1864]
... I went to Tenniel's, who showed me one drawing on wood, the only thing he had, of Alice sitting by the pool of tears, and the rabbit hurrying away. We discussed the book and agreed on about thirty-four pictures.

Oct: 28. (F). [1864]
... Then to Messrs. Dalziel [the engravers of Tenniel's drawings]. Mr. Dalziel showed me proofs of several of the pictures, including the four from "Father William," and decidedly advised my printing from the wood-blocks.

April 17. (M). [1865]
Settled with Macmillan the size of the book – 7x5.

May 11. (Th). [1865]
Met Alice and Miss Prickett [governess for the Liddell children] in the quadrangle: Alice seems changed a good deal, and hardly for the better – probably going through the usual awkward stage of transition.

May 26. (T). [1865]
Received from Macmillan a copy (blank all but the first sheet) of *Alice's Adventures in Wonderland* bound in red cloth as a specimen.

July 15. (Sat.). [1865]
Went to Macmillan's, and wrote in twenty or more copies of *Alice* to go as presents to various friends.

July 20. (Th). [1865]
Called on Macmillan, and showed him Tenniel's letter about the fairy-tale – he is entirely dissatisfied with the printing of the pictures, and I suppose we shall have to do it again.

Aug. 2. (W). [1865]

Finally decided on the re-print of *Alice*, and that the first 2000 shall be sold as waste paper. Wrote about it to Macmillan, Combe and Tenniel. That total cost will be:

Drawing pictures	138
Cutting	142
Printing (by Clay)	240
Binding and advertising (say)	80
	600 [£]

i.e. 6/-a copy on the 2000. If I make £500 by sale, this will be a loss of £100, and the loss on the first 2000 will probably be £100, leaving me £200 out of pocket. But if a second 2000 could be sold it would cost £300, and bring in £500, thus squaring accounts and any further sale would be a gain, but that I can hardly hope for. [Approximately 180,000 copies were actually sold during Carroll's lifetime.]

Nov. 9. (Th). [1865]

Received from Macmillan a copy of the new impression of *Alice* [printed by Richard Clay] – very *far* superior to the old, and in fact a perfect piece of artistic printing.

April 9. (M). [1866]

To Macmillan's, to get a copy of *Alice* for Constance Sant; I saw Mr. Craik, who told me they had had an offer from America, the man wanting to know what they would charge for "one or two thousand." He proposed sending out the Oxford impression, and I promised to ask Mr. Tenniel about it.... Then I called on Mr. Tenniel, who gave his consent to the American sale.

April 10. (Tu). [1866]

Called on Mr. Macmillan and empowered him to sell the Oxford impression of *Alice* in America.

May 29. (Tu). [1866]
Received from Macmillan two hundred of the fly-leaf adver-
tisements of *Alice*, which he has printed by my suggestion.

March 1. (Sun) [1885]
Sent off two letters of literary importance: one to Mrs. Hargreaves (Alice Liddell) to ask her consent to my publishing the
original MS. Of *Alice* in facsimile (the idea occurred to me the
other day): the other to Mr. Harry Furniss, a very clever illus-
trator in *Punch*, asking if he is open to proposals to draw pictures for me [for Carroll's novel, *Sylvie and Bruno*].

March 29. (Sun). [1885]
Never before have I had so many literary projects on hand at
once. For curiosity I will make a list of them: – [There follows
a list of fifteen items, including:]
(9) *Nursery Alice* – for which twenty pictures are now being
coloured by Mr. Tenniel.
(11) *Alice's Adventures Underground*, a facsimile of the MS. book
lent to me by "Alice" (Mrs. Hargreaves). I am now in corre-
spondence with Dalziel [the engraver] about it.

Dec: 22. (W). [1886]
Today begins the sale of *Alice's Adventures Underground*. Tomorrow is the first performance of *Alice in Wonderland* at the Prince
of Wales' Theatre. A tolerably eventful week for me!

Nov: 1. (Th). [1888]
Skene brought, as his guest, Mr. Hargreaves, (the husband of
"Alice"), who was a stranger to me, though we had met, years
ago, as pupil and lecturer. It was not easy to link in one's mind
the new face with the olden memory – the stranger with the
once-so-intimately known and loved "Alice," whom I shall
always remember best as an entirely fascinating little seven-
year-old maiden.

March 7. (F). [1890]

Received from Mr. E. Evans a finished set of the sheets of *The Nursery Alice*. It is a *great* success. We can now publish at Easter.

March 25. (Tu). [1890]

Have been laid up for a week with "synovitis" in left knee: but managed to go to London, to write in over a hundred copies of *The Nursery Alice*.

[Source: *The Diaries of Lewis Carroll*, ed. Roger Lancelyn Green (Westport, CT: Greenwood Press, 1971), 2 vols.: 1: 222,223, 229-31,233-36, 241-43; 2: 432-34. 445, 465, 476.]

2. Letters

To Tom Taylor
Christ Church, Oxford

December 20,1863

Dear Sir,

Do you know Mr. Tenniel enough to be able to say whether he could undertake such a thing as drawing a dozen wood-cuts to illustrate a child's book, and if so, could you put me into communication with him? The reasons for which I ask (which however can be of but little interest if your answer be in the negative) are that I have written such a tale for a young friend, and illustrated it in pen and ink. It has been read and liked by so many children, and I have been so often asked to publish it, that I have decided on doing so. I have tried my hand at draw-ing on the wood, and come to the conclusion that it would take much more time than I can afford, and that the result would not be satisfactory after all. I want some figure-pictures done in pure outline, or nearly so, and of all artists on wood, I should prefer Mr. Tenniel. If he should be willing to undertake them, I would send him the book to look over, not that he should at all follow my pictures, but simply to give him an idea of the sort of thing I want. I should be much obliged if you would find out for me what he thinks about it, and remain

Very truly yours,
C. L. Dodgson

[Source: *The Letters of Lewis Carroll*, ed. Morton N. Cohen, 2 vols. (New York: Oxford University Press, 1979) 1:62. This and the following letters Copyright (c) 1979 by Philip Dodgson Jaques and Elizabeth Christie. Used by permission of Oxford University Press, Inc.

Tom Taylor was a popular playwright, his most famous work being *Our American Cousin* (1858), performed at Ford's Theater in Washington, D.C. when Lincoln was assassinated. He was on the staff of *Punch* at the time of Carroll's letter, and later became the editor of the magazine. John Tenniel was the leading political cartoonist in *Punch*.]

To Tom Taylor
Christ Church, Oxford

June 10, 1864

... P.S. I should be very glad if you could help me in fixing on a name for my fairy-tale, which Mr. Tenniel (in consequence of your kind introduction) is now illustrating for me, and which I hope to get published before Xmas. The heroine spends an hour underground, and meets various birds, beasts, etc. (*no* fairies), endowed with speech. The whole thing is a dream, but *that* I don't want revealed till the end. I first thought of "Alice's Adventures Under Ground," but that was pronounced too like a lesson-book, in which instruction about mines would be administered in the form of a grill; then I took "Alice's Golden Hour," but that I gave up, having a dark suspicion that there is already a book called "Lily's Golden Hours." Here are the other names I have thought of:

$$\text{Alice among the} \begin{cases} \text{elves} \\ \text{goblins} \end{cases} \quad \text{Alice's} \begin{cases} \text{hour} \\ \text{doings} \\ \text{adventures} \end{cases} \text{in} \begin{cases} \text{elf-land} \\ \text{wonderland} \end{cases}$$

Of all these I at present prefer "Alice's Adventures in Wonderland." In spite of your "morality," I want something sensational. Perhaps you can suggest a better name than any of these.

[Source: *The Letters of Lewis Carroll*, ed. Morton N. Cohen, 1: 65.]

To Alice (Liddell) Hargreaves
Christ Church, Oxford

March 1, 1885

My dear Mrs. Hargreaves,
I fancy this will come to you almost like a voice from the dead, after so many years of silence – and yet those years have made no difference, that I can perceive, in *my* clearness of memory of the days when we *did* correspond. I am getting to feel what an old man's failing memory is, as to recent events and new friends (for instance, I made friends, only a few weeks ago, with a very nice little maid of about 12, and had a walk with her – and now I can't recall either of her names!) but my mental picture is as vivid as ever, of one who was, through so many years, my ideal child-friend. I have had scores of child-friends since your time: but they have been quite a different thing.

However, I did not begin this letter to say all *that*. What I want to ask is – would you have any objection to the original MS book of *Alice's Adventures* (which I suppose you still possess) being published in facsimile? The idea of doing so occurred to me only the other day. If, on consideration, you come to the conclusion that you would rather *not* have it done, there is an end of the matter. If, however, you give a favorable reply, I would be much obliged if you would lend it me (registered post I should think would be safest) that I may consider the possibilities. I have not seen it for about 20 years: so am by no means sure that the illustrations may not prove to be so awfully bad, that to reproduce them would be absurd.

There can be no doubt that I should incur the charge of gross egoism in publishing it. But I don't care for that in the least: knowing that I have no such motive: only I think, considering the extraordinary popularity the books have had (we have sold more than 120,000 of the two) there must be many who would like to see the original form.

Always your friend,
C. L. Dodgson

[*The Letters of Lewis Carroll*, ed. Morton N. Cohen, 1:560–61. Alice Liddell married Reginald Hargreaves on September 15, 1880 in Westminster Abbey. Although the wedding was much publicized, Carroll's diaries and letters remain silent about what must have been a painful occasion for him. The green leather notebook containing Carroll's hand-printed and illustrated *Alice's Adventures Under Ground* was subsequently reproduced in facsimile. Towards the end of her life, Alice Hargreaves sold this unique volume, along with inscribed first editions of the Alice books, in order to help her son, Caryl, pay off the debts on their estate. He invested the money unwisely and lost it all. In light of the fate of this manuscript volume, Carroll's letter to Gertrude Thomson, below, is especially poignant.]

To Alice (Liddell) Hargreaves
Christ Church, Oxford

March 21, 1885

Dear Mrs. Hargreaves,
I am indeed grateful to you for sending the MS book, which has just arrived. The greatest care shall be taken of it. Believe me

Always yours sincerely,
C. L. Dodgson

[Source: *The Letters of Lewis Carroll*, ed. Morton N. Cohen, 1:568]

To E. Gertrude Thomson
Christ Church, Oxford

July 16, 1885

... My original plan for this Long Vacation, was to go to East-bourne as soon after July 1 as my rooms (I always go to the same) should be vacant. This, however, did not happen, till July 9th, so I took them from that day, and have been paying for the empty rooms for a week now, not being able to go myself, or to find a couple of lady-friends (or even a single one) to put in as my guests. What keeps me here is a grand piece of photo-zincography which is being done (at least the photography-part) in my studio, by a man who has come, with assistant and a mass of boxes of chemicals, etc., all the way from Essex. It has taken some time and trouble to find a really good man for this: and I was resolved to have the thing done in first-rate style, or not at all. But you will be wondering, all this while, what this important work can be! The germ of *Alice's Adventures in Wonderland* was an extempore story, told in a boat to the 3 children of Dean Liddell: it was afterwards, at the request of Miss Alice Liddell, written out for her, in MS print, with pen-and-ink pictures (*such* pictures!) of my own devising: without the least idea, at the time, that it would ever be published. But friends urged me to print it, so it was re-written, and enlarged, and published. Now that we have sold some 70,000 copies, it occurred to me that there must be a good many people, to whom a facsimile of the MS book would be interesting: and that is my present task. There are 92 pages, and, though we do them 2 at a time, it is a tedious business: and I have to stay in all day for it, as I allow no hands but mine to touch the MS book. Workmen's hands would soon spoil it, and it is not my proper-ty now, so I feel a terrible responsibility in having it lent me by the owner, who (I am happy to believe) sets a certain value on it as something unique. Luckily (as it will avoid confusion) the name is different from the published book, and is *Alice's Adventures Under Ground*.

[*The Letters of Lewis Carroll*, ed. Morton N. Cohen, 1:591. Gertrude Thomson was an artist friend of Carroll's who did the colored drawing for the cover of *The Nursery "Alice."*]

Appendix F: Remembering Lewis Carroll

1. Alice's Recollections of Carrollian Days As Told to her Son, Caryl Hargreaves

This article is the result of a game. Some years ago, before the sale of the manuscript which made my mother's identity more generally known, we were playing one of the many guessing games in a country house. I was one of the guessers, and the required answer, as it happened, was Alice in Wonderland. I thought I had spotted the right answer, and, to make sure, asked whether she had ever existed as a real person. I was told that she had never really lived: that she was mythical. It struck me as being so unusual, to say the least of it, that anybody should become mythical while still alive and still under eighty (for her eightieth birthday only fell on May 4, 1932), that I then and there determined to try and get my mother to put down some notes on her early life and recollections of Lewis Carroll. I never succeeded in getting her to do it herself, but what follows my sketch of her childhood at Oxford is her own story in her own words.

Alice Liddell was born on May 4, 1852, in the house next door to Westminster Abbey, occupied by her father as Headmaster of Westminster School. She was accordingly christened in Westminster Abbey (and incidentally married there. I have often wondered how many people have been both christened and married in the Abbey!), but she has no recollections of their life at Westminster, as when she was about four years old her father was made Dean of Christ Church, and the family moved to Oxford.

While on the subject let me give a few facts about the Liddell family in order to correct some misapprehensions which came to light in the press at the time of the Centenary. The Dean and Mrs. Liddell had, besides three sons, the following five daughters: (1) Lorina, always called Ina, who married Mr. Skene of Pitlour, and died in 1930; (2) Alice; (3) Edith, who was engaged to Aubrey Harcourt of Nuneham, but died, before she was married, in 1876; (4) Rhoda, still alive; (5) Violet, who died in 1927.

Soon after they went to Oxford, the three little girls were put in charge of Miss Prickett, whom they called "Pricks." Her father had some position at Pembroke College, and lived in Floyd's Row, near Folly Bridge, just behind Christ Church. She was not the highly educated governess of the present day, but she brought up the Liddell children successfully according to the ideas of those days, and, that done, married Mr. Foster. She died proprietress of the Mitre Hotel, Oxford. On one occasion when Oxford was very full, my grandfather persuaded Mrs. Foster to turn out of her own rooms in the hotel in order to provide accommodation for Lord Rosebery. The latter, who knew all the Liddell family well, said to the Dean that he was surprised to find the rooms of the proprietress of the Mitre Hotel full of photographs of the Liddells, and wondered how she had got them! Like everyone else, "Pricks" had her likes and dislikes, and Alice was not one of her favourites: Ina the eldest, the imperious Prima of the poem, was. In addition to being taught by her, the girls had masters for French, German, and Italian, and mistresses for music. When much older, they went to the School of Art for drawing. This school was later taken over by Mr. Ruskin, who taught my mother to sketch. On one occasion he was telling her she had done a drawing very badly. "I'm sorry," said Alice. "Don't be sorry, Alice, but don't do it again," was Mr. Ruskin's reply. Such were the gentler arts which produced the generation of the sixties and seventies, but my mother also had some more practical instruction, such as cooking lessons. Then there were dancing lessons, and they became proficient at the Quadrille which was considered essential in those days. What they would have done if they had been asked to dance a Lobster Quadrille, I don't know!

Let us now go into Christ Church by Tom Gate. On the other side of the quadrangle we see three little girls, all dressed exactly alike in white cotton dresses, white openwork socks and black shoes, walking with their nurse along the gravel path which led from the Deanery to the Hall archway. A stone parapet and pavement has long since replaced the gravel path which in those days ran along the top of a grass bank. If we follow them, we shall find that they are going to the buildings called the Old Library which have since been pulled down to make way for Meadow Buildings – (what an awful thought!). Arrived there they go up the staircase which leads to Mr. Dodgson's rooms. These looked out over the old Broad Walk, which was very different from what it now is. The present Broad Walk did not exist, and the way down to the river and to the boats was alongside the Till Mill stream, an evil-smelling and altogether undesirable approach to the river, though at the time when the new Broad Walk was made, leading straight from Meadow Buildings to the river, many protests were raised. But, if you can wait, in a minute I shall be able to introduce you to the party.

Here they come; the two men carrying luncheon-baskets, with the three little girls in shady hats clinging to their hands. The man with the rather handsome, and very interesting face is Mr. Dodgson, while the other one is Mr. Duckworth, afterwards Canon of Westminster, who gave his name to the "Duck" in "The Pool of Tears." Ina, the tallest of the three girls, has brown hair, and very clean-cut features; Alice, the second, has almost black hair cut in a fringe across her forehead; while Edith arrests our attention by her bright auburn hair. Lorina Charlotte, the eldest sister, becomes the Lory in "The Pool of Tears," while her initials make the name Elsie (L.C.) in the story of the three sisters who lived at the bottom of a well; Lacie, the second "well" sister, is merely what would nowadays be called an anagram for Alice; Edith becomes Tertia in the dedicatory poem, the Eaglet in "The Pool of Tears," and Tillie in "The Three Sisters." This last was because the other two sisters often called her Matilda, a nickname they had invented for her. Being now introduced, we can follow them down to Salter's, where the rowing boats are kept, and watch them choose a nice roomy boat, and plenty of comfortable cushions. Now Alice can tell us her story free from the many interruptions which would have been sure to come from the other two seventy years ago.

"Soon after we went to live in the old grey stone-built Deanery, there were two additions to the family in the shape of two tiny tabby kittens. One called Villikens, was given to my eldest brother Harry, but died at an early age of some poison. The other, Dinah, which was given to Ina, became my special pet, and lived to be immortalised in the *Alice*. Every day these kittens were bathed by us in imitation of our own upbringing. Dinah I was devoted to, but there were some other animals of which we were terrified. When my father went to Christ Church, he had some carved lions (wooden representations of the Liddell crest) placed on top of each of the corner posts in the banisters going upstairs and along the gallery. When we went to bed we had to go along this gallery, and we always ran as hard as we could along it, because we knew that the lions got down from their pedestals and ran after us. And then the swans on the river when we went out with Mr. Dodgson! But, even then, we were always much too happy little girls to be really frightened. We had some canaries, but there was never a white rabbit in the family. That was a pure invention of Mr. Dodgson's.

"We were all very fond of games, and our favourite card games were Pope Joan, and Beggar my Neighbour, followed later by Whist. About the time when the *Alice* was told, we used to spend a good many happy hours in the Deanery garden trying to play croquet. Chess came later. The deanery is a fair-sized house, one side of which looks out into Tom Quad, while the other looks on to a garden which is also overlooked by the Christ Church Library. It was very modern for those days in that it had a big bath, but with the unmodern limitation that only cold water was laid on! So the young ladies had a cold bath every morning! It was in this house, built by Cardinal Wolsey, but adapted to the comforts of the day, that we spent the happy years of childhood.

"... But my great joy was to go out riding with my father. As soon as we had a pony, he used to take one of us out with him every morning. The first pony we ever had was one given to my eldest brother Harry, called Tommy. Harry was away at school most of the time, and in any case did not care much about riding, so we always kept his pony exercised for him. I began to ride soon after we went to Oxford. We were taught up and down a path running at an angle to the Broad Walk (the triangular piece of grass between the two paths called the Dean's Ham) by Bultitude [the family's coachman]. With my father we used to ride on Port Meadow, or to go to Abingdon through Radley, and there were the most lovely rides through Wytham Woods.... When Tommy got too old, my father bought a bigger pony for us. One Boxing Day this pony crossed its legs, and came down with me on the Abingdon road. My father had to leave me by the side of the road while he went off to get help. While he was gone, some strangers, out for an excursion, passed, and were kind enough to send me back to Oxford in their wagonette, lying on a feather bed, borrowed from a nearby farm. The bottom of the wagonette was not quite long enough when the door was shut, and this caused me great pain, so perhaps I was not as grateful as I should have been, for, when I got home and Bultitude was carrying me indoors, I said to him, 'You won't let them hurt me any more, will you?' at which, as he told my mother afterwards, he 'nearly let Miss Alice drop.' As it was, I was on my back for six weeks with a broken thigh. During all these weeks Mr. Dodgson never came to see me. If he had, perhaps the world might have known some more of Alice's Adventures. As it is, I think many of my earlier adventures must be irretrievably lost to posterity, because Mr, Dodgson told us many, many stories before the famous trip up the river to Godstow. No doubt he added some of the earlier adventures to make up the difference between *Alice in Wonderland* and *Alice's Adventures Underground*, which latter was nearly all told on that one afternoon. Much of *Through the Looking Glass* is made up of them too, particularly the ones to do with chessmen, which are dated by the period when we were excitedly learning chess. But even then, I am afraid that many must have perished for ever in his waste-paper basket, for he used to illustrate the meaning of his stories on any piece of paper that he had handy.

"The stories that he illustrated in this way owed their existence to the fact that Mr. Dodgson was one of the first amateur photographers, and took many photographs of us. He did not draw when telling stories on the river expeditions. When the time of year made picnics impossible, we used to go to his rooms in the Old Library, leaving the Deanery by the back door, escorted by our nurse. When we got there, we used to sit on the big sofa on each side of him, while he told us stories, illustrating them by pencil or ink drawings as he went along. When we were thoroughly happy and amused at his stories, he used to pose us, and expose the plates before the right mood had passed. He seemed to have an endless store of these fantastical tales, which he made up as he told them, drawing busily on a large sheet of paper all the time. They were not always entirely new. Sometimes they were new versions of old stories; sometimes they started on the old basis, but grew into new tales owing to the frequent interruptions which opened up fresh and undreamed-of possibilities. In this way the stories, slowly enunciated in his quiet voice with its curious stutter, were perfected. Occasionally he pretended to fall asleep, to our great dismay. Sometimes he said 'That is all till next time,' only to resume on being told that it was already next time. Being photographed was therefore a joy to us and not a penance as it is to most children. We looked forward to the happy hours in the mathematical tutor's rooms.

"But much more exciting than being photographed was being allowed to go into the dark room, and watch him develop the large glass plates. What could be more thrilling than to see the negative gradually take shape, as he gently rocked it to and fro in the acid bath? Besides, the dark room was so mysterious, and we felt that any adventure might happen there! There were all the joys of preparation, anticipation, and realisation, besides the feeling that we were assisting at some secret rite usually reserved for grown-ups! Then there was the additional excitement, after the plates were developed, of seeing what we looked like in a photograph. Looking at the photographs now, it is evident that Mr. Dodgson was far in advance of his time in the art of photography and of posing his subjects.

"We never went to tea with him, nor did he come to tea with us. In any case, five-o'clock tea had not become an established practice in those days. He used sometimes to come to the Deanery on the afternoons when we had a half-holiday. At the time when we first went to Oxford, my parents, having had luncheon at one o'clock, did not have another meal until dinner, which they took at 6.30 p.m.... In those days, instead of five-o'clock tea, coffee and tea were served after dinner in the drawing-room. It was not until we were nearly grown up that afternoon tea was started, and then only as a treat. When the weather was too bad to go out, we used to say, 'Now then, it's a rainy day, let's have some tea.' On the other hand, when we went on the river for the afternoon with Mr. Dodgson, which happened at most four or five times every summer term, he always brought out with him a large basket full of cakes, and a kettle, which we used to boil under a haycock, if we could find one. On rarer occasions we went out for the whole day with him, and then we took a larger basket with luncheon – cold chicken and salad and all sorts of good things. One of our favourite whole-day excursions was to row down to Nuneham and picnic in the woods there, in one of the huts specially provided by Mr. Harcourt [William Vernon Harcourt, a scientist and Canon of York, owned the Nuneham estate] for picnickers. On landing at Nuneham, our first duty was to choose the hut, and then to borrow plates, glasses, knives and forks from the cottages by the riverside. To us the hut might have been a Fairy King's palace, and the picnic a banquet in our honour. Sometimes we were told stories after luncheon that transported us into Fairyland. Sometimes we spent the afternoon wandering in the more material fairyland of the Nuneham woods until it was time to row back to Oxford in the long summer evening. On these occasions we did not get home until about seven o'clock.

"The party usually consisted of five – one of Mr. Dodgson's men friends as well as himself and us three. His brother occasionally took an oar in the merry party, but our most usual fifth was Mr. Duckworth, who sang well. On our way back we generally sang songs popular at the time, such as,

'Star of the evening, beautiful star,'

and

'Twinkle, twinkle, little star,'

and

'Will you walk into my parlour, said the spider to the fly,' all of which are parodied in the *Alice*.

"On one occasion two of Mr. Dodgson's sisters joined the party, making seven of us, all in one boat. They seemed to us rather stout, and one might have expected that, with such a load in it, the boat would have been swamped. However, it was not the river that swamped us but the rain. It came on to pour so hard that we had to land at Iffley, and after trying to dry the Misses Dodgson at a fire, we drove home. This was a serious party, no stories nor singing: we were awed by the 'old ladies,' for though they can only have been in their twenties, they appeared dreadfully old to us.

"In the usual way, after we had chosen our boat with great care, we three children were stowed away in the stern, and Mr. Dodgson took the stroke oar. A pair of sculls was always laid in the boat for us little girls to handle when being taught to row by our indulgent host. He succeeded in teaching us in the course of these excursions, and it proved an unending joy to us. When we had learned enough to manage the oars, we were allowed to take our turn at them, while the two men watched and instructed us…. I can remember what hard work it was rowing upstream from Nuneham, but this was nothing if we thought we were learning and getting on. It was a proud day when we could 'feather our oars' properly. The verse at the beginning of the *Alice* describes our rowing. We thought it nearly as much fun as the stories. Sometimes (a treat of great importance in the eyes of the fortunate one) one of us was allowed to take the tiller ropes: and, if the course was a little devious, little blame was accorded to the small but inexperienced coxswain.

"Nearly all of *Alice's Adventures Underground* was told on that blazing summer afternoon with the heat haze shimmering over the meadows where the party landed to shelter for awhile in the shadow cast by the haycocks near Godstow. I think the stories he told us that afternoon must have been better than usual, because I have such a distinct recollection of the expedition, and also, on the next day I started to pester him to write down the story for me, which I had never done before. It was due to my 'going on' and importunity that, after saying he would think about it, he eventually gave the hesitating promise which started him writing it down at all. This he referred to in a letter written in 1883 in which he writes of me as the 'one without whose infant patronage I might possibly never have written at all.' What a nuisance I must have made of myself! Still, I am glad I did it now; and so was Mr. Dodgson afterwards. It does not do to think what pleasure would have been missed if his little bright-eyed favourite had not bothered him to put pen to paper. The result was that for several years, when he went away on vacation, he took the little black book about with him, writing the manuscript in his own peculiar script, and drawing the illustrations. Finally the book was finished and given to me. But in the meantime, friends who had seen and heard bits of it while he was at work on it, were so thrilled that they persuaded him to publish it. I have been told, though I doubt its being true, that at first he thought that it should be published at the publisher's expense, but that the London publishers were reluctant to do so, and he therefore decided to publish it at his own expense. In any case, after Macmillans had agreed to publish it, there arose the question of the illustrations. At first he tried to do them himself, on the lines of those in the manuscript book, but he came to the conclusion that he could not do them well enough, as they had to be drawn on wood, and he did not know how. He eventually approached Mr. (later Sir John) Tenniel. Fortunately, as I think most people will agree, the latter accepted. As a rule Tenniel used Mr. Dodgson's drawings as the basis for his own illustrations and they held frequent consultations about them. One point, which was not settled for a long time and until after many trials and consultations, was whether Alice in Wonderland should have her hair cut straight across her forehead as Alice Liddell had always worn it, or not. Finally it was decided that Alice in Wonderland should have no facial resemblance to her prototype.

"Unfortunately my mother tore up all the letters that Mr. Dodgson wrote to me when I was a small girl. I cannot remember what any of them were like, but it is an awful thought to contemplate what may have perished in the Deanery waste-paper basket. Mr. Dodgson always wore black clergyman's clothes in Oxford, but, when he took us out on the river, he used to wear white flannel trousers. He also replaced his black top-hat by a hard white straw hat on these occasions, but of course retained his black boots, because in those days white tennis shoes had never been heard of. He always carried himself upright, almost more than upright, as if he had swallowed a poker.

"On the occasion of the marriage of King Edward and Queen Alexandra, the whole of Oxford was illuminated, and Mr. Dodgson and his brother took me out to see the illuminations. The crowd in the streets was very great, and I clung tightly on to the hand of the strong man on either side of me. The colleges were all lit up, and the High Street was a mass of illuminations of all sorts and kinds. One in particular took my fancy, in which the words 'May they be happy' appeared in large letters of fire. My enthusiasm prompted Mr. Dodgson to draw a caricature of it next day for me, in which underneath those words appeared two hands holding very formidable birches with the words 'Certainly not.' Even if the joke was not very good, the drawing pleased me enormously, and I wish I had it still! Little did we dream then that this shy but almost brilliant logic tutor, with a bent for telling fairy stories to little girls, and for taking photographs of elderly dons, would before so many years be known all over the civilised world, and that his fairy stories would be translated into almost every European language, into Chinese and Japanese, and some of them even into Arabic! But perhaps only a brilliant logician could have written *Alice in Wonderland*!"

[Source: *The Cornhill Magazine*, n.s. (July, 1932) 1-12]

2. Isa Bowman, *Lewis Carroll, As I Knew Him*

[Carroll first met Isa Bowman in September, 1887. He was fifty-five years old and she was thirteen. She was a child actress who had a minor part in Savile Clarke's adaptation of the Alice books for the stage. For the next eight years she became an important part of Carroll's life. Her last visit to Carroll was in May, 1895, shortly after which she was married. Her memoir is a rich source for the magical influence Carroll had upon young girls.]

Lewis Carroll was a man of medium height. When I knew him his hair was a silver-grey, rather longer than it was the fashion to wear, and his eyes were a deep blue. He was clean shaven, and, as he walked, always seemed a little unsteady in his gait. At Oxford he was a well-known figure. He was a little eccentric in his clothes. In the coldest weather he would never wear an overcoat, and he had a curious habit of always wearing, in all seasons of the year, a pair of grey and black cotton gloves.

But for the whiteness of his hair it was difficult to tell his age from his face, for there were no wrinkles on it. He had a curiously womanish face, and, in direct contradiction to his real character, there seemed to be little strength in it. One reads a great deal about the lines that a man's life paints in his face, and there are many people who believe that character is indicated by the curves of flesh and bone. I do not, and never shall, believe it is true, and Lewis Carroll is only one of many instances to support my theory. He was as firm and self-contained as a man may be, but there was little to show it in his face.

Yet you could easily discern it in the way in which he met and talked with his friends. When he shook hands with you –

he had firm white hands, rather large – his grip was strong and steadfast. Every one knows the kind of man of whom it is said, "his hands were all soft and flabby when he said 'How-do-you-do.'" Well, Lewis Carroll was not a bit like that. Every one says when he shook your hand the pressure of his was full of strength, and you felt here indeed was a man to admire and to love. The expression in his eyes was also very kind and charming.

He used to look at me, when we met, in the very tenderest, gentlest way. Of course on an ordinary occasion I knew that his interested glance did not mean anything of any extra importance. Nothing could have happened since I had seen him last, yet, at the same time, his look was always so deeply sympathetic and benevolent, that one could hardly help feeling it meant a great deal more than the expression of the ordinary man.

He was afflicted with what I believe is known as "House-maid's knee," and this made his movements singularly jerky and abrupt. Then again he found it impossible to avoid stammering in his speech. He would, when engaged in an animated conversation with a friend, talk quickly and well for a few minutes, and then suddenly and without any very apparent cause would begin to stutter so much, that it was often difficult to understand him. He was very conscious of this impediment, and he tried hard to cure himself. For several years he read a scene from some play of Shakespeare's every day aloud, but despite this he was never quite able to cure himself of the habit. Many people would have found this a great hindrance to the affairs of ordinary life, and would have felt it deeply. Lewis Carroll was different. His mind and life were so simple and open that there was no room in them for self-consciousness, and I have often heard him jest at his own misfortune, with a comic wonder at it.

The personal characteristic that you would notice most on meeting Lewis Carroll was his extreme shyness. With children, of course, he was not nearly so reserved, but in the society of people of maturer age he was almost old-maidishly prim in his manner. When he knew a child well this reserve would vanish completely, but it needed only a slightly disconcerting incident to bring the cloak of shyness about him once more, and close the lips that just before had been talking so delightfully.

I shall never forget one afternoon when we had been walking in Christ Church meadows. On one side of the great open space the little river Cherwell runs through groves of trees towards the Isis, where the college boat-races are rowed. We were going quietly along by the side of the "Cher," when he began to explain to me that the tiny stream was a tributary, "a baby river" he put it, of the big Thames. He talked for some minutes, explaining how rivers came down from hills and flowed eventually to the sea, when he suddenly met a brother Don at a turning in the avenue.

He was holding my hand and giving me my lesson in geography with great earnestness when the other man came round the corner.

He greeted him in answer to his salutation, but the incident disturbed his train of thought, and for the rest of the walk he became very difficult to understand, and talked in a nervous and preoccupied manner. One strange way in which his nervousness affected him was peculiarly characteristic. When, owing to the stupendous success of "Alice in Wonderland" and "Alice Through the Looking-Glass," he became a celebrity, many people were anxious to see him, and in some way or other to find out what manner of man he was. This seemed to him horrible, and he invented a mild deception for use when some autograph-hunter or curious person sent him a request for his signature on a photograph, or asked him some silly question as to the writing of one of his books, how long it took to write, and how many copies had been sold. Through some third person he always represented that Lewis Carroll the author and Mr. Dodgson the professor were two distinct persons, and that the author could not be heard of at Oxford at all. On one occasion an American actually wrote to say that he had heard that Lewis Carroll had laid out a garden to represent some of the scenes in "Alice in Wonderland," and that he (the American) was coming right away to take photographs of it. Poor Lewis Carroll, he was in terror of Americans for a week!

Of being photographed he had a horror, and despite the fact that he was continually and importunately requested to sit before the camera, only very few photographs of him are in existence. Yet he had been himself a great amateur photographer, and had taken many pictures that were remarkable in their exact portraiture of the subject.

It was this exactness that he used to pride himself on in his camera work. He always said that modern professional photographers spoilt all their pictures by touching them up absurdly to flatter the sitter. When it was necessary for me to have some pictures taken he sent me to Mr. H. H. Cameron, whom he declared to be the only artist who dared to produce a photograph that was exactly like its subject. I thought that Mr. Cameron's picture made me look a dreadful fright, but Lewis Carroll always declared that it was a perfect specimen of portrait work.

... Yet, despite his love for the photographer's art, he hated the idea of having his own picture taken for the benefit of a curious world. The shyness that made him nervous in the presence of strangers made the idea that any one who cared to stare into a shop window could examine and criticise his portrait extremely repulsive to him.

I remember that this shyness of his was the only occasion of anything approaching a quarrel between us.

I had an idle trick of drawing caricatures when I was a child, and one day when he was writing some letters I began to make a picture of him on the back of an envelope. I quite forget what the drawing was like – probably it was an abominable libel – but suddenly he turned round and saw what I was doing. He got up from his seat and turned very red, frightening me very much. Then he took my poor little drawing, and tearing it into small pieces threw it into the fire without a word. Afterwards he came suddenly to me, and saying nothing, caught me up in his arms and kissed me passionately. I was only some ten or eleven years of age at the time, but now the incident comes back to me very clearly, and I can see it as if it happened but yesterday – the sudden snatching of my picture, the hurried striding across the room, and then the tender light in his face as he caught me up to him and kissed me.

I used to see a good deal of him at Oxford, and I was constantly in Christ Church. He would invite me to stay with him and find me rooms just outside the college gates, where I was put into charge of an elderly dame, whose name, if I do not forget, was Mrs. Buxall. I would spend long happy days with my uncle, and at nine o'clock I was taken over to the little house in St. Aldates and delivered into the hands of the landlady, who put me to bed.

In the morning I was awakened by the deep reverberations of "Great Tom" calling Oxford to wake and begin the new day. Those times were very pleasant, and the remembrance of them lingers with me still. Lewis Carroll at the time of which I am speaking had two tiny turret rooms, one on each side of his staircase in Christ Church. He always used to tell me that when I grew up and became married he would give me the two little rooms, so that if I ever disagreed with my husband we could each of us retire to a turret till we had made up our quarrel!

And those rooms of his! I do not think there was ever such a fairy-land for children. I am sure they must have contained one of the finest collections of musical-boxes to be found anywhere in the world. There were big black ebony boxes with glass tops, through which you could see all the works. There was a big box with a handle, which it was quite hard exercise for a little girl to turn, and there must have been twenty or thirty little ones which could only play one tune. Sometimes one of the musical-boxes would not play properly, and then I always got tremendously excited. Uncle [Carroll] used to go to a drawer in the table and produce a box of little screw-drivers and punches, and while I sat on his knee he would unscrew the lid and take out the wheels to see what was the matter. He must have been a clever mechanist, for the result was always the same – after a longer or shorter period the music began again. Sometimes when the musical-boxes had played all their tunes he used to put them into the box backwards, and was as pleased as I at the comic effect of the music "standing on its head," as he phrased it.

There was another and very wonderful toy which he sometimes produced for me, and this was known as "The Bat." The ceilings of the rooms in which he lived at the time were very high indeed, and admirably suited for the purposes of "The Bat." It was an ingeniously constructed toy of gauze and wire, which actually flew about the room like a bat. It was worked by a piece of twisted elastic, and it could fly for about half a minute.

I was always a little afraid of this toy because it was too life-like, but there was a fearful joy in it. When the music-boxes began to pall he would get up from his chair and look at me with a knowing smile. I always knew what was coming even before he began to speak, and I used to dance up and down in tremulous anticipation.

"Isa, my darling," he would say, "once upon a time there was some one called Bob the Bat! and he lived in the top left-hand drawer of the writing-table. What could he do when uncle wound him up?"

And then I would squeak out breathlessly, "He could really FLY!"

Bob the Bat had many adventures. There was no way of controlling the direction of its flight, and one morning, a hot summer's morning, when the window was wide open, Bob flew out into the garden and alighted in a bowl of salad which a scout was taking to some one's rooms. The poor fellow was so startled by the sudden flapping apparition that he dropped the bowl, and it was broken into a thousand pieces. There! I have written "a thousand pieces," and a thoughtless exaggeration of that sort was a thing that Lewis Carroll hated. "A thousand pieces?" he would have said; "you know, Isa, that if the bowl had been broken into a thousand pieces they would each have been so tiny that you could have hardly seen them."

[Source: Isa Bowman, *Lewis Carroll as I Knew Him* (New York: Dover, 1972) 7-23.]

Appendix G: Contemporary Reviews of Alice's Adventures in Wonderland

1. The *Press* 25 November 1865

[*Alice* is reviewed along with *Balderscourt; or Holiday Tales*, by the Rev. C.H. Adams and *Old Merry's Annual*.]

Each of these volumes is suitable as a gift-book for our young friends. In old age, when the memory becomes treacherous, the early prayers, religious truths, and fairy tales taught in the best class of nursery books, are recollected, whilst almost every thing else may be forgotten. These volumes are written in a simple and attractive style, and all of them inculcate good principles. The first-named, whilst suited for very young children, is nevertheless more elaborately "got up" than the others. It is printed on toned paper, the illustrations, by Tenniel, are beautiful, and the binding good and attractive. Little Alice falls asleep by the side of her elder sister, and dreams that she enters a rabbit-hole, and encounters all sorts of wonderful adventures in the society of a rabbit, hare, lizzard, dodo, turtle, gryphon, king, queen, knave, and other imaginary characters. It is most amusingly written, and a child, when once the tale has been commenced, will long to hear the whole of this wondrous narrative.

2. The *Publishers' Circular* 8 December 1865

Among the two hundred books for children which have been sent to us this year, the most original and most charming is Alice's Adventures in Wonderland, by Lewis Carroll, illustrated with no less than forty-two pictures by John Tenniel. What the great advocates for the progress of scientific knowledge will say to this book it is difficult to imagine. It is a piece of delicious nonsense – the story of a simple loving child, who allows her imagination to paint fairy-like pictures of a white rabbit with pink eyes, a frightened mouse, a March hare, a pig-baby, and divers other creatures, who hold wonderful conversations with her. Mr. Tenniel has helped little Alice with his best pencil, and has produced for her the most humorous set of pictures which we have seen for many a day.

3. The *Bookseller* 12 December 1865

> "How doth the little crocodile
> Improve his shining tail,
> And pour the water of the Nile
> On every golden scale!"

This version of a not unknown song caught our eye on opening this beautiful book for children. We were struck by the fine poetic strain, and read on; and we must fain say we were delighted. Now, we are not going to tell how little Alice became a fairy; and, after her transformation, had curious conversations with the rabbit, the caterpillar, the pet pig, the lobster and the mock-turtle; nor how she was astonished at her own wonderful memory, her remarkable knowledge, and the easy way in which she changed and changed again. But this we may say, that a more original fairy tale – and original fairy tales are by no means common now-a-days – it has not lately been our good fortune to read. And when we add that it is beautifully printed on fine paper, and illustrated by Tenniel, the great art-draughtsman of *Punch*, with two score of most mirth-provoking sketches, we have said enough to excite the curiosity of boys and girls, and make them impatient to possess this book.

4. The *Guardian* 15 December 1865

Every one knows how gravely in our dreams we take part in the most absurd transactions, unconscious of their absurdity; but it is not every one who can reproduce this unconsciousness in waking hours, like the author of *Alice's Adventures in Wonderland* (Macmillan). The story, or dream, is absolute nonsense; but nonsense so graceful and so full of humour that one can hardly help reading it through. The illustrations, by Tenniel, are, if anything, still better than the story; together they furnish children with materials for many a hearty laugh, which older children may very easily share.

5. *Illustrated Times* 16 December 1865

In Mr. Carroll's book we have recounted the extraordinary story of a little girl who, having been sitting for some time in the open air with her sister, suddenly falls into dreamland, and in her dream beholds all sorts of grotesque objects – such as a rabbit dressed in coat and waistcoat, a dodo carrying a walking-stick, a caterpillar smoking a hookah, a "Cheshire cat" with a veritable grin, the figures on a pack of cards endowed with life, &c.; and goes through a succession of adventures, which certainly prove the author to possess a most fertile imagination, but which are too extravagantly absurd to produce more diversion than disappointment and irritation. The end of the dream is that that which the child thought was a pack of cards "flying down upon her," after indulging in the eccentricities of a trial at law, in which the king is the judge and the knave of hearts is the prisoner, turns out to be a collection of dead leaves that had fluttered down from the trees upon her face whilst she was asleep. The two sisters agree that Alice's dream has been a very wonderful one, and – that is all; for the reader looks in vain for any immediate reason why Alice should have dreamt such a dream or for any very edifying result arising from it. But, regarding the book in the more genial light in which the younger generation would wish to view it, there can be little question that it will bear favourable comparison with many of those eccentric flights of fancy which enrich our literature at merry Christmas time. The illustrations by Mr. Tenniel not only serve to elucidate the text with considerable humour, but, at the same time, amply testify to the advance which his long and successful connection with *Punch* has enabled him to make in that department of art to which the term "comic" is generally applied. Amongst the more grotesque designs are some instances of animals, clothed in human guise, which may be called worthy the pencil of Grandville, and which certainly constitute the best guarantee for the success of the book.

6. The *Athenaeum* 16 December 1865

Somehow we do not feel as if the writers of books for children had made any great advance on the author of "Philip Quarll," or those who provided Mr. Newbery, of St. Paul's Churchyard, with the matter of his "gilt books," how pretty, and strange, and fairy-like in their gaudy Dutchpaper binding! It may be a superstition, but "The Perambulations of a Mouse," thumbed and got by heart by the fire-light, in the days when we were tiny, has not been exceeded by any late product of ingenuity addressed to the small people of today.

One notable and delightful exception to our remark, however, is to be found in Herr Andersen's stories. Here we have another collection: *What the Moon Saw; and other Tales.* Translated by W.H. Dulcken, Ph.D. With Eighty Illustrations by A.W. Bayes. Engraved by the Brothers Dalziel. (Routledge & Sons.) – In this, together with many old favourites, we have some new ones; and the best of these are addressed to a grown-up audience. On the quaintness and pathos of the author – only approached or excelled by those of Hawthorne – we need not descant anew. The illustrations are moderately good; not more.

Alice's Adventures in Wonderland. By Lewis Carroll. With Forty-two Illustrations by John Tenniel. (Macmillan & Co.) This is a dream-story; but who can, in cold blood, manufacture a dream, with all its loops and ties, and loose threads, and entanglements, and inconsistencies, and passages which lead to nothing, at the end of which Sleep's most diligent pilgrim never arrives? Mr. Carroll has laboured hard to heap together strange adventures, and heterogeneous combinations; and we acknowledge the hard labour. Mr. Tenniel, again, is square, and grim, and uncouth in his illustrations, howbeit clever, even sometimes to the verge of grandeur, as is the artist's habit. We fancy that any child might be more puzzled than enchanted by this stiff, over-wrought story.

7. The *Spectator* 22 December 1865

Alice's Adventures in Wonderland. By Lewis Carroll. With forty-two illustrations by John Tenniel. (Macmillan). – This is the book for little folks, and big folks who take it home to their little folks will find themselves reading more than they intended, and laughing more than they had any right to expect. Alice is a charming little girl (witness Mr. Tenniel *passim*), with a delicious style of conversation, who runs down a rabbit-hole one fine day and finds herself in Wonderland. She is amongst all sorts of small creatures, rabbits, mice, &c., that have a tongue and use it, and contradict her shamefully; then she cannot eat or drink anything without changing her size, and, as she says pathetically, "being so many different sizes in a day is very confusing"; then she has to take advice from a very rude Caterpillar, who is smoking a hookah upon a toadstool (here is a charming illustration of Mr. Tenniel's), and then she takes tea with the March Hare and the Mad Hatter (here the fun waxes rather furious); finally, after an interview with a Cheshire Cat, she mixes in the proceedings of a pack of cards, who move about in great state, and do many funny things which are amusingly illustrated, and at last, being treated with disrespect by her, all rise up into the air and come flying down upon her, and awaken her out of her pleasant but exciting dream. Mr. Carroll's story is very funny, but we wish that he had left out the hatter; this personage is *de trop* also in Mr. Tenniel's illustrations, which without him are always graceful or quaintly humorous.

8. The *Spectator* 22 December 1866

[A further review, for the next Christmas season. The review appears under the heading "Children's Books." *Little Alice in Wonderland* (sic) is the third of 21 books reviewed, the first two being Hans Andersen's *Stories for the Household*, translated by W. H. Dulcken, and *Aunt Judy's Christmas Volume*.]

We really think that most people who wish to please or profit the little folks will find something suitable in this goodly collection. The first three books upon the list we take upon ourselves, in its entirety, the responsibility of recommending; families provided with these may pick and choose amongst the rest; but these three, there is no doubt about it, they should have. The first of them is our old friend, and everybody's, Hans Andersen, in a complete edition....

Little Alice in Wonderland, we are not surprised to see, has reached a fifth thousand; so much clever and yet genuine fun in the letter-press, and so much grace and humour in the illustrations have never before been found within the same compass. The sweet figure of little Alice contrasts delightfully all through the book with the funny creatures and people she encounters in her most exciting journey; and as she never makes a slip in her manners or loses her sense of propriety in the most trying situations, her story may be considered as strictly moral as it is exquisitely amusing. This is the last of the three books that every child ought to have. We now reach a medley of which the merits vary, and with regard to which people are at liberty to consult their own tastes....

9. The *London Review* 23 December 1865

"Alice's Adventures in Wonderland" is a delightful book for children – or, for the matter of that, for grown-up people, provided they have wisdom and sympathy enough to enjoy a piece of downright hearty drollery and fanciful humour. Alice is a little girl who falls down a rabbit-hole into some strange subterranean region, where she meets all kinds of odd people and things, and goes through a world of marvellous adventures. The style in which these things are related is admirable for its appearance of wondering belief, as if the mind of the child were somehow transfused into the narrative; and the book, small as it is, is crammed full of curious invention. Exquisite also are the illustrations (forty-two in number) by Mr. Tenniel – a most charming contrast, in their grace, delicacy, finish, and airy fancy, to the ugly phantasmagoria in which so many of the artists of the present day indulge.

Some people are remarkably fond of telling their dreams, and indeed, can often become quite animated in the recital of them. They like to relate at breakfast the odd adventures and escapes and sights and marvellous experiences of all sorts which befell them in the night, and the happy or painful unreality of which was only gently or roughly broken to them by the tap at the door or the opening of the shutters. And others like to listen to these heroes, and then become heroes, too, in their turn. Dreams, indeed, will ever be held in honour. They are our gratifying "stretches of imagination," which we are forbidden to indulge in daily life. Often, certainly, do they sorely try us, yet often, too, enchant. Perhaps this morning some member of the House of Commons awoke from the last row in the House to the sound of the horn on the summit of the Right, and his ecstasy when his eyes opened upon the curious sunrise made him more than half doubt whether he was not, after all, still dozing under Mr. Ayrton, and only dreaming of the mountain tops he hoped to climb. Or did he one day go off in the House, while thinking of his trip to Switzerland in store, to gaze upon the Alps from Westminster Tower?

There are two books which have been sadly wanting to the world – the one, a good selection of dreams, and the other, its sister volume, of the dream-like reflections and sayings of children. Such books could not fail to be attractive and popular; more so, a good deal than half the story-books and most of the novels in the world. And especially would the latter be delightful, not only to mammas and grandmammas and aunts, but to many a man, steeped head over ears in dull realities, who finds his best treat and beguilement in playing his leisure hour away with children, and becoming himself a child again, as he tells them a story, or answers their quaint guesses, or listens to them soberly fraternizing with a bird, or a cat, or a fly.

Alice's Adventures in Wonderland is neither the one nor the other of the books we speak of; but it is akin to both, and is a very charming production. It is the picture of a child's simple and unreasoning imaginations illustrated in a dream, and is extremely well and pleasantly written. What more happy place than that chosen for the scene of these adventures? What child does not wonder when it looks down a rabbit-hole and fancy to itself all sorts of odd things going on at the bottom? – all the uncongenial creatures of the world in perfect harmony together there. "Down, down, down." … "Curiouser and curiouser." Who will say that it was not the supreme aspiration of his childhood's ambition – perhaps it is his ambition still – to find some fine day something – of course in the shape of a delicious eatable – which would at once enable him to shut up or expand like a telescope, to pop through the keyhole, or stride over a house?

Down below, little Alice, naturally enough, forms a wide acquaintance with all the animals and insects that be, whether of the land or the sea – a Cheshire Puss, a March Hare, a Dodo, a Mock Turtle, &c., – and the little disputations, conversations and philosophical reflections of the dream-child among these strange companions she meets are most droll. Now and then, perhaps, the drollery is excessive, and somewhat mars the natural simplicity of what lies beneath; but the vein below is always attractive. The child identifies itself with all things that breathe: human beings, animals, and insects are all in companionship, – this is the beautiful idea of the childish mind. Alice may grow larger and smaller, so as not to be able to "explain herself," "because I'm not myself, you see"; and may find that "being so many different sizes in a day is very confusing." But it is all proper enough. The caterpillar changes, too, and is probably likewise confused at his transformation. "When you have to turn into a chrysalis – you will some day, you know – and then after that into a butterfly, I should think, you'll feel a little queer, won't you?"

A great merit of this book is the novelty of its character, seen, perhaps, with best advantage at the Mad Tea Party….

Certainly we enjoy the walk with Alice through Wonderland, though now and then, perhaps, something disturbing almost causes us to wake from our dream. That it is a little bit too clever every here and there seems to us to be the fault of a very pretty and highly original book, sure to delight the little world of wondering minds, and which may well please those who have, unfortunately, passed the years of wondering.

11. *John Bull* 20 January 1866

The above is *facile princeps* of the Christmas (children's) Books that have come before us during the present prolific season, and fairly deserves a notice to itself. It is quite a work of genius, and a literary study; for, if the reputed author be the true one (and Lewis Carroll is of course a *nom de plume*), it effectually dispels the notion that first-rate mathematical talent and ability are inconsistent with genuine humour and imagination. Some have so accounted for the differential qualities of the Cambridge and Oxford character; and it may be, after all, that the prevalent *classical* atmosphere of the latter University, habitually breathed by our author, has neutralized somewhat the unpoetical fumes of his own special lucubrations, and placed him in such strong contrast with the hard *exact-scientific* mind of, say, Bishop Colenso. Certainly a more genial and exuberant fancy seldom ranged through dreamland than the narrator of "Alice's Adventures." The result is a nursery tale, which, like Kingsley's *Water-Babies*, or one of Hans Christian Andersen's stories, combines so much meaning and method with its racy broad humour – which it is a great mistake to describe, as we have seen it done in some review or other, as absolute and unmitigated nonsense – that it supplies a fund of almost equal amusement to the juvenile and adult reader. We freely confess to have indulged (despite our editorial gravity and decorum) in many a peal of loud laughter and a continuous irrepressible titter while carried along irresistibly through its two hundred pages of unceasing fun, diversified by the as admirable Tenniel illustrations, which so happily embody the grotesque conceptions of the writer. It is in truth as tickling as a pantomime in the briskness and richness of it satirical jocularity.

The probable impossibilities, monstrous absurdities, and incongruous situations of a childhood dream are the subject of the comedy, and must have required a childlike mind to rehabilitate them. Everybody remembers to have dreamt of the world coming in at the window, of men made of sealing-wax or India-rubber, of looking at one's self being hung, drawn and quartered, of floating about in the air. These are the *sort* of adventures Alice meets with in her dreamland. She goes to sleep and falls down a rabbit-hole, – down, down, to the centre of the earth, clutching at bookshelves and jam-pots in her way. She meets there with all sorts of extinct and fabulous animals, such as dodos, griffins, and mock turtles – and among the rest with a curious specimen of the human genus, a hungry and tea-drinking hatter, the intimate friend of a March hare. We do not know but that there is a cunning covert allusion in this late character to the famous Oxford man in the moon, and the increased payment for his hats at the time of a city election. Certainly the author's political proclivities seem to be in an opposite direction, – and, though good naturedly, in an *extremely* opposite direction. "'Off with her head!' the Queen shouted at the top of her voice. Nobody moved. 'Who cares for you?' said Alice, (she had grown to her *full size* by this time.) '*you're nothing but 'a pack of cards!*'" The trial-scene at which this sentiment occurs is one of the cleverest and most amusing in the book. We must conclude in drawing attention to several clever parodies – e.g., "'Tis the voice of the lobster," "How doth the little crocodile," and best of all, "You are old, Father William."

12. The *Literary Churchman* 5 May 1866

A capital child's book of clever nonsense, without aim or object other than pure amusement, and unburdened by any moral whatsoever. Children of an historical and conservative turn of mind (and children almost always are conservatives), will probably be scandalized at the unauthorized departure from the received account of the famous tart-stealing case at the court of the King of Hearts. But doubtless the author can plead formidable precedents for his boldness in undertaking to rehabilitate that hitherto much-suspected character the Knave of Hearts.

The illustrations are really admirable, and it is almost invidious to select among them, but perhaps the Dodo distributing the prizes, and the Cheshire Cat, which vanished gradually till only its grin was left, are two of the best, and the very pretty little girl is a charming relief to all the grotesque appearances which surround her.

13. The *Sunderland Herald* 25 May 1866

This very pretty and funny book ought to become a great favourite with children. It has this advantage, that it has no moral, and that it does not teach anything. It is, in fact, pure sugar throughout, and is without any of that bitter foundation of fact which some people imagine ought to be at the bottom of all children's books. It is certainly nonsense from beginning to end, but it is just that nonsense which no one but a clever man could have written. Alice, the little heroine of the book, in a dream goes into Wonderland with a vengeance. At one time she is nearly drowned in a pool of her own tears, at another she holds a conference with a caterpillar seated on a mushroom. Then we find her one of a mad tea-party, her companions those traditionary lunatics a March hare and a hatter. She plays a game of croquet with a live flamingo for a hammer, a hedgehog for a ball, and doubled-up soldiers for hoops, and soon after, with a mock turtle and a gryphon, she looks in at a lobster quadrille, during which a song is sung, of which we give one verse as a sample: –

> "Will you walk a little faster?" said a whiting to a snail,
> "There's a porpoise close behind us, and he's treading on my tail.
> See how eagerly the lobsters, and the turtles all advance!
> They are waiting on the shingle – will you come and join the dance?"

Tenniel's illustrations are some of them extremely pretty, and are all thoroughly according to the spirit of the book. The picture representing "Alice and mouse swimming in the pool of tears," and Alice with a pig in her arms, show her as the perfection of a charming and pretty child. Mr. Carroll has in one place described a Cheshire cat, of which nothing was left but the grin, and this Mr. Tenniel has attempted to illustrate, and has, strange to say, succeeded. We can confidently recommend this book as a present for any children who are in the habit of spending a part of each day in "doing their lessons," and who may therefore be fairly allowed a little unalloyed nonsense as a reward. The book is printed and issued in a style which fully sustains the reputation that Macmillan & Co. have justly obtained.

14. *Aunt Judy's Magazine* 1 June 1866

Forty-two illustrations by Tenniel! Why there needs nothing else to sell this book, one would think. But our young friends may rest assured that the exquisite illustrations only do justice to the exquisitely wild, fantastic, impossible, yet most natural history of "Alice in Wonderland." For the author (Mr. Lewis Carroll, of course – you see his name on the title-page, do you not?) has a secret, and he has managed his secret so much better than any author who ever "tried on" a secret of the same sort before, that we would not for the world let it out. No; the young folks for whom this charming account is written must go on and on and on till they find out the secret for themselves; and then they will agree with us that never was the mystery made to feel so beautifully natural before.

Of Mr. Tenniel's illustrations we need only say that he has entered equally into the fun and graceful sentiment of his author, and that we are as much in love with little Alice's face in all its changes as we are amused by the elegant get up of the white rabbit in ball costume, the lobster quadrille on the sands, or the concourse of animals fresh from the "Pool of Tears" drying themselves in the mouse's most dry historical memories.

The above hints will probably make "parents and guardians" aware that they must not look to "Alice's Adventures" for knowledge in disguise.

15. The *Examiner* 15 December 1866

A good, well-constructed child's story well told, though of entirely human interest, with no more in it than an opening legend and a faint suggestion of the supernatural, is Mr .David Smith's "Karl-of-the-Locket and his Three Wishes." A character just the reverse of this will fit "Alice's Adventures in Wonderland." Here there is no plot to speak of, the jest lying in the incessant opposition of unexpected ideas, through a long train of delightfully whimsical fancies that admit only the faintest suggestion of reality. It is a child's dream of wonders, and drifts like a dream through nearly two hundred pages of some of the best nonsense ever written for children by an Englishman. Mr. Tenniel has furnished three or four dozen pictures that are quite as clever and amusing as the text. They enter thoroughly into the spirit of the jesting, in which almost every line will tickle a child's imagination, and almost every page contains something that may stir a clever and light-hearted man to laughter. The want of construction is a little felt towards the end, if one reads the book, as we could not help doing, straight through at a sitting. But it is all so clever, and so deliciously purposeless, so happy an example of the effect produced by incessant surprise of whimsical and unexpected incidents or turns of dialogue, that the only thing not wonderful within the cover of the volume is the announcement on the title page that it is now in its "fifth thousand." We have hope for the future of the children who can enjoy writing of this sort; and we respect the five thousand uncles, aunts, and others, who have thought it a more profitable gift book than the lumps of hard fact turned into the shape of literary sweetmeats that are every year presented for their choice.

16. The *Daily News* 19 December 1866

It certainly cannot be said that the young people are neglected in the matter of literary and artistic entertainment at this bountiful season of the year. The issue of children's books is a department by itself – and a very important department – in the publishing trade. Some houses are almost entirely given up to the production of children's literature; while some for generations have had a famous name for books suited to the young. Of late years a great advance has been made both in the writing and the illustrating of children's books. Fifty years ago – excepting in the excellent stories and essays of Mrs. Barbauld,

Miss Edgeworth, and one or two others – the literature of the young had a violent, bitter, and puritanical tone, calculated rather to harden and contract than to expand and vivify the minds of its readers; and of the "art" exhibited in the woodcuts and steel plates, it is sufficient to say that it was barbarous. Then the external appearance of the books, in their dull brown calf-skin, was sombre and depressing. All this has been amended for several years; but we may add that the improvement is progressive. Speaking generally, children's books at the present day leave little to be desired. Occasionally we may and do come across a story in which the religious element is introduced to an extent or in a manner objectionable, because apparently factitious, and in excess of the simple needs of childhood. But for the most part the tone of our juvenile literature is pure, healthy, genial, cheerful, kindly, and unobtrusively reverential. The pictures are often excellent, and seldom actually bad; and the covers are such as to make the happy young possessors think they have got hold of so many jewelled caskets. A very large number of these books have been issued for the present Christmas; so large indeed, that our table is flooded with them, and we can do little more than enumerate their titles…

Tales are, of course, in abundance; among them we find a new edition of "Alice's Adventures in Wonderland," a charming tale, by Mr. Lewis Carroll, with equally charming illustrations by Mr. Tenniel, overflowing with grace, fancy, and humour (Macmillan and Co.);….

17. The *Scotsman* 22 December 1866

[*Alice* is considered along with *The Fountain of Youth*, translated from the Danish by H.W. Freeland.]

In external beauty these volumes are models; and "Alice's Adventures" are, further, exquisitely printed and illustrated. Nor is the story unreadable; but it is dull. There is no flow of animal spirits in its fur, which is forced and over-ingenious. Mr. Carroll seems to have said to himself, "Go to, now, I shall write a child's book"; and forthwith he has done it; whereas true children's literature is really of the poetical order, and must be born, not made. But Mr. Tenniel's admirably clever and grotesque illustrations carry us well through "Wonderland."

18. The *Contemporary Review* May 1869

Mr. Lewis Carroll, though he certainly does not possess anything like Mr. [George] MacDonald's commanding phantasy, has yet a peculiar power in slipping away unseen from the every-day world into a world of strange wonders. But his *spécialité* is that he carries the breath of real world with him wherever he goes, so that a whiff of it ever and anon passes over what is strangest. Under his disguises of kings and queens, rabbits and eagles, fish-footmen, and the rest, the child must constantly feel himself thrown back, as with a sudden rebound, upon the characters and the scenes of every day. The real and the grotesque, suddenly paired, rub cheeks together, and scuttle off to perform the same serio-farcical play in various ways and with other company. Mr. Carroll's world is not a distant and misty one. What puzzles Alice, and what will delight every youngster with her Fairyland, is the quaint way in which the most familiar things jostle and rub shoulders with the oddest, queerest and most fantastic. Even in the bits of jaunty rhyme thrown so skilfully into the story there is the near echo of familiar favourites. Throughout we have the best of all proof that Mr. Carroll has clearly caught the law on which the necessity rests for this association; and we have most effective surprises, and no lingering over separate points, nor over much explanation or detail. And together with the queerest, most surprising associations of figures and characters, we have also the oddest play of phrases in the Duchess's *penchant* for morals, which is made to yield the most grotesque lights, in which old sayings are set and illuminated, like well-known but insignificant faces suddenly stricken with the grotesque lights from the coloured bottles in a chemist's window. Mr. Carroll is just a little forced and artificial now and then, and verges too closely upon direct and earnest social caricature, as, for instance, in the matter of the jurors, where the practical drift of his picture pertains to a sphere of which children have no knowledge, and with which they consequently can have no sympathy. This is a matter which he should be on his guard against, as it has at several points marred this beautiful children's book. In "The Rose and the Ring" Mr. Thackeray carried this sort of hard, stringent, sustained criticism of conventional social regulations too far, and the book has permanent value from precisely the same elements as his other works, rather than as a genuine child's book.

19. "Alice Translated," The *Spectator* 7 August 1869

There is much complaint nowadays of the dearth of original production in this country. Fiction and poetry seem to be in danger of becoming lost arts through the multitude of verse-writers and novel-writers. Our drama is notoriously an imported commodity. Even the more adventurous spirits at our seats of learning are said to cast off the fetters of native tradition only to deliver themselves to a new bondage under the rule of the last German book, the more readily if it happens to contradict the last but one. For the comfort of those Englishmen whom the sight of these things tempts to despair of their country, it is well that we can point to at least one notable victory in a field which, though it may not be very wide, is among those where it is most difficult to command success, and where ignominious defeats are most common.

Alice in Wonderland is, beyond question, supreme among modern books for children. We do not forget the *Water-Babies*, but we exclude it from competition, as being not simply a child's book, but something more. Not that we would gainsay any one who should discover treasures of hidden wisdom in "Alice's Adventures." Indeed, we have reason to believe that nothing has prevented them from being adopted as a textbook at Cambridge, but the insuperable jealousy of Oxford mathematics which notoriously prevails at that university, and which has discovered in the theory of Muchness suggested by the Dormouse a connection with certain speculations on Determinants. At present, however, we cannot enter into the minute analysis which would be required for the proper treatment of this question. We find, then, that Alice, having already made all

English-speaking children her subjects is about to extend her dominion to the nurseries of France and Germany. We confess that our first hasty impulse was to exclaim, "Translate *Alice*? Impossible!" But we were straightway rebuked by the philosophical rejoinder of the caterpillar, "Why not?" And presently reason added, when the shock of surprise had passed off, "Not only it may be, but it must be." For what are in fact the qualities which are the marks of a really good child's book? Imprimis, it must amuse children; item, it must have no obvious moral; but this is not enough. The best children's tales, the tales which have already lived among the people, address themselves to all ages; witness the treasures preserved for us by the Brothers Grimm. If any readers are too old to sympathise with the many disappointments of the youth who went out to learn to shiver, to admire the irony of fate which again and again exalts the despised Dummling above his more favoured brethren, or to shudder at the unknown crime which combined all the powers of nature against Herr Korbes, we are heartily sorry for them. But further, not only is the true child-mind of no age in particular; it is also cosmopolitan. There is no delight in local colouring for its own sake, and we seldom find more of it than is unavoidably imposed by the limits of the storyteller's experience. In the fairy world there are no foreign parts, and in the centre of the earth or on the other side of the moon we are as much at home as on the Thames or the Weser. It follows that a child's book of genuine worth ought to suffer less by translation than any other kind of book; and the volumes now before us may to that extent be considered a further test of the excellence of the original. If any person objects to any part of the foregoing argument on the score of paradox or otherwise, we are willing to refer the dispute to the Cheshire Cat.

[These and other reviews of *Alice's Adventures in Wonderland* are reprinted in the following issues of *Jabberwocky*: Winter 1979/80, Spring 1980, Summer, 1980, and Autumn 1980.]

Appendix H: Poems Parodied in Alice's Adventures in Wonderland

1. "Against Idleness and Mischief," Isaac Watts (1674-1748).

[Carroll's parody is "How doth the little crocodile."]

> How doth the little busy bee
>   Improve each shining hour,
> And gather honey all the day
>   From every opening flower!
>
> How skillfully she builds her cell!
>   How neat she spreads the wax!
> And labors hard to store it well
>   With the sweet food she makes.
>
> In works of labour or of skill,
>   I would be busy too;
> For Satan finds some mischief still
>   For idle hands to do.
>
> In books, or work, or healthful play,
>   Let my first years be passed,
> That I may give for every day
>   Some good account at last.

2. "The Old Man's Comforts and How He Gained Them," Robert Southey (1774-1843). First published in *The Annual Anthology* in 1799.

[Carroll's parody is "You are old, father William."]

> "You are old, father William," the young man cried,
>   "The few locks which are left you are grey;
> You are hale, father William, a hearty old man;
>   Now tell me the reason, I pray."

"In the days of my youth," father William replied,
    "I remember'd that youth would fly fast,
And abus'd not my health and my vigour at first,
    That I never might need them at last."

"You are old, father William," the young man cried,
    "And pleasures with youth pass away.
And yet you lament not the days that are gone;
    Now tell me the reason, I pray."

"In the days of my youth," father William replied,
    "I remember'd that youth could not last;
I thought of the future, whatever I did,
    That I never might grieve for the past."

"You are old, father William," the young man cried,
    "And life must be hast'ning away;
You are cheerful and love to converse upon death;
    Now tell me the reason, I pray."

"I am cheerful, young man," father William replied,
    "Let the cause thy attention engage;
In the days of my youth I remember'd my God!
    And He hath not forgotten my age."

3. "Speak Gently," David Bates. An American poem, published anonymously in *Sharpe's Magazine* (London) in 1848
and collected in his volume *The Eolian* (Philadelphia) in
1849.

[Carroll's parody is "Speak roughly to your little boy."]

Speak gently! It is better far
    To rule by love than fear;
Speak gently; let no harsh words mar
    The good we might do here!

Speak gently! Love doth whisper low
    The vows that true hearts bind;

And gently Friendship's accents flow;
    Affection's voice is kind.

Speak gently to the little child!
    Its love be sure to gain;
Teach it in accents soft and mild;
    It may not long remain.

Speak gently to the young, for they
    Will have enough to bear;
Pass through this life as best they may,
    'Tis full of anxious care.

Speak gently to the aged one,
    Grieve not the care-worn heart;
Whose sands of life are nearly run,
    Let such in peace depart!

Speak gently, kindly, to the poor;
    Let no harsh tone be heard;
They have enough they must endure,
    Without an unkind word!

Speak gently to the erring; know
    They may have toiled in vain;
Perchance unkindness made them so;
    Oh, win them back again!

4. "The Star," Jane Taylor. First published in *Rhymes for the Nursery* in 1806.

[Carroll's parody is "Twinkle, twinkle, little bat!"]

    Twinkle, twinkle, little star,
    How I wonder what you are!
    Up above the world so high,
    Like a diamond in the sky.

When the blazing sun is gone,
When he nothing shines upon,
Then you show your little light,
Twinkle, twinkle, all the night.

Then the traveller in the dark
Thanks you for your tiny spark:
He could not see which way to go,
If you did not twinkle so.

In the dark blue sky you keep,
And often through my curtains peep,
For you never shut your eye
Till the sun is in the sky.

As your bright and tiny spark
Lights the traveller in the dark,
Though I know not what you are,
Twinkle, twinkle, little star.

5. "The Spider and the Fly," Mary Howitt. First published in *Sketches of Natural History* in 1834.

[Carroll's "'Will you walk a little faster?' said a whiting to a snail" parodies the first line and replicates the meter of Howitt's poem, the first stanza of which follows.]

"Will you walk into my parlour" said the spider to the fly.
"'Tis the prettiest little parlour that ever you did spy.
The way into my parlour is up a winding stair,
And I've got many curious things to show when you
                                                    are there."
"Oh no, no," said the little fly," to ask me is in vain,
For who goes up your winding stair can ne'er come
                                                    down again."

6. "The Sluggard," Isaac Watts.

[Carroll's parody is "'Tis the voice of the lobster."]

'Tis the voice of the sluggard; I heard him complain,
"You have wak'd me too soon, I must slumber again."
As the door on its hinges, so he on his bed,
Turns his sides and his shoulders and his heavy head.

"A little more sleep, and a little more slumber;"
Thus he wastes half his days, and his hours without number,
And when he gets up, he sits folding his hands,
Or walks about sauntering, or trifling he stands.

I pass'd by his garden, and saw the wild brier,
The thorn and the thistle grow broader and higher;
The clothes that hang on him are turning to rags;
And his money still wastes till he starves or he begs.

I made him a visit, still hoping to find
That he took better care for improving his mind:
He told me his dreams, talked of eating and drinking;
But he scarce reads his Bible, and never loves thinking.

Said I then to my heart, "Here's a lesson for me,"
This man's but a picture of what I might be:
But thanks to my friends for their care in my breeding,
Who taught me betimes to love working and reading.

7. "Star of the Evening," James M. Sayles. Author of both the lyrics and the music; dates unknown.

[Carroll's parody is "Beautiful Soup."]

> Beautiful star in heav'n so bright,
> Softly falls thy silv'ry light,
> As thou movest from earth afar,
> Star of the evening, beautiful star.

chorus:
>Beautiful star,
>Beautiful star,
>Star of the evening, beautiful star.

>In Fancy's eye thou seem'st to say,
>Follow me, come from earth away.
>Upward thy spirit's pinions try,
>To realms of love beyond the sky.

>Shine on, oh star of love divine,
>And may our soul's affection twine
>Around thee as thou movest afar,
>Star of the twilight, beautiful star.

8. "Alice Gray," William Mee. Published about 1815.

[The verses read out by the White Rabbit as evidence in the trial of the Knave of Hearts are from Carroll's nonsense poem, "She's All My Fancy Painted Him," published in the *Comic Times* in 1855, and significantly revised for inclusion in *Wonderland*. This earlier version starts off with a parody of the opening stanzas of William Mee's song, "Alice Gray."]

>She's all my fancy painted her,
>>She's lovely, she's divine,
>But her heart it is another's,
>>She never can be mine.

>Yet loved I as man never loved,
>>A love without decay,
>O, my heart, my heart is breaking
>>For the love of Alice Gray

9. "She's All My Fancy Painted Him," Lewis Carroll. From the *Comic Times* (1855).

She's all my fancy painted him
    (I make no idle boast);
If he or you had lost a limb,
    Which would have suffered most?

He said that you had been to her,
    And seen me here before;
But, in another character,
    She was the same of yore.

There was not one that spoke to us,
    Of all that thronged the street:
So he sadly got into a 'bus,
    And pattered with his feet.

They sent him word I had not gone
    (We know it to be true);
If she would push the matter on,
    What would become of you?

They gave her one, they gave me two,
    They gave us three or more;
They all returned from him to you,
    Though they were mine before.

If I or she should chance to be
    Involved in this affair,
He trusts to you to set them free,
    Exactly as we were.

It seemed to me that you had been
    (Before she had this fit)
An obstacle, that came between
    Him, and ourselves, and it.

Don't let him know she liked them best,
    For this must ever be
A secret, kept from all the rest,
    Between yourself and me.

Appendix I: Contemporary Children's Literature

1. William Makepeace Thackeray, from *The Rose and the Ring* (1855)

[William Makepeace Thackeray's *The Rose and the Ring* (1855) was the last and most successful of the series of Christmas books he wrote between 1846 and 1855. Set in the mythical land of Paflagonia, the story tells of the fairy Blackstick, who gives a magical ring to Giglio's mother and a magical rose to the mother of Prince Bulbo, the son of the Duke of Padella. These objects make whoever owns them irresistably attractive. After receiving the ring from Prince Giglio, Princess Angelica (daughter of King Valoroso) becomes everyone's favorite, but Giglio falls out with her and takes back his ring. Lady Gruffanuff, the old and ugly villain in the tale, acquires the ring and traps Giglio into marrying her. Blackstone, who years earlier had turned Gruffanuff's rude footman husband into a door knocker, turns him back into a human being and again Gruffanuff's husband, thereby freeing Giglio to marry his beloved Princess Rosalba (the daughter of the King of Crim Tartary).]

The King, dancing the twenty-fifth polka with Rosalba, remarked with wonder the ring she wore; and then Rosalba told him how she had got it from Gruffanuff, who no doubt had picked it up when Angelica flung it away.

"Yes," says the Fairy Blackstick, who had come to see the young people, and who had very likely certain plans regarding them. "That ring I gave the Queen, Giglio's mother, who was not, saving your presence, a very wise woman; it is enchanted, and whoever wears it looks beautiful in the eyes of the world. I made poor Prince Bulbo, when he was christened, the present of a rose which made him look handsome while he had it; but he gave it to Angelica, who instantly looked beautiful again, whilst Bulbo relapsed into his natural plainness."

"Rosalba needs no ring, I am sure," says Giglio, with a low bow. "She is beautiful enough, in my eyes, without any enchanted aid."

"Oh, sir!" said Rosalba.

"Take off the ring and try," said the King, and resolutely drew the ring off her finger. In *his* eyes she looked just as handsome as before!

The King was thinking of throwing the ring away, as it was so dangerous and made all the people so mad about Rosalba; but being a Prince of great humour, and good-humour too, he cast his eyes upon a poor youth who happened to be looking on very disconsolately, and said—

"Bulbo, my poor lad! come and try on this ring. The Princess Rosalba makes it a present to you." The magic properties of this ring were uncommonly strong, for no sooner had Bulbo put it on, but lo and behold! he appeared a personable, agreeable young Prince enough – with a fine complexion, fair hair, rather stout, and with bandy legs; but these were encased in such a beautiful pair of yellow morocco boots that nobody remarked them. And Bulbo's spirits rose up almost immediately after he had looked in the glass, and he talked to their Majesties in the most lively, agreeable manner, and danced opposite the Queen with one of the prettiest maids of honour, and after looking at Her Majesty, could not help saying – "How very odd; she is very pretty, but not so *extraordinarily* handsome."

"Oh no, by no means!" says the Maid of Honour.

"But what care I, dear sir," says the Queen, who overheard them," if you think I am good-looking enough!"

His Majesty's glance in reply to this affectionate speech was such that no painter could draw it. And the Fairy Blackstick said, "Bless you, my darling children! Now you are united and happy; and now you see what I said from the first, that a little misfortune has done you both good. *You*, Giglio, had you been bred in prosperity, would scarcely have learned to read or write – you would have been idle and extravagant, and could not have been a good king, as you now will be. You, Rosalba, would have been so flattered, that your little head might have been turned like Angelica's, who thought herself too good for Giglio."

"As if anybody could be good enough for *him*!" cried she.

"Oh, you – you darling!" says Giglio. And so she was; and he was just holding out his arms in order to give her a hug before the whole company, when a messenger came rushing in, and said, "My Lord, the enemy!"

"To arms!" cries Giglio.

"Oh, mercy!" says Rosalba, and fainted, of course. He snatched one kiss from her lips, and rushed *forth to the field* of battle!

The fairy had provided King Giglio with a suit of armour, which was not only embroidered all over with jewels, and blinding to your eyes to look at, but was water-proof, gun-proof, and sword-proof; so that in the midst of the very hottest battles His Majesty rode about as calmly as if he had been a British Grenadier at Alma. Were I engaged in fighting for my country, *I* should like such a suit of armour as Prince Giglio wore; but, you know, he was a Prince of a fairy tale, and they always have these wonderful things.

Besides the fairy armour, the Prince had a fairy horse, which would gallop at any pace you please; and a fairy sword, which would lengthen, and run through a whole regiment of enemies at once. With such a weapon at command, I wonder, for my part, he thought of ordering his army out; but forth they all came, in magnificent new uniforms; Hedzoff and the Prince's two college friends each commanding a division, and His Majesty prancing in person at the head of them all.

Ah! if I had the pen of a Sir Archibald Alison, my dear friends, would I not now entertain you with the account of a most tremendous shindy? Should not fine blows be struck? dreadful wounds be delivered? arrows darken the air? cannon-balls crash through the battalions? cavalry charge infantry? infantry pitch into cavalry? bugles blow; drums beat; horses neigh; fifes sing; soldiers roar, swear, hurray; officers shout out, "Forward, my men!" "This way, lads!" "Give it 'em, boys!" "Fight for King Giglio, and the cause of right!" "King Padella for ever!" Would I not describe all this, I say, and in the very finest language, too? But this humble pen does not possess the skill necessary for the description of combats. In a word, the overthrow of King Padella's army was so complete, that if they had been Russians you could not have wished them to be more utterly smashed and confounded....

"I should like to know who else is going to be married, if I am not?" shrieks out Gruffanuff. "I should like to know if King Giglio is a gentleman, and if there is such a thing as justice in Paflagonia? Lord Chancellor! my Lord Archbishop! will your Lordships sit by and see a poor, fond, confiding, tender creature put upon? Has not Prince Giglio promised to marry his Barbara? Is not this Giglio's signature? Does not this paper declare that he is mine, and only mine?" And she handed to his Grace the Archbishop the document which the Prince signed that evening when she wore the magic ring, and Giglio drank so much champagne. And the old Archbishop taking out his eyeglasses, read – "'This is to give notice that I, Giglio, only son of Savio, King of Paflagonia, hereby promise to marry the charming and virtuous Barbara Griselda, Countess Gruffanuff, and widow of the late Jenkins Gruffanuff, Esq.'"

"H'm," says the Archbishop, "the document is certainly a – a document."

"Phoo," says the Lord Chancellor, "the signature is not in His Majesty's handwriting." Indeed, since his studies at Bosforo, Giglio had made an immense improvement in calligraphy.

"Is it your handwriting, Giglio?" cries the Fairy Blackstick, with an awful severity of countenance.

"Y–y–y–es," poor Giglio gasps out, "I had quite forgotten the confounded paper: she can't mean to hold me by it. You old wretch, what will you take to let me off? Help the Queen, some one; Her Majesty has fainted."

"Chop her head off!" "Smother the old witch!" "Pitch her into the river!" exclaim the impetuous Hedzoff, the ardent Smith, and the faithful Jones.

But Gruffanuff flung her arms round the Archbishop's neck, and bellowed out, "Justice, justice, my Lord Chancellor!" so loudly, that her piercing shrieks caused everybody to pause. As for Rosalba, she was borne away lifeless by her ladies; and you may imagine the look of agony which Giglio cast towards that lovely being, as his hope, his joy, his darling, his all in all, was thus removed, and in her place the horrid old Gruffanuff rushed up to his side, and once more shrieked out, "Justice, justice!"

"Won't you take that sum of money which Glumboso hid?" says Giglio: "two hundred and eighteen thousand millions, or thereabouts. It's a handsome sum."

"I will have that and you too!" says Gruffanuff.

"Let us throw the crown jewels into the bargain," gasps out Giglio.

"I will wear them by my Giglio's side!" says Gruffanuff.

"Will half, three-quarters, five-sixths, nineteen-twentieths, of my kingdom do, Countess?" asks the trembling monarch.

"What were all Europe to me without *you* my Giglio?" cries Gruff, kissing his hand.

"I won't, I can't, I shan't, – I'll resign the crown first," shouts Giglio, tearing away his hand; but Gruff clung to it.

"I have a competency, my love," she says, "and with thee and a cottage thy Barbara will be happy."

Giglio was half mad with rage by this time. "I will not marry her," says he. "Oh, Fairy, Fairy, give me counsel!" And as he spoke, he looked wildly round at the severe face of the Fairy Blackstick.

"'Why is Fairy Blackstick always advising me, and warning me to keep my word? Does she suppose that I am not a man of honour?'" said the Fairy, quoting Giglio's own haughty words. He quailed under the brightness of her eyes; he felt that there was no escape for him from that awful inquisition.

"Well, Archbishop," said he, in a dreadful voice, that made his Grace start, "since this Fairy has led me to the height of happiness but to dash me down into the depths of despair, since I am to lose Rosalba, let me at least keep my honour. Get up, Countess, and let us be married; I can keep my word, but I can die afterwards."...

"Are you determined to make this poor young man unhappy?" says Blackstick.

"To marry him, yes! What business is it of yours? Pray, madam, don't say 'you' to a Queen," cries Gruffanuff.

"You won't take the money he offered you?"

"No."

"You won't let him off his bargain, though you know you cheated him when you made him sign the paper?"

"Impudence! Policemen, remove this woman!" cries Gruffanuff. And the policemen were rushing forward, but with a wave of her wand the Fairy struck them all like so many statues in their places.

"You won't take anything in exchange for your bond, Mrs. Gruffanuff ?" cries the Fairy, with awful severity. "I speak for the last time."

"No!" shrieks Gruffanuff, stamping with her foot. "I'll have my husband, my husband, my husband!"

"You SHALL HAVE YOUR HUSBAND!" the Fairy Blackstick cried; and advancing a step, laid her hand upon the nose of the KNOCKER.

As she touched it, the brass nose seemed to elongate, the open mouth opened still wider, and uttered a roar which made everybody start. The eyes rolled wildly; the arms and legs uncurled themselves, writhed about, and seemed to lengthen with each twist; the knocker expanded into a figure in yellow livery, six feet high; the screws by which it was fixed to the door unloosed themselves, and JENKINS GRUFFANUFF once more trod the threshold off which he had been lifted more than twenty years ago!

"Master's not at home," says Jenkins, just in his old voice; and Mrs. Jenkins, giving a dreadful *youp*, fell down in a fit, in which nobody minded her. For everybody was shouting, "Huzzay! huzzay!" "Hip, hip, hurray!" "Long live the King and Queen!" "Were such things ever seen?" "No, never, never, never!" "The Fairy Blackstick for ever!"

The bells were ringing double peals, the guns roaring and banging most prodigiously. Bulbo was embracing everybody; the Lord Chancellor was flinging up his wig and shouting like a madman; Hedzoff had got the Archbishop round the waist and they were dancing a jig for joy; and as for Giglio – I leave you to imagine what *he* was doing, and if he kissed Rosalba once, twice, twenty thousand times, I'm sure I don't think he was wrong.

So Gruffanuff opened the hall door with a low bow, just as he had been accustomed to do, and they all went in and signed the book, and then they went to church and were married, and the Fairy Blackstick sailed away on her cane, and was never more heard of in Paflagonia.

And here ends the Fireside Pantomime.

[Source: William Makepeace Thackeray, *The Rose and the Ring or, the History of Prince Giglio and Prince Bulbo* (New York: Frederick Stokes, 1854) 133-37, 148-51, 155-58.]

2. George MacDonald, from *Phantastes* (1858) and *The Light Princess* (1864)

[George MacDonald (1824-1905), the author of several novels about life in rural Scotland, is best remembered for his fairy stories for children. His most notable works in that genre include *Phantastes* (1858), *At the Back of the North Wind* (1871), *The Princess and the Goblin* (1872), and *The Princess and Curdie* (1882). Carroll was a close friend of MacDonald and his wife, Louisa, and in 1863, trusting their taste and literary judgment, he asked them to read his manuscript copy of *Alice's Adventures Under Ground*. They read the story to their children, and shortly afterwards wrote Carroll urging him to publish the tale. Greville MacDonald later recalled that "he asked my mother to read his first 'Alice' book to us, just to see how we took it and thus to gauge its worth if published.... I remember that first reading well, and also my braggart avowal that I wished there were 60,000 volumes of it.... Uncle Dodgson's method was more potent than he knew, and it made him very dear to us. We would climb about him as, with pen and ink, he sketched absurd or romantic or homely incidents, the while telling us their stories with no moral hints to spoil their charm." Carroll was quite familiar with *Phantastes* and *The Light Princess*. He appears to have read the latter in manuscript form in 1862, before it was published two years later as part of the loosely constructed novel *Adela Cathcart*. The excerpts from these two stories, printed below, will give some idea of the influence these tales had upon Carroll's creation of *Alice's Adventures in Wonderland*. MacDonald's stories are richly imaginative, with little conventional moralizing. His hero's adventures in Fairy Land in *Phantastes* take place in a romantic and, at times, dark dream, populated by curious creatures and people, including a white rabbit and animals he could hear speak.]

i. From *Phantastes*

While these strange events were passing through my mind, I suddenly, as one awakes to the consciousness that the sea has been moaning by him for hours, or that the storm has been howling about his window all night, became aware of the sound of running water near me; and looking out of bed, I saw that a large green marble basin, in which I was wont to wash, and which stood on a low pedestal of the same material in a corner of my room, was overflowing like a spring; and that a stream of clear water was running over the carpet, all the length of the room, finding its outlet I knew not where. And, stranger still, where this carpet, which I had myself designed to imitate a field of grass and daisies, bordered the course of the little stream, the grass-blades and daisies seemed to wave in a tiny breeze that followed the water's flow; while under the rivulet they bent and swayed with every motion of the changeful current, as if they were about to dissolve with it, and, forsaking their fixed form, become fluent as the waters.

My dressing-table was an old-fashioned piece of furniture of black oak, with drawers all down the front. These were elaborately carved in foliage, of which ivy formed the chief part. The nearer end of this table remained just as it had been, but on the further end a singular change had commenced. I happened to fix my eye on a little cluster of ivy-leaves. The first of these was evidently the work of the carver; the next looked curious; the third was unmistakably ivy; and just beyond it a tendril of clematis had twined itself about the gilt handle of one of the drawers. Hearing next a slight motion above me, I looked up, and saw that the branches and leaves designed upon the curtains of my bed were slightly in motion. Not knowing what change might follow next, I thought it high time to get up; and, springing from the bed, my bare feet alighted upon a cool green sward; and although I dressed in all haste, I found myself completing my toilet under the boughs of a great tree, whose top waved in the golden stream of the sunrise with many interchanging lights, and with shadows of leaf and branch gliding over leaf and branch, as the cool morning wind swung it to and fro, like a sinking sea-wave.

After washing as well as I could in the clear stream, I rose and looked around me. The tree under which I seemed to have lain all night, was one of the advanced guard of a dense forest, towards which the rivulet ran. Faint traces of a footpath, much overgrown with grass and moss, and with here and there a pimpernel even, were discernible along the right bank. "This," thought I, "must surely be the path into Fairy Land, which the lady of last night promised I should so soon find." I crossed the rivulet, and accompanied it, keeping the footpath on its right bank, until it led me, as I expected, into the wood.

★　★　★　★　★　★　★　★　★　★　★

But as I went further into the wood, these sights and sounds became fewer, giving way to others of a different character. A little forest of wild hyacinths was alive with exquisite creatures, who stood nearly motionless, with drooping necks, holding each by the stem of her flower, and swaying gently with it, whenever a low breath of wind swung the crowded floral belfry. In like manner, though differing of course in form and meaning, stood a group of harebells, like little angels waiting, ready, till they were wanted to go on some yet unknown message. In darker nooks, by the mossy roots of the trees, or in little tufts of grass, each dwelling in a globe of its own green light, weaving a network of grass and its shadows, glowed the glowworms. They were just like the glowworms of our own land, for they are fairies everywhere; worms in the day, and glowworms at night, when their own can appear, and they can be themselves to others as well as themselves. But they had their enemies here. For I saw great strong-armed beetles, hurrying about with most unwieldy haste, awkward as elephant-calves, looking apparently for glowworms; for the moment a beetle espied one, through what to it was a forest of grass, or an underwood of moss, it pounced upon it, and bore it way, in spite of its feeble resistance. Wondering what their object could be, I watched one of the beetles, and then I discovered a thing I could not account for. But it is no use trying to account for things in Fairy Land; and one who travels there soon learns to forget the very idea of doing so, and takes everything as it comes; like a child, who, being in a chronic condition of wonder, is surprised at nothing.

★   ★   ★   ★   ★   ★   ★   ★   ★   ★   ★

I walked on, in the fresh morning air, as if new-born. The only thing that damped my pleasure was a cloud of something between sorrow and delight, that crossed my mind with the frequently returning thought of my last night's hostess [a genial fairy in whose cottage he spent the night]. "But then," thought I, "if she is sorry, I could not help it; and she has all the pleasures she ever had. Such a day as this is surely a joy to her, as much at least as to me. And her life will perhaps be the richer, for holding now within it the memory of what came, but could not stay. And if ever she is a woman, who knows but we may meet somewhere? there is plenty of room for meeting in the universe." Comforting myself thus, yet with a vague compunction, as if I ought not to have left her, I went on. There was little to distinguish the woods to-day from those of my own land; except that all the wild things, rabbits, birds, squirrels, mice, and the numberless other inhabitants, were very tame; that is, they did not run away from me, but gazed at me as I passed, frequently coming nearer, as if to examine me more closely. Whether this came from utter ignorance, or from familiarity with the human appearance of beings who never hurt them, I could not tell. As I stood once, looking up to the splendid flower of a parasite, which hung from the branch of a tree over my head, a large white rabbit cantered slowly up, put one of its little feet on one of mine, and looked up at me with its red eyes, just as I had been looking up at the flower above me. I stooped and stroked it; but when I attempted to lift it, it banged the ground with its hind feet, and scampered off at a great rate, turning, however, to look at me, several times before I lost sight of it. Now and then, too, a dim human figure would appear and disappear, at some distance, amongst the trees, moving like a sleep-walker. But no one ever came near me.

This day I found plenty of food in the forest – strange nuts and fruits I had never seen before. I hesitated to eat them; but argued that, if I could live on the air of Fairy Land, I could live on its food also. I found my reasoning correct, and the result was better than I had hoped; for it not only satisfied my hunger, but operated in such a way upon my senses, that I was brought into far more complete relationship with the things around me. The human forms appeared much more dense and defined; more tangibly visible, if I may say so. I seemed to know better which direction to choose when any doubt arose. I began to feel in some degree what the birds meant in their songs, though I could not express it in words, any more than you can some landscapes. At times, to my surprise, I found myself listening attentively, and as if it were no unusual thing with me, to a conversation between two squirrels or monkeys. The subjects were not very interesting, except as associated with the individual life and necessities of the little creatures: where the best nuts were to be found in the neighbourhood, and who could crack them best, or who had most laid up for the winter, and such like; only they never said where the store was. There was no great difference in kind between their talk and our ordinary human conversation. Some of the creatures I never heard speak at all, and believe they never do so, except under the impulse of some great excitement. The mice talked; but the hedgehogs seemed very phlegmatic; and though I met a couple of moles above ground several times, they never said a word to each other in my hearing. There were no wild beasts in the forest; at least, I did not see one larger than a wild cat. There were plenty of snakes, however, and I do not think they were all harmless; but none ever bit me.

$$\star \quad \star \quad \star \quad \star \quad \star \quad \star \quad \star \quad \star \quad \star \quad \star \quad \star$$

[After killing an evil monster in Fairy Land, the hero is slain and buried. He then awakes from his dream.]

Sinking from such a state of ideal bliss, into the world of shadows which again closed around and infolded me, my first dread was, not unnaturally, that my own shadow [his feared demonic self] had found me again, and that my torture had commenced anew. It was a sad revulsion of feeling. This, indeed, seemed to correspond to what we think death is, before we die. Yet I felt within me a power of calm endurance to which I had hitherto been a stranger. For, in truth, that I should be able if only to think such things as I had been thinking, was an unspeakable delight. An hour of such peace made the turmoil of a life-time worth striving through.

I found myself lying in the open air, in the early morning, before sunrise. Over me rose the summer heaven, expectant of the sun. The clouds already saw him, coming from afar; and soon every dewdrop would rejoice in his individual presence within it. I lay motionless for a few minutes; and then slowly rose and looked about me. I was on the summit of a little hill; a valley lay beneath, and a range of mountains closed up the view upon that side. But, to my horror, across the valley, and up the height of the opposing mountains, stretched, from my very feet, a hugely expanding shade. There it lay, long and large, dark and mighty. I turned away with a sick despair; when lo! I beheld the sun just lifting his head above the eastern hill, and the shadow that fell from me, lay only where his beams fell not. I danced for joy. It was only the natural shadow, that goes with every man who walks in the sun. As he arose, higher and higher, the shadow-head sank down the side of the opposite hill, and crept in across the valley towards my feet.

Now that I was so joyously delivered from this fear, I saw and recognised the country around me. In the valley below, lay my own castle, and the haunts of my childhood were all about me. I hastened home. My sisters received me with unspeakable joy; but I suppose they observed some change in me, for a kind of respect, with a slight touch of awe in it, mingled with their joy, and made me ashamed. They had been in great distress about me. On the morning of my disappearance, they had found the floor of my room flooded; and, all that day, a wondrous and nearly impervious mist had hung about the castle and grounds. I had been gone, they told me, twenty-one days. To me it seemed twenty-one years. Nor could I yet feel quite secure in my new experiences. When, at night, I lay down once more in my own bed, I did not feel at all sure that when I awoke, I should not find myself in some mysterious region of Fairy Land. My dreams were incessant and perturbed; but when I did awake, I saw clearly that I was in my own home.

My mind soon grew calm; and I began the duties of my new position, somewhat instructed, I hoped, by the adventures that had befallen me in Fairy Land. Could I translate the experience of my travels there, into common life? This was the question. Or must I live it all over again, and learn it all over again, in the other forms that belong to the world of men, whose experience yet runs parallel to that of Fairy Land? These questions I cannot yet answer. But I fear.

Even yet, I find myself looking round sometimes with anxiety, to see whether my shadow falls right away from the sun or no. I have never yet discovered any inclination to either side. And if I am not unfrequently sad, I yet cast no more of a shade on the earth, than most men who have lived in it as long as I. I have a strange feeling sometimes, that I am a ghost, sent into the world to minister to my fellow-men, or, rather, to repair the wrongs I have already done. May the world be brighter for me, at least in those portions of it, where my darkness falls not.

ii. From *The Light Princess*

[Because she is not invited to the christening of the princess, the King's sister casts a spell depriving his child of gravity and the ability to weep tears.]

Where Is She?

One fine summer day, a month after these her first adventures, during which time she had been very carefully watched, the princess was lying on the bed in the queen's own chamber, fast asleep. One of the windows was open, for it was noon, and the day was so sultry that the little girl was wrapped in nothing less ethereal than slumber itself. The queen came into the room, and not observing that the baby was on the bed, opened another window. A frolicsome fairy wind, which had been watching for a chance of mischief, rushed in at the one window, and taking its way over the bed where the child was lying, caught her up, and rolling and floating her along like a piece of flue, or a dandelion seed, carried her with it through the opposite window, and away. The queen went down-stairs, quite ignorant of the loss she had herself occasioned.

When the nurse returned, she supposed that her Majesty had carried her off, and, dreading a scolding, delayed making inquiry about her. But hearing nothing, she grew uneasy, and went at length to the queen's boudoir, where she found her Majesty.

"Please, your Majesty, shall I take the baby?" said she.

"Where is she?" asked the queen.

"Please forgive me. I know it was wrong."

"What do you mean?" said the queen, looking grave.

"Oh! don't frighten me, your Majesty!" exclaimed the nurse, clasping her hands.

The queen saw that something was amiss, and fell down in a faint. The nurse rushed about the palace, screaming, "My baby! my baby!"

Every one ran to the queen's room. But the queen could give no orders. They soon found out, however, that the princess was missing, and in a moment the palace was like a beehive in a garden; and in one minute more the queen was brought to herself by a great shout and a clapping of hands. They had found the princess fast asleep under a rose-bush, to which the elvish little wind-puff had carried her, finishing its mischief by shaking a shower of red rose-leaves all over the little white sleeper. Startled by the noise the servants made, she woke, and, furious with glee, scattered the rose-leaves in all directions, like a shower of spray in the sunset.

She was watched more carefully after this, no doubt; yet it would be endless to relate all the odd incidents resulting from this peculiarity of the young princess. But there never was a baby in a house, not to say a palace, that kept the household in such constant good humour, at least below-stairs. If it was not easy for her nurses to hold her, at least she made neither their arms nor their hearts ache. And she was so nice to play at ball with! There was positively no danger of letting her fall. They might throw her down, or knock her down, or push her down, but couldn't *let* her down. It is true, they might let her fly into the fire or the coal-hole, or through the window; but none of these accidents had happened as yet. If you heard peals of laughter resounding from some unknown region, you might be sure enough of the cause. Going down into the kitchen, or *the room*, you would find Jane and Thomas, and Robert and Susan, all and sum, playing at ball with the little princess. She was the ball herself, and did not enjoy it the less for that. Away she went, flying from one to another, screeching with laughter. And the servants loved the ball itself better even than the game. But they had to take some care how they threw her, for if she received an upward direction, she would never come down again without being fetched.

What Is to Be Done?

But above-stairs it was different. One day, for instance, after breakfast, the king went into his counting-house, and counted out his money.

The operation gave him no pleasure.

"To think," said he to himself, "that every one of these gold sovereigns weighs a quarter of an ounce, and my real, live, flesh-and-blood princess weighs nothing at all!"

And he hated his gold sovereigns, as they lay with a broad smile of self-satisfaction all over their yellow faces.

The queen was in the parlour, eating bread and honey. But at the second mouthful she burst out crying, and could not swallow it.

The king heard her sobbing. Glad of anybody, but especially of his queen, to quarrel with, he clashed his gold sovereigns into his money-box, clapped his crown on his head, and rushed into the parlour.

"What is all this about?" exclaimed he. "What are you crying for, queen?"

"I can't eat it," said the queen, looking ruefully at the honey-pot.

"No wonder!" retorted the king. "You've just eaten your breakfast – two turkey eggs, and three anchovies."

"Oh, that's not it!" sobbed her Majesty. "It's my child, my child!"

"Well, what's the matter with your child? She's neither up the chimney nor down the draw-well. Just hear her laughing."

Yet the king could not help a sigh, which he tried to turn into a cough, saying –

"It is a good thing to be light-hearted, I am sure, whether she be ours or not."

"It is a bad thing to be light-headed," answered the queen, looking with prophetic soul far into the future.

"'Tis a good thing to be light-handed," said the king.

"'Tis a bad thing to be light-fingered," answered the queen.

"'Tis a good thing to be light-footed," said the king.

"'Tis a bad thing – " began the queen; but the king interrupted her.

"In fact," said he, with the tone of one who concludes an argument in which he has had only imaginary opponents, and in which, therefore, he has come off triumphant – "in fact, it is a good thing altogether to be light-bodied."

"But it is a bad thing altogether to be light-minded," retorted the queen, who was beginning to lose her temper.

This last answer quite discomfited his Majesty, who turned on his heel, and betook himself to his counting-house again. But he was not half-way towards it, when the voice of his queen overtook him.

"And it's a bad thing to be light-haired," screamed she, determined to have more last words, now that her spirit was roused.

The queen's hair was black as night; and the king's had been, and his daughter's was, golden as morning. But it was not this reflection on his hair that arrested him; it was the double use of the word *light*. For the king hated all witticisms, and punning especially. And besides, he could not tell whether the queen meant light-*haired* or light-*heired*; for why might she not aspirate her vowels when she was exasperated herself?

He turned upon his other heel, and rejoined her. She looked angry still, because she knew that she was guilty, or, what was much the same, knew that he thought so.

"My dear queen," said he, "duplicity of any sort is exceedingly objectionable between married people of any rank, not to say kings and queens; and the most objectionable form duplicity can assume is that of punning."

"There!" said the queen, "I never made a jest, but I broke it in the making. I am the most unfortunate woman in the world!"

She looked so rueful, that the king took her in his arms; and they sat down to consult.

"Can you bear this?" said the king.

"No, I can't," said the queen.

"Well, what's to be done?" said the king.

"I'm sure I don't know," said the queen. "But might you not try an apology?"

"To my old sister, I suppose you mean?" said the king.

"Yes," said the queen.

"Well, I don't mind," said the king.

So he went the next morning to the house of the princess,

and, making a very humble apology, begged her to undo the spell. But the princess declared, with a grave face, that she knew nothing at all about it. Her eyes, however, shone pink, which was a sign that she was happy. She advised the king and queen to have patience, and to mend their ways. The king returned disconsolate. The queen tried to comfort him.

"We will wait till she is older. She may then be able to suggest something herself. She will know at least how she feels, and explain things to us."

"But what if she should marry?" exclaimed the king, in sudden consternation at the idea. "Well, what of that?" rejoined the queen.

"Just think! If she were to have children! In the course of a hundred years the air might be as full of floating children as of gossamers in autumn."

"That is no business of ours," replied the queen. "Besides, by that time they will have learned to take care of themselves."

A sigh was the king's only answer.

He would have consulted the court physicians; but he was afraid they would try experiments upon her.

Look at the Rain!

The princess burst into a passion of tears, and *fell* on the floor. There she lay for an hour, and her tears never ceased. All the pent-up crying of her life was spent now. And a rain came on, such as had never been seen in that country. The sun shone all the time, and the great drops, which fell straight to the earth, shone likewise. The palace was in the heart of a rainbow. It was a rain of rubies, and sapphires, and emeralds, and topazes. The torrents poured from the mountains like molten gold; and if it had not been for its subterraneous outlet, the lake would have overflowed and inundated the country. It was full from shore to shore.

But the princess did not heed the lake. She lay on the floor and wept, and this rain within doors was far more wonderful than the rain out of doors. For when it abated a little, and she proceeded to rise, she found, to her astonishment, that she could not. At length, after many efforts, she succeeded in getting upon her feet. But she tumbled down again directly. Hearing her fall, her old nurse uttered a yell of delight, and ran to her, screaming, –

"My darling child! she's found her gravity!"

"Oh, that's it! is it?" said the princess, rubbing her shoulder and her knee alternately. "I consider it very unpleasant. I feel as if I should be crushed to pieces."

"Hurrah!" cried the prince from the bed. "If you've come round, princess, so have I. How's the lake?"

"Brimful," answered the nurse.

"Then we're all happy."

"That we are indeed!" answered the princess, sobbing.

And there was rejoicing all over the country that rainy day. Even the babies forgot their past troubles, and danced and crowed amazingly. And the king told stories, and the queen listened to them. And he divided the money in his box, and she the honey in her pot, among all the children. And there was such jubilation as was never heard of before.

Of course the prince and princess were betrothed at once. But the princess had to learn to walk, before they could be married with any propriety. And this was not so easy at her time of life, for she could walk no more than a baby. She was always falling down and hurting herself.

"Is this the gravity you used to make so much of?" said she one day to the prince, as he raised her from the floor. "For my part, I was a great deal more comfortable without it."

"No, no, that's not it. This is it," replied the prince, as he took her up, and carried her about like a baby, kissing her all the time. "This is gravity."

"That's better," said she. "I don't mind that so much."

And she smiled the sweetest, loveliest smile in the prince's face. And she gave him one little kiss in return for all his; and he thought them overpaid, for he was beside himself with delight. I fear she complained of her gravity more than once after this, notwithstanding.

It was a long time before she got reconciled to walking. But the pain of learning it was quite counterbalanced by two things, either of which would have been sufficient consolation. The first was, that the prince himself was her teacher; and the second, that she could tumble into the lake as often as she pleased. Still, she preferred to have the prince jump in with her; and the splash they made before was nothing to the splash they made now.

The lake never sank again. In process of time, it wore the roof of the cavern quite through, and was twice as deep as before.

The only revenge the princess took upon her aunt was to tread pretty hard on her gouty toe the next time she saw her. But she was sorry for it the very next day, when she heard that the water had undermined her house, and that it had fallen in the night, burying her in its ruins; whence no one ever ventured to dig up her body. There she lies to this day.

So the prince and princess lived and were happy; and had crowns of gold, and clothes of cloth, and shoes of leather, and children of boys and girls, not one of whom was ever known, on the most critical occasion, to lose the smallest atom of his or her due proportion of gravity.

[Source: George MacDonald, *The Light Princess* (New York: Farrar, Straus and Giroux, 1969) 12-23, 106-10.]

3. Charles Kingsley, from *The Water-Babies* (1862-63)

[Charles Kingsley (1819-75), the author of social protests novels, historical fiction, and several books for children, was a Christian socialist and professor of history at Cambridge University. His most enduring work was *The Water-Babies*, first published in serial form in *Macmillan's Magazine* (Aug. 1862-March 1863) and then in book form in 1863. It tells the story of Tom, a child chimney sweep who, reborn as a water-baby, experiences several adventures with marine creatures and with the occasional human being. Began as a story for Kingsley's youngest child, Grenville Arthur, it was later expanded to include Kingsley's strong views on science, society, and education. Concerned with good hygiene, Kingsley has his hero drown in a river not only to cleanse his soot-covered body but to suggest his spiritual purification. His final redemption comes through his difficult journey to Other-end-of-Nowhere. It is here that he aids in the redemption of his cruel former master, Mr. Grimes. Despite these social and religious themes, the story sparkles with wit, clever word play, a self-conscious, play-ful narrator, surprising transformations, a talking turnip and stick, and bristling irony – making it a significant predecessor to Carroll's creative nonsense.]

Ah, now comes the most wonderful part of this wonderful story. Tom, when he woke, for of course he woke – children always wake after they have slept exactly as long as is good for them – found himself swimming about in the stream, being about four inches, or – that I may be accurate – 3.87902 inches long, and having round the parotid region of his fauces a set of external gills (I hope you understand all the big words) just like those of a sucking eft, which he mistook for a lace frill, till he pulled at them, found he hurt himself, and made up his mind that they were part of himself, and best left alone.

In fact, the fairies had turned him into a water-baby.

A water-baby? You never heard of a water-baby. Perhaps not. That is the very reason why this story was written. There are a great many things in the world which you never heard of; and a great many more which nobody ever heard of; and a great many things, too, which nobody will ever hear of, at least until the coming of the Cocqcigrues, when man shall be the measure of all things.

"But there are no such things as water-babies."

How do you know that? Have you been there to see? And If you had been there to see, and had seen none, that would not prove that there were none. If Mr. Garth does not find a fox in Eversley Wood – as folks sometimes fear he never will – that does not prove that there are no such things as foxes. And as is Eversley Wood to all the woods in England, so are the waters we know to all the waters in the world. And no one has a right to say that no water-babies exist, till they have seen no water-babies existing; which is quite a different thing, mind, from not seeing water-babies; and a thing which nobody ever did, or perhaps ever will do.

     ★   ★   ★   ★   ★   ★   ★   ★   ★   ★   ★

Am I in earnest? Oh dear no! Don't you know that this is a fairy tale, and all fun and pretence; and that you are not to believe one word of it, even if it is true?

But at all events, so it happened to Tom. And, therefore, the keeper, and the groom, and Sir John made a great mistake, and were very unhappy (Sir John at least) without any reason, when they found a black thing in the water, and said it was Tom's body, and that he had been drowned. They were utterly mistaken. Tom was quite alive; and cleaner, and merrier, than he ever had been. The fairies had washed him, you see, in the swift river, so thoroughly, that not only his dirt, but his whole husk and shell had been washed quite off him, and the pretty little real Tom was washed out of the inside of it, and swam away, as a caddis does when its case of stones and silk is bored through and away it goes on its back, paddling to the shore, there to split its skin, and fly away as a caperer, on four fawn-coloured wings, with long legs and horns. They are foolish caperers, and fly into the candle at night, if you leave the door open. We will hope Tom will be wise now he has got safe out of his sooty old shell....

Now you may fancy that Tom was quite good, when he had everything that he could want or wish: but you would be very much mistaken. Being quite comfortable is a very good thing; but it does not make people good. Indeed, it sometimes makes them naughty, as it has made the people in America; and as it made the people in the Bible, who waxed fat and kicked, like horses overfed and underworked. And I am very sorry to say that this happened to little Tom. For he grew so fond of the sea-bullseyes and sea-lollipops that his foolish little head could think of nothing else: and he was always longing for more, and wondering when the strange lady would come again and give him some, and what she would give him, and how much, and whether she would give him more than the others. And he thought of nothing but lollipops by day, and dreamt of nothing else by night and what happened then?

★ ★ ★ ★ ★ ★ ★ ★ ★ ★ ★

But people do not yet believe that Mother Carey is as clever as all that comes to; and they will not till they, too, go the journey to the Other-end-of-Nowhere.

"And now, my pretty little man," said Mother Carey, "you are sure you know the way to the Other-end-of-Nowhere?"

Tom thought; and behold, he had forgotten it utterly.

"That is because you took your eyes off me."

Tom looked at her again, and recollected; and then looked away, and forgot in an instant.

"But what am I to do, ma'am? For I can't keep looking at you when I am somewhere else."

"You must do without me, as most people have to do, for nine hundred and ninety-nine thousandths of their lives; and look at the dog instead; for he knows the way well enough, and will not forget it. Besides, you may meet some very queer-tempered people there, who will not let you pass without this passport of mine, which you must hang round your neck and take care of; and, of course, as the dog will always go behind you, you must go the whole way backward."

"Backward!" cried Tom. "Then I shall not be able to see my way."

"On the contrary, if you look forward, you will not see a step before you, and be certain to go wrong; but, if you look behind you, and watch carefully whatever you have passed, and especially keep your eye on the dog, who goes by instinct, and therefore can't go wrong, then you will know what is coming next, as plainly as if you saw it in a looking-glass."

Tom was very much astonished: but he obeyed her, for he had learnt always to believe what the fairies told him.

★　★　★　★　★　★　★　★　★　★　★

Then Tom came to a very famous island, which was called, in the days of the great traveller Captain Gulliver, the Isle of Laputa. But Mrs. Bedonebyasyoudid has named it over again, the Isle of Tomtoddies, all heads and no bodies.

And when Tom came near it, he heard such a grumbling and grunting and growling and wailing and weeping and whining that he thought people must be ringing little pigs, or cropping puppies' ears, or drowning kittens: but when he came nearer still, he began to hear words among the noise; which was the Tomtoddies' song which they sing morning and evening, and all night too, to their great idol Examination –

"I can't learn my lesson: the examiner's coming!"

And that was the only song which they knew.

And when Tom got on shore the first thing he saw was a great pillar, on one side of which was inscribed, "Playthings not allowed here;" at which he was so shocked that he would not stay to see what was written on the other side. Then he looked round for the people of the island: but instead of men, women, and children, he found nothing but turnips and radishes, beet and mangold wurzel, without a single green leaf among them, and half of them burst and decayed, with toad-stools growing out of them. Those which were left began crying to Tom, in half a dozen different languages at once, and all of them badly spoken, "I can't learn my lesson; do come and help me!" And one cried, "Can you show me how to extract this square root?"

And another, "Can you tell me the distance between δ Lyræ and β Camelopardalis?"

And another, "What is the latitude and longitude of Snooksville, in Norman's County, Oregon, U.S.?"

And another, "What was the name of Mutius Scaevola's thirteenth cousin's grandmother's maid's cat?"

And another, "How long would it take a school-inspector of average activity to tumble head over heels from London to York?"

And another, "Can you tell me the name of a place that nobody ever heard of, where nothing ever happened, in a country which has not been discovered yet?"

And another, "Can you show me how to correct this hopelessly corrupt passage of Graidiocolosyrtus Tabenniticus, on the cause why crocodiles have no tongues?"

And so on, and so on, and so on, till one would have thought they were all trying for tide-waiters' places, or cornetcies in the heavy dragoons.

"And what good on earth will it do you if I did tell you?" quoth Tom.

Well, they didn't know that: all they knew was the examiner was coming.

Then Tom stumbled on the hugest and softest nimblecome-quick turnip you ever saw filling a hole in a crop of swedes, and it cried to him, "Can you tell me anything at all about anything you like?"

"About what?" says Tom.

"About anything you like; for as fast as I learn things I forget them again. So my mamma says that my intellect is not adapted for methodic science, and says that I must go in for general information."

Tom told him that he did not know general information, nor any officers in the army; only he had a friend once that went for a drummer: but he could tell him a great many strange things which he had seen in his travels.

So he told him prettily enough, while the poor turnip listened very carefully; and the more he listened, the more he forgot, and the more water ran out of him.

Tom thought he was crying: but it was only his poor brains running away, from being worked so hard; and as Tom talked, the unhappy turnip streamed down all over with juice, and split and shrank till nothing was left of him but rind and water; whereat Tom ran away in a fright, for he thought he might be taken up for killing the turnip.

But, on the contrary, the turnip's parents were highly delighted, and considered him a saint and a martyr, and put up a long inscription over his tomb about his wonderful talents, early development, and unparalleled precocity. Were they not a foolish couple? But there was a still more foolish couple next to them, who were beating a wretched little radish, no bigger than my thumb, for sullenness and obstinacy and wilful stupidity, and never knew that the reason why it couldn't learn or hardly even speak was, that there was a great worm inside it eating out all its brains. But even they are no foolisher than some hundred score of papas and mammas, who fetch the rod when they ought to fetch a new toy, and send to the dark cupboard instead of to the doctor.

Tom was so puzzled and frightened with all he saw, that he was longing to ask the meaning of it; and at last he stumbled over a respectable old stick lying half covered with earth. But a very stout and worthy stick it was, for it belonged to good Roger Ascham in old time, and had carved on his head King Edward the Sixth, with the Bible in his hand.

"You see," said the stick, "they were as pretty little children once as you could wish to see, and might have been so still if they had been only left to grow up like human beings, and then handed over to me; but their foolish fathers and mothers, instead of letting them pick flowers, and make dirt-pies, and get birds' nests, and dance round the gooseberry bush, as little children should, kept them always at lessons, working, working, working, learning week-day lessons all week-days, and Sunday lessons all Sunday, and weekly examinations every Saturday, and monthly examinations every month, and yearly examinations every year, everything seven times over, as if once was not enough, and enough as good as a feast – till their brains grew big, and their bodies grew small, and they were all changed into turnips, with little but water inside; and still their foolish parents actually pick the leaves off them as fast as they grow, lest they should have anything green about them."

"Ah!" said Tom, "if dear Mrs. Doasyouwouldbedoneby knew of it she would send them a lot of tops, and balls, and marbles, and ninepins, and make them all as jolly as sandboys."

"It would be no use," said the stick. "They can't play now, if they tried. Don't you see how their legs have turned to roots and grown into the ground, by never taking any exercise, but sapping and moping always in the same place? But here comes the Examiner-of-all-Examiners. So you had better get away, I warn you, or he will examine you and your dog into the bargain, and set him to examine all the other dogs, and you to examine all the other water-babies. There is no escaping out of his hands, for his nose is nine thousand miles long, and can go down chimneys, and through keyholes, upstairs, downstairs, in

my lady's chamber, examining all little boys, and the little boys'
tutors likewise.

★　★　★　★　★　★　★　★　★　★　★

MORAL

*AND now, my dear little man, what should we learn from this para-
ble?*

*We should learn thirty-seven or thirty-nine things, I am not exactly
sure which: but one thing, at least, we may learn, and that is this —
when we see efts in the pond, never to throw stones at them, or catch
them with crooked pins, or put them into vivariums with sticklebacks,
that the sticklebacks may prick them in their poor little stomachs, and
make them jump out of the glass into somebody's work-box, and so
come to a bad end. For these efts are nothing else but the water-babies
who are stupid and dirty, and will not learn their lessons and keep
themselves clean; and, therefore (as comparative anatomists will tell you
fifty years hence, though they are not learned enough to tell you now),
their skulls grow flat, their jaws grow out, and their brains grow small,
and their tails grow long, and they lose all their ribs (which I am sure
you would not like to do), and their skins grow dirty and spotted, and
they never get into the clear rivers, much less into the great wide sea, but
hang about in dirty ponds, and live in the mud, and eat worms, as they
deserve to do.*

*But that is no reason why you should ill-use them: but only why
you should pity them, and be kind to them, and hope that some day
they will wake up, and be ashamed of their nasty, dirty, lazy, stupid
life, and try to amend, and become something better once more. For, perhaps, if they do so, then after 379,423 years, nine months, thirteen days,
two hours, and twenty-one minutes (for aught that appears to the contrary), if they work very hard and wash very hard all that time, their
brains may grow bigger, and their jaws grow smaller, and their ribs come
back, and their tails wither off, and they will turn into water-babies
again, and perhaps after that into land-babies; and after that perhaps
into grown men.*

You know they won't? Very well, I daresay you know best. But you see, some folks have a great liking for those poor little elfs. They never did anybody any harm, or could if they tried; and their only fault is, that they do no good — any more than some thousands of their betters. But what with ducks, and what with pike, and what with sticklebacks, and what with water-beetles, and what with naughty boys, they are "sae sair hadden down," as the Scotsmen say, that it is a wonder how they live; and some folks can't help hoping, with good Bishop Butler, that they may have another chance, to make things fair and even, somewhere, somewhen, somehow.

Meanwhile, do you learn your lessons, and thank God that you have plenty of cold water to wash in; and wash in it too, like a true Englishman. And then, if my story is not true, something better is; and if I am not quite right, still you will be, as long as you stick to hard work and cold water.

But remember always, as I told you at first, that this is all a fairy tale, and only fun and pretence: and, therefore, you are not to believe a word of it, even if it is true.

[Source: Charles Kingsley, *The Water-Babies* (New York: A. Wessels, 1900) 45, 52, 145, 187-88, 207-11, 230-31.]

4. Julia Horatia Ewing, from "Amelia and the Dwarfs" (1870)

[Julia Horatia Ewing (1841-85), novelist and author of numerous books for children, first published "Amelia and the Dwarfs" in *Aunt Judy's Magazine* in 1870 and later included it with other stories in a volume entitled *The Brownies and Other Tales* (1870). The editor of *Aunt Judy's Magazine* was Margaret Gatty, Julia's mother. Carroll contributed several pieces to the magazine about this time, including *Castle-Croquet* (1867), *Bruno's Revenge* (1867), and *Puzzles from Wonderland* (1870). Ewing's popular story is an amalgam of Carroll's subterranean fantasy and conventional nineteenth-century moralizing. Her editor mother wrote of the story: "You are rather singular in keeping the domestic part so *real* in spite of the introduction of supernatural machinery." The first part of the tale, omitted here, details all of the bad habits of the unruly Amelia who, by story's end, is transformed into a proper Victorian child.]

... It was summer, and haytime. Amelia had been constantly in the hayfield, and the haymakers had constantly wished that she had been anywhere else. She mislaid the rakes, nearly killed herself and several other persons with a fork, and overturned one haycock after another as fast as they were made. At tea-time it was hoped that she would depart, but she teased her mamma to have the tea brought into the field, and her mamma said: "The poor child must have a treat sometimes," and so it was brought out.

After this she fell off the haycart, and was a good deal shaken, but not hurt. So she was taken indoors, and the haymakers worked hard and cleared the field, all but a few cocks which were left till the morning.

The sun set, the dew fell, the moon rose. It was a lovely night. Amelia peeped from behind the blinds of the drawing-room windows, and saw four haycocks, each with a deep shadow reposing at its side. The rest of the field was swept clean, and looked pale in the moonshine. It was a lovely night.

"I want to go out," said Amelia. "They will take away those cocks before I can get at them in the morning, and there will be no more jumping and tumbling. I shall go out and have some fun now."

"My dear Amelia, you must not," said her mamma; and her papa added: "I won't hear of it." So Amelia went upstairs to grumble to nurse; but nurse only said: "Now, my dear Miss Amelia, do go quietly to bed, like a dear love. The field is all wet with dew. Besides, it's a moonlight night, and who knows what's abroad? You might see the fairies – bless us and sain us! – and what-not. There's been a magpie hopping up and down near the house all day, and that's a sign of ill-luck."

"I don't care for magpies," said Amelia; "I threw a stone at that one to-day."

And she left the nursery, and swung downstairs on the rail of the banisters. But she did not go into the drawing-room; she opened the front door and went out into the moonshine.

It was a lovely night. But there was something strange about it. Everything looked asleep, and yet seemed not only awake but watching. There was not a sound, and yet the air seemed full of half sounds. The child was quite alone, and yet at every step she fancied someone behind her, on one side of her, somewhere, and found it only a rustling leaf or a passing shadow. She was soon in the hayfield, where it was just the same; so that when she fancied that something green was moving near the first haycock she thought very little of it, till, coming closer, she plainly perceived by the moonlight a tiny man dressed in green, with a tall, pointed hat, and very, very long tips to his shoes, tying his shoe-string with his foot on a stubble stalk. He had the most wizened of faces, and when he got angry with his shoe, he pulled so wry a grimace that it was quite laughable. At last he stood up, stepping carefully over the stubble, went up to the first haycock, and drawing out a hollow grass stalk blew upon it till his cheeks were puffed like footballs. And yet there was no sound, only a half-sound, as of a horn blown in the far distance, or in a dream. Presently the point of a tall hat, and finally just such another little wizened face poked out through the side of the haycock.

"Can we hold revel here to-night?" asked the little green man.

"That indeed you cannot," answered the other; "we have hardly room to turn round as it is, with all Amelia's dirty frocks."

"Ah, bah!" said the dwarf; and he walked on to the next haycock, Amelia cautiously following.

Here he blew again, and a head was put out as before; on which he said:

"Can we hold revel here to-night?"

"How is it possible," was the reply, "when there is not a place where one can so much as set down an acorn cup, for Amelia's broken victuals?"

"Fie! fie!" said the dwarf, and went on to the third, where all happened as before; and he asked the old question:

"Can we hold revel here to-night?"

"Can you dance on glass and crockery shreds?" inquired the other. "Amelia's broken gimcracks are everywhere."

"Pshaw!" snorted the dwarf, frowning terribly; and when he came to the fourth haycock he blew such an angry blast that the grass stalk split into seven pieces. But he met with no better success than before. Only the point of a hat came through the hay, and a feeble voice piped in tones of depression: "The broken threads would entangle our feet. It's all Amelia's fault. If we could only get hold of her!"

"If she's wise, she'll keep as far from these haycocks as she can," snarled the dwarf angrily; and he shook his fist as much as to say: "If she did come, I should not receive her very pleasantly."

Now with Amelia, to hear that she had better not do something, was to make her wish at once to do it; and as she was not at all wanting in courage, she pulled the dwarf's little cloak, just as she would have twitched her mother's shawl, and said (with that sort of snarly whine in which spoilt children generally speak): "Why shouldn't I come to the haycocks if I want to? They belong to my papa, and I shall come if I like. But you have no business here."

"Nightshade and hemlock!" ejaculated the little man, "you are not lacking in impudence. Perhaps your Sauciness is not quite aware how things are distributed in this world?" saying which he lifted his pointed shoes and began to dance and sing:

> "All under the sun belongs to men,
> And all under the moon to the fairies.
> So, so, so! Ho, ho, ho!
> All under the moon to the fairies."

As he sang "Ho, ho, ho!" the little man turned head over heels; and though by this time Amelia would gladly have got away, she could not, for the dwarf seemed to dance and tumble round her, and always to cut off the chance of escape; whilst numberless voices from all around seemed to join in the chorus, with:

"So, so, so! Ho, ho, ho!
All under the moon to the fairies."

"And now," said the little man, "to work! And you have plenty of work before you, so trip on, to the first haycock."

"I shan't!" said Amelia.

"On with you!" repeated the dwarf.

"I won't!" said Amelia.

But the little man, who was behind her, pinched her funny-bone with his lean fingers, and as everybody knows, that is agony; so Amelia ran on, and tried to get away. But when she went too fast, the dwarf trod on her heels with his long-pointed shoe, and if she did not go fast enough, he pinched her funny-bone. So for once in her life she was obliged to do as she was told. As they ran, tall hats and wizened faces were popped out on all sides of the haycocks, like blanched almonds on a tipsy cake; and whenever the dwarf pinched Amelia, or trod on her heels, the goblins cried "Ho, ho, ho!" with such horrible contortions as they laughed, that it was hideous to behold them.

"Here is Amelia!" shouted the dwarf when they reached the first haycock.

"Ho, ho, ho!" laughed all the others, as they poked out here and there from the hay.

"Bring a stock," said the dwarf; on which the hay was lifted, and out ran six or seven dwarfs, carrying what seemed to Amelia to be a little girl like herself. And when she looked closer, to her horror and surprise the figure was exactly like her – it was her own face, clothes, and everything.

"Shall we kick it into the house?" asked the goblins.

" No," said the dwarf; "lay it down by the haycock. The father and mother are coming to seek her now."

When Amelia heard this she began to shriek for help; but she was pushed into the haycock, where her loudest cries sounded like the chirruping of a grasshopper.

It was really a fine sight to see the inside of the cock.

Farmers do not like to see flowers in a hayfield, but the fairies do. They had arranged all the butter-cups, etc., in patterns on the haywalls; bunches of meadow-sweet swung from the roof like censers, and perfumed the air; and the ox-eye daisies which formed the ceiling gave a light like stars. But Amelia cared for none of this. She only struggled to peep through the hay, and she did see her father and mother and nurse come down the lawn, followed by the other servants, looking for her. When they saw the stock they ran to raise it with exclamations of pity and surprise. The stock moaned faintly, and Amelia's mamma wept, and Amelia herself shouted with all her might.

"What's that?" said her mamma. (It is not easy to deceive a mother.)

"Only the grasshoppers, my dear," said papa. "Let us get the poor child home."

The stock moaned again, and the mother said, "Oh dear! oh dear-r-Ramelia!" and followed in tears.

"Rub her eyes," said the dwarf; on which Amelia's eyes were rubbed with some ointment, and when she took a last peep she could see that the stock was nothing but a hairy imp, with a face like the oldest and most grotesque of apes.

" – and send her below," added the dwarf. On which the field opened, and Amelia was pushed underground.

She found herself on a sort of open heath, where no houses were to be seen. Of course there was no moonshine, and yet it was neither daylight nor dark. There was as the light of early dawn, and every sound was at once clear and dreamy, like the first sounds of the day coming through the fresh air before sunrise. Beautiful flowers crept over the heath, whose tints were constantly changing in the subdued light; and as the hues changed and blended, the flowers gave forth different perfumes. All would have been charming but that at every few paces the paths were blocked by large clothes-baskets full of dirty frocks. And the frocks were Amelia's. Torn, draggled, wet, covered with sand, mud, and dirt of all kinds, Amelia recognized them.

"You've got to wash them all," said the dwarf, who was behind her as usual; "that's what you've come down for – not because your society is particularly pleasant. So the sooner you begin the better."

"I can't," said Amelia (she had already learnt that "I won't" is not an answer for every one); "send them up to nurse, and she'll do them. It is her business."

"What nurse can do she has done, and now it's time for you to begin," said the dwarf. "Sooner or later the mischief done by spoilt children's wilful disobedience comes back on their own hands. Unto a certain point we help them, for we love children, and we are wilful ourselves. But there are limits to everything. If you can't wash your dirty frocks, it is time you learnt to do so, if only that you may know what the trouble is you impose on other people. *She* will teach you."

The dwarf kicked out his foot in front of him, and pointed with his long toe to a woman who sat by a fire made upon the heath, where a pot was suspended from crossed poles. It was like a bit of a gipsy encampment, and the woman seemed to be a real woman, not a fairy which was the case, as Amelia afterwards found. She had lived underground for many years, and was the dwarfs' servant.

And this was how it came about that Amelia had to wash her dirty frocks. Let any little girl try to wash one of her dresses; not to half wash it, not to leave it stained with dirty water, but to wash it quite clean. Let her then try to starch and iron it in short, to make it look as if it had come from the laundress and she will have some idea of what poor Amelia had to learn to do. There was no help for it. When she was working she very seldom saw the dwarfs; but if she were idle or stubborn, or had any hopes of getting away, one was sure to start up at her elbow and pinch her funny-bone, or poke her in the ribs, till she did her best. Her back ached with stooping over the wash-tub; her hands and arms grew wrinkled with soaking in hot soapsuds, and sore with rubbing. Whatever she did not know how to do, the woman of the heath taught her. At first, whilst Amelia was sulky, the woman of the heath was sharp and cross; but when Amelia became willing and obedient, she was good-natured, and even helped her.

The first time that Amelia felt hungry she asked for some food.

"By all means," said one of the dwarfs; "there is plenty down here which belongs to you"; and he led her away till they came to a place like the first, except that it was covered with plates of broken meats; all the bits of good meat, pie, pudding, bread and butter, etc., that Amelia had wasted beforetime.

"I can't eat cold scraps like these," said Amelia, turning away.

"Then what did you ask for food for before you were hungry?" screamed the dwarf, and he pinched her and sent her about her business.

After a while she became so famished that she was glad to beg humbly to be allowed to go for food; and she ate a cold chop and the remains of a rice pudding with thankfulness. How delicious they tasted! She was surprised herself at the good things she had rejected. After a time she fancied she would like to warm up some of the cold meat in a pan, which the woman of the heath used to cook her own dinner in, and she asked for leave to do so.

"You may do anything you like to make yourself comfortable, if you do it yourself," said she; and Amelia, who had been watching her for many times, became quite expert in cooking up the scraps.

As there was no real daylight underground, so also there was no night. When the old woman was tired she lay down and had a nap, and when she thought that Amelia had earned a rest, she allowed her to do the same. It was never cold, and it never rained, so they slept on the heath among the flowers.

They say that: "It's a long lane that has no turning," and the hardest tasks come to an end some time, and Amelia's dresses were clean at last; but then a more wearisome work was before her. They had to be mended. Amelia looked at the jagged rents made by the hedges: the great gaping holes in front where she had put her foot through; the torn tucks and gathers. First she wept, then she bitterly regretted that she had so often refused to do her sewing at home that she was very awkward with her needle. Whether she ever would have got through this task alone is doubtful, but she had by this time become so well behaved and willing that the old woman was kind to her, and, pitying her blundering attempts, she helped her a great deal; whilst Amelia would cook the old woman's victuals, or repeat stories and pieces of poetry to amuse her.

"How glad I am that I ever learnt anything!" thought the poor child: "everything one learns seems to come in useful some time."

At last the dresses were finished.

"Do you think I shall be allowed to go home now?" Amelia asked of the woman of the heath.

"Not yet," said she; "you have got to mend the broken gim-cracks next."

"But when I have done all my tasks," Amelia said; "will they let me go then?"

"That depends," said the woman, and she sat silent over the fire; but Amelia wept so bitterly that she pitied her and said: "Only dry your eyes, for the fairies hate tears, and I will tell you all I know and do the best for you I can. You see, when you first came you were – excuse me! – such an unlicked cub; such a peevish, selfish, wilful, useless, and ill-mannered little miss, that neither the fairies nor anybody else were likely to keep you any longer than necessary. But now you are such a willing, handy, and civil little thing, and so pretty and graceful withal, that I think it is very likely that they will want to keep you altogether. I think you had better make up your mind to it. They are kindly little folk, and will make a pet of you in the end."

"Oh, no! no!" moaned poor Amelia; "I want to be with my mother, my poor dear mother! I want to make up for being a bad child so long. Besides, surely that "stock," as they called her, will want to come back to her own people."

"As to that," said the woman, "after a time the stock will affect mortal illness, and will then take possession of the first black cat she sees, and in that shape leave the house, and come home. But the figure that is like you will remain lifeless in the bed, and will be duly buried. Then your people, believing you to be dead, will never look for you, And you will always remain here. However, as this distresses you so, I will give you some advice. Can you dance?"

"Yes," said Amelia; "I did attend pretty well to my dancing lessons. I was considered rather clever about it."

"At any spare moments you find," continued the woman, "dance, dance all your dances, and as well as you can. The dwarfs love dancing."

"And then?" said Amelia.

"Then, perhaps some night they will take you up to dance with them in the meadows above ground."

"But I could not get away. They would tread on my heels oh! I could never escape them.""I know that," said the woman; "your only chance is this. If ever, when dancing in the meadows, you can find a four-leaved clover, hold it in your hand, and wish to be at home. Then no one can stop you. Meanwhile I advise you to seem happy, that they may think you are content, and have forgotten the world. And dance, above all, dance!"

And Amelia, not to be behindhand, began then and there to dance some pretty figures on the heath. As she was dancing the dwarf came by.

"Ho, ho!" said he, "you can dance, can you?"

"When I am happy, I can," said Amelia, performing several graceful movements as she spoke.

"What are you pleased about now?" snapped the dwarf suspiciously.

"Have I not reason?" said Amelia. "The dresses are washed and mended."

"Then up with them!" returned the dwarf. On which half a dozen elves popped the whole lot into a big basket and kicked them up into the world, where they found their way to the right wardrobes somehow.

As the woman of the heath had said, Amelia was soon set to a new task. When she bade the old woman farewell, she asked if she could do nothing for her if ever she got at liberty herself.

"Can I do nothing to get you back to your old home?" Amelia cried, for she thought of others now as well as herself.

"No, thank you," returned the old woman; "I am used to this, and do not care to return. I have been here a long time – how long I do not know; for as there is neither daylight nor dark we have no measure of time – long, I am sure, very long. The light and noise up yonder would now be too much for me. But I wish you well, and, above all, remember to dance!"

The new scene of Amelia's labours was a more rocky part of the heath, where grey granite boulders served for seats and tables, and sometimes for workshops and anvils, as in one place, where a grotesque and grimy old dwarf sat forging rivets to mend china and glass. A fire in a hollow of the boulder served for a forge, and on the flatter part was his anvil. The rocks were covered in all directions with the knick-knacks, ornaments, etc., that Amelia had at various times destroyed.

"If you please, sir," she said to the dwarf, "I am Amelia."

The dwarf left off blowing at his forge and looked at her.

"Then I wonder you're not ashamed of yourself," said he.

"I am ashamed of myself," said poor Amelia, "very much ashamed. I should like to mend these things if I can."

"Well, you can't say more than that," said the dwarf, in a mollified tone, for he was a kindly little creature; "bring that china bowl here, and I'll show you how to set to work."

Poor Amelia did not get on very fast, but she tried her best. As to the dwarf, it was truly wonderful to see how he worked. Things seemed to mend themselves at his touch, and he was so proud of his skill, and so particular, that he generally did over again the things which Amelia had done after her fashion. The first time he gave her a few minutes in which to rest and amuse herself, she held out her little skirt, and began one of her prettiest dances.

"Rivets and trivets!" shrieked the little man, "how you dance! It is charming! I say it is charming! On with you! Fa, la fa! La, fa la! It gives me the fidgets in my shoe points to see you!" and forthwith down he jumped, and began capering about.

"I am a good dancer myself," said the little man. "Do you know the 'Hop, Skip, and a Jump' dance?"

"I do not think I do," said Amelia.

"It is much admired," said the dwarf, "when I dance it"; and he thereupon tucked up the little leathern apron in which he worked, and performed some curious antics on one leg.

"That is the hop," he observed, pausing for a moment. "The skip is thus. You throw out your left leg as high and as far as you can, and as you drop on the toe of your left foot you fling out the right leg in the same manner, and so on. This is the jump," with which he turned a somersault and disappeared from view. When Amelia next saw him he was sitting cross-legged on his boulder.

"Good, wasn't it?" he said.

"Wonderful!" Amelia replied.

"Now it's your turn again," said the dwarf.

But Amelia cunningly replied: "I 'm afraid I must go on with my work."

"Pshaw!" said the little tinker. "Give me your work. I can do more in a minute than you in a month, and better to boot. Now dance again."

"Do you know this?" said Amelia, and she danced a few paces of a polka mazurka. "Admirable!" cried the little man. "Stay" – and he drew an old violin from behind the rock – "now dance again, and mark the time well, so that I may catch the measure, and then I will accompany you."

Which accordingly he did, improvising a very spirited tune, which had, however, the peculiar subdued and weird effect of all the other sounds in this strange region.

"The fiddle came from up yonder," said the little man. "It was smashed to atoms in the world and thrown away. But, ho, ho, ho! There is nothing that I cannot mend, and a mended fiddle is an amended fiddle. It improves the tone. Now teach me that dance, and I will patch up all the rest of the gimcracks. Is it a bargain?"

"By all means," said Amelia; and she began to explain the dance to the best of her ability. "Charming, charming!" cried the dwarf. "We have no such dance ourselves. We only dance hand in hand, and round and round, when we dance together. Now I will learn the step, and then I will put my arm round your waist and dance with you."

Amelia looked at the dwarf. He was very smutty, and old,

and wizened. Truly, a queer partner! But "handsome is that handsome does"; and he had done her a good turn. So when he had learnt the step, he put his arm round Amelia's waist, and they danced together. His shoe points were very much in the way, but otherwise he danced very well.

Then he set to work on the broken ornaments, and they were all very soon "as good as new." But they were not kicked up into the world, for, as the dwarfs said, they would be sure to break on the road. So they kept them and used them; and I fear that no benefit came from the little tinker's skill to Amelia's mamma's acquaintance in this matter.

"Have I any other tasks?" Amelia inquired.

"One more," said the dwarfs; and she was led farther on to a smooth mossy green, thickly covered with what looked like bits of broken thread. One would think it had been a milliner's work-room from the first invention of needles and thread.

"What are these?" Amelia asked.

"They are the broken threads of all the conversations you have interrupted," was the reply; "and pretty dangerous work it is to dance here now, with threads getting round one's shoe points. Dance a hornpipe in a herring-net, and you'll know what it is!"

Amelia began to pick up the threads, but it was tedious work. She had cleared a yard or two, and her back was aching terribly, when she heard the fiddle and the mazurka behind her; and looking round she saw the old dwarf, who was playing away, and making the most hideous grimaces as his chin pressed the violin.

"Dance, my lady, dance!" he shouted.

"I do not think I can," said Amelia; "I am so weary with stooping over my work."

"Then rest a few minutes," he answered, "and I will play you a jig. A jig is a beautiful dance, such life, such spirit! So!"

And he played faster and faster, his arm, his face, his fiddle-bow all seemed working together; and as he played, the threads danced themselves into three heaps.

"That is not bad, is it?" said the dwarf; "and now for our own dance," and he played the mazurka. "Get the measure well into your head. La, la fa la! La, la fa la! So!"

And throwing away his fiddle, he caught Amelia round the waist, and they danced as before. After which, she had no difficulty in putting the three heaps of thread into a basket.

"Where are these to be kicked to?" asked the young goblins.

"To the four winds of heaven," said the old dwarf. "There are very few drawing-room conversations worth putting together a second time. They are not like old china bowls."

By Moonlight

Thus Amelia's tasks were ended; but not a word was said of her return home. The dwarfs were now very kind, and made so much of her that it was evident that they meant her to remain with them. Amelia often cooked for them, and she danced and played with them, and never showed a sign of discontent; but her heart ached for home, and when she was alone she would bury her face in the flowers and cry for her mother.

One day she overheard the dwarfs in consultation.

"The moon is full to-morrow," said one ("Then I have been a month down here," thought Amelia; "it was full moon that night"), "shall we dance in the Mary Meads?"

"By all means," said the old tinker dwarf; "and we will take Amelia, and dance my dance."

"Is it safe?" said another.

"Look how content she is," said the old dwarf; "and, oh! how she dances; my feet tickle at the bare thought."

"The ordinary run of mortals do not see us," continued the objector; "but she is visible to any one. And there are men and women who wander in the moonlight, and the Mary Meads are near her old home."

"I will make her a hat of touchwood," said the old dwarf, "so that even if she is seen it will look like a will-o'-the-wisp bobbing up and down. If she does not come, I will not. I must dance my dance. You do not know what it is! We two alone move together with a grace which even here is remarkable. But when I think that up yonder we shall have attendant shadows echoing our movements, I long for the moment to arrive."

"So be it," said the others; and Amelia wore the touchwood hat, and went up with them to the Mary Meads.

Amelia and the dwarf danced the mazurka, and their shadows, now as short as themselves, then long and gigantic, danced beside them. As the moon went down, and the shadows lengthened, the dwarf was in raptures.

"When one sees how colossal one's very shadow is," he remarked, "one knows one's true worth. You also have a good shadow. We are partners in the dance, and I think we will be partners for life. But I have not fully considered the matter, so this is not to be regarded as a formal proposal." And he continued to dance, singing, "La, la, fa, la, la, la, fa, la." It was highly admired.

The Mary Meads lay a little below the house where Amelia's parents lived, and once during the night her father, who was watching by the sick bed of the stock, looked out of the window.

"How lovely the moonlight is!" he murmured; "but, dear me! there is a will-o'-the-wisp yonder. I had no idea the Mary Meads were so damp." Then he pulled the blind down and went back into the room.

As for poor Amelia, she found no four-leaved clover, and at cockcrow they all went underground.

"We will dance on Hunch Hill to-morrow," said the dwarfs.

All went as before; not a clover plant of any kind did Amelia see, and at cockcrow the revel broke up.

On the following night they danced in the hayfield. The old stubble was now almost hidden by green clover. There was a grand fairy dance – a round dance, which does not mean, as with us, a dance for two partners, but a dance where all join hands and dance round and round in a circle with appropriate antics. Round they went, faster and faster, the pointed shoes now meeting in the centre like the spokes of a wheel, now kicked out behind like spikes and then scamper, caper, hurry! They seemed to fly, when suddenly the ring broke at one corner, and nothing being stronger than its weakest point, the whole circle were sent flying over the field.

"Ho, ho, ho!" laughed the dwarfs, for they are good-humoured little folk, and do not mind a tumble.

"Ha, ha, ha!" laughed Amelia, for she had fallen with her

fingers on a four-leaved clover. She put it behind her back, for the old tinker dwarf was coming up to her, wiping the mud from his face with his leathern apron.

"Now for our dance!" he shrieked. "And I have made up my mind – partners now and partners always. You are incomparable. For three hundred years I have not met with your equal." But Amelia held the four-leaved clover above her head, and cried from her very heart: "I want to go home!"

The dwarf gave a hideous yell of disappointment, and at this instant the stock came tumbling head over heels into the midst, crying: "Oh, the pills, the powders, and the draughts! Oh, the lotions and embrocations! Oh, the blisters, the poultices, and the plasters! Men may well be so short-lived!"

And Amelia found herself in bed in her own home.

At Home Again

By the side of Amelia's bed stood a little table, on which were so many big bottles of medicine, that Amelia smiled to think of all the stock must have had to swallow during the month past. There was an open Bible on it too, in which Amelia's mother was reading, whilst tears trickled slowly down her pale cheeks. The poor lady looked so thin and ill, so worn with sorrow and watching, that Amelia's heart smote her, as if someone had given her a sharp blow.

"Mamma, mamma! Mother, my dear, dear mother!"

The tender, humble, loving tone of voice was so unlike Amelia's old imperious snarl, that her mother hardly recognized it; and when she saw Amelia's eyes full of intelligence instead of the delirium of fever, and that (though older and thinner and rather pale) she looked wonderfully well, the poor worn-out lady could hardly restrain herself from falling into hysterics for very joy. "Dear mamma, I want to tell you all about it," said Amelia, kissing the kind hand that stroked her brow.

But it appeared that the doctor had forbidden conversation; and though Amelia knew it would do her no harm, she yielded to her mother's wish and lay still and silent.

"Now, my love, it is time to take your medicine."

But Amelia pleaded: "Oh, mamma, indeed I don't want any medicine. I am quite well, and would like to get up."

"Ah, my dear child!" cried her mother, "what I have suffered in inducing you to take your medicine, and yet see what good it has done you."

"I hope you will never suffer any more from my wilfulness," said Amelia; and she swallowed two tablespoonfuls of a mixture labelled: "To be well shaken before taken," without even a wry face.

Presently the doctor came.

"You're not so very angry at the sight of me today, my little lady, eh?" he said.

"I have not seen you for a long time," said Amelia, "but I know you have been here, attending a stock who looked like me. If your eyes had been touched with fairy ointment, however, you would have been aware that it was a fairy imp, and a very ugly one, covered with hair. I have been living in terror lest it should go back underground in the shape of a black cat. However, thanks to the four-leaved clover, and the old woman of the heath, I am at home again." On hearing this rhodomontade, Amelia's mother burst into tears, for she thought the poor child was still raving with fever. But the doctor smiled pleasantly, and said: "Aye, aye, to be sure," with a little nod, as one should say, "We know all about it"; and laid two fingers in a casual manner on Amelia's wrist.

"But she is wonderfully better, madam," he said afterwards to her mamma; "the brain had been severely tried, but she is marvellously improved: in fact, it is an effort of nature, a most favourable effort, and we can but assist the rally; we will change the medicine." Which he did, and very wisely assisted nature with a bottle of pure water flavoured with tincture of roses.

"And it was so very kind of him to give me his directions in poetry," said Amelia's mamma; "for I told him my memory, which is never good, seemed going completely, from anxiety, and if I had done anything wrong just now, I should never have forgiven myself. And I always found poetry easier to remember than prose" which puzzled everybody, the doctor included, till it appeared that she had ingeniously discovered a rhyme in his orders:

> To be kept cool and quiet,
> With light nourishing diet.

Under which treatment Amelia was soon pronounced to be well.

She made another attempt to relate her adventures, but she found that not even nurse would believe in them.

"Why, you told me yourself I might meet with the fairies," said Amelia reproachfully.

"So I did, my dear," nurse replied, "and they say that it's that put it into your head. And I'm sure what you say about the dwarfs and all is as good as a printed book, though you can't think that ever I would have let any dirty clothes store up like that, let alone your frocks, my dear. But for pity sake, Miss Amelia, don't go on about it to your mother, for she thinks you'll never get your senses right again, and she has fretted enough about you poor lady; and nursed you night and day till she is nigh worn out. And anybody can see you've been ill, miss, you've grown so, and look paler and older like. Well, to be sure, as you say, if you'd been washing and working for a month in a place without a bit of sun, or a bed to lie on, and scraps to eat, it would be enough to do it; and many's the poor child that has to, and gets worn and old before her time. But, my dear, whatever you think, give into your mother; you'll never repent giving in to your mother, my dear, the longest day you live."

So Amelia kept her own counsel. But she had one confidant.

When her parents brought the stock home on the night of Amelia's visit to the haycocks the bull-dog's conduct had been most strange. His usual good-humour appeared to have been exchanged for incomprehensible fury, and he was with difficulty prevented from flying at the stock, who on her part showed an anger and dislike fully equal to his.

Finally the bull-dog had been confined to the stable, where

he remained the whole month, uttering from time to time such howls, with his snub nose in the air, that poor nurse quite gave up hope of Amelia's recovery.

"For indeed, my dear, they do say that a howling dog is a sign of death, and it was more than I could abear."

But the day after Amelia's return, as nurse was leaving the room with a tray which had carried some of the light nourishing diet ordered by the doctor, she was knocked down, tray and all, by the bull-dog, who came tearing into the room, dragging a chain and dirty rope after him, and nearly choked by the desperate efforts which had finally effected his escape from the stable. And he jumped straight onto the end of Amelia's bed, where he lay, *thudding* with his tail, and giving short whines of ecstasy. And as Amelia begged that he might be left, and as it was evident that he would bite any one who tried to take him away, he became established as chief nurse. When Amelia's meals were brought to the bedside on a tray, he kept a fixed eye on the plates, as if to see if her appetite were improving. And he would even take a snack himself, with an air of great affability.

And when Amelia told him her story, she could see by his eyes, and his nose, and his ears, and his tail, and the way he growled whenever the stock was mentioned, that he knew all about it. As, on the other hand, he had no difficulty in conveying to her by sympathetic whines the sentiment: "Of course I would have helped you if I could; but they tied me up, and this disgusting old rope has taken me a month to worry through."

So, in spite of the past, Amelia grew up good and gentle, unselfish and considerate for others. She was unusually clever, as those who have been with the "little people" are said always to be.

And she became so popular with her mother's acquaintances that they said: "We will no longer call her Amelia, for it is a name we learnt to dislike, but we will call her Amy, that is to say, "'Beloved.'"

★　　　★　　　★　　　★　　　★

"And did my godmother's grandmother believe that Amelia had really been with the fairies, or did she think it was all fever ravings?"

"That, indeed, she never said, but she always observed that it was a pleasant tale with a good moral, which was surely enough for anybody."

[Source: *The Brownies and Other Tales*, ed. Doris A. Pocock (Letchworth, England: Temple Press, 1939) 140-70.]

Appendix J: Lewis Carroll's Photographs of Alice, Lorina, and Edith Liddell

1. Alice Liddell as "The Beggar-Maid" (*c.* 1859). Princeton University Library.

2. Alice in profile (1858). Princeton University Library.

3. Alice feigning sleep. Princeton University Library.

4. Lorina and Alice in Chinese dress. Princeton University Library.

5. Edith, Lorina, and Alice on sofa (c. 1858). Princeton University Library.

6. Edith, Lorina, and Alice eating cherries: "Open your mouth, and shut your eyes" (1860). Princeton University Library. Carroll's title for this photograph was probably taken from William Mulready's painting of the same name, which depicts a young man feeding a girl a bunch of cherries. The title comes from the proverb, "Open your mouth, shut your eyes, and see what Providence will bring you."

Select Bibliography

Works by Lewis Carroll

Alice's Adventures in Wonderland. London: Macmillan, 1866.

Alice's Adventures under Ground, Being a Facsimile of the Original Ms. Book Afterwards Developed into "Alice's Adventures in Wonderland." London and New York: Macmillan, 1886.

Curiosa Mathematica, Part 1. A New Theory of Parallels. London: Macmillan, 1888.

Curiosa Mathematica, Part 2. Pillow Problems. London: Macmillan, 1893.

Euclid and His Modern Rivals. London: Macmillan, 1879.

The Game of Logic. London: Macmillan, 1887.

The Hunting of the Snark. London: Macmillan, 1876.

The Nursery Alice. London: Macmillan, 1889.

Phantasmagoria and Other Poems. London: Macmillan, 1869.

The Rectory Umbrella and Mischmasch. Foreword by Florence Milner. New York: Dover, 1971.

Rhyme? And Reason? London: Macmillan, 1883.

Sylvie and Bruno. London and New York: Macmillan, 1889.

Sylvie and Bruno Concluded. London and New York: Macmillan, 1893.

Symbolic Logic, Part 1. London and New York: Macmillan, 1896.

A Tangled Tale. London: Macmillan, 1883.

Three Sunsets and Other Poems. London: Macmillan, 1898.

Through the Looking-Glass, and What Alice Found There. London: Macmillan, 1872.

Diaries, Journals, and Letters

The Diaries of Lewis Carroll. Ed. Roger Lancelyn Green. 2 vols. London: Cassell, 1953.

The Letters of Lewis Carroll. Ed. Morton N. Cohen. 2 vols. New York: Oxford University Press, 1979.

Lewis Carroll and the House of Macmillan. Eds. Morton N. Cohen and Anita Gandolfo. New York: Cambridge University Press, 1987. Carroll's letters to his publisher.

Lewis Carroll and the Kitchens. Ed. Morton N. Cohen. New York: The Lewis Carroll Society of North America, 1980. Twenty-five letters, nineteen photographs.

Lewis Carroll's Diaries: the Private Journals of Charles Lutwidge Dodgson. With notes and annotations by Edward Wakeling and an introduction by Roger Lancyln Green. 4 vols. Luton, England: The Lewis Carroll Society, 1993-97.

The Russian Journal and Other Selections from the Works of Lewis Carroll. Ed. John Francis McDermott. New York: Dutton, 1935.

The Selected Letters of Lewis Carroll. Ed. Morton N. Cohen. New York: Pantheon, 1982.

A Selection from the Letters of Lewis Carroll to His Child Friends. Ed. Evelyn Hatch. London: Macmillan, 1933.

Editions and Collections

Alice's Adventures in Wonderland: A Critical Handbook. Ed. Donald Rackin. Belmont, Calif.: Wadsworth Publishing, 1961. Reproduces the Rosenbach facsimile of *Alice's Adventures Under Ground* and the text of *Alice's Adventures in Wonderland.*

Alice in Wonderland. Ed. Donald J. Gray. Norton Critical Edition. New York: Norton, 1992.

Alice's Adventures in Wonderland and Through the Looking-Glass. Ed. Roger Lancyln Green. Oxford: Oxford University Press, 1982.

The Annotated Alice: "Alice's Adventures in Wonderland" and "Through the Looking-Glass." Ed. Martin Gardner. New York: W. W. Norton, 2000. Called the "Definitive Edition," it is a composite of the 1960 edition and *More Annotated Alice,* with updated introduction and notes.

The Annotated Snark. Ed. Martin Gardner. New York: Simon and Schuster, 1962.

The Collected Verse of Lewis Carroll. London: Macmillan, 1932. Reprinted as *The Humorous Verse of Lewis Carroll.* New York: Dover, 1960.

The Complete Works of Lewis Carroll. With an introduction by Alexander Woollcott. New York: Vintage Books, 1976. Misleading title: there is no complete collection to date.

The Lewis Carroll Picture Book. A Selection from the Unpublished Writings and Drawings of Lewis Carroll. Ed. Stuart Dodgson Collingwood. London: T. Fisher Unwin, 1899. Reprinted in facsimile as *The Unknown Lewis Carroll.* New York: Dover, 1961.

Lewis Carroll's *"The Hunting of the Snark."* Eds. James Tanis and John Dooley. Los Altos, CA: William Kaufman, 1981. Centennial edition.

Lewis Carroll's Symbolic Logic. Ed. William Warren Bartley, III. New York: Clarkson N. Potter, 1977.

The Magic of Lewis Carroll. Ed. John Fisher. New York: Simon and Schuster, 1973. Carroll's games and puzzles.

Mathematical Recreations of Lewis Carroll. 2 vols. New York: Dover, 1938. Volume I reprints *Symbolic Logic* and *The Game of Logic*; volume 2 reprints *Pillow Problems* and *A Tangled Tale.*

More Annotated Alice. Ed. Martin Gardner. New York: Random House, 1990. Supplements his earlier annotated edition, with Tenniel's drawings replaced by those of Peter Newell.

The Wasp in a Wig: A "Suppressed" Episode of "Through the Looking-Glass and What Alice found There." Ed. Martin Gardner. New York: The Lewis Carroll Society of North America, 1977.

The Works of Lewis Carroll. Ed. Roger Lancelyn Green. Feltham: Spring Books, 1965.

The Works of Lewis Carroll. Ed. Edward Guiliano. Longmeadow Press, 1982.

Collections of Criticism

Gray, Donald J., ed. *Alice in Wonderland*. New York: Norton Critical Edition, 1992. Contains ten critical essays.

Guiliano, Edward, ed. *Lewis Carroll: A Celebration*. New York: Clarkson N. Potter, 1982. Fifteen essays on the occasion of the 150th anniversary of Carroll's birth.

———, ed. *Lewis Carroll Observed*. New York: Clarkson N. Potter, 1976. A collection of unpublished photographs, drawings, and poetry by Carroll, and fifteen essays about his work.

Guiliano, Edward, and James R. Kincaid, eds. *Soaring with the Dodo*. New York: The Lewis Carroll Society of North America, 1982. Ten essays on Carroll's life and art.

Phillips, Robert, ed. *Aspects of Alice: Lewis Carroll's Dreamchild as Seen Through the Critics' Looking-Glasses*. New York: Vanguard, 1971. The largest single collection of critical essays; includes a useful bibliography of items from 1865 through 1971.

Rackin, Donald, ed. *Alice's Adventures in Wonderland: A Critical Handbook*. Belmont, CA: Wadsworth Publishing, 1961. Contains eleven critical articles.

Books About Carroll

Bakewell, Michael. *Lewis Carroll, a Biography*. New York: Norton, 1996.

Blake, Kathleen. *Play, Games and Sport: The Literary Works of Lewis Carroll*. Ithaca, N.Y.: Cornell University Press, 1974. Examines Carroll's philosophy of play.

Bowman, Isa. *Lewis Carroll as I Knew Him*. New York: Dover, 1972. The reminiscence of one of Carroll's child friends.

Braithwaite, R.B. *Lewis Carroll as Logician*. London, 1932.

Clark, Anne. *Lewis Carroll*. London: J.M. Dent, 1979. A thorough, well-researched biography; sympathetic, but lacking in analysis.

Cohen, Morton N. *Reflections in a Looking-Glass: A Centennial Celebration of Lewis Carroll, Photographer.* New York: Aperture, 1998.

———. *Lewis Carroll.* New York: Knopf, 1995. The definitive biography by the foremost Carroll scholar.

———. *Lewis Carroll, Photographer of Children: Four Nude Studies.* New York: Clarkson N. Potter, 1979.

Collingwood, Stuart Dodgson. *The Life and Letters of Lewis Carroll.* London: T. Fisher Unwin, 1898. The standard family biography, by Carroll's nephew.

De la Mare, Walter. *Lewis Carroll.* Philadelphia: R. West, 1977.

Fordyce, Rachel. *Lewis Carroll: a Reference Guide.* Boston: G.K. Hall, 1988.

Gattegno, Jean. *Lewis Carroll: Fragments of a Looking-Glass.* Trans. Rosemary Sheed. New York: Crowell, 1976. A potpourri of analytical snippets that probe Carroll's psychology. Stimulating, but highly speculative, readings.

Gernsheim, Helmut. *Lewis Carroll, Photographer.* New York: Chanticleer Press, 1949. Contains 64 photographic plates.

Greenacre, Phyllis. *Swift and Carroll: A Psychoanalytical Study of Two Lives.* New York: International Universities Press, 1955. The most intelligent and provocative psychoanalytical study of Carroll to date.

Hancher, Michael. *The Tenniel Illustrations to the "Alice Books."* Columbus: Ohio State University Press, 1985. Traces the artistic roots of Tenniel's illustrations of the *Alice* books to his work for *Punch*, the paintings of various artists, photographs, and Carroll's own drawings.

Hudson, Derek. *Lewis Carroll: An illustrated Biography.* New York: New American Library, 1978. The best biography to date, despite its defensive attitude towards psychological interpretations of Carroll's life and work.

Huxley, Francis. *The Raven and the Writing Desk.* London: Thames and Hudson, 1976.

Kelly, Richard. *Lewis Carroll.* Boston: Twayne, 1990. A critical study of Carroll's life and his major works.

Lennon, Florence Becker. *Victoria through the Looking-Glass: The Life of Lewis Carroll.* London: Cassell, 1947. A somewhat disorganized study that contains much information found in no other biography and offers some excellent literary criticism and psychological insights.

Ovenden, Graham, ed. *The illustrators of "Alice in Wonderland" and "Through the Looking-Glass."* New York: St. Martin's, 1972. Provides a good sampling of the drawings of various artists but a scanty and inadequate examination of their work.

Pudney, John. *Lewis Carroll and His World.* London: Thames and Hudson, 1976. A brief biography enriched with many illustrations and photographs.

Reed, Langford. *The Life of Lewis Carroll.* Philadelphia: R. West, 1978.

Reichertz, Ronald. *The Making of the Alice Books: Lewis Carroll's Uses of Earlier Children's Literature.* Montreal: McGill-Queen's University Press, 1997.

Sewell, Elizabeth. *The Field of Nonsense.* London: Chatto and Windus, 1932. A brilliant and influential study of the principles of nonsense, based upon logical and linguistic considerations.

Stern, Jeffrey, ed. *Lewis Carroll's Library.* Silver Spring, Md.: The Lewis Carroll Society of North America, 1981. Lists books in Carroll's personal library.

Sutherland, Robert. *Language and Lewis Carroll.* The Hague: Mouton, 1970.

Taylor, Alexander L. *The White Knight.* London: Oliver and Boyd, 1932. Relates the *Alice* books to contemporary religious controversies.

Tenniel's Alice: Drawings by Sir John Tenniel for "Alice's Adventures in Wonderland" "Through the Looking-Glass." Cambridge, Mass.: Harvard College Library and the Metropolitan Museum of Art, 1978. Reproduces many of Tenniel's pencil drawings and preliminary sketches.

Thomas, Donald. *Lewis Carroll: a Portrait with Background.* London: John Murray, 1996.

Weaver, Warren. *Alice in Many Tongues; the Translations of Alice in Wonderland*. Madison: University of Wisconsin Press, 1964.

Willams, Sidney Herbert, and Falconer Madan, eds. *The Lewis Carroll Handbook*. Revised by Roger Lancelyn Green; further revised by Denis Crutch. Kent, England: Dawson, 1979. A bibliographic account of Carroll's writings and a history of their composition and development.

Wood, James Playsted. *The Snark Was a Boojum*. New York: Pantheon, 1966. A biography of Carroll distinguished mainly by David Levine's excellent drawings.